DYING BREATH

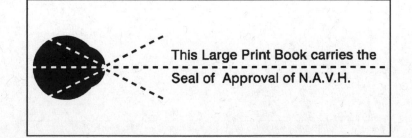

This Large Print Book carries the
Seal of Approval of N.A.V.H.

DYING BREATH

HEATHER GRAHAM

THORNDIKE PRESS
A part of Gale, Cengage Learning

Farmington Hills, Mich • San Francisco • New York • Waterville, Maine
Meriden, Conn • Mason, Ohio • Chicago

GALE
CENGAGE Learning®

Copyright © 2017 by Heather Graham Pozzessere.
Krewe of Hunters.
Thorndike Press, a part of Gale, Cengage Learning.

Thorndike Press® Large Print Core.
The text of this Large Print edition is unabridged.
Other aspects of the book may vary from the original edition.
Set in 16 pt. Plantin.

LIBRARY OF CONGRESS CATALOGING-IN-PUBLICATION DATA

Names: Graham, Heather, author.
Title: Dying breath / by Heather Graham.
Description: Large print edition. | Waterville, Maine : Thorndike Press, 2017. |
    Series: Krewe of hunters | Series: Thorndike Press large print core
Identifiers: LCCN 2017017109 | ISBN 9781410498137 (hardcover) | ISBN 1410498131
    (hardcover)
Subjects: LCSH: Government investigators—Fiction. | Women mediums—Fiction. |
    Serial murder investigation—Fiction. | Boston (Mass.)—Fiction. | Large type
    books. | GSAFD: Suspense fiction.
Classification: LCC PS3557.R198 D947 2017 | DDC 813/54—dc23
LC record available at https://lccn.loc.gov/2017017109

Published in 2017 by arrangement with Harlequin Books, S.A.

Printed in the United States of America
1 2 3 4 5 6 7 21 20 19 18 17

To the great and amazing state of
Massachusetts and my family there.

Some people marry for money . . .
When I was eighteen and madly in love,
I could have married to acquire
my in-law family, the most wonderful
group of people one could imagine,
stemming from the Miro and
Pozzessere tribes. All in all now, that
is well over a hundred people — and
every one of them is wonderful!

This book, though, is especially
in memory of Uncle George,
my whist partner, cribbage instructor
and so much more. He taught about
decency, kindness, generosity and
compassion in the best possible way —
simply by very quietly maintaining
all those qualities himself.

For Auntie Dee, the best aunt
anyone could imagine,
who has always called me her niece,
and never her in-law.

For Kenny, Doreen, John, Bill,
Ashley, Eric, Anna and Alex —
I am privileged to have you
all in my life.

CAST OF CHARACTERS

Victoria (Vickie) Preston — historian, author and youth-group leader

Griffin Pryce — special agent with the FBI's Krewe of Hunters

Jackson Crow — field director, Krewe of Hunters

Bertram Aldridge — serial killer, in prison

Chrissy and George Ballantine — family friends of Vickie's

Dylan Ballantine — Chrissy and George's teenaged son, now a ghost

Noah Ballantine — Chrissy and George's young son, nine years old

FRIENDS AND FAMILY

Lucy and Dr. Philip Preston — Vickie's parents

Roxanne Greeley — Vickie's best friend

Hank Fremont — Vickie's high school boyfriend

7

Mario Caro — runs local family restaurant Pasta Fagioli

LOCAL LAW ENFORCEMENT
Detective David Barnes — Boston PD
Lenora Connor — hypnotist
Carl Lumley — private security
Donald Baugh — private security

STUDENTS IN VICKIE'S YOUTH GROUP
Art Groton, Hardy Richardson, Cheryl Taylor, Cathy MacDonald, Jan, Frank, Ivan, Gio, Cindy and Sasha

PROLOGUE

The side door was open just a hair, but that little bit brought a hint of wintry air that sent a chill racing down Vickie Preston's spine. She shivered. She moved closer to the door and found herself looking out at the day through the double-paned window.

It was gray. Turning darker quickly as the day waned into the late afternoon.

Nothing unexpected, since it was winter, and still . . .

She felt unnerved. The wind seemed to have a keening sound about it — a sound that made her think of her granny O'Malley talking about banshees wailing.

Or maybe it was the fact that the door was open — even though she didn't know why it would be. But she knew it was all right. Mr. and Mrs. Ballantine hadn't even left for their night out yet. She would just ask him about the door — maybe he'd been taking something out to the car.

9

Still, oddly trembling, she closed the door and locked it. As she did so, Chrissy Ballantine came sailing into the kitchen, adjusting her gloves.

"Choose any of those little packets of food you'd like," Mrs. Ballantine said. "You know where they all are. Noah will probably need to eat about 8:30 tonight and there's a six-ounce bottle he can have after he eats his food. He'll most likely fall asleep after that. The baby monitor is next to the crib, of course. The diapers are next to the crib . . . and well, you know the drill. You have my number, and you have George's number, and . . ."

"Chrissy, can we go, please!" George Ballantine said, coming up behind his wife, slipping an arm around her waist. "My dear, as we know, Vickie is the most amazing baby-sitter in the world and if you torture her to death with commonsense details, she'll leave us!"

Vickie Preston smiled at them both.

God bless the Ballantines!

They were both in their midforties; Noah was, truly, a miracle child for them.

It had never been easy for her, Chrissy had once told Vickie. It seemed like a gift from above that she had finally gotten pregnant again. Fertility drugs before —

and now? Just a miracle.

Yes, Noah was a miracle.

And *before* . . .

Even though they had little Noah, tears often sprang to Chrissy's eyes when she referred to an earlier time — and the son they had lost. After all their first efforts twenty years ago, they had finally had a child: Dylan. Dylan had been great, a son any parent could adore. Good in school, good in sports, but more — a great sport himself, happy when he won, able to shrug it off and smile when he or his team lost.

A year shy of his eighteenth birthday, Dylan had been killed by a drunk driver. His death had nearly killed his parents as well; it had devastated a community. George Ballantine had left his high-tech job in New York City — too many memories — and relocated in Boston. And while his wife had still been in mourning, she'd suddenly found out that she would have the second child she had always wanted.

Vickie knew all about the Ballantines because the families knew each other through church. Chrissy Ballantine had called Vickie's mom, and Vickie had been interviewed. She had been in awe when she'd heard how much she could make, just baby-sitting a sweet child. And while she

11

was very happy about Noah, she also felt terrible for the couple, and she thought about the young man she saw in pictures about the house — Dylan Ballantine — often enough. She was now just about the age he had been when he died, almost eighteen. She found herself wondering what his life had been like — he'd been popular, certainly. Had he dreamed about college, being on his own, the places he might go, the things he might do in life?

Dylan was gone, but it was just sixteen months and three days ago that Noah Ballantine had made his stunning and miraculous arrival into the world.

For the first six months of his life, Chrissy had refused to leave his side. Her psychiatrist had finally convinced her she would smother her poor child, herself and her marriage if she didn't learn to trust someone. Vickie was always grateful they had chosen her.

"Yes, yes, of course, we can go," Chrissy said. "I'll just look in on the baby one more time, though, I know, of course Vickie will be fine."

"Vickie will be fine — whether you go stare at Noah again or not!" George said firmly.

Vickie could easily understand how precious the child was to both Chrissy and George. She loved the baby herself, as well as both of the Ballantines — and loved babysitting for them. They had a great old historic house that was one of the few listed on the National Historic Register and still a private residence in the midst of the explosion of Boston as a city. When she babysat in the afternoon, she would walk part of the Freedom Trail and, despite the fact she was a city native, still marvel at the Old South Meeting House, the Granary Burial Ground and other local wonders.

Her own house was old, but not nearly so old — or distinguished — as the Ballantine house. It had been built in 1790, combining the Georgian and Federal styles, and the architecture itself was amazing. The house was on most walking tours of the city. It had hosted Samuel Adams at one time, along with John Hancock and a number of other Revolutionary notables. Her home was nice — mid-1800s — but it had been built as apartments and was an apartment building to this day. Nothing like this.

"Oh, but his clothes!" Chrissy said. "I need to show Vickie where everything he might need can be found."

"Vickie knows where everything Noah has can be found. Details — you're going to

13

drive the poor girl crazy!" George said.

"Darling, I don't get crazy on details," Chrissy protested. "Okay, I do," she admitted, looking at Vickie. "But —"

"I'm fine. I don't mind details," Vickie assured her.

From his play area in the living room, Noah suddenly let out a demanding cry. Chrissy Ballantine immediately jumped and turned to go to him.

Her husband caught her arm. "Vickie is here now. She'll get Noah. And we'll head out to our dinner with my boss, huh?"

"Yes, of course, of course." Chrissy smiled at Vickie, hugged her impetuously and allowed her husband to steer her to the kitchen door.

A blast of cold air swept in; the house didn't have a garage, but rather a porte cochere, or covered drive, once a carriage entry. It was small and tight to the house, allowing for one car. But then they didn't need more than one car where they were in Boston. Public transportation on the T was great.

George Ballantine looked back at Vickie and winked. She smiled and waved and headed to the door to close and lock it behind them.

But Chrissy was suddenly back, rapping

14

on the window. "The alarm!" she said.

"I've got it!" Vickie assured her. And she keyed in the alarm.

As she did so, she remembered that she had forgotten to ask George Ballantine why the side door had been open. She rekeyed the alarm to Off and threw open the door.

But their silver Mercedes had already driven into the night.

She heard Noah let out another wail and she quickly locked the door and keyed in the alarm again before hurrying back to the grand parlor.

She wasn't really sure why any kid would be crying or wanting to leave this play space. His "playpen" was constructed to cover an area that was a good fifteen-by-fifteen feet long and wide. He could crawl onto his scooter, play with his toddler walker — or any number of the amazing toys in the carefully constructed play box in the play area.

Despite being spoiled rotten, Noah Ballantine was a sweet and affectionate baby. He had taken to Vickie right away, which had helped her earn the position. She adored him in turn.

He wasn't screaming or crying out with his few words when she reached the parlor; he was staring into what appeared to be blank space. And then he began to laugh —

15

the way he did when they watched *Little Baby Bum* videos and clapped and played.

His interaction with blank space made Vickie curious — and uncomfortable. She told herself that she was just spooked. She silently cursed herself for not asking George Ballantine about the open door — he would have said something to reassure her.

"What ya doing, my little love?" Vickie said, stepping over the playpen gate and hunkering down by the baby. He truly was a sweetheart. He looked at her and gave her a brilliant smile and clapped his hands.

He was blessed with huge hazel eyes and a thatch of rich sandy hair and couldn't possibly have been a cuter boy.

He clapped his hands again.

"Pat-a-cake, pat-a-cake, baker man! Bake me a cake as fast as you can!" she said. "Roll it, and poke it, and mark it with a *B,* and then put it in the oven for my baby and me!"

He responded with more laughter and smiles, and then looked aside again — as if someone else was there.

"Okay, okay, creeping me out there, kid!" Vickie said. "And, by the way — P.U.! You stink-um, dink-um!" she told him. "You need a diaper change."

She swept him up, climbed over the playpen gate and headed for the stairs.

16

She stopped halfway there, hearing a tapping at the window. It seemed that her heart caught in her throat.

Just branches in the wind, branches in the wind . . .

But if she didn't check it out, she'd scare herself all night. Cuddling Noah to her, she headed to the window and held her breath as she drew back the drapery.

"As I expected!" she said, keeping her voice filled with fun — she wasn't about to scare the baby. "Branches! Rude! How rude of them to tap at the window like that."

Noah thought it was all great.

"Up the stairs we go!"

Noah's room was a fantasy playland. His crib and dressing table, changing table, floor mat and toy chest were all done up in a jungle motif in pastel blues with an elephant theme. She grabbed a diaper and the wipes and made quick work of the change.

She felt her cell phone buzzing and answered it quickly, balancing Noah in the crook of her left arm. Her mom always called to make sure she was okay. Vickie was always afraid if she didn't answer quickly, her mom would have cops at the door. But it wasn't her mom, it was Roxanne Greeley, one of her best friends.

"So, the cats are gone, eh? Party, party?"

Roxanne asked her.

"No parties. I'm earning my money for college."

Roxanne giggled. "I know you — just teasing. If I were to head over for a wild and wicked party, that would be the two of us doing our toenails once the little guy fell asleep. But . . ."

"But what?" Vickie asked.

"Hank Fremont does think you should spend more time with him. I overheard him talking about his brother getting him some beer and then him heading over to surprise you," Roxanne said. "Some of the guys he hangs with were egging him on. Telling him he's the coolest dude in the school and if he's dating you, well, you should be cool, too."

"Not to worry. I informed Hank this is serious work for me. College is serious for me."

"Ah, well, one day maybe you'll be president of the country! And then I'll have wild, wicked parties doing my toenails with the president! Anyway, I warned you."

"I told him not to come. He won't. So I'll see you tomorrow? Shopping, right? We're going to the mall. Sushi at the ridiculously good place in the food court?"

"We're on."

Her phone was ringing again as she finished with Roxanne; it was Hank. She shook her head, smiled at the baby, and answered.

"I'm on my way, my love," Hank said, trying to make his voice husky — deeply, manly rich. Vickie shook her head at the baby with exasperation. He loved it.

"Don't be. I told you — I won't let you in," Vickie said. "Hank, this is serious for me. You need to be more serious. If you don't hit a few books instead of beer bottles, not even your athletics will get you into college."

"Hey, we're only young once! I already have beer and a pizza. Come on, that's a super-cool house. I'll be there —"

"Come, and I'll call the cops," she threatened.

"Bitch!"

"I mean it, Hank."

"Well, you know, we could be over."

"We will be eventually. Maybe now is a good enough time."

Vickie hung up, aggravated, and set her phone on the baby's dresser.

They'd been through this before. He'd apologize tomorrow. He'd beg her to stay with him. But everything she had said was true.

"Maybe this is the right time to end it,

huh, Noah?"

Noah laughed and clapped.

And then they both heard a thump. Noah's eyes widened; Vickie jumped.

It had come from the attic — she was certain.

Now she did freeze. For a moment, she couldn't even remember to shake it off quickly for the baby.

She waited. Nothing more.

Had a branch fallen on the house?

Or had Hank Fremont not taken her refusal seriously? Could he possibly be there already, up in the attic, or outside? Maybe, like in the movies, he'd actually called her from inside the house or right outside the house!

No, he'd been a jerk tonight, but usually he kind of listened to her. But he was a high school senior surrounded by a few guys who were taking a long time to reach anything that resembled maturity.

No. Hank would not be that big a jerk. But the house was closely surrounded by big trees.

"That's it — a branch," she managed to say at last, realizing that her hold on Noah was tight — and right when he looked at her, his little face puckered into what might have turned into a cry.

He smiled instead. "Bick-bick!" he said. It was his name for her. He was beginning to talk — sometimes his words made sense. He was good with *mama, dada, bye-bye,* and *kit-kat.* The Ballantines didn't have pets, but Noah had a great stuffed kitten that sang songs and told nursery rhymes and he knew to ask for his *kit-kat* when he wanted the toy.

"Let's go back downstairs," she murmured. "Maybe we'll look at your food packs and you can point at one and we'll choose your late-night snack that way!"

Noah clapped his hands. He was, however, looking past Vickie — toward the door. There was something about the way that he was looking that caused her to spin around and stare.

But no one stood in the doorway.

"You know, Noah, Bick-bick is going to have to stop this. There are a lot of horror stories about babysitters. The phone rings, and there's no one there. Just breathing, or something like that. We, however, have a great alarm on this house!"

Except the door had been ajar. Before the alarm had been set.

She was really doing it: scaring herself. If she went off the deep end, the Ballantines would never ask her back.

21

"Television! We will turn the television on. It will talk and be . . . well, it will be fine," she said.

Once downstairs, she couldn't find the remote control for the mammoth television screen that was just the right distance from the play area to make certain Noah wasn't too close.

She looked all over the room — in Noah's toy box, everywhere.

Shaking her head, she took the baby with her and headed for the kitchen.

The door remained locked. She couldn't help but check.

The phone rang and she nearly jumped a mile high. It was the house phone.

This was it — where the babysitter answered the home phone and someone just breathed into her ear.

She let it ring. And ring.

She heard the message machine kick in out in the parlor. And then her mother's voice.

"Victoria? Victoria, are you there, sweetheart?"

She picked the phone up. "Mom?"

"Yes, it's your mom — remember me?" Her mother asked dryly.

Her muscles were so tense she had to pray the baby didn't feel her fear.

She forced herself to breathe. "Mom, why didn't you call my cell?"

"I did. You didn't answer," her mother said.

Vickie felt in her pockets. Nope, her phone wasn't on her. Where the heck had she left it? Oh, yeah, she'd set it down upstairs after talking to Roxanne.

"Sorry. It's here somewhere. Anyway, what's up?"

"You were supposed to call and tell me that you got there okay."

"Mom, I thought you were planning on calling me. Also, I graduate in June. And I'm going to college. You just won't be able to check on me every minute."

"I know, I know. But that's June. I'll get a grip by then. It's just . . . well, when you go to the Ballantine house, I can't help but think about their son . . . their older son."

"Well, I'm here, I'm fine, baby is as well. I haven't bounced him off the roof yet or anything."

Her mother laughed softly. "You're a great babysitter, Vickie. And dog-walker and student and daughter. You've worked very hard. You're going to love going to NYU. Mrs. Ballantine will be almost as heartbroken as me when you head off."

"Mom, I'll be in New York. It's only a four

or five hour drive. Look, I promise I'll bring home lots of laundry and come home for food and the whole bit, okay?"

Noah let out a squeal of delight. He was looking over Vickie's shoulder again.

"I hear the little darling. Okay, sweetie. Go and take care of him!" her mother said.

"Love you, Mom."

"Okay, take care of the little one!"

Noah let out a delighted laugh once again.

Vickie barely managed to hang up the phone. She spun around. There was nothing there.

Nothing.

No one.

She almost picked up the phone to call her mom and ask her to come over. Or maybe she could call Roxanne back. Nope. She had assured Mr. and Mrs. Ballantine she did nothing but babysit. She didn't have friends over.

Including male friends?

Not to worry — she especially didn't have male friends over!

She took a deep breath and headed back into the parlor.

There, on the footstool in front of one of the antique rockers, sat the remote control.

And her cell phone.

She hadn't put them there!

24

This time, fear shot through her with electric sparks. She set Noah down quickly in his play area, afraid she would startle, scare or hurt him.

She made herself breathe — and breathe again.

"Okay, I just didn't see it before," she murmured to herself. "Right there — right on the footstool, but somehow, I've gone blind. What do you think, Noah? I didn't set the phone down upstairs, I did that down here. And I just didn't really look for the remote control. I'm too into you!"

He was such a delightful baby. He looked at her and clapped his hands together. She forced a smile and looked at her watch.

Six o'clock. Full dark on a wintry Boston night. Mr. and Mrs. Ballantine wouldn't come home for hours.

And now, because she'd seen too many horror movies, she was allowing herself to let her imagination run wild.

George and Chrissy Ballantine had been there when she arrived. There was no one else in the house.

"Breathe, kid, breathe," she told herself. "Ah! Well, it's here." She grabbed the remote control as if it were a lifeline. "Why didn't your parents get one of those remotes that just lets you talk to the TV and turn it

25

on, huh? You know, like, 'TV! Go on. Bring me to a really cute little kids' show!' "

Noah clapped and made a few oohing noises.

Vickie turned on the television. From the corner of her eye, she felt as if someone passed by her. She spun around, looking everywhere; there was no one there.

"Crazy. Your Bick-bick is going crazy, Noah!" she said.

She didn't know why, but she found herself looking at the family portraits that flanked the massive granite mantle.

Mr. and Mrs. Ballantine to the right.

Dylan and Noah to the left.

She swallowed hard and turned her attention to the flat-screen television.

It was tuned to a news channel. A reporter stood before a huge building in Suffolk County, warning listeners that two prisoners had escaped that morning from the South Bay House of Correction.

They had feigned illness in a planned escape; they had taken the guns used in their escape from guards they had left critically wounded.

One, Reginald Mason, had already been captured after a shootout with police at a convenience store. Two civilians had been wounded in the gunfire.

26

Residents of the Greater Boston area were warned to be extremely careful. Mug shots of the men were shown, with the footage then zooming in on the face of one Bertram Aldridge. Six years ago, he'd terrorized the area, becoming known as the Southside Slasher for the horrible way he'd murdered his seven known victims. He'd liked to tease law enforcement with letters to the newspapers, telling them FBI stood for Fat-Butt Intelligence and BPD stood for Billie-Prick-Dicks.

Police were out in force, and they expected to find the second man quickly, since he was local and had ties to the area. Past associates of the man were under investigation.

She realized she and the baby were staring at the screen as the reporter continued to numerate the violent crimes committed by the men. Bertram Aldridge, still on the loose, was known for butchering his victims with a knife, but he was familiar with firearms and had shot several officers during his original arrest.

"No, no!" she said aloud, and she began to flick the button to change the channel.

There were tons of news channels. Every one of them seemed to be covering the escape.

At last, she found a Disney cartoon, one that she loved herself — *The Little Mermaid.*

Singing crustaceans — yep. They were good for now.

Then the air in the room seemed changed, and again she felt as though someone else was there. Right there with her in the room.

The baby was clapping and laughing.

That was good, of course. Because, inwardly, she was freaking out.

The door was locked; she'd checked.

But it hadn't been before. She'd heard a bump. And her phone . . .

She could remember — at least she thought she could remember — putting it down upstairs.

"It's because I'm scared silly, little one — freaking here. I'm about to call my mommy!" she said to Noah, trying to smile all the time.

He laughed at her.

And then turned and laughed and clapped again, seemingly seeing someone else there.

"Okay, I've had it!" she said. "Kid, we're going to head into the kitchen. Nice and cozy there, and we have a door —"

Her words broke off. She heard something. For sure this time. From upstairs.

Then suddenly she screamed. There was something right in front of her. What — she didn't know. At first, it just seemed like clouds forming in air. Then there seemed to be a face, and then a form, and a full figure. Her mouth opened; she felt like fire and ice in one. Terror ripped through her with a painful vengeance.

And she heard the sound again. Something up the stairs. As if someone was moving, as if they were close to the stairs, perhaps to come down them . . .

And in front of her . . .

The figure and face had formed. Her gaze jerked up to the pictures above the mantle. She looked at the portrait of Dylan Ballantine.

And she looked at the strange thing that had formed out of the air before her.

"Go!" she heard. It was a rustle; it might have been leaves.

It might have been the terror that ruled her brain.

And it might have been the ghostly image of Dylan Ballantine standing before her now.

And still, she heard that sound . . . someone moving furtively, taking a step on the staircase, moving in a way she could sense . . .

And then . . .

She felt as if she was suddenly slapped

hard by an icy hand.

"Get Noah and get out!"

Like a whisper, like a whisper, like a sound that played only in her mind . . .

"Move! Move — now!"

At that point, she acted. She grabbed the baby. She forgot about his ultrawarm knit hat and his mittens and his outside shoes.

She held him to her chest, raced to the front door, threw it open and raced out into the street.

It was dark and it was cold and no tourists were traveling the Freedom Trail. She heard a pounding behind her.

She was terrified to look back.

She did.

A man was there, behind her, coming after her. A man with a gun.

She turned and ran again — toward the Paul Revere House.

There were still people there! A group milling, talking about where to go to dinner.

"Help, help!" she cried.

Someone heard her! A tall Boston policeman had suddenly appeared on the sidewalk.

"Down, miss, down!" he shouted.

She gripped Noah even more tightly to her and ducked low.

She heard an explosion and a scream at the same time. Turning back, she saw the man with the gun on the ground.

He had fired, but he had apparently tripped over his own two feet. His gun had gone off . . . But his bullet had aimed into the sky. He was struggling up, taking aim again . . .

But he'd been shot.

The young policeman had fired at almost the same time.

Standing next to the collapsed man was the image of the boy she had seen in the house. Dylan Ballantine, dead nearly three years, dead before his baby brother had been born.

The policeman rushed by Vickie and the baby, his own weapon aimed at the man — *the convict!* — who had evidently tripped . . .

The man on the ground screamed as the cop's bullet exploded again; his gun went flying from his hand. He was disarmed, bleeding.

But only because he had tripped over the leg of a dead boy! Over Dylan Ballantine.

And as she continued to stare back in terror, the image of Dylan Ballantine began to fade.

And then he was gone.

The icy darkness of the wintry night began to settle in, and Noah began to cry at last.

CHAPTER ONE

Boston, Massachusetts
The North End
Summer

Griffin Pryce ran hard and as fast as he could, ahead of Jackson Crow by maybe ten feet. Not that it mattered. The clue had led them to the historic old cemetery, but once there, they'd have to look.

Thankfully it was summer. There was no abundance of multicolored autumn leaves to cover the ground; they would hopefully find an area that had been disturbed easily enough.

This was the first time the kidnapper/killer known as the Undertaker had actually left his victim in a cemetery. At least, so Griffin believed.

He was known to box his victims, nail them into wooden coffin-like crates.

Now, the box might well *be* a coffin.

There — behind dozens of slate stone

markers, few really over the bodies they memorialized anymore and even fewer that had been rechiseled so that the words honoring the dead were legible — he saw where the ground had been ripped up.

He raced to the area — then swore when he hit a soft spot in the ground and went down — straight down — a good four feet.

"Here!" he shouted, though, of course, shouting was rather inane since Jackson surely recognized that Griffin had fallen into some kind of a pit.

Not so strange, he knew. In 2009, a woman had fallen into the stairway of a long forgotten tomb at the Granary cemetery. Time had a way with slate seals and old granite and the earth. Thousands had been buried here throughout time; all kinds of vaults lay beneath the surface.

He just prayed that they had found the right place, right now; that they were in time.

He heard Jackson coming up behind him as he frantically worked to dislodge more dirt from underneath himself. He doubted that the kidnapper would have had enough time to dig too deeply.

Thank God, he hadn't. He found the poor wooden coffin in which the victim had been buried alive. As he worked to remove heavy clods of dirt and bracken, Jackson was already on the phone calling for backup and an ambulance.

Backup wasn't far behind them. But before others arrived, Jackson joined him in the hole. They pried open the coffin lid.

And found Barbara Marshall.

She was pale beyond death; her lips were blue.

For a split second, Griffin and Jackson stared at one another. Then Jackson braced the coffin as Griffin pulled the woman from it, crawled from the hole with her in his arms, eased her gently to the ground and began resuscitation. He counted, he prayed, applied pressure and tried to breathe life into the woman.

Even in the midst of his efforts, a med tech arrived; Griffin gave way to the trained man who moved in to take his place.

"We may have been too late!" he said, the words a whisper, yet fierce even in their quiet tone.

"Maybe not," Jackson said.

The emergency crew worked quickly. Griffin stood there, almost numb, as Barbara Marshall was moved, as a gurney was brought, as lifesaving techniques went into play with a rush of medical equipment.

Then she was whisked away, and he and

Jackson were left gasping for breath as their counterpart from the police department arrived, while uniformed officers held back the suddenly growing crowd — and the press.

At last, with enough breath, Griffin looked at Jackson. "Think she'll make it?"

"She may."

"Think he's watching?" Griffin asked.

"Hard to tell. Whoever is doing this is also leading the semblance of a normal life," Jackson said.

"So he — or they — could be at work, picking kids up from school, or so on," Griffin murmured.

"But I think that, yes, watching will be part of the pleasure, whenever they can watch," Jackson said.

Griffin stood, fighting anger and disgust, and looked around at the buildings that surrounded them.

Boston was, to him, one of the most amazing cities in America. Modern finance and massive skyscrapers dominated the downtown area — along with precious gems of history. Boston Common, King's Chapel, Faneuil Hall, the Paul Revere House, the Old North Church and more were within easy walking distance. Centuries of history within blocks. Colonial architecture, Gothic churches, Victorian; Boston was a visual display of American eras.

But the multitude of what was newer and contemporary in building might well afford the kidnapper a fine vantage point for watching as the police and FBI agents ran around like ants on the ground following the clues he so relished sending to the media.

This time, the clue had been, "James II, sadly not long for the throne. Still, a thief. Ah, Old Boston!"

A crew had been sent to King's Chapel, as well. But Griffin had been convinced that their kidnapping victim would be found in the cemetery. This Undertaker liked drama.

And history and dirt, so it seemed.

Barbara Marshall was his fourth victim. Griffin prayed she survived.

The first victim, Beverly Tatum of Revere, had not.

But then, no one had heard of the Undertaker when she'd been taken.

When they had so desperately searched.

And searched.

Beverly Tatum had been found by police two weeks later, locked in an old freezer in a dump.

Jennifer Hudgins of Lynn had also died. The family had notified the police, who'd suspected her husband was responsible for her disappearance. They'd tailed him, questioned his coworkers . . . and then they'd run out of leads. The husband's alibi had been proven true.

Jennifer had eventually been found inside a locker at an abandoned school in Brookline.

Then, Angelina Gianni of Boston had been taken.

The FBI had been called in for help — the Krewe, specifically, because Angelina's husband, Anthony, had been certain that his wife's mother had been speaking to him from the grave, telling him that he must dig to find her.

By then, the major television and internet news agency that had received the first two clues — and had originally considered them to be nothing but odd statements from a kook — had determined that they might be from the real criminal.

The clues had been received in plain white envelopes — mailed from Boston's largest post office, no matter what other towns, cities or suburbs had been involved. No fingerprints of course. They contained a simple line or two lines giving a clue as to the whereabouts of the victims. The first clue had been "Where the old is discarded, where one may find what was once cold." The second clue had read "No longer may one learn; is all learning but kept locked away?"

They'd found the third victim, Angelina, before it was too late. Griffin could be grateful that his knowledge of his Massachusetts home had helped. The clue had read "Fire away, and so it begins!"

He'd focused on Lexington and an old house that had served as a bed-and-breakfast near the first famous battle site. Of course, even then, he might not have found her if it hadn't been for a dream. Or rather, the ghost who had entered his dream. The ghost of the missing woman's mother. Eva, her name had been. Even in his dream, she'd switched to Italian now and then.

Though Griffin had known since he'd been a child that the dead could sometimes speak, it was sometimes difficult to admit. Even now — even belonging to the Krewe of Hunters. Even working with Jackson Crow, who seemed to think their strange and very often useful "gifts" were nothing unusual.

And so Angelina had lived. Her family had been grateful and they would have done anything to help the police. But Angelina had no memory of what had happened to her.

All she remembered was the darkness of being locked away.

This time, no ghost had come to him. The kidnapper or kidnappers — while the press had decreed one man and dubbed him the Undertaker, Griffin couldn't rule out there wasn't more than one person involved — had come straight to Boston. Having grown up on Beacon Hill, and walked these streets on his beat as a Boston cop before joining the FBI, Griffin had been certain about the message.

He was grateful that he and Jackson and the Krewe, as representatives of the FBI, had helped. He was incredibly grateful that one victim had lived; maybe Barbara Marshall would make it as well.

But they were no closer to the kidnapper — or kidnappers, as he suspected. Jackson knew that Griffin believed it had to be more than one person executing the crimes, but since the press had gone with "Undertaker," they referred to *the* kidnapper themselves.

A shout suddenly went up from the street and echoed back to them. An officer in uniform came running back to them as they heard the sirens from the ambulance moving away through the city.

"She breathed on her own!" the officer said, his face alight. "They think she's going to make it."

Griffin looked over at Jackson and nodded his appreciation. Then he looked up at the buildings again, certain they were, indeed, being watched. Jackson leaped up and offered Griffin a hand; Griffin realized he was still somewhat in a hole. Accepting Jackson's hand, he stepped out.

"We'll find him," Jackson said quietly. He had a right to be confident. The Krewe solved their cases. Griffin knew that; he was extremely grateful to be a part of the unique and special unit.

"Sure," he said. He knew their minds were on similar tracks.

They would find the sick criminal doing this. But would they find him, and stop him, before someone else died?

As he joined Jackson, walking toward the street entrance of the cemetery, he saw Detective David Barnes, Boston Police, on his phone, looking ashen and tense.

Griffin had only just met Barnes on this case. The man had been with the BPD over fifteen years, but when Griffin had been a cop, Barnes had been *Southie,* working patrol out of South Boston. The man had studied him intently when they had first met

— he'd obviously heard Griffin had once been with the BPD, and that he'd been the patrolman to bring down escaped convict Bertram Aldridge. The dramatic takedown had been all over the news at the time, and had made Griffin's reputation.

Barnes seemed to be a decent man and a good detective; he'd welcomed their assistance and had been glad to have them on the team. Griffin figured he was about forty-five — with the wear and tear of someone a few years older.

"Victory — and yet short-lived," Barnes said, deep furrows lining his brow. "We've gotten a call from a nearby resident, George Ballantine. His wife didn't show up after their son's Little League practice — then he found out she never even made it to her garden club meeting earlier in the day." He stared at Griffin, nodding, and added, "Yeah. Ballantine."

Something inside clicked hard against Griffin's chest.

Ballantine.

He could remember too clearly when the killer, Bertram Aldridge, had made an attempt on the life of the Ballantine's toddler son and their young babysitter. He could remember seeing the terrified girl, running, and the killer in the street, raising his weapon . . .

"Aldridge is still incarcerated — maximum security," Griffin said.

"Yeah. And Aldridge liked to play with knives. This guy likes to let his victims smother slowly. Apparently, he's not even that worried when we find them still alive — he just heads out for another victim. Aldridge liked to write taunting notes to the police, too, though. But . . . this tone is different. Can't be Aldridge — absolutely impossible."

"If we know he's locked up," Griffin said.

"First thing I checked — couldn't help myself," Barnes said.

"How long has Mrs. Ballantine been missing?" Jackson asked.

"Her meeting was at noon. She wasn't there when George arrived home at 3:30 p.m.," Barnes told them.

"That's not a very long time," Jackson said.

It was barely four-something, Griffin thought. In any other circumstances, the situation wouldn't cause much alarm. Yet. There were a dozen explanations. Mrs. Ballantine's phone might not be working. She'd stopped to see a friend and hadn't even realized her ringer wasn't on. She'd had a flat tire and a friendly driver had stopped and called roadside assistance for her — and she was still waiting. The police wouldn't have even taken a report.

Ballantine. The family targeted again?

"It's him," Griffin said quietly. "It's the Undertaker. We need to get over to the Ballantine house as quickly as possible. Get ahold of the media; find out about a note — a clue."

Jackson studied him and nodded.

"Detective Barnes?" Jackson said.

Barnes didn't argue. "I'll get my car."

"No need. It's a short sprint from here," Griffin said.

"You remember the house?" Barnes asked him.

"I remember it well," Griffin said.

"Step light, my friend, for here I lie
Just steps away from a place to die
Boston Neck, and about the neck,
A rope I was forced to wear,
Years later was I found and cleared
By children bright and oh so dear
So now I rest in hallowed ground,
My story to be found.
No witch was I, no cause to die."

Vickie Preston read the words from the monument aloud to her group of older

44

teens, glad her dramatics — and simple, sad history — seemed to have them enthralled.

She had a group of ten with her: teens who had nearly been lost in the system. She had case files on all of them — if they hadn't been neglected or abused by their own parents, they had fallen prey to the evil vices of others.

Most had bounced about in foster care. They would all turn eighteen soon and enter the world on their own, where statistically they didn't seem to have much of a chance. Vickie had come home to Boston after college to work with a private charity called Grown Ups that was trying very hard to give such young people a better chance at survival in the real world as adults.

It had also just been a good move on her part. She'd split ways with her boyfriend, Jared Norton, several months ago; he'd liked to surprise her by waiting on the doorstep of her brownstone apartment in New York, convinced that she wanted him back in her life.

It wasn't going to happen, and he needed to move on.

It was still nice to have a home with an address he didn't know — and where he wouldn't show up.

"Miss Preston!"

"Yes," she said quickly.

"I thought they only killed witches in Salem!" One of the boys, Hardy Richardson, said, shaking his head in disbelief. He was a handsome kid, dark-haired, tall and broad-shouldered, with a quick and boyish smile. It was nice that he had maintained his smile; without it, he appeared to be years older than his true chronological age.

"Ah, no. The 'craze,' as we consider it, happened in Salem. Salem was part of the Massachusetts Bay Colony. And, sadly, while the Puritans came to the New World in search of religious freedom, they were the least tolerant people one could imagine. Quakers and members of other religious groups were banished or punished severely — several were hanged at Boston Neck. Also, there were a number of people who lived here who were hanged for witchcraft — even before the horrific events began in Salem," Vickie said. "A woman named Anne Hibbins was hanged in 1656 — long before the trials began in Salem. We don't know the name of the woman buried here, honored by this tombstone. That's because she wasn't legally buried here."

"Right. So, how can she be buried here?" Hardy asked. "I thought they dumped the bodies right by the hanging tree or in some marsh plot nearby?"

"Sometimes, a brave and intrepid family member went out and found the body. If you study this stone, you'll see there is a date carved into the stone — 1733. She was probably found and buried here secretly by the family — and they marked her grave when they dared," Vickie said. "But that doesn't mean she's down there — progress and decades and then centuries mean that stones get moved around sometimes. Still, I love this memorial."

"Vicious people," Cheryl Taylor, a petite — but very pretty and well-built — brunette murmured, before looking over at Vickie. "Do you think that's why we have such a bad reputation now?" she asked Vickie. "I mean, Bostonians, we do have a reputation for being snobby. Think that dates back to the Puritans?"

Vickie grinned. "Maybe — who knows? It was an extremely repressive society. In fact, when King James II ordered that an Anglican chapel be built in Boston, he had a hard time getting land. The cemetery was here first — he took part of the cemetery to build the chapel. We're standing in the oldest cemetery in the city. You can actually learn a tremendous amount about people and society by visiting graveyards. Of course, remember, a lot of original old grave markers would have been wood — long gone now. Time and the elements take their toll. But you can see on some of the oldest stones that the art is severe — a skeletal head with wings, rather scary-looking. The stones, for such a serious people, could be expensive to buy and carve. Over time, the appearance becomes more that of a cherub or angel — life itself becoming more valuable, the terrors of death less extreme."

"Whoa, those Puritans!" Cheryl said, shaking her head. "Still I don't get it — when did they begin to die out? I mean, if everyone was banished or hanged for not being a Puritan . . ."

"All legal machinations, as well as religious. Charters came and went. James II of England was forced to abdicate his throne; William and Mary became King and Queen of England. They opened the colonies to others. Actually, it's complicated, but — as in many cases — it had to do with politics and government," Vickie said. "But in my mind, William and Mary made the greatest changes when they came to the throne of England in 1689 after the Glorious Revolution."

"The Salem witch trials were 1692! So, William and Mary let that happen."

Vickie nodded. "True. A large part of the world believed in the evil of witchcraft back then. Communications were very slow. William and Mary turned it over to their royal governor, William Phips. Phips set up the trials of *oyer and terminer* — which meant *to see and to hear.* When the dregs of society were being accused, William Stoughton, a tough old buzzard who wholeheartedly believed in Satan and witchcraft, allowed spectral evidence. Then suddenly everyone was being accused — including the governor's wife. So, in a way, public opinion turned the tide. And Phips — when his wife was accused. Rather than going out with a bang, it rather all ended with a whimper. In the years following, there were many changes in the entire colony, by law, by religion and by people. Like most things, change came about slowly. And the land for King's Chapel was actually taken during the rule of James II. Like I said, it had a lot to do with charters and laws and who was running what when. What's actually good here is that execution for witchcraft was far less frequent in the colonies than in Europe. And, when we did create our American Constitution, we set forth a separation of church and state. That guaranteed freedom

49

of religion when we became our own country."

"Right. Now we just have weirdo cults!"
Hardy said.

"True, but they don't run the country,"
Vickie said.

"Thank God, have you seen some of the
stuff on some cults? Scary!" Cheryl said.

"Really scary," Hardy said. "If spectral
evidence was allowed in court and the dregs
of society were killed first, we'd be goners,"
he said. "I mean, heck, the right person just
had to accuse you and your ass was in jail."

"Pretty much — but you're not the dregs
of society. You're about to be adults and
choose your own course," Vickie said.
"There will always be room to improve, but
laws do protect us now."

"Speaking of us as a country, though, is
Paul Revere here?"

The question was voiced by Art Groton.
Like Hardy, he was nearly eighteen. He was
tall, blond and wiry strong. In Vickie's
mind, he was just beginning to come out of
his shell.

Art still seldom spoke. He had a truly sad
personal history. Both parents had died in a
blaze they'd created themselves while free-
basing heroin. The uncle who had taken him
in had beaten him; his psychiatrist suspected

50

sexual abuse as well, but Art wouldn't say. According to Art's records, the uncle was also long dead due to drug abuse. Art seemed to have bounced around the system through several counties, but he now lived with the kindest couple Vickie knew working with foster children. And she was glad when they told her Art's excursions with her were something that seemed to awaken him. He talked about them constantly; he said he wanted to make his way through college and work with the system as well.

Who better to understand an abused and neglected kid than an abused and neglected kid?

"Paul Revere," Vickie told them, "is buried in the Granary cemetery along with Samuel Adams and John Hancock and many other notable people. Not far, of course. Boston is a small city — an old city! The three oldest burial grounds are King's Chapel, where we are now, Copp's Hill, and the Granary. All are on the Freedom Trail."

"Yah, Boston!" Hardy said. "And we have the oldest college, right? Harvard?"

"Yes, Harvard is the oldest university," Vickie agreed, "1636."

"And then Yale, right?" Hardy asked.

Vickie shook her head and smiled. "Nope. Harvard was followed by the College of William and Mary in Williamsburg, Virginia, St. John's College, Annapolis — and then Yale, 1701."

Cheryl laughed and said, "Man, you are a walking encyclopedia, Miss Preston!"

"I just like history," Vickie told her. She glanced at her watch, knowing it was time to break for the day. Her students returned to their various foster homes on their own after their meetings. It was part of their agreements with the Commonwealth of Massachusetts. She was careful, always, to make sure she finished up in time for them to make their way home.

"Next week," she told them, "we're touring the Paul Revere house, and I've arranged for dinner after at a great restaurant in Little Italy. Courtesy of an anonymous benefactor, I'll have you know. Maybe someone who made it well in life — after having a rough start like many of you."

"Cool!" Art called.

"Go! See you next week — meet right in front of the Paul Revere house."

Her charges scattered, waving. Vickie watched them go. She liked each and every one of them, and deeply hoped she could make a positive change for their future.

As she made her own way to the street,

she tried to keep focused on the entrance ahead.

There were days when the old cemetery was quiet — very quiet.

There were also days when she saw the dead walking. Mostly they just eyed her curiously — and suspiciously. Sometimes, someone would smile. She would smile in return, but hurry on. She wasn't fond of seeing the dead — at least, not so many dead.

Dylan Ballantine — or the ghost of Dylan Ballantine — suddenly fell into step beside her. She glanced at him, arched a brow, shook her head, and hurried on.

"Hey! That was great," he told her.

"I hope so. The plan is that I get them really interested in history or something useful," she murmured.

An old couple, following the Freedom Trail, most probably, paused and looked at her, frowning. Of course. It appeared to them that she was talking to herself.

"Please, Dylan, let me get out of here, huh?" she asked.

"Of course, of course," he said.

But he wasn't going away.

It wasn't that she wasn't accustomed to seeing Dylan now.

They were old friends.

They'd established rules.

He'd terrified her when he continued to appear to her years before — even when she realized that she and little Noah might well have been murdered if it hadn't been for Dylan's spiritual presence. He'd saved them; he'd gotten her and the baby out of the house when a serial killer had been watching them, biding his time, playing with them as he waited, amused, before showing himself to torture and kill them — as he had other victims before.

She could still feel a cold shiver of fear grip her heart when she thought back to that night.

But she'd had to put that behind her. Despite Dylan appearing here and there — startling and scaring her terribly at first, then begging for her recognition and friendship, and then actually seeming to take up residence with her when she'd headed down to NYU — she'd gotten dual degrees in history and literature. She'd published her first book on the tombstones of New England and was happily writing one on the decline of Puritanism in New England. She was making herself be very fair — she tended to hate the codes by which they had lived and their absolute lack of tolerance for others.

They were, on the one side, her ancestors.

Her mother's grandmother had come over from Ireland, and her great-grandfather had been a fresh-off-the boat Norwegian actor. But her father's family could trace roots back to the mid-1600s; they'd arrived on a ship just a few decades after the arrival of the *Mayflower.* Dylan loved to tease her about that.

His family had actually been New Yorkers. Sane.

"Don't you have someone better to haunt?" she asked him.

He shook his head gravely. "Not today. Followed you to the cemetery, thinking I might find someone to chat up. Other ghosts, you know. People who lived in different decades and centuries can be really interesting. But whoa! Those people. Straight-laced to the core. They don't seem to want to talk to strangers."

"Don't go blaming it all on the Puritans," Vickie told him. "This cemetery also houses those who died well after the Puritan days."

"Yeah, well, it's no fun to hang around a cemetery anyway. Unless you're you, of course, looking up the lives of all those who came before!"

"I'm ignoring you!" Vickie said, hurrying on ahead.

Naturally, he caught up to her.

On the street, she looked around, and then turned to him, speaking firmly. "Hey! I'm going to my parents' place. If you come, you behave. You understand."

He grinned. Dylan was still not quite eighteen. Charming, boyish and handsome. If she was going to have a continual haunt — or a crazed personality — she could have been plagued by a far worse ghost, she was certain. But some days, he was truly and mischievously out to make her appear to have gone daft.

"Sure," he said.

A cop car went by, sirens blazing. And then another. Dylan looked after the cop cars.

"Hey, something is going down — over by the Granary cemetery. Want to check it out?"

"No," she said flatly. "You feel free to do so."

"I will," he told her.

"See you then," she said.

He laughed. "Oh, yeah. Don't worry. I know where your parents live."

"Yes, of course, you do," she said.

It wasn't much of a walk to her parents' home in Little Italy. They'd moved when she'd gone to college, but they hadn't moved far. They were now in a refurbished building that dated back to the 1820s but had been meticulously updated and turned into state-of-the-art condos.

They loved it; her father was now retired after thirty years as a history professor at Harvard, and her mom had left her position as first-grade teacher just last year. Their apartment had everything they could desire and they were close to all the restaurants they loved — especially a certain cannoli shop.

When Vickie arrived, the two were studying a travel website.

"Italy! The real thing," Lucy Preston said, her smile wide and her words excited as she opened the door. "Dad and I are really doing it! Rome, Florence, Venice . . . we're going! Doing the booking right now."

"Great!" Vickie told her mother, giving her a hug.

"Want to come?" Lucy asked.

"No," Vickie said with a laugh. "Join you two lovebirds on a romantic trip? Nope, thank you, but no thank you. Besides, you two kids are retired now. You can come and go as you like."

"That wouldn't be a bad idea," her dad, Philip, said. "It would really get you away from Jared."

"That terrible man!" her mother said.

"Mom, he isn't a terrible man. He's just — not right for me."

"Well, you could come to Italy for a few days. I mean, you're writing now. You can write anywhere."

"Ah, but I can't find those persnickety Puritans just anywhere, can I? My research is here, in this area, Mom, you know that."

"We've created a monster, Lucy," her dad said, coming up behind her mom. "She has a work ethic, dear Lord!" he teased, kissing her cheek. "Seriously, though? You'd love this trip, Vickie. I know. You would absolutely love it! You could do research in Italy."

"Dad, the Puritans came from England, not Italy."

"Ahha! But later, Italians flocked in and now, we're living in what they call Little Italy!" her father said triumphantly.

"That's not the point. You two need to go on alone and have a wonderful and really romantic trip!"

Vickie smiled. She loved her parents deeply. They were so savvy in many ways, and just a little bit clueless in others. They sometimes reminded her of a pair of children — incredibly responsible children, but in their enthusiasm, they frequently appeared on fire. As parents went, they were comparatively young and in excellent health.

The trip they were planning was to celebrate the fact that they'd both turn sixty that year. In her mind, her dad — the esteemed Dr. Philip Preston — was as handsome and cool-looking as a rogue pirate — he kept his head clean-shaven and wore a tiny gold stud in one ear. He was well over six feet tall, lean and wiry. Her mom, on the other hand, was about five-two with a froth of blond curls and cat's eyes — a hazel color that changed constantly. Her parents were attractive and energetic and she could just see the two of them cuddling in the back of a gondola.

Nope — she definitely didn't want to go with them!

"I'm excited for you two," she said.

"Coffee is on — want some?" her dad asked.

"Love it!"

"Come see what we're planning," her mother told her, urging her over to the dining room table where they'd set up their computer.

"Venice!" her mom said. "We'll stay right on St. Mark's Square. And in Rome, well you won't believe this, but one of dad's old students works as a tour guide and he's going to take us on a special tour of the Forum and the Coliseum, and we're meeting friends at a little restaurant near the Vatican . . . You know, you could meet us for just part of the trip, if you wanted."

"My darling parents, I'm delighted that your health is great and that you're off on an adventure," Vickie said. "It will be wonderful. How long are you going for?"

"Twenty-one days," her dad said. "I know you love Italy. It was all you talked about after that college trip you took. But," he said, smiling at his wife, "I think you're right to stay home. We both love that you're working with young people now. It's great for them."

"I do love Italy. And I'll go back with you one day," she promised them.

"You staying here . . . does it have anything to do with Jared Norton?" he mother asked.

Vickie was surprised by the question.

"Mom, no — I'm just busy right now. And you guys need time to enjoy each other. Italy, so romantic! You two need to go. I need to stay and work."

Her mother sighed deeply, and then accepted her words.

"Come on, then! Coffee. And, of course, I've got a pie," her mom said. "Oh, wait — we should have dinner first. You're here! Oh, and don't make faces at me. I know I can't really cook, but I do make the best clam chowder to be found anywhere, even you say that!"

Lucy grinned at her daughter. And Vickie laughed. "Yep, your clam chowder is to die for, it is, Mom. I'm totally wiped out, though."

Naturally, her mom served up the clam chowder anyway. Vickie had a spoonful almost to her mouth when the ghost of Dylan Ballantine came streaking through the walls with a trail of mist, not unlike a dust storm in a cartoon.

Vickie dropped her spoon, startled. Clam chowder hopped out of the bowl in little droplets.

Her mother and father stared at her; then her mother shivered and frowned and looked uneasily about the room.

"Sorry! Clumsy me," Vickie said.

Dylan paid no mind to her words or her parents. He was intent on her attention.

"Vickie, Vickie, you've got to help, you've got to do something. Dammit, Vickie!"

She kept smiling at her confused parents, refusing to look in his direction.

"Vickie, that killer, that Undertaker. He's taken my mother, Vickie. You've got to do something!"

She couldn't help herself. She jerked around to stare at him, horrified.

61

"Yes! They found the last woman who'd gone missing and right after, my dad called in about my mom. We have to find her fast, Vickie. Somehow, we have to find her. Now. Before he kills her, too! Please, Vickie, don't let this happen to my mother!"

He was still speaking when there was a knock at the door. A heavy knock, pounding and insistent.

"FBI! Folks, please open up!" came a voice.

"What in the world?"

Philip Preston rose and strode to the door; he looked through the peephole before frowning and opening it.

Two men stepped in.

The first was tall and dark and had the high cheekbones and golden skin tone of a Native American, along with striking blue eyes.

The second man . . .

Vickie had started to rise. She froze by the table.

She knew him.

He had aged nine years, of course. His features were still striking, but they seemed cleaner cut, leaner, more rugged. His shoulders were broader. He'd been wearing the blue uniform of the Boston Police Department that day; now he was in a blue suit he wore with casual ease.

Yet she remembered him so clearly. He'd seen her . . . and he'd warned her to get down. He'd taken a shot, and he'd disarmed the man who had been after her and little Noah on that fateful day. He'd been tall and strong and ridiculously macho and beautiful to her. Detectives had interviewed her, but he'd been there with coffee and a blanket, and he'd held her when she started to shake and had nearly fallen because she was so nervous. He'd been called to be there when she brokenly described everything that had happened that day.

She had thanked him for saving her.

"But it wasn't really me, was it?" he'd asked her.

She hadn't answered; she'd never known what to say, how much he knew, how much he had seen . . . if maybe he actually spoke to the dead himself.

She'd watched him interviewed on the news. He'd stopped a stone-cold killer. He had done nothing any man on the beat wouldn't have done, he had told reporters. He'd just been there when escaped convict Bertram Aldridge had burst out of the Ballantine house.

She could have been brutally murdered that day. Bertram Aldridge had come after her with a gun. That wasn't his customary means of murder. He liked to slice up his victims and write messages in their blood. He liked to write notes to the police and smear them with blood.

She had been lucky; so damned lucky. Time had allowed her to walk and talk normally again. To head down to NYC for college, to take work there as a researcher, but now . . .

She'd come home. And there he was. Griffin Pryce. He was standing next to the tall dark-haired man who was explaining that Chrissy Ballantine had been taken and they'd like to speak with Victoria for just a few minutes.

As Vickie continued to stare while her father explained that she hadn't worked for the Ballantine family since she'd been in college, she saw that Dylan had gone to the men, that he was speaking a blue streak at the same time.

"You have to find my mother. This isn't fair. My family has lost too much. Whatever the hell it takes, you have to find my mother."

It was almost as if Griffin Pryce had heard him. Because he spoke next, almost interrupting Philip Preston.

"We will find Chrissy Ballantine. We will,"

he said with conviction.

"But what makes you think that Vickie could help?" her father asked, frustrated.

And then Griffin Pryce looked at her. His eyes were older, harder than she remembered, though still determined and macho and beautiful and . . .

"Because her name is part of the clue that was sent to the media," he said softly.

CHAPTER TWO

Taker — as he had determined his code name to be — stood watching the commotion. Cops, reporters, medics — you name it.

It was good. So good. The woman, it seemed, was alive. People everywhere were talking. A tall blonde next to him smiled at him radiantly. "Can you believe it? They saved her! Dug her right out of the ground — and saved her!"

"Hallelujah," he said, nodding seriously. "Thank God!"

The blonde moved on.

He became aware that *Under* was coming to stand next to him. Under thought that being Under meant being the leader — and that Taker had agreed with that, since, in the name the press had given them — *Undertaker* — *Under* came first. Taker knew that Under was a lackey; he was the smart one. He was the one with the plan. And —

though he refrained from saying it — being a Taker was far better than being Under.

No matter. His accomplice was good — and loyal. Loyal, he knew, mattered most.

"So, they saved her ass!" Under said.

"Doesn't matter, does it?" Taker asked.

"Not when we've got a big one all boxed up!" Under said, and laughed.

Taker started moving down the street. Under followed in his footsteps.

"Think we'll get to see what happens with that one? I got to admit, I'm hoping your clue doesn't work. That's one I'd love to see go bad."

"Yeah," Taker agreed. "But hey, not the prize we're really looking for, right?"

"But a thread to the prize," Under said, and paused in the street, smiling as they watched the growing throng of reporters in the area. "Love this, love it, love it . . . and best of all . . ."

"Best of all, what?" Taker asked.

Under grinned. "We've got the dough to keeping going and going." Under paused, frowning. "Hey, what happens when we've taken down the prize, huh? I mean, this is cool, really cool. But I mean, you have an objective. And that's okay. But . . ."

"You change. You change your direction. Your style, your signature. And start all over again. You become someone else."

"So, this never has to end?"

"No, it never has to end," Taker said.

It would end, of course. He did have an objective. And as to his good friend Under . . .

Well, friendships often — and tragically — came to an end.

But for now . . .

His eye was on the prize. And as for Under . . . at the moment, Under was loyal, like a lapdog, and had assets and abilities Taker did not. Under could, upon occasion, behave in a superior manner, but . . .

Really. It was all just a matter of time.

"Where Preston ran and good old Paul rode."

Vickie sat frozen in her chair as Griffin Pryce read the words.

The two men had declined to take seats; therefore, her parents had refused to sit again. They were like a pair of puppies, blindsided by a couple of whacks to the head.

Not that Vickie felt any different. Or, perhaps, she did. She felt *frozen.*

"This is wrong, just wrong," Philip Preston said. "I mean, Preston is not an uncommon name. This clue may not refer to Vickie in any way. You're asking my daughter to become involved with a killer. A killer who might target her. You can't mean —"

"Yes, Mr. Preston," Jackson Crow said.

Vickie's father was not ready to give in. "Victoria was almost killed once. That man, that awful man — it's him? Aldridge! Bertram Aldridge. She won't be involved. I'll get her out of the country, I'll —"

"Bertram Aldridge is sitting in prison," Griffin said. "He will be there for life."

"This is someone who likes to taunt the police with notes," Jackson Crow said. "Most probably, they simply remembered and took her name from the newspapers or media at the time."

"They can't mean Vickie," her mother murmured.

"They mean Vickie," Griffin added quietly.

"Oh, no, no, no, no . . ." the ghost of Dylan Ballantine said, hands pressed to his temples. "My mom, they're talking about my mom."

"I know you!" Vickie's mother gasped suddenly. "You — you're Officer Pryce. You were the cop who was there the day that . . ."

"The day I was nearly killed, Mom," Vickie said.

"Yes, yes, you've been at our home before, and we're grateful, but . . . no, not again.

69

My husband is right. You'll get Vickie targeted by this sick person," Lucy replied.

"She may help save a woman's life. We don't like bringing anyone into harm's way, Mrs. Preston," Griffin said. "But I'm afraid that whoever is responsible, they know about the attempt by Bertram Aldridge on Vickie's life. The Ballantine house is near the Paul Revere house. And Vickie ran from that house."

"Look!" Philip Preston said angrily, "I won't have it! I won't have you use her."

"Dad!" she said, standing up suddenly. "Dad, please. I know you're talking out of love for me. But I'm an adult. I can make my own choices. And if there's anything I can do, I'm willing to do it."

"No!" her mother said, her face going as pale as ash.

"Mom, Dad, it will be all right. These men are FBI. There are cops everywhere. I'm going to go with them and see if I can do anything."

"Then you're going to Italy with us!" her father said firmly.

"Dad, we'll talk later. But time may be of the essence here. Please. I'm going to go with them," Vickie said firmly. She rose and looked at Griffin and said, "Shall we? I mean, I will be with the two of you at all times, right?"

"Absolutely," Griffin said, looking at her. He had, she thought, the darkest eyes she had ever seen. Dark eyes, dark hair, bronzed, rugged face. For a moment, their gazes seemed to be locked. He didn't like this, she knew. He wasn't happy to be drawing her in.

She realized that he and the other agent, Jackson Crow, were here because they were desperate to save a woman's life.

And she could help.

"You'll call me, you'll call us, the minute . . . I mean, you'll keep in touch, you'll let us know where you are every step of the way," her father said.

"We're wasting time," Dylan's ghost said urgently.

"Hey, it's going to be okay," Vickie assured her parents. She looked from Griffin Pryce to Jackson Crow and said, "We need to go."

"Go where? Vickie —"

"Where Preston ran and Paul rode," Vickie said. "The corner where the Ballantine house is — down the street from the Paul Revere house. They have her there somewhere. If I see the site, I might know what the clue means."

It had been some time since Griffin had

71

seen Victoria Preston.

Over eight years.

He had never forgotten her.

She had matured well.

When he had first met her — terrified at the scene when he had shot and wounded Bertram Aldridge — she had still been a kid. At least basically. She'd already been about five-eight back then, willowy, with long black hair and tremendous green eyes and fine, slim features. She'd been a beautiful girl — but beautiful girls like her abounded, and he might have seen dozens like her at any sorority party or teen gathering.

He'd immediately felt an affinity for her.

And she'd needed to talk. Which was good, because there was paperwork. Lots of it. She'd explained about the door being slightly open, but Mr. and Mrs. Ballantine had been home. She'd made sure it was locked and the alarm on after they had gone.

He hadn't been a detective back then; he'd been on the force three years, gathering experience, and had already started the application process with the FBI.

Detectives had taken over along with the FBI. Bertram Aldridge had gone back to being incarcerated with another trial in his future. He'd killed two guards during his escape.

Griffin shouldn't have had anything else to do with Victoria Preston. But he hadn't been able to leave it alone. He'd had to check on her.

Because he wouldn't have been on time — he wouldn't have saved her life — if Bertram Aldridge hadn't gone down. His shot might have killed Bertram instead of wounding him, but Victoria Preston would have been shot as well if Bertram Aldridge's shot hadn't gone wild . . .

He hadn't liked to think about it back then. He didn't like to think about it now.

But he'd seen the kid who had been with Vickie.

The ghost.

Seen him, and then he'd been gone. Griffin never knew if Vickie had seen what he'd seen that day, if she hadn't been saved to a far greater degree by a dead boy than she had been saved by his own actions.

He'd never point-blank asked her if she'd seen the boy; he hadn't been sure of what he'd seen himself, despite his own past.

Now, of course, he knew. Yes, she saw the boy.

And the boy was still with her.

Chrissy Ballantine's older son.

Griffin was doing the driving; he was the Bostonian, who knew where he was going, which streets were open, which were closed, which only went in one direction. They could have easily walked. But under the circumstances, the car was quicker — and more official.

And, thankfully, due to government tags, could be left anywhere, even in the narrow streets of Old Boston.

He'd suggested that they head to the corner street of the Ballantine house. Naturally, police were still in the house. George Ballantine was there with his son, and crime scene techs and detectives were going over the house and the grounds and trying to ascertain how the kidnapper/killer got in — and how he or she got out.

Jackson Crow was fast to get out of the car, but Vickie Preston was already out the back door. She stood for a moment, looking around. Griffin hurried around to her side, looking around as well.

The Paul Revere house was just down the street. They were on the Freedom Trail. When Griffin had been growing up, he'd had lots of friends who lived in other areas and the suburbs who came here just to shop for their Italian sausages and cannoli.

It was Old Boston. Centuries of history

unfolded in a number of fairly centralized streets; giant skyscrapers stood among cemeteries where founding fathers had long lain at rest. Great Gothic houses of worship stood among the modern, built in defiance of restrictions long before the Constitution affording a separation of church and state had been penned. Boston was, in Griffin's mind, a perfect example of the making of a country — and, in this particular area, there were treasures to be found.

It was also a mammoth haystack. How to find a woman among the new and the old — and the many giant buildings that rested here and there between those crafted at a time when a skyscraper had yet to be imagined?

"You think that she's here — somewhere near the house?" Jackson asked Vickie.

She stood looking up, thoughtful, distraught. Then she glanced Griffin's way.

"I'm a writer and researcher," she murmured. "I don't know much about the mind of a killer, I'm afraid. But . . ."

"But what?" Griffin heard himself ask, a little too sharply.

"Yeah, what, what?"

The ghost of Dylan Ballantine was with them, anxious. Griffin hadn't felt his presence in the car — Dylan must have come

75

on foot. Or through the air — or however the dead managed to travel.

None of them actually responded to the boy.

Griffin glanced at Jackson.

Apparently, none of them were going to acknowledge the fact that the others also saw Dylan.

"The clue is, 'Where Preston ran and old Paul rode.' I mean, he might have ridden on any of the streets around here, and maybe it doesn't mean anything. The reference to 'Preston' could also mean anything, but 'where old Paul rode' might suggest that she's somewhere Paul Revere might have been."

Griffin looked around the street. He tried to judge the age of the buildings they saw. The apartments across from them had 1830 chiseled into the stone. They were near Boston Common, and they were near a few of the very old churches, and, of course, burial grounds.

But he didn't think they'd find her in a cemetery or vault. Their last victim had been found so. Maybe the killer thought that they'd start digging, with such a clue.

"The Ballantine house," Vickie said. "It was here before the Revolution."

"The Ballantine house is crawling with

cops," Jackson pointed out.

"The basement?" Dylan said.

"They haven't found anything to explain how the killer might have spirited her out," Jackson said to Griffin. "It's easy enough for a determined criminal to watch people coming and going — and to notice they might have forgotten to lock a door or haven't found time to lock it and set an alarm. No one saw or heard anything. It wouldn't be surprising if a criminal had just slipped in and even out. But it'd be more surprising if someone came out carrying something the size of a woman, even if Chrissy Ballantine is a small woman."

Dylan was already running across the street.

"Vickie?" Griffin asked.

"They have a basement. Only part of it has been finished. The foundation is really big — so, as you can imagine, there's a lot to the basement."

Griffin studied Vickie. He was pretty sure that she had something of a "gift." Intuition, or something stronger that helped her. Like her ability to see the dead.

A gift . . . that some people might consider a curse or a sickness! Whichever. At the moment, he had to think that they were working with a gift — one that could save lives.

The three of them headed toward the house. Men in uniform stood outside, blocking entrance to it, but Griffin and Jackson quickly showed their credentials. They were allowed through.

George Ballantine was seated on the couch in the grand parlor of the house; it was a large room, tastefully furnished with antiques. He had a cup of coffee in front of him that he hadn't touched. When they entered, he was talking aloud, rambling, just to talk and try to figure out why this would have happened to him.

"Chrissy is smart, she doesn't just open the door. I mean, my God, we had a maniac in here once. She's careful." He paused, breaking off in pain. "We lost my older son — we nearly lost Noah. And now Chrissy . . ."

He broke off, staring across the room.

"Vickie?"

"Mr. Ballantine," she said, hurrying forward.

George stood, a distinguished man in his tailored suit, and reached out for Vickie. She hurried forward and he enveloped her in a trembling hug.

"Mr. Ballantine, we think that Vickie can help," Jackson said.

George Ballantine looked at Jackson and

then at Griffin.

They'd met at the house, briefly, before heading over to pick up Vickie. George Ballantine hadn't really seemed to recognize Griffin from the past, but then, they hadn't had much interaction. The detectives and FBI agents on the case had dealt with the family. He'd looked at Griffin strangely, but hadn't seemed to have grasped the connection.

Vickie — he knew.

"Vickie, dear, so good of you to come . . . it's been so long. Noah . . . Noah is in his room. I'm trying to keep him from everything going on. Of course, I haven't managed that at all. He's nine now, still a kid, but . . . I'm going to have to explain. He just knows that his mom is missing. He had baseball today, Little League, you know? They called me because Chrissy wasn't there to get him, and then I came home, and she wasn't here, but she had a cup of tea out . . . Chrissy doesn't leave things out like that. Her purse is here, her keys . . . it's as if she's vanished into the thin air. And that clue, Vickie, I mean, thank you. No one can know that 'Preston' means you, but . . . oh, God! I can't believe this. My family, Chrissy, she's amazing . . . you know Chrissy. Oh, God."

Vickie Preston drew gently away from him. "Mr. Ballantine, we need to search the basement."

"The basement? The cops have been down there — they've been everywhere," he said.

"Yes, Mr. Ballantine, but we need to look, please," Griffin told him.

The man still looked dazed. "Of course. Whatever. But shouldn't you be out there looking for her?"

"We're working on it, Mr. Ballantine. Please," Jackson said quietly.

"What about the other woman — the other woman who was just saved? It's all over the news — you just saved her. Can't she tell you anything — tell you who did this? She could help, she could give us something!" George said.

"We keep checking in," Griffin assured him. "I'm afraid she's still unconscious. We need your help, sir."

Ballantine nodded. "Sure." He frowned as he stared at Griffin. "I know you," he said.

"I used to be a Boston police officer," Griffin said.

"Yeah, yeah, you were here . . ." George Ballantine seemed confused, and then angry. "Are you the reason this madman took my Chrissy?"

"I don't believe so, sir. I haven't worked

here in years," Griffin said.

"Then what the hell are you doing here?" Mr. Ballantine demanded. Then he looked at Vickie as if it all might somehow be her fault. "Both of you . . . maybe it's because of you."

Vickie was visibly shaken; Griffin fought his anger. The man was in no condition to be rational.

"I'm with the FBI now, Mr. Ballantine," Griffin said. "Excuse us. We're hoping that something in the basement will help."

He turned; he didn't know the Ballantine house, but Vickie did. She took his cue and walked away from Ballantine, heading to the kitchen.

Vickie opened the door that led to the basement. Griffin and Jackson followed her down. It was evident the police and techs had been down there already. Shelves that lined the brick walls had been gone through; the door to a half bath stood open.

One door led to the water heater and cooling system, another to other mechanics. The first room held a pool table and old comfortable chairs. There was a half bar that had been built to one side.

Structural components blocked off various areas.

They walked through the different rooms

in the basement, between giant brick columns, leaving behind the finished section and moving into a raw work area. They all searched.

Vickie stood in the middle of the floor, baffled.

Dylan Ballantine appeared at her side.

"Vickie, please, please, think!"

She was thinking; that was painfully evident.

"I'm not sure what else . . . where else. The clue seems so evident. Where Paul rode . . . this house would have stood then. I'm not sure what else . . . there's the Paul Revere house down the street, but too many people are in and out. And the churches . . . there are so many tourists around."

"And we just found a woman in one of the cemeteries," Jackson said quietly, encouraging her train of thought.

"She's here. She's here — I'm sure she's here," Vickie murmured.

Griffin looked around. A pile of wood was neatly stacked against a far wall. He closed his eyes and tried to see with his mind's eye. Yes, there could be someone beneath it. But with just the wood piled on top?

Had the killer changed his ways, and strangled or stabbed her first?

He strode firmly over to the woodpile and

began to toss the large and small logs to the side. He became more frantic, and then he was joined by Jackson and Vickie.

But as they neared the bottom of the pile, he felt his frustration grow. There was no woman there.

"Beneath, beneath!" Vickie cried. "There's a door to a deeper pit . . . they used to store way more wood down here before, decades ago, long before modern heating systems came in."

And there was a door. Griffin saw a little metal ring in the middle of it. He jerked so hard on it that he almost ripped the thin wood portal out of its sockets.

And there she lay. Chrissy Ballantine, covered in the minutiae of dust and chips and dirt that had fallen upon the place where she'd been entombed . . .

"Get her out," Jackson said.

"Mom, Mom!" the ghost of Dylan sobbed.

Griffin dropped low on his knees and lifted Chrissy Ballantine from the little pit in her own home. He was prepared to resuscitate; Jackson was shouting to the cops upstairs to get a paramedic down to him.

Vickie stood by, silent, watching, as if she were frozen.

Chrissy Ballantine took a deep breath and

coughed and sputtered on her own.

Resuscitation wasn't necessary.

Chrissy Ballantine was alive and breathing on her own.

And her eyes opened. She looked up and smiled.

"Vickie . . . Dylan." Her eyes closed. She was alive.

And the paramedics were hurrying down to tend to her.

Griffin closed his own eyes for a minute, silently thankful that they'd found a second woman alive — on the same day.

Then he realized that Dylan's mother had said his name.

He looked up where Vickie was standing. She stood alone, staring at him with enormous green eyes. He tried to smile and rose and moved away from the paramedics and Chrissy Ballantine. They could hear George Ballantine above, fighting with the cops to get to his wife. They could hear a policeman urging him to let the paramedics work.

"She'll be okay, Mr. Ballantine. She'll be okay. You can come along. They're going to get her to the hospital now," one of the officers assured him.

"We've got to go to the hospital, too," Jackson told him.

"Yeah," he said. "But first, we have to get

Miss Preston home."

Vickie shook her head. "I should go back to my parents' house, Agent Pryce. They need to know — I mean, I can call them, but they're parents and need to see me, to know that I'm just fine and that Chrissy Ballantine has been found. Alive."

"Of course," Jackson told her. "But we'll get an officer to escort you."

"And," Griffin added, "please assure them that we'll have officers outside their building."

"Do you think Chrissy Ballantine will know what happened?"

"Two victims were found alive today, Miss Preston," Jackson said. "We can certainly hope that one of them is able to give us something. Mrs. Ballantine owes her life to you, and we got lucky with the other victim. We're working to find real answers soon."

The med techs were getting Chrissy onto a stretcher. Boston med techs were among the finest in the country, Griffin was certain. Chrissy Ballantine already had an IV in her arm and an oxygen mask over her nose and mouth. Her color was already better; she was going to make it just fine, he believed.

When they had cleared the room, Vickie headed toward the stairs.

Detective David Barnes was on his way down.

He almost ran straight into Vickie.

"Miss Preston?" he asked.

"Yes."

"I'm Detective Barnes. You found her — you found her already?"

Griffin wasn't sure if the note in Barnes's voice was amazement — or skepticism.

"Logical, Detective," Jackson said, stepping forward. "And thank God for Miss Preston. She went the historical and reasonable route. No one saw anything. Hard to slip the woman out in a neighborhood like this without someone seeing something. And as for the clue — where old Paul rode. This house was here. Victoria Preston was pretty amazing."

"Of course — and still, wow. Amazing — that's the word," Barnes said. "Thank you for your help, Miss Preston. Naturally, there's paperwork."

"There always is," Vickie said.

"Miss Preston would like to get to her parents' home and let them know that she's fine and that Mrs. Ballantine is alive as well," Griffin said.

"Yes, of course. But . . ." Barnes said.

"I'll go with Miss Preston and take her statement," Jackson said. "You and Griffin can head to the hospital and speak with Mrs. Ballantine as soon as it's possible without endangering her health."

"All right," Barnes said. Griffin was sure the man was still looking at the three of them suspiciously, as if they shared something that he wasn't in on.

And they did.

"Let's go then," he said to Barnes. He paused and turned to Vickie.

She looked tired, covered in sawdust and damp from exertion. Her dark hair was disarrayed and her eyes seemed incredibly large and green in the garish light of the unfinished area of the basement.

"Thank you," he told her.

"Of course," she said. "Of course."

That should have been it. He should have moved instantly.

He didn't. He stood there a few seconds longer. There was more to say.

He didn't know how to say it.

When he finally turned to head out, he knew that he'd see her again.

He had to. He had to because . . .

He simply had to.

"Bick-bick! Vickie, Victoria!"

Vickie was almost out the door, escorted by a nice big cop on one side and the rock of a man who was Jackson Crow on the other, when she heard Noah Ballantine calling to her.

She turned, and it felt as if her heart melted in her chest. Though the families had stayed friends since the night of the traumatic events — they'd seen each other now and then at church or other social events — it had now been years since she had seen Noah.

She would have recognized Noah Ballantine, now a nine-year-old, anywhere. He hadn't changed much. His dad was a truly dignified-looking man, and somehow, Noah was just as dignified. His mother was beautiful, and Noah was still a beautiful kid.

He remembered her. And that was truly amazing. He'd been so young the last time they'd seen one another.

He was tall for his age, lean, with a thatch of sandy hair and hazel eyes. He stared at Vickie gravely, and yet with a look of hope that was humbling. He wasn't a particularly big kid, but something about his face and eyes seemed way older than his years.

His father, Vickie knew, had just headed for the hospital. Griffin and Detective Barnes would be following. She hoped that everyone hadn't just forgotten Noah in their anxiety for his mother and determination to talk to her.

"Noah!" she said, and she walked back to him as he raced into her arms.

She hugged him tightly for a minute. When he pulled away at last, he looked at her and said, "I knew you would come. I knew you would save my mother. The way you saved me."

Vickie flushed, humbled. "Noah, it wasn't just me, lots of people were involved."

He smiled at her. "But I knew you would come." There was suddenly an oddly mischievous look about him. "And, of course, I know there are others involved. But Bickbick . . . wow, gotta quit calling you Bickbick." He laughed. "I mean I'm older now. And so are you."

"Thanks."

"Not that old!" Noah said quickly.

"Thanks again. And, well, I'm not so sure you're so grown-up they need to throw you out on the streets with the work force," she told him. "And you may call me anything you like. Noah, it's so good to see you."

"My mom . . . she's going to be all right, isn't she?"

"I believe so, Noah. And, hopefully, she'll be able to tell the officers what happened, and all this will be over," Vickie said.

Griffin Pryce and Detective Barnes came

up behind Noah, waiting patiently before heading out to follow the ambulance to the hospital.

Noah swung around and headed to Griffin to shake his hand.

"Thank you. Thank you. Twice now. You're really good, I figure. You knew to bring Victoria in. Somehow, sir, I think all this must be that awful man from before," he said.

Vickie liked the way Griffin smiled down at Noah. He apparently had a nice soft spot for kids.

"We're just super grateful, Noah, that your mom is going to be okay. And the man before — we made certain — he is in prison. So. What are we going to do about you right now? I think your dad was pretty eager to go be with your mom. Do you have any other family here?"

"No, sir. My parents were kind of old when they had me. Late-life kid, I've heard people say. My grandparents are dead. I think I have cousins in Baltimore. But I'll be okay. This house has an alarm system — and I watch cop shows, even though I'm really not supposed to," Noah said. "I know as soon as he can, my dad will come back and get me so I can see my mom."

"You know what, Noah? If you want,

Detective Barnes and I are on our way to the hospital — we'll take you with us," Griffin told him.

"Really? That would be great."

Barnes looked at Griffin and frowned.

"We'll have someone from social services sit with you until you can see her," Griffin said.

"I can do better than that — just let me see my parents and I'll head to the hospital and sit with Noah," Vickie offered. She could have called them, of course. Under the circumstances, it seemed best to actually see them and speak with them in person.

"Miss Preston, you've been invaluable," Detective Barnes said. "I'm sure that —"

"Noah and I are old friends," Vickie said. "It will be my pleasure."

"It is set then," Jackson Crow said firmly. "I'll see to it that Miss Preston visits her parents, and then gets to the hospital. Vickie, if you will?" he asked, indicating the door.

Vickie smiled at the others and spun around to head out the door. The big cop was patiently waiting for them. A crowd had gathered; traffic was snarled.

News, it seemed, traveled fast. Maybe people just gathered any time an ambulance

91

and cop cars appeared. "Duck your head — we'll keep your involvement out of the press," Jackson Crow told her.

She ducked her head.

The cop drove; Vickie was next to him, aware of Jackson Crow behind her.

The cop stayed with the car, Jackson politely thanking him.

Up in her parents' apartment, Vickie was nearly crushed to death by her mom and dad. She told them happily that Mrs. Ballantine was going to be fine, they were fairly certain. She would spend at least one night in the hospital.

"We should really visit when we can, Phil," her mother told her father. "It is sad — we were close with George and Chrissy for so long. And then the thing happened with that maniac Bertram Aldridge. We just . . . I guess we just drifted apart lately. Anytime we saw one another . . . I guess all we could think about was that our children might have . . . died."

"Of course we'll visit!" Phil said. He still had an arm around Vickie's shoulders. He stared at Jackson as if daring the man to take her away from him.

"Actually, Dad, I'm going to the hospital now. I'm going to stay with Noah Ballantine," Vickie told them.

"No," her mother said. "No, no, Vickie."

"Mom, it will be okay," she said firmly. "Noah is nine and he doesn't have any family here and he might wind up hanging with child services."

"Which isn't terrible!" her dad said.

"Which isn't happening," she said firmly. "I came right here so we could tell you what happened and so you could see I was okay. Hey, you know how to work the Skype on your phones. I'll keep in touch — visually! — okay? I know you're scared, too. But we're talking about a little boy who has to be in some real trauma right now."

She kissed her dad's cheek and then her mom's.

Her dad stared at Jackson Crow. "Don't you let anything happen to her!"

"Sir, we will not," Crow promised.

"This is all too much. Vickie isn't a cop or an agent or —"

"Dad, I'm just going to hang with Noah. It will be fine," Vickie said, determined. "Love you both. We have a cop double-parked downstairs. We have to go."

Her parents kissed her again. She glanced at Jackson Crow, flushing slightly. She was surprised at how overprotective her folks were behaving.

"I'll be in touch," she promised.

They managed to escape to the hallway. In the elevator, she looked over at Jackson. "I'm sorry. I mean, I've been away from home a long time. I've just moved back and . . ."

"Never be sorry that you have people who love you so much," he told her, indicating that the elevator door had opened.

She smiled uneasily and headed out.

They didn't speak in the cop car; Jackson Crow received a call. When they reached the hospital, Jackson knew just which way to go after receiving clearance from the hospital's security. Chrissy was already out of the emergency room and on a floor above.

There was a waiting room; Griffin Pryce was there with Noah Ballantine. He rose when they arrived, nodding at them all. "Jackson, I'll head back in. Chrissy has been in and out of consciousness. Detective Barnes is there. We haven't pressed her yet."

"Great. Noah, how are you doing?" Jackson asked.

"I'm fine, sir. Griffin talked to the doctors — my mom is really going to be okay. Whoever did this to her gave her a really good conk on the head. They want her to stay here tonight and probably tomorrow night. But she's going to be okay."

Griffin looked at Vickie. She had no idea what he was thinking; he seemed to have acquired the ability to look as stoic as Jackson Crow. Maybe it was FBI training, not to give anything away.

"So, Noah, here we are," Vickie said. "I'm so glad — so grateful about your mom."

"Bick-bick," he said, smiling. "I'm so glad you're with me."

"Okay, we have some time to kill," she said. "Tell me what's up with you."

They sat in the waiting room. Jackson Crow took up a position by the door. Griffin went out.

Noah told her about school and Little League and everything that he was doing. She, in turn, told him about school in New York and coming back and working with some of the older kids in the system. They managed to pass time — until Noah fell asleep with his head on her lap.

A police officer in uniform came in and Jackson Crow went out. When she looked down at her lap, Vickie saw that Noah had woken up and was staring at her.

"You see Dylan," he said softly.

She didn't mean to jerk with her surprise at his words, but she did.

He smiled. "We haven't seen a lot of each other since you went to New York, but I know that you see Dylan! I mean, he told me that he hangs with you a lot. He comes home now and then, too. Did he help you find Mom? He wasn't at the house."

"No, he wasn't at the house when it happened. But . . ." She hesitated. She had certainly agreed that she saw him. "I'm sure he's in with her now," she said simply.

Noah nodded and began to whisper quickly. "I don't tell anybody — they'd think that I was crazy. And we never got a chance to talk about it. Or, I guess we just didn't talk about it."

"You were so young. And I thought that I was crazy," Vickie said.

"I tried to tell my dad once and then I heard him talking to my mom and they were both worried that I was still troubled subconsciously by all the stuff that happened when I was a toddler. They wanted to have me like picked apart at some institute — and I was never a dumb kid, Vickie. They meant a loony bin. I never told anybody after that. Not my friends, not my teachers . . . not the priest. I didn't tell anybody. I didn't want to get locked up. And I knew that nobody else saw what I saw. But I did know that you saw him, too, because Dylan told me that he had a good time 'haunting' you, though he hitched a ride back up here

96

on the train a lot."

Vickie looked at him and nodded and actually managed a slight smile. She'd gotten Dylan to knock — mind over matter, he'd told her. He hadn't been so good at first, but he'd learned to make noise rapping at the door. She'd always had a bad time when he thought that she was dating the wrong guy. He had no problem telling her, and — she was quick to discover — Dylan tended to be right in his character assessments.

"I see Dylan, yes, and he's still my friend, and way back when, you really can't possibly remember, but . . . Dylan kept us both from being killed."

"I do remember," he said. "Odd, huh? They say you can't possibly remember when you were so little. But I guess, maybe . . . I always saw Dylan."

"I didn't, until that day. And then . . . after a while of seeing him, I realized that sometimes, I saw other ghosts as well. I think I realized it first when I was walking by a cemetery. Not that I've found that the dead really want to hang out in graveyards all the time."

Noah looked at her somberly.

"Right — like, I mean, really, who would? I'm sure there are more fun places to be.

But, you know, Agent Pryce sees him, too," he said. "I know Griffin sees Dylan. He just can't say anything. Maybe Agent Crow sees him, too. But I know for sure that Griffin does. And you know what?"

"What?"

"You need to ask him about it. Because it's important. I know I'm a kid, and people don't listen to kids, but . . . I think it's going to matter. I think Dylan is going to help again. And I think you're going to have to tell Griffin that you see Dylan. Because I know . . ."

"You know what?"

"I know this isn't over."

"Noah, your mom is fine, she's going to be fine, and —"

"My mom will be fine. That's not it, Vickie."

"What is it, then?"

"Vickie, I'm afraid that it's not over for *you*."

Taker watched the news. He really hadn't given a damn that a few of the women had been found alive. Why bother taunting the police and sending the clues if they didn't want them to have some hope?

But this . . .

They'd found Chrissy Ballantine so

damned quickly. How the hell . . . ?

For a moment, he felt a rush of unease — almost bordering on fear.

Had he really learned his lessons well? Yes, always be on the lookout. Take care of cameras, know the lay of the land, know the victim, know timing, always wear gloves, never let the thrill — the rush of pleasure over a kill — get in the way of a controlled crime scene.

His unease suddenly turned to anger; his anger to raw fury.

He stared at the television screen.

Control. Care. Organization.

He waited until the rush of fury was gone, and then he dialed Under.

"The party is alive and swinging," Under said.

"Yep, so . . . I think we need to find another cool party, huh? Have you checked out any?" he asked.

"I know just the place. You ready?"

"Hell, yeah. Time to dance!" Taker said.

Was he ready?

Absolutely. Oh, yes, absolutely. And this time . . .

This time, well, he'd just have to tighten up his "party" package.

CHAPTER THREE

Chrissy Ballantine appeared dazed — and brilliantly awake.

Griffin wasn't sure he'd ever seen anyone so grateful to be alive.

George Ballantine had spent the night in a hospital chair at her side. His tender care for his wife was touching; Griffin had seen couples ripped apart by far less. He wasn't sure exactly what the statistics were, but he knew couples who lost children often found themselves split apart by their grief, rather than brought closer together.

Not so with George and Chrissy. Maybe Noah had saved them.

"Griffin, Officer Pryce!" Chrissy said, reaching out her hands to him.

"He's not Officer Pryce now," George reminded her. "He's Special Agent Pryce."

"Whatever his title, a godsend!" Chrissy said.

He stepped close to the bed, taking her

hands. "You look well," he told her quietly.

"Thanks to you," she said. "And to you, Special Agent Crow," she added, looking past Griffin to where Jackson waited just inside the hospital room door.

"And, really Victoria Preston," Griffin told her.

"I know!" she said softly, looking over at her husband. She added in a rush, "I understand that Vickie went above and beyond. George said he gave her permission to take Noah to her apartment for the night and they'll be back here soon. And that an officer watched over them through the night. I'm very grateful. I'll never be able to tell you how grateful I am."

"We need anything that you can remember about yesterday morning, Mrs. Ballantine," Griffin said. "Anything."

"I know!" she told him, her smile fading, her voice dismayed. "I don't know . . . I mean, I was in the kitchen, taking salad fixings out of the refrigerator. And then . . . I don't know! I remember waking up and realizing that I was penned in and it was dark and I could smell wood and oldness and dampness — and I knew I was in the old log pit in the basement. I screamed at first, and I tried to claw my way out and then . . . No one heard my screams and I couldn't breathe and I couldn't move and . . . and then I was here, waking up in this bed, disoriented . . ."

Neither Griffin nor Jackson had expected much; she'd woken during the night a few times, but been so disoriented they'd left her to the doctors and her husband.

Luckily, Barbara Marshall, rescued from the cemetery yesterday, was in the same hospital.

Barbara had become coherent at about three this morning; they'd spent time with her — and heard the same story. Nothing. Barbara had been slipping a pod into her coffeemaker — that was the last thing she'd remembered.

Both houses had been equipped with alarms.

The alarms had been set; the codes had been keyed in. The kidnapper — or kidnappers — had managed to find the alarm codes and slip into the houses without missing a beat on the codes — or being seen whatsoever.

Griffin pulled up a chair next to Chrissy. He was fully aware that the ghost of Dylan Ballantine was near his mother as well, standing by the bedside table, next to his father.

He was certain that the ghost had stood

guard through the night. At the moment, however, he completely ignored the spirit. His attention was for Chrissy.

"You didn't see anything, and you can't let that distress you. This person — or these persons — are very good at what they do. And it may take you some time. But what I'd like you to do is think. Try to remember anything at all — especially involving your other senses. Did you hear anything that might have been a little odd? Did you smell anything? A cologne, a soap, anything . . . ?"

He was afraid Chrissy was going to cry. He squeezed her hand. "Please, please, I know it's upsetting. Just try to think about these things. Something may come back to you."

She nodded. "Thank you!" she whispered again. "Thank you so much. I can't believe that you're here again. I mean, George said he didn't even recognize you at first. But you were really the one who saved Noah. If anything had happened to Noah, I wouldn't have wanted to live. A wood pit grave would have been a blessing!" she said softly.

"Chrissy," George said, sounding anguished.

"Mrs. Ballantine, I was the beat cop who happened to be on the street at the time," he told her. "But I'm grateful to have been there."

"Of course, of course, and now you're back," she said.

"Yes, he's back," George said.

"The FBI was called in to help. I know Boston, so I was a natural to take the case," Griffin said.

"Boston has its own FBI office," George said gruffly.

"We're part of a special unit," Jackson said. He was leaning against the doorframe, his arms crossed over his chest, but he had obviously listened to every word that had been said. "We deal with riddles and puzzles and cases that have strange elements regarding them."

"So far, this has all been in Massachusetts," George muttered. "But I suppose we're lucky we have the FBI in on it, right?"

"You have good cops, too, sir," Griffin said. "But we've been assigned — and the more officers working a case like this, well, the better." He smiled at Chrissy. "We won't stop until we know the truth."

"The truth is that we were targeted. And, we were probably targeted because of Vickie!" George announced, emotion in his voice.

"George!" Chrissy remonstrated. "You let

Noah go with her last night," she reminded him.

"Her — *and* a cop!" George said firmly.

"Victoria Preston was very nearly the victim of a horrendous crime. She got out of your house with your child. I was there, remember?" Griffin said, trying to control the growing anger he felt. "Vickie was just the babysitter. Your house might have been targeted. Noah might have been the targeted one — just as Chrissy was targeted now."

"I don't mean to be ungrateful!" George said. He suddenly rose, agitated, running his fingers through his hair. "I'm upset. Does anyone but me not think it's crazy that Vickie was *named* in the clue when my wife disappeared? It has to be that Bertram Aldridge. He's involved, somehow."

"Naturally, sir, the Bureau and the police have been exploring that angle," Jackson said flatly. "But Aldridge remains in maximum security."

"He should have died!" Chrissy said suddenly. "He should have been hanged or burned or electrocuted or given a needle or gas or whatever they do now in death penalty states. If he had died, those other poor women might still be alive."

Everyone was silent for a minute.

Griffin realized everyone there was struggling with morality — and truth. Men did get out of prison — even maximum security prisons. Too often, they killed again. In the situation years ago, Aldridge had aimed to kill.

If he had died that day, would any of this be happening? But Aldridge was still safely locked away in prison and could not be guilty of kidnapping and murder.

"They used the name Preston in the clue," George said. "And Victoria Preston was at our home when that maniac Aldridge broke in."

Griffin swung on him, got his temper in check, and said politely. "Yes, sir. When that maniac Aldridge broke into *your* home. And, now, sir, *your* wife was taken. Perhaps you need to think about what *you* might have done in *your* past, Mr. Ballantine. What it is *you* might have done that has attracted psychotic killers?"

Vickie's mom had implored her to stay at their apartment with Noah.

But she didn't want her own parents involved any more than they already were.

She also wanted time alone with Noah.

He was extraordinary for a nine-year-old boy. And yet, as she packed him up for the overnight stay, she discovered that he was still, despite everything, at heart, a child.

They didn't want to bring too many things, but they looked for his Thor pajamas and collected a number of his superhero action figures along with a box of Lego bricks and, for good measure, his tablet.

He'd read every one of the Harry Potter books, and enthusiastically assured her that he was a massive fan of Rick Riordan.

She wondered if he was enchanted by superheroes, magic and mythology because he knew he was unusual. While he didn't have extraordinary powers, he did speak with his dead brother. In fact, once they were alone in his room, stuffing a change of clothes into his backpack, he told her he considered Dylan to be his best friend. He told Dylan everything. "But," he told her, "Dylan tells me that you're really cool, and it's a sad thing that you moved away because going back and forth wasn't all that easy."

"I think he takes the train — for real," Vickie told him.

"Oh, yeah, he told me that he'd kind of liked hitchhiking at first — just jumping into cars on the road," Noah said. "But every once in a while, someone would kind of know that he was there. He was afraid that he'd freak somebody out or something and cause an accident. Dylan wouldn't want that to happen to anyone."

Dylan had died because of an accident. Vickie smiled and moved on, telling him, "You know what Dylan can do?"

"What?"

"He can push a soda can across the table to me when I ask him."

"Wow! I've never seen him do that!"

"Ask him sometime," Vickie said, smiling.

She realized that the toddler she had once adored had grown into a great kid. She was glad to be with him.

And glad to share the fact that she saw the ghost of Dylan Ballantine.

The next morning when they reached the hospital, Vickie held back in the waiting room, letting the officers bring Noah to see his mother.

A couple of televisions were on, and Vickie went to stand before one of them. The news was on. The reporter was announcing that FBI and BPD forces had found both of the most recent victims of the Undertaker, an assailant who was kidnapping his victims and leaving them with just enough air to live — or not. They had shots of the old cemetery being dug up and shots of an ambulance. There were interviews with witnesses from the streets, but as yet, no interviews with either Barbara Marshall or her family, or Chrissy Ballantine or her family.

Vickie was staring at the screen as the woman recapped the previous victims of the Undertaker; Angelina Gianna was doing well. Sadly, the first two victims were lost, mourned by their families. And any leads in the Undertaker crimes were being kept close. As far as news sources went, law enforcement was no closer to catching the Undertaker than they had been when the first victim went missing. Everyone was, of course, grateful that Chrissy Ballantine, latest victim, was doing well at an undisclosed hospital; she and her family had been targeted previously by the killer Bertram Aldridge. Thankfully, their young son had survived, especially since the family had already tragically lost one son.

Vickie was staring at the screen, trying to determine if the anchorwoman had been helpfully informative for the public — or if she hadn't somewhat sensationalized the Ballantine name — when she felt someone behind her.

She turned quickly. One of the policemen who had stood guard over her and Noah was still by the door. She was alone in the waiting room.

Except, she saw, for Dylan.

He threw his hands up in the air. "My parents! Such good people to be so ignorant at times! Oh, don't get me wrong, Vickie. I love my mom. I'm so grateful she's alive."

"Everyone is grateful, Dylan," she whispered.

"Of course. They're scared, that's it. First I die, then you and Noah are nearly killed — and now this. But scared or not. They should think before they talk."

"So, what is it?" Vickie pressed.

"It is wonderful," Dylan said, ignoring her. "I mean, you should be with them in there with Noah now. Precious. My baby bro is really great, isn't he? Smart as a whip. You'd think he was a teenager."

"He's very smart — and perceptive," Vickie said. "So, what —"

"They think you have something to do with the family being attacked again," Dylan told her.

"What?" Vickie burst out with the word, drawing the attention of the cop at the door. She pursed her lips and lowered her head; she'd learned how not to look crazy by never visibly reacting to Dylan in any way — now she was doing so.

"Everything all right, miss?" the officer called to her.

"Yes, fine, thank you!" she called back,

and turned her gaze again before repeating softy but fervently to Dylan, "What?"

"They're just scared," Dylan said quickly. "It's just that you were there when Noah was nearly kidnapped or killed, and then your name . . . your name was on the clue."

Vickie could feel the hot red flush that covered her cheeks. "Are they forgetting that I might have been killed that day as well? And that the Undertaker was after your mom — not me?" she asked.

"Vickie, Vickie, please, not you, too. Don't fly off the handle. I shouldn't have said anything. I'm sorry. I'm really sorry. I've never seen you so angry. Not even when I made the pile of books fall over on that one guy you were dating. By the way — he was a jerk. Vickie . . ."

"I'm sorry, Dylan. Yeah, they're scared. That's okay. They're all together now. I think I'm going to go ahead and go home. Gee. Go figure, I do have to work for a living. I have a pile of books and old transcripts and other things to go through. Noah is fine; your folks are fine. I'm going home," she told him.

"Vickie, it's my fault, please, don't be mad — they're good people. Honest. My parents are good people," Dylan said.

"And they're fine now, and I do have

things to do. I'll see them again soon, I'm sure. I'm not mad."

"You are mad. You're wicked mad."

"Just a little. I will get over it."

"Vickie . . . !" Dylan had such a look of distress on his face that she paused.

He'd died as a teenager. He'd never be any older. He'd been a great young man. He always would be. She was sure he'd had no idea of just how deeply he had offended her.

"I'm really fine — I honestly understand," she said.

As she headed toward the door, the cop stepped into it. "Miss Preston, may I escort you somewhere? Did you want to go down to the cafeteria, or would you like some coffee?"

"Officer, Noah is safe with his parents. Chrissy Ballantine needs her rest. I think I'd like to go home. I have to work," she said.

She saw him frown. She supposed nothing about her going home had been in his orders that day.

"Please," she said.

He didn't have to deal with the dilemma. FBI Special Agent Griffin Pryce came walking into the waiting room.

"Hey," he said, smiling at the officer and

112

then her.

"I'd like to go home," Vickie said. She was braced; she expected trouble.

"I hurt her feelings. I didn't mean to," Dylan said.

Special Agent Griffin Pryce gave no sign that he heard Dylan speak. "I'm sure that's fine. It was good of you to take such special care of Noah last night."

"Taking care of Noah is a pleasure and no hardship," Vickie said. "But he's fine now. In with his parents."

"Of course. I'll see you there myself, Vickie," he said.

"Thank you, Special Agent Pryce," she said.

"It's all right, Officer Murphy. Thank you," Griffin told the cop. He indicated the open waiting room door to Vickie; she headed on out.

He joined her in the hallway. "Special Agent Pryce?" he repeated, glancing at her as they headed to the elevators. "We used to be friends."

"Were we? Not that I mean to be rude or offensive in any way," Vickie said. "But I'm not sure we were friends. You saved my life — and Noah's. And then you came to my house and checked up on me a few times. And then I graduated and went to college

113

and never saw you again. Until now. I mean, we're not *not* friends, but . . . you have a very formal job now. I think I'm being rude. Or babbling. I may just be tired . . . forgive me."

He wasn't looking at her as they stepped into the elevator. She thought that he was subtly smiling. "Of course," he said. "And, you know, of course, that we — the FBI and the police — are indebted to you."

She waved a hand in the air. "Honestly — I'm so sorry about the other women. The two who died before they were found," she added softly. "But for me, it's over now. I just want to go home and maybe have an early glass of wine and start working on some of the materials on my desk."

"Working at your desk. That's good. You don't have to be with your kids today, working for Grown Ups, right?"

She looked at him as the elevator door opened. "How do you know about my kids?"

"Obviously, once your name was mentioned in a clue and it had to do with the Ballantine family? Our office immediately pulled up all kinds of information on you."

"Great. You thought I was somehow involved?"

"Nope. We just needed to find you. And

we did, at your parents' house."

She laughed suddenly. "I must be tired. It just now occurred to me how easily you found me. I wasn't at my own apartment, and my parents have moved since . . . since that night."

"We are the Federal Bureau of Investigation," he said with a shrug. "It would have been sad if we hadn't been able to find you. Neither you nor your parents were in hiding."

"No," she murmured.

"That's our black SUV there," Griffin said, indicating a vehicle that was double-parked.

"You have a driver."

"At the moment."

"You have come far."

"I'm in the right place," he said simply.

"And, of course, you know where my apartment is," Vickie murmured.

"Yes."

"Good. I won't have to give anyone directions," she said.

He opened the back door of the big black vehicle for her, and Vickie slid in before he walked around to the other side. He quickly gave directions to the driver.

When they reached the front of her building — another brownstone she had found in the downtown district; she did seem to have a thing for brownstones — he asked the driver to wait.

"I'm okay to go on my own, really," she told him, surprised. "You must be very busy right now."

"We are busy, but I'll see you up. And, for the next few days at least, don't worry — you won't have an officer breathing over your shoulder, but you will have a patrol around the building."

Vickie decided not to argue.

Actually, she wasn't against some kind of protection.

Although . . . She hadn't really considered herself to be in danger! Her name had been used as a clue. It was like sports stars or actors or actresses being used in trivia games . . . wasn't it?

Deadly games.

"You're on the ground floor," Griffin commented, looking up at the building.

"Yes, I am. Well, almost. The basement rises above the street level a bit, so technically, I'm a bit off the street. And the basement is finished with apartments as well," she told him.

Vickie didn't know why she was so nervous as she slipped her key into the main door. She seemed to be fumbling with it.

She opened the front door, and crossed the small entryway to her own inner door. It was located to the left of the stairs that led to the apartments on the second and third floors of the old building, two on each floor.

Griffin was still right behind her.

"I'd ask you in, but —"

"I'd love to come in."

He followed her into her apartment. Once inside, she realized that he was instantly assessing it.

"Alarm system?" he asked her.

"I haven't been here that long. I'm in a pretty popular area, lots of people —"

"You should have an alarm system. Everyone should."

"Well, I don't at the moment . . ."

He moved through her apartment. It wasn't small — and it wasn't especially large. She had a full parlor that stretched into a dining room; the kitchen was visible over the counter that separated it from the dining and living area. There was a hallway that led to her bedroom in the back, and the guest room — which she used as her office — just across from the kitchen.

He didn't ask permission; he walked through the place.

Back in the parlor, he looked at her and said, "At least you have storm windows and they have sound locks."

"That was the first thing I looked for when I came up here to rent a place," she said.

"Really?"

"No."

He laughed out loud at that; he wasn't the entirely severe man he had seemed when she had first seen him again at her parents' apartment. But then, at that time, a woman's life had lain in the balance.

"Would you like coffee or tea, a drink, soda . . . a bottle of water?" she asked.

"Coffee would be great."

"Um, it'll just take a minute. I like a Hawaiian bean. Is that okay?"

"Whatever."

"Black?"

"Yep."

She headed into the kitchen, wondering what had made her ask him to stay. He would have left, gone back to do his job. Then she wouldn't have seen him again.

It wasn't as if they had really been . . . anything. He'd come to see her after the Aldridge attack. He'd been a good cop; he'd made sure she was doing well. He'd wanted to see how she had been dealing with the events that had occurred. And then, he had disappeared from her life.

She'd been an adolescent, of course —

not quite eighteen. He'd been in his early or midtwenties. She'd had something of a man-who-saved-me crush on him back then — as had her friends. Griffin Pryce was very good-looking. Tall and broad-shouldered. Great eyes. Great body. Yep, at the time, all of her friends, including Roxanne, had dreamed about him a little, giggling — they'd giggled a lot at that age. They'd liked to tease one another. Imagine love — and sex — with just such a man.

She managed to make coffee without her hands trembling or giving any other indication of where her thoughts had strayed. She prepared herself a cup as well. He took a seat at one of the stools by the counter.

She kept the counter between them, leaning against it from the other side.

She was glad Dylan wasn't there.

"Other than all that's going on, it's really good to see you," Griffin told her. "You're doing well?"

She smiled at that. "Define *well*! I'm happy to be home in Boston. The Cradle of Liberty, and all that. College was great — New York is amazing, too. I enjoy what I do. They aren't exactly bestsellers, but my history books do okay and . . . I honestly love the work I'm doing with Grown Ups. So many kids just need a chance, someone to care, someone to open doors in their minds. I hope I make some kind of difference." She paused for a breath. "I may be answering you with way more than you were asking. You. What about you? I mean, patrolman to agent. Special Agent."

He laughed. "We're all 'Special Agent.' But I love my unit and I love what I do."

"You were a good cop."

"Hopefully I'm a good agent."

"Obviously, you are. Strange, I'd just finished with the kids when we heard all the commotion over by the cemetery. I'd heard about the other women who were kidnapped, but . . . that was terrible and unusual, wasn't it? Two women taken . . . just hours apart?"

"Strange and very scary. Barbara Marshall was taken at night — Chrissy Ballantine the following afternoon — in broad daylight." He looked up from his mug, pinning her with his dark eyes from across the counter. "We need to get him."

"Was Chrissy Ballantine any help? What about the other woman?"

"Neither has been much help — not yet. Chrissy doesn't remember anything. She never saw her attacker. He came from behind. We're hoping she'll get some kind of memory back, think of something."

"Yes, hopefully. And the other woman?"

"Barbara Marshall. She's taking a little longer to come around. Hopefully, too, one of them will think of something that might be helpful."

"Not that I know a lot about forensics, but . . . what about DNA? Fingerprints? Footprints?"

"Nothing so far. Fingerprints are easily obscured. This person is wearing gloves. Still, we have good teams. Maybe they'll come up with a hair or a fiber or something that will help. Then, of course, you have to have something to match your evidence to . . . But we're on it."

"Two women died," Vickie said, remembering the news. "But another one lived, right?"

"Yes, Angelina Gianni, very sweet woman," he said. He looked at her steadily, sipping his coffee. "Very interesting case. Local police were frustrated and the different cities and townships involved — along with the state — decided it was time they brought in the FBI. Anthony Gianni — Angelina's husband — believed that he was visited by Angelina's late mother."

And was she?

Vickie was so tempted to say the words. She didn't.

"And you found her — because of the clues, though, right?"

"We found her," he said, watching her closely.

"Would you like something to eat?" Vickie asked nervously. "Do you guys take time to eat? Well, you must, of course. But I have the feeling you're hanging around because you're worried I'm not all right. I'm fine. Truly. I'm a lot older than when you last knew me. Much steadier! Hey, some of the kids I work with barely made it out of juvenile hall, and they have tales to tell that would make the hair at the back of your neck stand up. I'm good. I'll be okay, really. Except, of course, I could make you something to eat."

He was smiling.

Still older, wiser, more experienced. Comfortable with himself. Confident as hell.

"I'm good," he told her. "They do let us eat."

She started to speak; she was saved as she heard a buzzing and he pulled his phone out of the pocket of his jacket.

There was no way of telling who he was talking to or what was going on. His responses went from "Pryce, here" to "good" and "I'll be right there."

He rose, still looking at her. "Hopefully,

we'll get something soon. I can keep you in the loop, if you want."

"Please," she told him.

He was heading to the door. He paused there, looking back.

"There will be a patrolman around your door. If you have any trouble . . . if you're frightened in any way . . ."

"I'll run out of the apartment screaming blue blazes," she promised him.

He was about to go out when he paused again.

"You have my number?"

"Number? What? Oh, phone number. No, I . . ."

"Here's my card. Please, put it in your phone right away. And call me — that way I'll have your number in my phone."

She would have laughed if it weren't for the rugged contours of his face and the intensity in his dark eyes. No one had ever asked for her number so seriously before.

This wasn't a pickup line.

He was all business.

"In case you need me," he said.

"Um, thank you," she murmured. "But really, you don't need to worry about me. I'm sure this case is really time consuming and . . . remember, they do let you eat." She tried to smile and add a little lightness

123

to the conversation.

She failed miserably.

"I'll be fine," she told him.

He was still looking at her.

"But," she promised, holding the card and her phone. "I'll put the number in right away. See? Dialing you already."

He nodded, stared at her a moment longer — thinking God alone knew what.

And then he was gone.

The minute he was out the door, she felt oddly alone.

And ever-so-slightly afraid.

Taker stood on the sidewalk just down the street from the old home-turned-apartment-building where Vickie Preston lived.

He stood in the shadows, pretending to give his attention to his phone.

He watched as the FBI guy came and went.

He noted the patrolman on the street, keeping careful guard. The patrolman was worrisome, but not too much so.

The FBI guy.

Taker knew all about him. Bizarre that he was back; bizarre that he'd been *the* cop on patrol duty in the Ballantine neighborhood the night Bertram Aldridge had been caught — and now he was back. No matter; obstacles were just things to be overcome. They were challenges. In fact, he was a good challenge.

Like Victoria Preston and the kid, he deserved to die.

Patience, control and care.

Taker turned and headed down the street. He glanced at his watch. Time was everything; he still had a little time tonight. But time was also put best to use in planning.

He loved the game; the cleverness of the game. Deciding whom to take, and how and when, and finding each nook and cranny where he'd do his hiding. He loved the clues, thinking of just what he wanted to say. So few words, yet each one important.

He wasn't much on torture. It was the glee that followed a successful maneuver that was the high for him.

No, he wasn't much on torture, although, of course, there were those who might think that being buried alive was a form of torture . . .

But, it wasn't. Not compared to what torture might be!

And in Victoria Preston's case . . .

He just might change the game.

CHAPTER FOUR

Anthony Gianni was waiting for Griffin and Jackson to arrive, standing in front of the cannoli shop that took up a large portion of the ground floor of his apartment building.

Griffin was in the lead and Anthony took his hands first, thanking him for coming.

"She's home now, my wife, my poor Angelina, she's home again. And I wouldn't have called you, wouldn't have bothered you, if I hadn't thought we might help. I knew you had the police watching our place and I was so grateful. And the officer, he was so fine — he got us to the hospital right away when she started having the asthma attack . . . I'm still so worried. I want you to speak with her, but you must understand — she's still having trouble breathing. Whatever she inhaled . . . she's still having trouble. The doctors let her come home, but she has to be quiet, you know, let all the medicines work?"

"We will leave the minute your wife appears to be in the least distressed," Griffin assured him.

"I want to help, we want to help. Angie wouldn't be alive without you," Anthony told him.

Anthony Gianni was a first-generation American — as was his wife. Sixtysomething now, Gianni was a tall broad-shouldered man who moved with dignity. While he'd been born in the United States, he'd grown up with his heritage here in Little Italy and his first language had been Italian. His English was just as fluent, but had an accent which slipped into his conversation at times. When he was emotional — as he was now — he seemed to speak volumes with his hands, as well. Griffin and Jackson had both liked the man since they had met him. Even when he was desperate to find his wife — and was thinking that he was going crazy — he had been courteous and helpful in every way. Now he kissed his fingers and shook his hands into the sky and spoke in Italian before adding, "Holy Mother Mary, I pray that I remain sane in all this!"

"You're fine, sir. Dreams work in mysterious ways," Griffin said.

"So, I was dreaming. Hmm. I tell you, she

was as real as flesh in my dreams, but there she was, Mama D'Onofrio, there before me, telling me what I must say to you! And yes, sir, Special Agent Pryce, you knew Lexington, Massachusetts. I'd have never thought. You — you two." He looked from Jackson to Griffin. "How you knew . . ."

"I guessed," Griffin said.

"Special Agent Pryce does know the state," Jackson added.

"And to watch for dug-up ground, thanks to your dream," Griffin said. "But you've called us because of something that Mrs. Gianni said."

Gianni nodded. "Come in, come in, please."

There was a door to the apartments above the cannoli shop. Anthony Gianni led the way.

They found the apartment was surprisingly plush, once they reached it. Tastefully decorated, it boasted a very large living room and fine art on the walls. Anthony didn't stop in the living room and they followed him down a hallway, past a few doors and to a large bedroom at the end with picture windows and a view of the city beyond.

Angelina Gianni was a slim woman with narrow features and a beautiful smile. She lay in a hospital bed, raised so that she could breathe more easily.

"Agents, thank you for coming, thank you for . . . thank you for believing," she said, reaching out a hand to greet them. "I'm sorry to greet you from a bed again, but . . . it seems that my asthma has come back."

"She was buried, in a basement by a coal vault," Anthony said. "Her breathing . . . it still hasn't recovered. The doctors though . . . they are good. She can be home, as long as we keep a good eye on her! But last night, we had to head to the emergency room. Now we have breathing treatments; she is doing much better."

"We're so sorry for your pain," Jackson said.

A sparkle lit Angelina's eyes. "And I am so grateful to be alive. And, it's like a miracle, yes? You found me — like a needle in a haystack."

"You were found. We're very grateful," Griffin said.

"And you saved the next two women. But there may be more," Anthony said.

"We will find whoever did this," Jackson told them firmly.

"I believe you," Angelina said softly. She flushed and looked away for a minute. "I am so glad that they brought you in. The police . . . the police are good, but . . ."

"But they thought I was crazy when I told them Mama D'Onofrio said to dig," Anthony said.

"Yes, Anthony saw my dear mother. He saw her in a dream. I wish that I could see her. I feel her, often. I think she feels me, maybe," Angelina said. She shook her head. "But enough to do with dreams of those long dead — I have been trying to remember, but . . . it's so hard. I was down at the Italian meat market, I was coming home. It was dark, but there were people on the streets. I was just walking and then . . . then it hit me. I didn't know I had been hit, of course. I don't even remember the pain. It was as if I was walking, and then I wasn't. And when I woke up in panic, trying to scream . . ."

"Angie, don't upset yourself!" Anthony pleaded.

She shook her head. "I am remembering bits and pieces. I am remembering something that smells like the woods — you told me to remember scents, right, Agent Pryce?"

"Yes, Mrs. Gianni."

"So, I remember something like the woods. But what's important, I think, is that I remember voices."

130

"Voices? Male — female?" Griffin asked.

"Male, I think. I'm not sure — they were hushed, they were whispers. I think now — especially knowing they entered the old inn by an outside coal drop — they were in a hurry. They had to make sure I was confined and couldn't move and that I would smother in a few hours, but they were worried about being caught. Two, Agent Pryce, Agent Crow. I know that there were two people there who were involved. There is not *an* Undertaker. There are two."

Griffin glanced over at Jackson.

Jackson nodded. "Mrs. Gianni, we're going to let that information out to the press, with your permission. We won't mention dreams or your mother's words or anything else. But I do believe it's important for people to be aware that a victim heard two voices."

"Of course," Angelina and Anthony said in unison.

Anthony wanted to get the agents coffee and food. They thanked him, but said that they had to move on. When they were outside the apartment and on the streets of Little Italy, Jackson asked, "Well?"

Griffin shook his head. "Nothing. You?"

"Nothing," Jackson said. "If the ghost of Mama D'Onofrio is in that house, I didn't

131

get a feel for her in any way."

"Think they can just live in dreams?" Griffin asked.

"I gave up thinking about the power of life and death years ago," Jackson told him. "Any time I have an opinion or think I know something, it changes. You?"

"I just leave my eyes open, and my mind open," Griffin said, "and I'm very grateful for any clue, physical or from the mouths of the dead, however they may speak."

"I wish Mama D'Onofrio would pop into one of my dreams," Jackson said.

"Me, too. I'd like to ask her how she knew her daughter was buried," Griffin agreed.

They'd been heading for the car. Jackson stopped walking. He looked at Griffin for a moment and then said, "I hate to say this, but I don't think there's any way out of it. Victoria Preston is somehow on the killers' radar."

"Asking her to help is dangerous — to her."

"Not asking her to help might be more dangerous — for her," Jackson said quietly. "Honestly, for her sake, we need to keep her close."

"There was a home on this lot before the Paul Revere house was built, and — as is often true — that home connected to an earlier history. Increase Mather had a parsonage here for the Second Church — he lived here with his family from about 1670 until it was destroyed in the great fire of 1676," Vickie told her students.

Cheryl Taylor started waving her hand. "I know!"

"Okay?" Vickie said.

"Increase Mather, big Puritan dude. And his son, Cotton Mather, was the creepy bastard who said that they had to hang George Burroughs in Salem anyway, even after he could say the Lord's Prayer. Right?"

"Burroughs had been the minister in Salem from 1680 to 1683 — and he was the only minister to be executed during the Salem witch incident, yes," Vickie said, smiling. "I'm working on a book about the Mather family now, and sometimes it's hard to be unbiased. But it's always a great lesson in being careful. Burroughs was in trouble with the Putnam family because he'd borrowed money he couldn't return. He wasn't even in Salem — he'd headed up to Maine, but he was found there and arrested."

"And," Cheryl said, "it goes to support the theory that much of what went on had to do with the social climate — and those who didn't agree with one another managing to kill a whole pack of people. Those wretched girls were the evil ones."

"And they knew Paul Revere?" Hardy asked, looking quizzical.

"No, it's just an interesting piece of history. This house was built after the parsonage burned down. The first owner was a wealthy merchant named Robert Howard. Paul Revere bought the house in 1770," Vickie said.

"And it's been like this since?" Art asked her, grinning.

"No, the Revere family owned the house until about 1800. Then it became all kinds of things, including tenement housing, a cigar store . . . Well, I'll leave it to the guides to explain while you go through. The important thing, to me, is that one of Revere's descendants, John P. Reynolds Jr., bought the house when it was going to be demolished right around 1900 to keep it from being destroyed. He started the Paul Revere Memorial Association to preserve the home from which Revere made his historic ride. It's the oldest house in Boston. And thanks to Revere's descendant, it's been meticulously restored over the years — and we all get to see what it was like when Paul Revere made his famous ride," Vickie told them.

"I love being a Bostonian. We are so cool," Cheryl said.

Vickie realized Dylan Ballantine was with her when she heard him sniff by her side.

"So cool — are you kidding me? Boston comes from the Puritans. Those Puritans! Self-righteous idiots and bastards, I say!" Dylan muttered.

Vickie made a point of ignoring him and smiling at her students. "Tours are usually self-guided, but we have a friend of Grown Ups taking you through. Here's your guide through the house," Vickie told them. She waved at the colleague who also worked with Grown Ups. He was actually a visiting professor over at Harvard, specializing in military history, but like Vickie, he enjoyed donating hours each week to Grown Ups. He knew details down to belt buckles and shoe sizes of many historic persons — he also knew how to tell stories with passion and drama. Their young heads would be reeling by the time the tour was finished.

"See you all at Pasta Fagioli!" she said to the group, indicating that she'd meet them after their tour.

The kids traipsed off after their guide. Vickie turned to Dylan — carefully.

She knew she was still being watched by a cop. It was only a few days since Chrissy

Ballantine had been kidnapped.

"Your mom doing well?" she asked as she started down the street.

"Yeah, Mom is great. And they're feeling terrible. Of course, they don't know how you know they were offensive. And, of course, you know because of me, but . . . Wow, I do have a big mouth. Vickie, I swear . . ."

"I told you. It's all right."

"Yeah, but my mom has been calling you. And you haven't answered her messages."

"I'm sorry. I've been busy."

"Sure."

"Dylan, you forget *my* mom is in this town."

"Maybe she thinks the FBI agents said something to you," Dylan said hopefully.

"They didn't."

"Yes, but . . . Oh! She may think you're psychic."

"It doesn't matter, Dylan. She's doing well, right?"

"Yes, she's fine. But she's still scared. Do you think my mom was targeted for some reason? I mean, why? Yeah, they have money, but not like Trump or Rockefeller or anyone like that. And my dad is a good guy. There couldn't be any reason. The things that have happened to us can't be related. I mean, that creepy evil Bertram Aldridge just found any house to sneak into . . . Now Dad has hired private security. There's a guy watching the house twenty-four seven."

"That's good."

"Maybe you should go live at my house," Dylan said.

"Hey! I don't want to live with my *own* parents, Dylan," Vickie said, exasperated.

"Please, don't be enemies with mine."

"Dylan, I'm not enemies with anyone."

Looking across the street, she could see that the cop who had been carefully following her was now frowning.

He thinks he's been assigned to eight hours of watching over a lunatic!

She pulled out her phone and pretended to be talking on it.

"Dylan, I don't want to be enemies with anyone. Don't worry — I will call your mom. You might have noticed I'm a little busy today."

"Yeah. With those ballbusters."

"Underprivileged kids."

Dylan shook his head, looking at the sidewalk.

"Some cause their own problems."

"Like dope-addict parents?"

Dylan shrugged. "Sorry — I know most of your kids are really decent. I'm just being a dickwad because I want you to make it up with my folks, okay?"

"Yeah."

"I mean, really. It's not just them. It's Noah."

"Noah. You know, Dylan, he was sixteen months old when I was with him."

"And you took him home with you — he trusted and knew you."

"Because you must talk about the way you love to haunt me and tease me."

"He's a special kid, Vickie."

"I promise to call your mom!"

"Good!" Dylan said, and he headed off down the street, hands in his pockets, whistling.

She watched him go and remembered she was pretending to have a phone conversation. Swearing softly beneath her breath, she "pretended" to hang up and started down the street herself.

When she arrived at the restaurant, she greeted the owner, Mario, with a hug and a kiss. Mario Caro had been in her high school graduating class and was now managing the family restaurant, Pasta Fagioli. He had a little side room reserved for her group, and he told her he didn't mind if she sat around reading with a cappuccino while she waited for her students to finish at the

Paul Revere house. The room was already set and ready for whenever the kids arrived. As they walked back, she saw the cop who had been assigned to her entering the restaurant.

She smiled at Mario. "Will you give him your best cappuccino and a cannoli — and tell him it's on me."

"Guardian angel?" he asked.

"Yep."

Mario frowned. "So, you were involved in everything that went on."

"Involved with . . . ?"

"There was a whole article in the paper about the Ballantine family — and what happened eight years ago," Mario told her. "Everyone knows about the clues the kidnapper gives out. And everyone around here knew your name, and figured you were involved somehow. I mean, the cops and the FBI reported that Chrissy Ballantine was found, but — understandably, in my mind — they're not saying more. They're asking the public to remember that it's an ongoing investigation. And, you know, they're warning people to be careful. But from what has been reported, these poor women don't know what's hit them until it's hit them."

"I guess my name was in the paper —

although Preston is a common enough name."

"Sure. Unless it involves Chrissy Ballantine. I hear, though — get a lot of cops in here — that they're trying to keep a protective eye on the victims who survived. Wonder how long they'll be able to do that." He grimaced. "Citywide cutbacks, but . . . hey. I guess the Feds are involved. Better budgets, maybe. However, whatever, you know you've got friends in this city. And, hey, a lot of us are Italian, and while most of us just manage restaurants and make pasta, some of us are pretty tough."

He was teasing, of course. His mom was a librarian. His dad was the gentlest soul she'd ever known.

"Wise guy?" she asked him.

He grinned. "Hey, okay, so we're tough as overcooked ziti. Some people still think that if you're Italian, you're a hit man. Let's go with that — if it will work!"

She grinned and left him and wandered on in to the private side room he'd reserved for her. She took a seat at the end of the table and pulled out one of the books an antique dealer had found for her on Cotton Mather. It had been written in the 1700s and she'd spent a small fortune on it — even at a dealer discount, the book had been

140

hundreds of dollars. And then she'd had a cover made for it.

Books were a passion for her. She had collector's editions of many. Her mother had bought her a first printing of a Daniel Defoe novel for graduation, and, of course, her dad had laughed but been very happy. Most kids wanted help with a car, or maybe a nice watch. Not Vickie.

She couldn't have been more thrilled than she had been with her copy of *Robinson Crusoe.*

She'd also begun to learn that she could combine her love for old things — history and research — and make a living doing it.

She carefully opened her copy of *Cotton Mather — Saint or Ultimate Evil.* Having been born when she had been, the idea that people across half the world believed in and burned or hanged witches was absolutely ludicrous from the get-go. But she had to force herself to head back to that time.

Still didn't work for her. How did you leave one country for religious freedom — and then be totally intolerant of all others?

She was deep into her reading when she either sensed another presence — or simply realized that she could see the bottom half of a man below the book. She looked up, startled.

Griffin Pryce was there. She stared at him, surprised.

He'd called her once to check up on her. She'd assured him she was fine. He'd told her there was nothing new in the investigation. They'd said goodbye.

And now . . .

Now he was here.

"Hey," she said softly.

"You were so involved . . . I'm sorry to disturb you."

"It's fine. I'm killing time. My kids are due here in a bit. They're seeing the Paul Revere house."

"Nice." He drew up a chair in front of her. "I loved that old place growing up."

"Anything new?" she asked.

"Yes and no. Mainly yes."

"What's yes, and what's no?"

He leaned toward her. The intensity in his eyes was something she remembered from years before, when he had come to take her out for coffee and ask her if she was really doing okay.

"Anything I say, is, of course, confidential," he said.

She nodded.

"Barbara Marshall is out of the hospital and home. We're watching over her right now, of course. She manages a flower stall and she's single, so . . . no boyfriend in the picture, and her family is out in Warwick. Naturally, the police are watching over you."

Vickie smiled and said dryly, "I'm hoping that my currently assigned officer is enjoying his cappuccino and whatever else Mario decided to give him."

"We have to be careful," he said quietly.

"Oh, I'm not protesting. I'm grateful to have him."

"Good."

He didn't speak for a minute. Then he continued. "Chrissy Ballantine is also out of the hospital. Of course, they're quite comfortable, so George Ballantine has hired a full-time security service."

"That's good," Vickie murmured, looking downward and playing with her now empty cappuccino cup.

"She couldn't remember anything at all. She was in the kitchen. Then she was in the basement in the floor, semiconscious and too weak to be heard."

"I'm glad she's doing well, and that she's protected."

"We also spoke with Angelina Gianni, the first of the victims we found in time."

"And?"

"She doesn't believe there is one Undertaker. She believes there are two."

143

"Oh. Does that make it harder — or easier?"

"It makes it two," he said.

"I see," Vickie murmured. She didn't really see anything — and she wasn't sure why he was sitting there, or why she was remembering all of her friends teasing her about the cop who had saved her, macho, cute as could be . . . sexy.

He was a very attractive man. She hadn't seen him in so long. And when she had seen him, it had been in the emotional aftermath of a traumatic experience.

Is that why she felt a ridiculous bond with him? As if they should be much more than occasional acquaintances. Was it Noah's absolute certainty that Griffin shared her odd talent — that he was totally aware that Dylan was still with them — at least, Dylan's ghost or his spirit?

"How did you know I was here?" she asked him, and then she laughed. "Of course, never mind. I have my escort in the next room, and if I didn't . . . well. I guess you'd know anyway. You all seem to know everything."

He didn't answer that for a moment. Then he said softly, "If only . . . if we knew everything, I'd have a handle on what's going on here." He sounded frustrated at the end. "The killer — or killers, if Angelina is right — seem to be playing at this, almost. They're giving us a chance to find the women they're kidnapping — as if they don't really care if they live or die. The thing is, we've been lucky in the last three cases. If we don't stop them, they will keep going."

"I'm sure you'll find them," Vickie said, not sure what else she was about to say. Although, she almost added the word "eventually." She was very glad she hadn't.

"We don't stop until we do," he assured her. "Thing is, we don't know when they'll strike again."

"You're sure that they will?"

"Yes."

She hesitated and then asked, "Do you know why Chrissy or George Ballantine would blame me in any way for her having been taken?"

"Fear. And, of course, they don't want to believe anything they've said or done could have caused such a thing."

"Fear. Do you think the kidnappers will make another try at Chrissy? From what I've seen, it seems that they've chosen their victims randomly."

"They might have been victims of convenience, too."

"You mean . . ."

"I mean the kidnappers obviously watch their prey. They know when they're alone — or, in Angelina's case — when a street is empty and someone can be snatched up. In every case, the kidnapper or kidnappers have come from behind. Each woman has been taken before she had any clue whatsoever that she was being stalked. They have to be watching people; they've never come up to a situation where anyone has seen them or fought back."

"So any woman in the city is at risk."

"In the city, and anywhere near, so it seems. They haven't struck outside Massachusetts, yet."

"I do imagine that everyone — every law enforcement agency — is on the alert."

He nodded. "Of course. But I think you should know, we might have looked forever — looked until it was too late — for Chrissy Ballantine. You're the reason we found her."

"Well, no, I mean, not really, I know a fair amount about Boston. But of course, that didn't really matter — she was actually in the house all the time."

"And we might have been tearing apart every business and apartment building there — and we wouldn't have found her. She really does owe you her life. Vickie, your gut intuitions are . . . a talent. Like seeing the dead."

Vickie waved a hand in the air, feeling uncomfortable.

"Vickie, I'm wondering if you mind heading to the Boston Neck with me," he said quietly.

She stared at him in surprise. "To do with — this case? Griffin . . . Special Agent Pryce . . . I'm great with kids and young adults and I love history. But I don't think I had a single class in criminology. Everything I might know or think that I know comes from crime shows on television."

"I don't need a criminologist," he said quietly. "I need someone with special talents. Someone close there in the area who knows the lay of the land."

"I . . ."

Her students were arriving. Through the back windows of the restaurant, she could see that they were coming.

Art was quietly in the lead.

Hardy wasn't far behind him, but walking backward and flirting with Cheryl. Cheryl had an adoring look on her face — young love.

She seemed to care about him, but in exactly what way was hard to ascertain.

Behind them came the others: Jan, Frank

and Ivan — the three had lost both parents and had no family; Gio, Cindy, Cathy and Sasha — had all been taken from abusive homes. Cathy's dad had been so high on crack, he'd burned their house down. She'd barely escaped and still bore scars from the incident five years ago. Gio's name had been legally changed; he was the son of a multiple offender who was serving time in Leavenworth for counterfeiting, forgery and arms deals. Cheryl and Hardy had both come to Massachusetts via other states; they'd been runaways, street kids, just left to fend for themselves. A few of them had gotten into trouble. Sasha had been in juvenile court for shoplifting; Art had actually been found on the street, suffering from an overdose of heroin.

Doing anything that might change their lives for the better meant a great deal to her.

"I don't do this every day," she murmured, "only one or two days a week. And I don't miss. The kids count on me. I know people think that hey, she's a writer, her time doesn't matter, she's just at home, she doesn't really do anything, but . . ."

"I don't need a lot of your time. It wouldn't interfere with anything you do for the kids. Vickie, we don't know who has been taken yet, but the next clue has arrived at the paper. Out there, somewhere, we have another victim."

"Oh. So, yes — you do know they won't stop. That they do have someone else . . ."

"And your name is on the clue again," he said softly.

She gasped, stunned, and sat back, not sure at all on how to reply.

"What?" she managed in a frantic whisper.

" 'Vickie knows where some of the righteous met the Neck,' " he quoted.

"No," she murmured.

Then she saw Dylan was coming; he was hurrying ahead of her students, as if he knew Griffin Pryce was there, talking to her, and he wanted to beat the others.

He ran into the room and stood at the end of the table. She tried not to notice him because Griffin Pryce was staring at her.

"Vickie! You've got to help him because I'm afraid. For my folks. For Noah. Yes, he's taking women. Or, they're taking women. But they're killers. They don't care who they hurt."

She could see Mario greeting her group of young people out in the main part of the restaurant.

Griffin kept staring at her.

"I'd like to help," she said softly. "I really would."

"Then tell him that you'll go with him, that you will help!" Dylan said.

"Yes, please. Listen," Griffin said intensely, "we'll see to it that you're never in any danger. You will never be anywhere without one of us in the field, and when you're working at home or with the kids, you'll have a guard on you, twenty-four seven, until these men are caught. I know, of course, how your parents feel about this, and I'm really sorry to ask."

"It's not that I'm afraid," she said. "Well, I mean, I am afraid — I'm a horrible coward. But I do trust in you and the police, and I suppose I'm very lucky at this moment, actually having a guard when anyone might be in danger, it's just that, I'm not sure how I can help. I know Boston, and I know the Ballantine family, so . . ."

"You know Boston!" Dylan said.

Griffin smiled. "I'm sure you know all of the environs well."

"I do, but . . ."

"Please, Vickie," Dylan said. "Help us out here!"

"Yes, please help us out here," Griffin repeated.

She frowned and stared at him. Despite

what Noah had told her, and despite what she'd been certain about in her own mind, she nearly jumped out of her chair.

"You see Dylan," she said in a heated whisper. "You just heard him talking!"

"Yes," Griffin said simply.

"My name is in a new clue, you don't even know who was taken yet . . . and you spring this on me! And you see Dylan clearly. And you did . . . you did before. The day that . . . Bertram Aldridge was in the Ballantine house and you shot him . . . But he was down before he could shoot me and Noah because Dylan had tripped him. You saw him then."

"Yes."

"You — jerk! You bastard. I'm on the spot now, and back then, you didn't say a word."

"I didn't know if you'd seen Dylan then," Griffin said quietly. "You didn't tell me."

The kids were nearly there. He leaned closer. "Vickie, this concerns me. The killer — killers — know you. We can't figure it out. You do have special talents. We need you."

He and Dylan were both staring at her, waiting for her answer.

And uneasiness poured into her.

Her name, now her first name, on a clue.

Was she somehow involved? How could it

be? She knew the man who had nearly killed her and Noah was in prison. Why would someone else target her or the Ballantine family or . . . just use her name in a clue?

Was she in danger — and was Griffin Pryce saying that he needed her — exactly because he thought she might be in danger?

Her kids — or young almost-adults — were pouring in, excitedly talking about the house, about Paul Revere and the men who had signed the Declaration of Independence, risking their lives to put their names on a piece of paper.

"I can't believe I've never been there before!" Cheryl said, heading toward Vickie and then stopping as she saw Griffin, who had risen.

"Oh! Hello, um, hi. I'm Cheryl," she said, giving him her hand.

"How do you do, Cheryl. Griffin Pryce," he said. He turned to Vickie. "I'll give you a minute and wait for you just outside."

Then he was gone. And when he was fully out of the room, Cathy McDonald said, "Wow! He's fine, Miss Preston."

"Hot!" Cheryl teased.

"Miss Preston's got one on the line," Art teased.

"Who is cuter — wait, wrong word!" Cheryl teased. "Sexier? Yeah, that's it! Who is — whew! — more charming, adorable . . . whatever! Him or her?"

"Hey!" Vickie protested.

"Disrespectful, right?" Hardy asked.

"Griffin is a friend," Vickie said. "Come on, guys — this is a great restaurant, and a friend of mine manages it. I have to go, but you'll be all set. And you'll behave like great young adults!"

"No spitballs out of straw wrappers, huh?" Hardy teased.

"Nope, sit down."

"Come on, Miss Preston!" Hardy said. "We're in high school!"

"My point exactly," she told him. High school. Yes, they were physically adults; they could dress up and walk down the street and appear to be mature and complete, well beyond their ages.

She remembered being that age so well. Some of her friends were determined and excited to face the future, leave home, head to college. Some weren't leaving home; they were taking jobs, they were going to Boston-area schools, perhaps heading into the military.

Few were like this group — in many ways — far too wise regarding the world.

And in many ways, still just kids.

"There are set menus at the seats. Choose

from those, and make me proud, guys, huh?" Vickie said.

"Sure! Promise," Hardy said, sitting.

Griffin had gone outside.

Dylan had not.

He was at her side, grinning.

"Okay, so, Bick-bick, I'm surprised one of them hasn't said it yet."

She looked at him, a silent *"Said what?"* in her eyes.

"Miss Preston," Cheryl said. "No disrespect intended. That dude is *wicked hot.* You're really not going to tell us about him?"

Dylan laughed softly and headed on out of the restaurant.

CHAPTER FIVE

"Scholars disagree on exactly when the Puritans lost control of Boston and the Massachusetts Bay Colony," Vickie said. "The society was extremely repressive, and actually, the Pilgrims and Puritans were two different peoples in a way. The Pilgrims wanted to break from the Church; the Puritans wanted to reform it. Too much? Sorry. I'm trying to simplify all this. But when the Puritans were in power, they were the law. This was, of course, way before the formation of the United States of America and the separation of church and state. Okay, so, there was a problem with the Quakers. The Puritans banished them — if they came back, they'd be hanged by the neck until dead."

"Only way to hang someone," Dylan murmured.

Griffin watched Vickie and lowered his head, not to show a smile. She was excellent at pretending that she didn't hear or see the boy, and, of course, Barnes was still with them, hopeful that Vickie would miraculously have some kind of a sense for what they were trying to do. They had come out to the Boston Neck — once the tiny strip of land that had connected the peninsula with Boston as the tip to the mainland, and now a thriving area — not the actual geographic south of the city, but the South End, nevertheless — made possible by landfill in the marshes surrounding the Boston Neck.

"Now, of course, a whole new history has come around. We're looking at land changes, at the Victorian era. And a pretty cool place, too, really. This area is known for its diversity now, and has been for years and years," Vickie said.

"I used to be a patrolman here," Detective Barnes said. "You'd think I'd know where I was going or what I was doing. But this is always like looking for a needle in a haystack."

They stood on Washington Street, looking north. Barnes watched Vickie, hopeful and doubtful all in one.

Jackson Crow appeared to be certain that Vickie would discover the missing woman — although they didn't even know who she might be as yet.

The workaday world and the traffic of the busy city went on all around them.

"So, we try all kinds of locations," Griffin said. "But we forget the 'newer' history and concentrate on the older?"

"Yeah, that sounds weird," Vickie said. "There will obviously be new, but I think that we're looking at new that still pertains to the very old, as in built over the area where the gallows once stood or where bodies were thrown after hanging. If the clue is really meant to give us something, and so far, the clues have been real."

"Witches, huh?" Dylan murmured.

She managed to answer him and ignore him, all in one. "That's the thing, hanging wasn't all intolerance and it wasn't all during the Puritan hold on the city. There were people hanged who, through the years, weren't just of different faiths — they were hanged for murder and other serious crimes. The last gallows were located in the yard at the Charles Street Jail, starting 1826. But out here . . ."

She paused and shook her head. "I know of at least three areas where we could look. Bodies were dumped in the Common Grounds . . . not Boston Common, but an area referred to as the Common Grounds."

"Every word in these clues seems to mean

157

something, Vickie. *Righteous.* A murderer wouldn't likely have been righteous," Griffin pointed out.

"Okay. The Quakers, through their religious beliefs, thought it was their duty to return and spread what they saw as the true word of God. When they came back, they were hanged. Back then, Boston was nearly an island. Boston Neck had a gatehouse, so you couldn't just come and go. The gallows were moved a few times during the centuries, though. Obviously, there's landfill now where there used to be marshland."

"We don't even have a report regarding a missing woman as of yet," Detective Barnes muttered.

"We will," Jackson said quietly.

"So we're looking for a random woman," Barnes said.

"We're looking for a woman who is buried alive, boxed up somewhere, caged to smother to death," Griffin said evenly.

"Maybe they're playing with us," Barnes said.

"I don't think they are," Jackson told him.

"The Neck being capitalized, I'd say they do mean the Neck," Griffin said, his attention focused on Vickie.

She nodded, apparently not disturbed by Barnes's skepticism. But of course, she was accustomed to ignoring the ghost who haunted her.

She definitely had focus.

"Yes, okay. The Neck was fortified with a gatehouse. Just south of that area was what they called Gallows Hill — not much of a hill, slightly higher ground, mostly even now. Four Quakers — among others — met their demise there. William Robinson, Marmaduke Stevenson, William Leddra and Mary Dyer. Mary escaped the penalty once, but being a Quaker, had to come back again against the Puritan's 'bloody law.' So, they might have been righteous — in my mind, ridiculously foolhardy as well, not to take anything away from anyone's beliefs." She paused and pointed. "There are firsthand accounts of what happened. The deaths were circa 1660. Years later, someone got a stone up in memory, but that quickly came down. But in 1699 a Quaker came through on his way from Brookline to Boston and commented on someone pointing out the location to him. The Massachusetts charter was revoked in 1684, and in 1689, a Toleration Act was passed and the whole Puritan thing began to die out. But back to the likely location of the gallows — really a tree with a ladder and rope — where the Quakers or Friends were martyred, it would be somewhere around West Dedham and Washington Street."

"Let's see what we see," Griffin said.

It was hard to imagine the distant past; the area now was a nod to the Victorian era. Well-tended row houses in red brick were abundant. Industry was keen; with plentiful bars, coffeehouses and music venues.

"You keep a close eye on our civilian consultant," Jackson said. "I'll branch off at Dedham."

They heard the buzzing of a cell phone; Barnes excused himself to answer it.

The others started walking.

"Hey!" Barnes called to them. His features were grim — and very pale.

Jackson, Vickie and Griffin stopped. Barnes was white as he hurried to catch up with them.

"Fiona West, forty-three, of Brookline. She went missing yesterday. She works nights, so her husband didn't realize until he just got home from work himself that she never came back last night. He called her work; she never reported in. Her car was in the lot, but she never made it into the door. Five-five, brunette — they're sending the picture over the phone now . . . yes. Here she is."

He produced his phone for them all to see.

Fiona West had a great smile. She was dark-haired, blue-eyed, pretty with an enthusiasm for life that came alive, even in a bad picture over the phone.

"Let's find her," Griffin said.

"We're calling out the troops — I have several squads coming for a sweep. The Neck — the damned Boston Neck. It's not a pile of farms anymore, there are business, churches and homes . . . what the hell!" Barnes muttered. "Needle in a haystack!"

"We're looking for a place where bodies might have been dumped after they had been hanged," Vickie said.

"And no one knows precisely where those bodies might be," Barnes said. "Forgive me — it's not that I have no faith, Miss Preston, but we need an army on this. We don't have an army, but I'm taking every officer I can get."

"And that's good, Detective Barnes," Vickie said. "I'm not offended. I don't have a precise answer for you."

Barnes moved on, ready to meet with other officers.

Griffin and Jackson looked at Vickie.

"So an army is coming in — we'll stick together," Jackson said.

"Vickie?" Griffin asked quietly.

She pointed down Washington Street. "Let's head that way — I think."

It was a long, long late afternoon and evening.

The wear and tear, Griffin thought, was beginning to show on many of those called in to search.

Officers combed the area. For the most part, residents, shop owners and workers — white collar and blue — were more than willing to let the law in, to help, to try to think of any place where a woman might have been boxed up in a coffin-like manner and left.

Barnes worked the officers on a grid while Jackson, Vickie, the ghost of Dylan Ballantine and Griffin went on a different concept of a grid, following her rationale through history.

She spent some time speaking with the priest at the church — a history buff himself — and he talked about the earliest buildings in the area.

They searched the church and the crypts and all possible burial areas.

Lawns, T stations, waterworks, cables, roadways, homes and offices.

Near midnight, they were all exhausted.

162

Vickie looked tired and frustrated as they stood on the street, not far from the church. She was frowning, deep in thought.

"What is it?" he asked her.

She pointed across the street. "The Pine house, over there," she said.

"We were there earlier," he reminded her. "And, yes, it seemed just right. It's what remains of an old farm. Still owned by the family of the man who had it built in the nineteenth century. We did go in, remember? The guy just stores stuff there — he let us tear apart his basement."

"I know — it's just in the right place," Vickie said. "And . . . I just think we're missing something. It feels right," she added softly.

"Vickie knows her stuff," Dylan said softly. Even he looked weary. Griffin supposed ghosts could become just as tired and frustrated as — as when they had been living. He was actually surprised Dylan was still with them; he might have left at any time.

"The Pine house," Jackson murmured. "Between an ice cream shop with happy, dancing, cartoon cow stickers on the windows — and the biker bar. I guess there's kind of a break between the two. Vickie, we're going to have to call Mr. Pine back and it is nearly midnight."

"We've been everywhere," she said. "Well, it would be impossible for us to have been everywhere. But there's something we missed somehow. We're looking for holes in basement floors, recently dug graves, dump sites . . . I think these *Undertakers* changed up the game. I think we had to have missed something and the remains of that old farmhouse is where we're going to figure out what they did."

"I'll call Mr. Pine again," Griffin said. And he did so.

The ghost of Dylan Ballantine said softly, "When you've got a real feeling for something, you have to go with it."

"Well, it's not just me. Father Adair — the man I was speaking with at the church — said there was something about the house that always made him uneasy."

"Fiona West hasn't been missing that long," Jackson pointed out.

"No, but maybe . . . okay, this sounds weird. Maybe the house is old and therefore creepy and perhaps even invites bad things to happen," Vickie said.

Dylan sniffed loudly. "That's half of Boston!"

Vickie sighed with great patience. "Most places that are really old are well-preserved and well-tended," she said. "I do have a feeling. One of those intuition things, I guess. I didn't like it when we were in there. I swear — we missed something."

She seemed very certain. Griffin had felt his admiration for her growing throughout the day. She was tireless — frustration didn't seem to bring her to anger. When one solution didn't work, she looked for another.

Oliver Pine seemed to be a decent man. Griffin first woke his wife, and then the man came to the phone sounding as if he'd been disrupted from a deep sleep. He assured Griffin that he didn't live far at all — he'd be there in a matter of minutes.

They headed across the street and back over to the east side of Washington Street. As they did so, Vickie looked at him. "I'm sorry. I mean, if we don't find something . . ."

"If we don't find anything, it's okay. That's the way this works. We look and look. Sometimes we're lucky quickly. Sometimes, we have no luck at all. But when you feel as strongly as you do now, it's better to take the chance," he said.

"I'm just not sure where we didn't look," Dylan murmured.

They all ignored him; a car drove up. It was Oliver Pine. He parked and hurried out to open the locks on the house.

"Mr. Pine, we really can't thank you enough," Jackson told him.

"Hey!" the man said, shaking his head. "To be asked to help? No problem. I stand here a grateful man that it's not a member of my family. Anyway, I sure couldn't guarantee that there wasn't something in here; we never lived in the place. I inherited it from my grandfather, but it's not like it was really livable. Naked lightbulbs, horrible plumbing — I turn the water off in winter. There are two bathrooms from the 1940s . . . the house was chopped up years ago when plots were sold off for the buildings on either side. I guess I should just donate it to some historic board — if anyone wants it. There are some cool old fixtures, and stuff like that, but . . ." He broke off with a shrug. "I can just give you the keys. I really only come here when we need somewhere to put things. I actually keep the snowblower in the parlor — as you saw earlier."

"Thank you. We'll hopefully not be long," Jackson said. "If you want to get home, we will make sure your keys are returned."

"Thanks." Pine was young-looking. Griffin had looked him up to find out about him and the old structure earlier. He was actually forty; the father of three boys.

Jackson took the house keys from Pine and started to walk him to the door. Griffin was watching Vickie as she stared at a wall of chain-store half-empty bookcases across the room.

"Wait!" she said suddenly.

Pine and Jackson halted, swinging around to look at Vickie.

"Mr. Pine, you said that you're almost never here, right?"

"No, I'm sorry to say. I'm sure the historic board people don't like me very much. But it's Boston, and other places around here may be so much older. What's left of this place isn't really relevant to any major events in history, so you just kind of go on, you know what I mean?"

"Mr. Pine, what about those bookcases?"

"They're old, but not that old. I mean, they're not new or anything. My dad put them in when I was a kid — they came in one of those assemble-it-yourself kits. I don't think they're even real wood," Pine said.

"Do they attach to the wall?" Vickie asked him.

"Uh, no. They never did. We meant to work on this place. Then when my dad died, my mom just tried to keep it all together, you know?"

"Of course," Vickie said. She was already walking to the bookcases. Griffin, frowning, hurried over to her.

"No dust," he noted, "not here, not on this end. And there is dust on the other end."

He didn't have to say anything else — go into any kind of a lengthy explanation of the subtle signs that someone had been there, that the bookcases against the wall had been moved recently, and that they needed to look further.

Jackson was already by his side.

"They've been moved — those bookcases?" Oliver Pine said, confused. "The only people I know about who have been in here for years have been my wife and me. And my friend, Barney, when he helped me bring in the old refrigerator. We didn't even look at the bookcases. Maybe I am a terrible property owner, but the kids . . . life is busy, you know?"

"Sure. Sorry, we're messing up your place," Griffin said. But he didn't stop. A few of the dusty, old books in the cases fell out.

"Uh, whatever," Pine said.

The place had naked lightbulbs hanging on wires from the ceiling. The light was vivid and garish.

Vickie walked up to the wall. "It is paneling," she said, and turned to them all. "Looks like there's a strange crack in the wood there. Or not a crack . . . just a bad alignment."

"Bad alignment?" Dylan said, snorting. "A two-year-old could have done better work."

"Renovations here have been pretty cheap and — schlocky," Pine said, oblivious to the presence of Dylan Ballantine.

"Mr. Pine, we're about to rip up your wall," Jackson said. "If you wish us to stop, legally, we have to do as you ask, and then pursue a warrant."

"But," Griffin added, "if we take that time, a woman may die."

"She may only have minutes left," Vickie whispered.

Pine stared at them, shell-shocked, a man truly lost.

But then he spoke with conviction.

"Rip away," he said. "I don't live here, and hell, it needs to be fixed and spruced up a zillion times over as it is."

Griffin saw one of the plywood slats that should have been part of the bookcase leaning against an old vacuum. He picked it up to use as leverage, thinking it might well

169

break and shatter before it broke the paneling. To his surprise, it didn't; the paneling gave as if it had barely been set in place.

Behind the wall was a space that ran the length of the room — about fifteen feet. It was perhaps three feet deep.

There was definitely . . . a body.

Vickie let out a sharp gasp.

It wasn't Fiona West; this body had been in the wall a very long time. It was partially skeletal.

It also appeared to be partially mummified.

"Oh, my God!" Oliver Pine breathed.

Griffin began to tear at the paneling with his hands. Jackson joined in, then Oliver Pine — and then Dylan, ineffective with his ghostly hands, but so determined to help.

Then, suddenly, Dylan gave up at the tearing and working. He grinned at Vickie — and appeared to walk right through the wall.

He came back out.

"More bodies," he said grimly, as the others continued to work.

They kept at it with renewed energy.

Dylan was right.

Another body appeared. And then another.

They continued in something like a frenzy, ripping out the length of the poorly paneled wall to see the space behind.

The bodies were all in various stages of decay and natural preservation; they were braced up by wooden stakes, most with hair still falling around their macabre half skeletal, half stretched-skin faces.

Three, four, five, six . . .

They seemed to stare out with disarticulated jaws, eyes black and cavernous, as if they had walked out of a horror movie, macabre and horrifically eerie.

Seven, eight . . .

"Not Fiona," Vickie said, more anxious that they should find a living woman than shocked or terrified by what they had found so far. "We're running out of time."

Griffin glanced at Vickie; she was watching nervously. Every one of them was stunned, but she wasn't screaming, she wasn't running — nor was she getting in the way when it was apparent that another worker wasn't needed.

"There! There — right there!" Vickie gasped.

She was pointing to the far end of the wall. The last body.

And she was right. At the very last, at the end of the space behind the false wall, they found something different — a human-shaped bundle that might be Fiona West.

She was wrapped up as if in a shroud. They pulled her out as quickly and gently as possible, tearing the fabric from her.

Jackson instantly went for his phone, calling for an ambulance, as Vickie dropped down by Griffin's side, working at tearing away the material around the woman.

Vickie was on the floor, staring at him across the body of the woman, her green eyes immense. "She's breathing, right, she's breathing?"

Yes, the woman was breathing.

Griffin felt for a pulse; Fiona was alive. Her pulse was faint and weak, but it was there. And she was definitely breathing on her own.

"She's alive," he said.

Vickie closed her eyes and sank back on her haunches, letting out a swift sigh of relief.

"Can I do anything, can I help, should we . . . be doing something?" she asked.

"She's breathing on her own — we need to keep her still until the EMTs arrive," he said. "Just — just watch her."

"Oh, my God. Oh, my God. Oh, my God!" Oliver Pine said, half sinking and half falling to the floor.

"Yeah, you idiot! You are a lousy property owner," Dylan said.

"He's been trying very hard to help!" Vickie said, looking straight at Dylan.

"But there were already bodies in his wall!" Dylan said.

Thankfully, Oliver Pine wasn't hearing a word — he was just staring at the bodies that remained lined up in the space behind the false wall.

Luckily, they all seemed to have passed on peacefully — they weren't hanging around in ghostly form, not that Vickie could sense, anyway.

"Someone in my family was a mass murderer!" Pine wailed suddenly.

It was midnight and police were still combing the area. It seemed it wasn't more than two minutes before they heard sirens, and other officers began to arrive, Detective David Barnes at the head. Griffin helped Vickie to her feet so that they could draw away and leave the EMTs to work on Fiona West.

"What the bloody hell?" David Barnes demanded, reaching the room.

Jackson Crow stepped over to apprise him of the situation.

An officer escorted Oliver Pine outside. Griffin watched as he was led out.

"The historic board is really going to have something to say about this," he said as he walked away, appearing completely disoriented and stunned, a man in shock. "Are the bodies now historic? Who the hell were they?" He turned to the officer escorting him. "You know that I didn't do that, right? I mean, oh, my God!"

"Yes, sir. We know you couldn't have done — that," the officer said.

Jackson walked over to where Vickie and Griffin stood together. "I can deal with this. I'll write up a report. We can meet with Barnes at his station tomorrow for anything else that's needed. Why don't you two leave, and get some rest. Vickie, you've been invaluable to our team."

"I'm truly grateful I could help," she said, looking from Jackson to Griffin and then around the room, now flooded with police.

She lowered her voice.

"I never thought that this . . . *thing* with the dead could be useful, but . . . wait, actually, tonight it had nothing to do with the dead, it was the reverend I spoke to, it was where the house was, it was . . . maybe it was the dead. If we didn't all see Dylan . . ."

"You're welcome," Dylan said, proud of himself as he came to them. He didn't drift, or appear to float on the air. He seemed to swagger.

Setting ghostly arms around Vickie and

Griffin, he said, "I'm very happy to be of service — and you guys did save my mom. And I'm off — back to watch over the family. Call me when you need me. Oh, wait. I can't answer a phone. Not to worry. I'll be back."

Vickie watched him go. "How can a ghost be such a wiseass?" she murmured.

"He's still a teenager," Jackson reminded her. "You could probably use some rest."

"You could both use showers," she said, looking from Jackson to Griffin and managing something of a smile.

Griffin looked at Jackson — his partner on this case was covered in dust, plaster, wood chips and more.

He assumed he looked the same. And, observing Vickie again, he saw that she hadn't escaped the fallout from the false wall.

"Let me get you on home," he told Vickie.

"Thank you," she murmured.

She was staring at the wall again. Griffin followed her line of vision.

The panels were all down, only broken sections of balsa and plaster remained here and there along the structural segments.

It seemed that a field of dead stared out at them. Fragments and whole pieces of clothing clung to the oddly preserved bodies; some appeared as if they could walk right out. With others, it seemed that they would fall into a pile of bones at the slightest touch.

What the hell had happened here? When had it happened?

How had the killers stumbled upon the cache?

The dead just gaped at them in a reproach silenced by decades.

Vickie shivered.

Then she turned and hurried out the door.

Uncanny! Absolutely, frigging, unbelievably uncanny!

Taker had watched the developments for some time. He'd kept to the shadows, inside stores, along walls and crevices, but he hadn't been particularly concerned. If he'd been seen, there was no reason he shouldn't be where he was. The streets here were filled with coffeehouses, restaurants and shops.

At first, he'd watched with amusement. No, frankly, he'd watched with glee.

He'd even called Under to say how fantastic the find had been, how cool, and he'd described the police and the FBI running around like ants.

But now . . .

How the bloody hell . . .

The Master would be so disappointed! It was fine, just fine, that some of the women had been found alive, but this was really becoming a pattern now!

It was her, of course. Victoria Preston.

She was supposed to be involved, yes, of course, but . . .

She was annoyingly right on, far more so than they had expected.

He dialed Under. "Well, not so good. You failed."

"I failed? You're an ass! A jerk. Your clever writing. I didn't fail. The whole city is going to be in awe — in fact, I should have said screw you and screw this shit and given my find to the city."

"And been arrested for trespassing, huh?"

Under began to swear. "You ass! Quit with the clues that are maps, huh?"

"We'll tone it down — until we get something as good," Taker said. He still needed Under. But when he didn't . . .

He smiled. "Yeah, my clue was too good. Besides, we have an ace in the hole. Because people are stupid. We'll play that next, and then . . ."

"Then?"

"Maybe we'll start working on the end game."

He hung up and stared at the goings-on

at the Pine house, the plethora of cop cars and police techs and whoever else kept coming.

Uncanny. Absolutely, frigging, unbelievably — uncanny!

Vickie hadn't been afraid while she was in the Pine house.

On the contrary — when the first "old" corpse had appeared, she had been dismayed. She'd been so convinced that they would find Fiona West there. And then, of course, the men had kept tearing at the wall, and more and more old corpses had appeared, and then, finally, Fiona West.

She'd been so concerned for the woman who might still be living that she had barely noticed the dead.

But before they had left, she had stared at the sight of the corpses, all lined up in their terrible pageantry.

Bone, and fragments of bone. Dark, rotted, mummified flesh stretched tightly over that bone. How had they come to that stage? When had they been killed — and why?

And most importantly . . .

"How the hell did the kidnapper-slash-killers know about the Pine house? I mean, I'm no expert, but it appears that those bodies were shored up behind the — cheaply made, mind you — false wall of the Pine house. Apparently, no one else knew they were there. If someone had known they were there, they would have been removed ages ago," Griffin said, thoughtful as he drove through the streets of Boston.

It was after 2:00 a.m. The good thing was there wasn't the usual snarl of Boston traffic with which to contend.

"I don't know. I can't even imagine," Vickie said. She closed her eyes, thinking maybe she could re-create an image and try to get a fix on the remnants of clothing upon the bodies.

She could far too easily get a mental picture.

She couldn't get a fix on clothing. She could only see the disarticulated hanging jaws, the gaping, stygian stare of the empty eye sockets.

She shouldn't have felt so unnerved now. So frightened.

After all, she saw the dead walking around!

And yet, there had been something so sad, so terrible, about the victims in the wall. Long dead. She needed to be far more afraid of the present — and killers who were still at large.

"The city will have forensic anthropologists in there tomorrow," Griffin continued. "We'll have answers as to how they came to be there . . ." He paused, shrugging. "Poor Oliver Pine. He might have had a sadistic ancestor who was a serial killer, and he'll get to discover the truth."

"I wonder how the smell didn't alert someone when those bodies were going in the wall. Then again, it was one of the oldest farmhouses in the area. Maybe the bodies decomposed and mummified before there were a lot of people around to notice the smell of rot, or maybe there were dead animals, or the victims of hangings around to smell, or . . ."

"What remains most pertinent to our current situation," Griffin said, "is knowing how the Undertakers knew about the false wall and how easily it would be to add another body in at the end of the space."

"Do you think they might have discovered it by accident?" Vickie asked. "They obviously know the city and this area of Massachusetts and delight in coming up with their one-line clues to send law enforcement into a frenzy."

"The police and you," Griffin murmured.

They arrived at her apartment. Vickie automatically reached for the door handle to get out of the car. She was moving slowly.

Griffin had come around by the time she managed to get halfway out of the car.

"You okay?" he asked. "You're shaking."

"I'm fine — just a little unnerved," she told him.

And she was. More so than she had thought. She realized she'd accepted his assistance to get out of the car as if she were grabbing at a lifeline.

And he was a lifeline. He seemed vibrant, warm, strong . . . someone great to cling to.

She tried to breathe. She wasn't a clinger. She just wasn't. And yet she realized she wanted to throw herself into his arms and ask him to hold her until she wasn't afraid anymore. In truth, she really longed for more, she realized.

Standing on the sidewalk in front of her small complex, she pictured herself doing just that — leaning in to him, having his arms around her, letting her own curl around his neck. Maybe have her fingers thread through the rich darkness of his hair. Maybe she'd had a thing for him since she'd first seen him when she'd been seventeen years old. Her imagination began to run really wild as she thought about the places such an action could take them. He was rock solid, probably really beautiful naked.

She felt herself flush even though she

181

hadn't done a thing, and whether he saw the dead or not, she sincerely doubted that he could read her mind.

A car drove up behind them. She saw it was a police car.

"Officer Manetti will be outside all night," Griffin told him. "You have my number. I'll see you to your door — make sure everything is tight."

"Sure. Thanks," she said lightly.

He held her elbow as they headed down the short walk to the outside door of the complex. She prayed for her fingers to work on the lock; thankfully, they did. She then opened the door to her own apartment, painfully aware of him beside her.

Rock-hard, trustworthy, vibrant, filled with life and determination and heart and soul . . .

And simply sensual and masculine, and though she hated the very concept, yes, at this moment, she wanted to cling!

She refrained. He came into the apartment with her and immediately went about his inspection. She was in the kitchen when he finished, setting water on for tea.

"All clear," he told her, and asked quietly, "Are you okay? Tonight had to be pretty traumatic. We deal with this kind of thing all the time, but even I have rarely seen a sight quite like that row of bodies in the wall."

"I'm fine," she lied. "And it was a good night, really, right? I mean, the dead people in the walls were beyond help long ago. The woman who could be saved was saved."

"Yes."

He stayed there, close to her, but distant. She thought she should offer him tea; she thought he should go. They'd spent the day together; they'd spent other time together. There was a strange and undeniable bond between them. That was one thing. He also had an allure; a charisma. He appealed to her in every way possible, and thus the alarming run of her imagination.

She was just so afraid that he would see her as a victim, as the scared kid he had once saved, as the young woman plagued by the dead and the past and . . .

"Well, it's late. I should get going," he said.

"Of course. You'll keep me up on everything happening, please?"

"Actually, I intend to stay close — like this," he said, smiling and lifting his hand to show her his entwined fingers. Then his smile faded. "Vickie, I'm afraid we're going to be on top of you until these killers are brought to justice."

On top of her . . .

Bad, bad, bad. Her mind was moving in the really wrong direction . . .

"For some reason, they are using your name — they are taunting you. I am afraid you are involved with this, through nothing you did on your part. I'll be back tomorrow. You're working here, right, from your home?"

Leave it to the FBI. Yes, they even had her schedule. Not that it was any great secret.

"Yes."

"See you tomorrow, then."

"Thank you. Good night."

For a moment, they stood awkwardly. If she really let her imagination run, she could wonder if he was thinking the same thing. Forget it all for a minute, take a step forward, take her into his arms, indulge in a kiss, hot and wet and . . .

He walked to the door. "Lock up."

"Yep."

Then he was gone. And she locked the door.

Vickie brewed her tea and brought it into the bedroom. After a quick shower to get off the plaster and dust and who-knew-what-else from the Pine house, she prepared for bed. She started to turn on the television and then didn't. Tomorrow would be time for the news.

She was exhausted, but sleep wouldn't come. She tossed and turned for at least an hour.

When she slept, it was restlessly. When she started to dream, she was back at the Pine house and the skeletal and mummified bodies were staring at her — then they began to jerk and twitch and . . .

Step out of the walls.

In the garish light and shadow of the Pine house, they began to walk toward her. They gnashed their teeth, something she knew — even in her dream — was quite impossible. Their jaws were barely attached to their heads if they were still attached at all.

But . . .

They were moving. One by one, and as a small army.

Coming at her . . .

They seemed to lumber as they moved. Black goo . . . rotten blood . . . appeared to drip from the dark and withered, mummified flesh.

"Victoria . . ."

They whispered her name.

"Victoria, Victoria, Vickie . . ."

It became a chant.

A skeletal arm reached out for her.

She awoke with a startled scream.

It was morning; she hadn't drawn the

drapes and sunlight was pouring in.

And someone was banging at her door.

CHAPTER SIX

"We're still doing all kinds of testing," Dr. Theodore Loeb told Griffin. "But from what I've managed to ascertain so far, six of our victims were males, two were females. They have been in that wall for decades. Further testing will hopefully pinpoint a year, but I'm thinking that these murders took place back in the late 1800s."

"How were the victims killed?" Griffin asked him.

"Again, we're working with some bodies that have left little evidence behind. And, of course, this is speculation right now, but I believe the bodies in better shape were killed in winter and preservation began before they had time to rot."

"Dr. Loeb, how were they killed?" Griffin asked.

"Oh, well, we are still working on that as well. They weren't shot — no trace of bullets found — and don't seem to have borne knife wounds of any kind, not discernible by the remains. There is visible trauma on a number of the skulls, but I don't believe it was enough to have been a killing blow. Soft tissue is scarce, but it will be tested. At the moment, I believe they were either poisoned — a possibility — or they were simply smothered."

"In the wall itself, or before they were put in the wall?"

"I'm not sure how. We're still working on what was going on."

They were at the office of the chief medical examiner on Albany Street. Dr. Loeb and his assistants had been given a special room dedicated to the historic corpses. According to their home office back in Northern Virginia, Dr. Loeb was one of the most respected forensic anthropologists in the world. He was an older man, almost as skeletal as some of their victims. He was dignified and yet energetic; Griffin believed that, if they were out there, Loeb would find the answers.

"But what a find, what a find. What a mystery!" the man said.

"An amazing find, yes. Especially since we found a kidnapped victim there," Griffin said.

"Yes, yes, of course. Thank God! You

found the woman alive. And how extraordinary! How could they have known? Of course, I've been reading about this case. I'm no Sherlock Holmes, but I'm thinking this Undertaker might have lucked upon the situation. You know, he may sit around thinking, *just where do I leave my next victim?* And once you're out on the Boston Neck in the South End, you start looking for the right place," Dr. Loeb said.

"Maybe," Griffin told him. "Dr. Loeb, will you please keep me up on any information as you come across it?"

"Naturally, Special Agent Pryce," Dr. Loeb told him.

As Griffin left the office, he received the call he'd been expecting from Jackson Crow.

"Anything from Dr. Loeb?" Jackson asked.

"He thinks we're looking at the late 1800s, victims possibly disabled by conks on the head, and then poisoned or smothered."

"Too similar, huh?"

"Maybe. What have you got?"

"Fiona West can tell us nothing. She was locking her car — she felt a searing pain in her head. The good thing is that she doesn't even remember being bundled up and closed into a wall with a bunch of age-old corpses."

"That's good . . . for her," Griffin murmured. "Struck getting out of her car. She didn't see him — or them. Okay, so Angelina Gianni is certain that there are two criminals working together. I believe this is right — I always suspected two. Getting victims buried or into walls or boxes and Dumpsters and coal bins isn't that easy on your own, and not when you're trying to make sure you're not seen. We go back to *struck on the head.* Here's what scares me. The victims haven't been able to tell us anything. I believe that the kidnappers/killers know that their victims thus far were knocked out cold — they have complete confidence that the victims aren't going to be able to tell us anything. What frightens me is, what happens if they mess up before we find them? If they think that a victim can identify them, does that victim die right away?"

"We can't speculate on that — we have to find an answer here somewhere before the Undertakers strike again," Jackson said.

"I have an idea."

"And what's that?" Jackson asked.

"Bertram Aldridge."

"He's in prison — we've checked. And I've had Angela back at Krewe headquarters going through everything we can find in his prison correspondence and through his visitor list."

"Yep. Still say we need to see him," Griffin said.

"Well, it sure as hell can't hurt."

Griffin felt Jackson's hesitation over the line before he spoke again.

"What about Vickie Preston?" Jackson asked.

Something in Griffin's gut clenched. "What about Vickie? What do you mean?"

"Well, we have a situation here in which these people now seem to be going right for the jugular — her name in the clues. So, it's possible they are simply fans of Bertram Aldridge, or maybe they're on a payback mission for him."

"Payback — *I* shot the man," Griffin said. "Not Vickie."

"Yes, you did. You shot him when he should have still been in the house — torturing Vickie Preston and Noah Ballantine. Maybe you're not an easy target and maybe you are a target — they just haven't begun plaguing you as yet. They got you here, right? This whole thing might have been studied. But then again, maybe it's just Vickie they're after. The one who got away."

"So, copycats, of a form, who want revenge for Aldridge. But they're on a spree here, so it seems. Nothing new sent to the media as of yet, right? No riddles or clues?" Griffin asked.

"No. A killing spree, so it seems, but . . . no, we haven't heard about another victim yet. And right now, they're probably thinking how clever they are. Somehow, they knew about bodies in the wall from murders a century ago. I'm sure they're thinking they're very clever."

"It definitely points to killers from this area. I'd say someone who grew up here, who might have heard tales about the old Pine house — or maybe they broke in somewhere along the line and made the discovery themselves. Yeah, they've been ahead of us, all right. But they'll make a mistake."

"I believe they will, too. I agree that we need to see Aldridge," Jackson said.

"Right."

"But," Jackson added, "I think we need to bring Vickie with us."

Vickie was groggy getting up, and she couldn't help but be afraid — who pounded on your door like that if something wasn't the matter?

She grabbed a robe to slip over her pajamas and hurried to the door, her heart beating. She had to be all right; she knew that

Griffin Pryce would never leave her door unguarded.

She looked through the peephole. And then she smiled.

Actually, this was a visitor she should have expected already.

It was Roxanne Greeley at her door.

They'd been best friends in high school, and even when they'd gone on to their separate colleges — Vickie in New York City and Roxanne down in Florida — they'd kept in touch constantly and managed to make sure they'd spent time during holidays together. No one had been more thrilled that Vickie had come back to Boston than Roxanne.

She was a visual artist who also worked with Grown Ups.

"Hey! Let me in, let me in. Before that cop comes back and decides I'm not an innocent character!" Roxanne called to her through the door.

Vickie opened it, smiling.

Roxanne rushed in and hugged her, holding her tightly.

"You! Go figure, how do you get into these things?" Roxanne demanded.

"What do you mean —"

"Don't worry. You're not in the news. I talked to my mom who talked to your mom who is very concerned and doesn't understand why you don't just come home and live with them. Oh, and she — your mom — believes the Ballantine family is going to ask if you want to stay with them until this is all over, and your mom is all torn, she's your mom and wants you, but hey, the Ballantines do have more money and you might just be safer with them. Toss-up, huh?" Roxanne asked. Her initial enthusiasm seemed to go out of her as if a balloon had popped. "Are you okay?" she asked anxiously.

"I'm fine. Cop at the door — you saw him, right?" Vickie said. "Come on in. Hang tight for a minute, will you — I'm not even dressed."

"I'll make coffee. Pull on some clothes. You don't have Grown Ups today, right?"

"Nope."

"Will the cop come with us if we want to go to lunch?"

"Lunch?"

"It's almost noon."

"Okay. Yes, the nice policeman will follow us."

"Then get ready. I'll have a cup of coffee, and we can head out!"

Thirty minutes later, they were on their way out, walking along the street — followed by the nice man from the unmarked police car who was in plain clothing. Vickie had smiled and waved at him when they'd left the house; he'd smiled and waved back.

They chose to walk. Naturally, there were really great Italian restaurants in the neighborhood. They chose a family-run establishment that had been there since their school days. They decided to have a cup of Italian wedding soup each, and then split an antipasto and an order of ziti.

"And you're all right, really?" Roxanne asked her. "You really should have called me right away — I mean, as soon as you could after that clue came to the papers and the FBI came to your house. I know they're doing their best to keep your involvement hush-hush, but you can't stop the press. The clues have come in. There's speculation everywhere that Bertram Aldridge is somehow involved, but of course he's locked away. Copycat — at least, kind of a copycat. Or an admirer of Aldridge!" She waved a hand in the air. "Anyway, today's headline is all about Fiona West being found alive. *With* a ton of corpses, old murder victims. You were there, right? Your name was in the clue. What was that like? Horrible, of course, horrible. I shouldn't be asking. Okay, I am asking. You're my friend. I'm

worried. Really worried. About you, naturally. Not physically — I mean, I can see
the cop and I know the FBI is looking out
for you. Can't help it — you're my best
friend."

"I was there — it was horrible. I'm fine.
Fiona West is alive. There was nothing
anyone could do about the other people
who had been walled up — that happened
decades ago."

"Yeah."

"I'm fine. Really." If having nightmares
about long-dead corpses coming at her was
normal after such an evening, she really was
perfectly fine. "Honestly, fine. And glad to
be away, and out for lunch with you," Vickie
told her.

"Same menu as when we were kids,"
Roxanne noted. She laughed softly. "Not
that we're that old. But sometimes, doesn't
it feel as if we were young — really young
— like eons ago? I remember high school,
when everyone thought you were just crazy
and suffering from stress when you broke it
off with Hank Fremont. He was such a
hunk back then, cool sports guy, everyone
was kind of afraid of him. But you were
determined to get out of Boston and get to
NYC as quickly as you could. You were not
missing out on the college you wanted

because of him — or any other guy." Roxanne paused to take a sip of her iced tea. "He was out in Springfield, working for Sonia Camp's dad at an amusement park. Nothing wrong with amusement parks or even working for someone's dad, but . . . he'd have brought you down to not going to school at all, too, if you'd stayed with him. I think someone said he was back in Boston now — oh, yeah, I talked to Katie Austin the other day — Hank Fremont is back in Boston. Hey, well, there's something. He might be doing some work with Grown Ups, too. Not sure what he's going to teach the kids. *What not to do when you're super cool in high school and think it will last your whole life?* How could you be so smart at eighteen? I made it through school, but I was so insane over Trent Larson at the time." She laughed. "Oh, Lord. And Trent Larson is now doing time. But the point is, he broke up with me before heading to the south and beginning his life of crime. I'm lucky in life now *despite* myself."

"Trent Larson was an idiot to leave you brokenhearted. You were always not just stunning, but bright and kind and all the right things," Vickie assured her. And she meant it; Roxanne was a strawberry blonde with a sleek and athletic build, a smile like sunshine and an empathy for others that was contagious.

She laughed. "Ah, yes, but still. You were the leave-er. I was the left! Thank God, of course, with hindsight. I'm always a little in awe. You came through what happened — and you kept on course."

Vickie shrugged. "You came through just fine, too. As for me? I guess we were just both lucky. There was something about NYU. Once my dad took me down to New York City to look at colleges there, I knew I really wanted to go to school there and spend some time living in that atmosphere."

"I look at the kids we work with now and I think about how hard everything was at that age. I remember the 'mean girls' and peer pressure and the kids using drugs or alcohol already, and we can look back and see who was just goofing off, and who might have already been on a very bad track. I think how lucky we were because we had parents who cared. Every once in a while, I think about teenage angst — and wonder how the kids we work with will ever survive," Roxanne said solemnly.

"We give them the best support we can, in our small way."

"Ah, well. I can only imagine. I was out with a group when all the info came out

198

about Barbara Marshall being found — and Chrissy Ballantine having gone missing right at the same time. One of my kids said the whole thing was stupid, that if you were going to kidnap and possibly kill someone, you ought to at the very least make some big bucks — ask for a ransom. His attitude gave me chills!" Roxanne said.

"Did you talk to the kid's case worker about it?" Vickie asked.

"Of course."

Roxanne nibbled on an olive. "We never do know what life will bring." She seemed distracted for a minute, looking toward the door. "I was wondering, how much of what you do now and where you are do you think came about because of what happened? The whole bit with Bertram Aldridge and then the cop — now agent — Griffin Pryce?"

Vickie lowered her head to survey and spear a piece of cheese from the antipasto plate; she felt a rush of blood to her face and didn't want Roxanne to see her flush.

She didn't want to accept the feelings in herself that the question brought about.

"Why do you ask about him?" she murmured.

"Well, there was something about him. He was the kind who was all noble and honorable — friend to a scared young woman. There was some bond the situation seemed to cause between you."

"Well, he saved my life. And it's not that strange he's back here — he's with a special unit that was called in. He's not with the behavioral sciences unit, but a different group that deal with . . . strange cases like this. It's natural."

"Ah," Roxanne whispered knowingly. "Well, it's good. Your mom, of course, is scared of him — scared of this situation. Scared of you being with him."

"I'm not exactly with him."

"You're not?" Roxanne seemed to voice the question strangely.

"No, why?" Vickie asked.

Roxanne smiled, rising and waving as she said, "Because he's walking into the restaurant right now, apparently telling the hostess that he's going to join us."

Vickie swung around. Griffin Pryce was weaving through the tables toward them. He saw Roxanne waving at him and waved back as he headed over.

Vickie didn't have to initiate a greeting — Roxanne had that covered.

"Hi!" Roxanne said to Griffin, having no compulsion as she met him with a hug.

He returned it; if he was surprised or taken off guard, he didn't show it.

Roxanne pulled away, looking at him anxiously. "You're here for Vickie. I'm Roxanne. Roxanne Greeley. Do you remember me? I remember you? Well, of course, I remember you. We were all in shock and you were so right there when you needed to be there — and now you're back. Here. Which is kind of like 'there.' Hmm. Okay, sorry. It is good to see you. I think, of course. I personally feel Vickie is a lot safer when you're around."

"Sit, please," Griffin said, pulling back Roxanne's chair and sliding into the seat across from Vickie that wasn't occupied by their purses. "Of course, Roxanne, I remember you. Very well. You were a great friend. I see you still are. And you think it's good I'm around." He glanced at Vickie, a rather sad, grim smile somewhat curling his lips. "You okay?"

"Yes, sure," she told him. *Horrible nightmares about corpses, but . . .*

She forced a smile. "I'm more than fine. I'm very happy to have had a part in finding these women and in finding them alive."

He nodded, looking at her. "We're grateful that you feel that way."

Something else was coming.

Roxanne was leaned on an elbow, just staring at him. "Um, olive? Cappicola . . .

201

cheese?" she asked. "It's just a huge anti-pasto. Would you like something else?"

The waitress was actually hovering near their table.

"Coffee, please?" Griffin asked. The young woman nodded; he turned to Roxanne. "Thanks — that olive looks great."

"Please, help yourself!" Roxanne said.

"Roxie, you can quit being quite so nice — he's here for something," Vickie said, staring at Griffin.

He didn't deny it. He nodded slightly again.

"You are?" Roxanne asked.

Vickie sighed inwardly; she was looking at him much the way she had years ago, when they'd all had something of a schoolgirl crush on him.

"Vickie is key to this investigation," he said quietly.

"She is? Oh! Oh, she is, of course. Her name in the clues, twice. Oh, my God! If he weren't locked up, I'd say for sure that it was Aldridge. Out to get her — the one who got away. Vickie, you have to be so careful. I mean, I can see that you have people watching over Vickie — the cop in plain clothes was ready to shoot me, I swear! — but this is really, really scary. You have to watch over her, Special Agent Pryce. I mean — like a hawk. They're out to get her." Roxanne turned to look at Vickie. "Maybe you should go to Italy with your parents — the Undertaker might not have a passport. But then, if he did . . . wow. You wouldn't be protected there. Your dad would kill for you, but he's a professor. And what if . . ."

Vickie had thought Griffin might be impatient with Roxanne; but he picked up her train of thought.

"What if the killer or killers just stopped and waited for Vickie to eventually come back from Europe and start up all over again when the case has gone cold, and there isn't as much law enforcement around?" he finished.

Chills shot through Vickie and she realized law enforcement had a very real theory she was somehow involved in the end game, that she might *be* the end game.

"We do need to talk," Griffin said quietly.

Roxanne stood; Griffin stood politely as well.

"I've got my kids today. I'm with Grown Ups, too. We're going to sketch at the aquarium. Vickie, call me. Griffin — no matter what anyone else says, it's really nice to see you again."

"Thank you," he told her gravely.

"I'll see you soon," Vickie promised.

Roxanne waved, grabbed her bag, and was quickly out of the restaurant.

"I'm sorry. I really didn't mean to ruin your lunch," Griffin told her.

She waved a hand in the air. "We were really finished. High school rehashed, food almost eaten . . . we've just skipped the cannoli and cappuccino part."

She felt unnerved and off; her heart was thundering a million miles an hour and she was ridiculously glad to see him, even though that was stupid and dangerous. They couldn't be involved; he was at once tasked with the assignment of catching a criminal and, apparently, keeping her alive.

"So, you don't think me being around is just fun for these guys, part of their remarkable *clue*-giving method and madness. You think I really might be the main target?"

For a moment, he looked frustrated, and she was oddly gratified to see it — not the police, not the FBI, not his special unit, no one, as yet, seemed to have the answer. She wasn't the only one lost and in the dark.

"I don't know," he admitted. "I just don't know. Here's what I think I know — we're looking at someone native to the area, or who grew up here. Someone who either knows Bertram Aldridge, or is a massive fan of his work. This is a different type of kidnapper and killer — and still a sadist. Aldridge went to prison for butchering women with a knife. Maybe these people — and it is people, two of them, I'm certain, Angelina Gianni heard two voices during her ordeal — are just as sadistic, but they like the torture of knocking their victims out and then allowing them to suffocate, boxed in, buried. Somehow, they knew about eight victims — six men, two women — murdered and walled up in an old house, sometime during the late 1800s, according to the ME. They know about you. They know you survived when Bertram Aldridge broke into the Ballantine home. What they know may be just what anyone can pick up from social media and public records — but I do think that you've been studied."

Vickie leaned back, looking at him. "Why me? I was a scared kid who just ran. You shot Bertram Aldridge."

"Yes, but Vickie, you're the one who got away."

She felt sick suddenly, chilled to the bone, terrified on a base and primal level. Mentally, her defense mechanisms kicked in; she was protected. The FBI was watching her, the police were watching her . . .

But if these people really wanted her dead — wasn't she as good as dead? Eventually,

205

someone would slip up, time would go by, and she would have to live in fear forever . . .

No, she wouldn't.

She stared back at Griffin Pryce. "Well, then. You really have to catch these bastards, huh?"

He smiled. "Yes. You want to help?"

"You bet. So what do you need me to do? Is there a new clue that's arrived at the paper? Is there any evidence? Is there any way I can figure out who these people might be?"

He leaned closer to her as well. They might have appeared to be enjoying a romantic tête-à-tête, their attention on one another was so determined.

"Everything right now seems to be a fifty-fifty. Either the killers know Bertram, or they don't. They're disciples, or they're fans. He knows and has instigated what is going on — or he has no clue and is just gleefully watching," Griffin said. "What's known is they're smart — but maybe smart in that they've watched a dozen TV series about crimes and evidence, or they have been petty crooks before, learning the ropes by watching people, watching alarms and getting away with what they want. I believe they will slip up, but when . . . that's what's worrisome, and who will suffer and who will die while we're waiting for them to slip up is a very scary contemplation. We've naturally scoured Bertram Aldridge's prison correspondence. He's in maximum security, but even so, he gets a couple of calls a week. He is also allowed to write and receive letters, though they are read by prison authorities. We haven't found anything damning — but we have discovered that when he first went in, he didn't have much correspondence. Over the past few years, he's had a number of calls that, when traced, go to pay-as-you-go cell phones, discarded after two calls. So, it is highly likely he's been talking to someone."

"What about his family? I remember that when he escaped all those years ago, authorities — on the news, anyway — thought that he'd be in the area because he had family around here."

"Bertram Aldridge is a native Bostonian," Griffin told Vickie. "His parents died when he was young. He grew up with a grandmother who lived on the south side. She's been dead three years now. The house has been sold three times since and now belongs to a corporation — completely renovated and redone. I don't know if you really remember him — he was capable of being articulate and very charming. When he was committing his knife crimes, he lured his victims with a smile easily enough. The first go-round — fifteen years ago — he was finally brought down by an undercover Boston policeman in drag — the guy was so good he could make a stunning woman, and when Aldridge tried to seduce him out to the kill, he turned the tables and the plain-clothes officers on the stakeout along with him were able to hone in and they arrested Aldridge."

"I'd think the cop who brought him down would be on his radar, too."

"He'll never know who it was — the information was never made public."

"People talk."

"I'm sure he'd like to kill lots of police-men. But cops aren't usually easy targets. Average citizens just going about their lives — unaware that they're being stalked — can be taken by surprise." He hesitated. "They've gone for easy prey."

"And you're suggesting I'm easy prey."

"Maybe. Maybe not. Because they're mak-ing it pretty obvious they know you. You've had a police guard on you."

"But by myself, I'm easy prey."

"We can all be easy prey."

"You don't need to be diplomatic. I don't know how to use a gun. I've never taken a martial arts course. I can play chopsticks on a piano, run pretty decently, which just might come in handy, and I'm all right with a computer. But . . . yeah. I guess I'm pretty pathetic when it comes to the possibility of being prey."

Again, he hesitated. Then he smiled. "Massachusetts is a 'may issue' state, meaning authorities are not compelled to issue concealed carry licenses even if you meet the requirements. We could get around that — except I wouldn't. Not unless you're willing to go through training."

"I'm willing."

She was willing? She hated guns.

But she hated the concept of dying more.

"All right," he said slowly. "Here's the thing. If you don't know what you're doing, you're just as likely to shoot yourself or someone you love as you are to shoot a criminal. So, you really do have to get serious. Here's the other thing. The women who have been taken have all been victims of very sly attacks — they had no clue they were being stalked until they were struck on the head. If you're in your own home making tea, it's unlikely the gun will be in your hand. If you're walking down the street with groceries, you're unlikely to be ready for the guy who is after you. So, there's a lot more to this than just becoming savvy with a firearm. Over the years, I've seen good cops and good agents go down, because we're all off guard sometimes and a blitz attack doesn't give anyone the chance to be prepared."

"We're back to the fact these Undertakers have to be caught," Vickie said. "And I don't believe you came to see me today about becoming gun savvy or to make me feel better about the fact anyone can be taken by surprise."

"No."

"Then what?"

"I want you to come with Jackson and me to see Bertram Aldridge."

CHAPTER SEVEN

"I always think it's strange how we can remember certain incidents with almost perfect visual clarity in our minds — and forget what we had for lunch the day before," Vickie said, working at her range top with a steam coffeemaker. She glanced over at Griffin. "I mean, I think most people work that way."

Griffin had determined to walk Vickie back to her apartment. He'd nodded to the cop on guard duty, who had acknowledged and followed behind — he wouldn't be able to stay long. Yes, she'd still need protection.

People had smiled at them as they'd walked. They probably appeared to be a young couple — out to see the city sights. Maybe people just smiled at her in general. She wasn't a pushover, but — despite what had happened to her at an impressionable age — she seemed to like people in general. She had an easy way about her — she was quick to apologize if she brushed someone, to laugh if a child's ball rolled across the street to her and to smile and demur just as quickly if someone accidentally offended her. It was odd, just walking down the street with her. They shared a natural bond — they both spoke to the dead. But he worked with a "krewe" of wonderful people who also spoke with the dead. Yes, they had a natural friendship and bond. This was different. Of course, they shared that certain incident.

But he'd been drawn to her years before. She'd been wide-eyed and innocent — learning the harsh reality of just how cruel and brutal the world could be. He'd made a point to step away.

More than eight years had passed. They'd gone different ways, lived in different worlds. She'd changed; he'd changed.

And when he was with her, he still felt as if he'd always been near her.

Maybe, in his mind, he had been.

Maybe she had just grown up to be someone any man would want to know; stunning, naturally seductive, charming . . .

Instinct. He was sure some of it was human biology; she seemed to awaken everything primal in him. He'd thought it was the need to protect. He realized it was a need for much more. She stirred everything in his senses. He should walk away; leave this to others. But no matter what faith he might have in his fellow agents, he knew he couldn't trust that anyone else in the world would — or could — protect her as he could. Ego? No. In some pathetically caveman way, she was his; he would see this all to the end, see her to safety — or die trying.

He watched the way her hair fell over her face, the way she glanced up with a "coffee's almost ready" smile. A sizzle of heat ran through him and he nodded and he knew: yes, he should walk away — no, he never would.

Because she was right; there were certain things you never forget, that you could recall just as clearly as if you were watching them unfold on a movie screen.

Like the day Bertram Aldridge had nearly killed her.

And he had come to know her.

The coffee had steamed; she got two mugs and poured it out, bringing one to him, and indicating they should sit in the little parlor area of her apartment.

She had great artwork on the walls. Paintings of historic moments mixed with modern-art posters. Two of the walls were lined with bookshelves; her book collection was extensive, histories and biographies mixed with popular fiction and graphic novels.

"You do know what I mean, right?" she asked him, seated in an old rocker across from the position he'd taken on the sofa.

He nodded. "Yeah. I see you running out of the Ballantine house, gripping the baby — Noah. I see Bertram Aldridge. I take aim and he's taking aim and my heart is going a million miles an hour. He trips, his shot goes wild and my shot wings him in the shoulder. But they say, that's trauma. You remember trauma. Do we always remember it right? Who knows?"

She nodded. "I remember him in court, too. I remember the way he smiled at me, as if we were friends — almost as if we had dated! The day at Ballantine house . . . I saw his face fleetingly. I saw he meant to kill me, shoot me down. He had a smile on his face. And then again, in court — that one day I came in — he looked at me as if . . . as if he knew me. He kept smiling and grinning, as though we shared something . . ." She broke off, shaking her head. "You know, I really had gotten over it. I went to NYC. Everything was different. I loved my professors, I loved the school and the city and the history there — St. Paul's, Trinity, Wall Street — a lot like Boston, in a way. New York is a thriving and vibrant world of today — and yet there's so much in the architecture and the culture and all that led to it." She fell silent. "I'm sure there are bodies in the wall somewhere in NYC, too." She gazed over at him. "I am going to find out who was murdered and walled up. How did they go forever — until new sick killers found them?"

"Things — and people — wind up buried in time," Griffin told her. "Last night was . . . bad. For officers. You're not an officer."

She grinned at that. "Surreal," she told him. "At least they weren't . . . fresh victims. I mean, I've spent endless hours in museums where they often display bones and corpses from the past. Okay, okay, so I admit it! I had a dream about them. A nightmare. They came alive and came after me — maybe I've seen too many episodes of *The Walking Dead.*"

He laughed softly because she had spoken so lightly.

"I've dreamed of the dead coming alive, too. Well, to be honest, when I was a kid, I thought I was dreaming — and the dead were coming to see me."

She seemed to inch closer to him. "The first time I ever saw, spoke to or had my wits scared out of me by the dead was at the Ballantine house that day. It was like opening a door. I don't always see them walking around. Just sometimes. Sometimes they want to be seen — sometimes they don't. Sometimes they want to talk — and sometimes they don't. The thing is, a ghost was a human being and whatever makes us human beings — the soul I imagine — remains the same." She winced. "This sounds ridiculous, but I've met some really great ghosts. Often in cemeteries. They say they don't hang around where they're buried often, but . . . some have nice graves, I guess, and they like to check on them. Dylan, of course, seems to have decided to watch over me for life. I'm so accustomed to having him around."

"That's — actually nice," he said softly. "He seems to be a real friend — and real friends, dead or alive, are often hard to come by."

"And you?" she persisted.

"Ah, well, I was one of those kids who saw his first 'ghost' when I was really young. We lived in an old Revolutionary house just north of downtown. One of Washington's officers was stationed there and used the house during the Battle of Bunker Hill. Of course, I didn't know that at the time. He would just come and play with me — damned good ghost. He could move a kid's toy block! Anyway, when I was older and talked about him, I was whisked off to a psychiatrist. The doctor told my parents that a lot of kids had imaginary friends. So, I had an imaginary friend. But I had an aunt on my dad's side who has whatever it is that we have. She told me not to share my imaginary friends with others. They were special. She was great. Aunt Mathilda. She died about five years ago. She told me not to expect to see her. She was ready to go and meet up with Uncle Henry. I never have seen her. I like to think she is happy with Uncle Henry."

"What about your Revolutionary soldier? Is he still there? With your folks?"

"My parents are in Arizona — my dad had to go — bad asthma. But they still own the house, and come up sometimes. When they're not in it, relatives and friends might use it — and, they rent it out with an association sometimes."

"So . . . you were just always comfortable with the dead popping by?" she asked, a curious small smile curving her lips.

"Yeah, pretty much so. Like Noah," he

added softly.

Vickie sighed. "Well, nice. It all came as a bit of a surprise to me. I'm glad now, of course. I love Dylan. I can understand how losing him nearly destroyed Chrissy and George Ballantine." She paused for a minute, forming her words. "You see the dead — and Jackson Crow? What about the cops you've worked with? Other agents?"

"Well, to try to make a long story short — none of the cops I worked with saw the dead. But that was okay — I'd learned never to let on that I did. Jackson Crow, yes, of course. The entire special unit we're with are able to see and communicate with souls who have remained behind." He hesitated, shrugging. "I was always looking for an explanation for the people I saw that others didn't — and as a kid, I spent a lot of time searching newspapers, books and the internet. But actually, I didn't have to look for others — they found me. A man came into my life. Adam Harrison. I was still young when I first met him. He knew my aunt and Uncle Henry when they were still living. He came to dinner one night. He didn't say a word in front of my parents, but he came into my room with my aunt — under the pretense I could show them some of my new toys or books or something. And he sat down and seriously asked me questions and I told him all about my Revolutionary hero and a few of the other people — the dead ones — I'd met over time. Aunt Mattie was there, so I figured it had to be okay. Though, of course, I admit, I was afraid my parents had called in another shrink, at first. He was great. He told me he envied me — and other people like me. He said some of them helped him out at times — that they were able to help when bad things happened. Because sometimes, the dead know what we don't. Medical examiners are great — they do so often speak for the dead. But speaking with the dead themselves . . . well, that could really make a difference. Anyway, he told me to look him up when I was ready. He said to go to school and college and do well and maybe even join the police force and then aim for the FBI. And when I did, to call him."

"And this man is . . . ?"

"Adam Harrison is the overall supervisor for the Krewe of Hunters, our division. It's his creation. Adam's son, Josh, had a rare kind of sixth sense. Josh was killed in a car accident, but when he died, one of his best friends — who was with him at the time — apparently inherited the gift. Adam started working with her and other people around the country. He's from Northern Virginia and a wealthy man, a philanthropist — and very friendly with a number of people in power. The Krewe of Hunters is really just a special unit — it isn't an official title. The first people he chose for the units came together in New Orleans and so the 'krewe' part of it all began. I became a cop — as you know. Applied to the FBI, went through the academy, spent some time working with the criminal investigation unit in DC, and when I thought it was time to look up Adam, he sent for me."

Vickie was smiling. He wished he could just reach out and stroke her cheek. She seemed to love his story.

"Amazing!" she said softly.

It seemed they had moved closer. The intimacy between them was palpable. She was nearly touching him. He could touch her.

His phone began to buzz in his jacket pocket.

"Sorry," he murmured.

"Of course!" She rose, moving away to allow him to speak privately.

It was Jackson Crow.

Griffin braced himself, thinking they might have received another taunt, clue or riddle from the killers.

"Is Vickie okay with coming along with us to see Aldridge?"

"Yeah," he said to Jackson. "I believe Victoria Preston will be fine visiting Aldridge with us."

"I'm setting it up. But we've got another problem."

"There is another clue?"

"It's Barbara Marshall — the woman we dug out of the cemetery. We've tried to interview her before, but she had no memory of anything other than a conk on the head. We've received a call from the friend, Annie Harte, who has been staying with her — and Barbara fights something or someone in her sleep. Annie is hoping we can help. Barbara is still going through therapy, but apparently, she hasn't remembered anything during sessions — just in dreams. At any rate, Annie and Barbara want to see us. They're going to meet us and Detective Barnes down at the station."

"All right. I'm on the way."

Vickie had moved away, but she walked back toward him then. "Another woman? Already?" she asked, slightly pale.

"Not that we know about. I have to meet with Jackson and Detective Barnes."

"Oh."

She stood about five feet from him. Five

feet. He wished he could just cross that small bit of space and take her into his arms. Hold her. He wondered if she was thinking anything of the same.

"You'd best go. And you will . . ."

"Keep you apprised. Yes."

"And I will go with you to see Bertram Aldridge, of course."

"Thank you."

"It's the least I can do."

"It's above and beyond — and thank you."

"No," she murmured.

"Thank you for the coffee."

"Thank you for the conversation."

He was going to move by her. He imagined a strange and kinetic energy suddenly leaping through the air, drawing them together.

She stepped back.

"I'll see you soon," he managed huskily.

And then he was out the door. But even when he reached the car he had parked a few blocks back, he could swear the scent of her perfume still drifted on the air.

Talk about being haunted . . .

The Boston Police Department was the oldest in the nation. The first *night watch* was established in 1635 — not that one could consider that a police department. By 1703, officers were hired who were paid thirty-five shillings a month for their service. A reorganization took place at the end of the 1700s. Those serving carried a rattle-like creation that could summon help, a badge that proved a man to be on duty, a pole that was painted blue-and-white and had a hook — to catch and pull those evil-doers who were escaping, and a "bill" on the other end to be used as a weapon.

The *day police* didn't come into being until 1838, and they were not connected to the night watch, but answered to the city marshal. It was the year the General Court created the formal police department and disbanded both the night watch and the day police.

Vickie had a pile of books set out in front of her, opened to different pages. She was determined to find somewhere in her materials something about the murders that had been committed in the late 1800s. She'd found a number of books that proudly announced the history of the Boston Police Department.

What she needed was records of their work. And such records surely existed in readily available material — she even had the complete transcripts of the Salem witch trials, and those had taken place years before the victims of a long-dead killer had been sealed into a false wall in the Boston Neck.

She left her books and headed to the computer and began to key in the names of the police in the late nineteenth-century she found referenced in the books. She was alone, but she cried out with pleasure when she found a research site — constructed by a history major at Harvard — that had gathered together the notes of one Officer Joseph MacDonald, a man who had served from 1871 to 1901 — a thirty-year service that hit her time period exactly.

Night fell while she read and read — feeling triumphant. MacDonald first noted that a woman named Mary, a thirty-five-year-old prostitute had disappeared. Her friends had asked him to look for the woman; most of the officers in the department then had given her disappearance little thought. She was, after all, a "tippler" and a prostitute. Disappearance unsolved. A year later, a day laborer known around only as Flannigan suddenly failed to show up for a job.

It was assumed that he had moved on.

Four years later, MacDonald noted that a "goodly number" of people had vanished from the streets. When a man of some influence arrived in Boston, looking for his brother, a doctor who had been set on moving to Boston, and demanded police attention, MacDonald brought his suspicions of a murderer to his superiors.

But there was no proof that the young doctor had ever arrived in Boston. And as for the day laborers and others who had disappeared, well, they had probably just moved away.

If they had met with foul play, where were the bodies?

MacDonald had written in his final journal — he was quite a note-taker and had lived to the ripe old age of ninety-one — that he had served the Boston Police Department proudly — his one regret had been he was certain he had failed to find justice for those who had not been "in the fine graces of normal society, other than the man of medicine, who was not proved to be in or of the area."

She quickly keyed back to the title page of the paper and found the name of the grad student who had written the content on the research site. Alex Maple. She didn't know if Alex was a he or a she, or how to contact Alex. She couldn't find a web page; she reverted to Facebook and found several Alex Maples. But once she was certain she found the right one — Harvard and the current Beacon Hill address seemed to point in that direction — she wrote Alex a message. If the photos were any clue, Alex Maple was a young man in his late twenties.

She was startled to realize it had grown late and she was really tired. Glancing at her phone, she saw Griffin hadn't called her or sent any messages.

She was tempted to pick up the phone and call him.

Wincing, she determined she would not allow herself to do so.

She still jumped, her heart racing again, when her phone rang. "Yes?" she answered quickly, without glancing at the caller ID.

"Sweetheart?"

"Mom!"

"You haven't called — I've gotten so worried."

Vickie smiled, shaking her head. "All is well. A cop is outside my door. I had lunch with Roxanne. I'm good. And, of course, I love you and Dad. I'm sorry — I should have checked in."

"The news is full of information about that woman being found. With corpses! Oh, God, the poor thing . . . I don't want you involved in this. Oh, Vickie! Italy. You need to come to Italy."

"That won't solve anything. I'm protected.

Cop at the door. Cops here, there and everywhere. I'm good, I promise."

"You really should be staying here."

Maybe she should be staying with them. Making them feel secure in her safety. She just couldn't do it. What if . . . ?

She was glad she was speaking with her mother over the phone. Because, of course, it was at that moment she realized and admitted to herself that she wasn't leaving her own place because of Griffin. What if . . .

What if he did want what she wanted? A chance to forget the rest, and explore one another? Just let go and give in and let the years wash away and have everything?

"Mom, all is well, I promise."

"I don't understand why you're all mixed up in this."

"I help with history, Mom, that's all."

"This is very scary."

"I know, and I promise I'll be a better kid, check in twice a day — okay?"

"Dad says he loves you. He says you're more stubborn than a mule, and he loves you anyway."

She laughed softly. "Tell Dad I love him, too."

She hung up. It wasn't the call from Griffin she'd been hoping for, but she was blessed with great parents. Maybe she'd read a bit more, head back into the late nineteenth century.

And maybe he would still call.

She turned back to the internet.

They were at the station, and it was the first time Griffin has seen Barbara Marshall since she'd come out of the hospital; she'd been so lost and confused then, unable to remember anything at all. She'd been sweet and grateful, but had remembered nothing but the massive explosion of pain in her head.

He had been able to speak with Jackson and Barnes briefly before meeting with Barbara and her friend, Annie. Barbara had gone to a therapist; she hadn't yet been to a hypnotherapist.

They decided to call in a specialist who had often worked with the BPD, assuming that Barbara didn't mind.

"Barbara, I'm guessing you've heard of hypnotherapy," Jackson said, when all their greetings were finished and it was ascertained she thought she was doing very well — "Miraculously, alive!" she'd told them.

"Hypnotherapy. I'm not sure I can be hypnotized," she said.

"But you could try," Annie said. She was a heavy-set woman with great big brown eyes, dimples, a soft voice, and an ever-encouraging smile.

"Sure," Barbara said. "I'd do anything. I know some women haven't been so lucky," she added, a catch in her voice.

"We've got some leads," Griffin said, hunkering down by her. "But the thing is, there may be another time when we're not fast enough. Anything you can do to help us will be immensely appreciated."

"What about the other women? You found a lady named Fiona West last night, right? Does she know anything?"

"Fiona West is still in the hospital, but she was able to answer a few questions. She was heading to her car; she'd parked off Washington. She reached her car, put her key in the lock . . . and that was it. Searing pain at the back of her head," Jackson said.

"Yes, well, whoever this is, they really hit hard." She fell silent, perhaps caught up in the memory of her trauma.

"I came over to stay with Barbara," Annie explained.

"I'm not married or engaged, and I'm afraid the last guy I really cared about is in the military, deployed," Barbara said. "He corresponds when he can, but . . . anyway, I'm basically alone. Except for very good friends."

229

"The thing is, in her sleep, she fights with someone. And she whimpers and moans and says 'no, no, no . . . oh, God, buried alive.' "

Griffin stared at the two of them with surprise.

"Then, somehow, somewhere, at some point, you more or less regained consciousness," he said.

"The mind is awesome and terrible, huh, Special Agent Pryce?" Barbara asked softly. "But we know I was found in a cemetery, so how does that help?"

"It can help. Do you remember — were you carried in a box? Over someone's shoulder — lugged between two people?" Detective Barnes asked.

Griffin glanced at Jackson. They both liked Barnes, but he rose to impatience quickly.

"Easy, Miss Marshall," Griffin said.

"Please. I'm alive because of you and Special Agent Crow — and the Boston PD, of course, Detective Barnes," Barbara said. "Just call me Barbara."

"Barbara. You're not ever going to recall a step-by-step situation — you were knocked unconscious. But it sounds as if you did come around a bit here and there. If we try hypnotherapy, you just might remember something that would tell us more about the way you were taken — and delivered to the cemetery."

She nodded. "Sure. Anything that might help."

"Excellent," Jackson said.

"I'll call Lenora in," Barnes told them.

He quickly understood why Lenora Connor was so appreciated by the BPD; she was in her late fifties or early sixties, a small woman in a casual suit with salt-and-pepper hair and a calm and friendly manner that quickly put everyone at ease. She expressed her concern for Barbara, thanked Annie for being such a great friend and even discussed the weather — beautifully balmy, as it was. Then she explained to Barbara, "This isn't about silly things like you barking like a dog or anything like that. It's just setting your mind at ease and rest, and your body at ease and rest. Our brains are the original computers, really. And you know how cluttered up computers can become, far too many windows open, too many pictures, space taken . . . we just try to clear up the clutter, okay?"

"Do I need to lie down?" Barbara asked.

"You need to be comfortable. Are you comfortable sitting?"

"Perfectly," Barbara said.

"Then we'll begin!"

The therapist talked, describing an idyllic scene so well Griffin was convinced he could almost hear the trickling water of a stream. Barbara closed her eyes.

So did Annie.

Slowly, Lenora brought Barbara Marshall back to the night she'd been kidnapped. Sitting in her chair, the young woman began to twitch in distress. He was about to leap forward and stop what was going on, but the therapist lifted a hand and talked her through it.

"I smell the earth. And I hear something . . . something being dragged. And someone swearing. I know that a box is being dragged and I can't move, can't fight, can't see . . . But I hear them. I smell the earth. And she's whispering, she's whispering . . ."

Griffin, Jackson and Barnes exchanged glances.

Lenora looked over at them.

"She?" Griffin mouthed silently.

"You hear a woman's voice?" Lenora asked.

"She's the one swearing," Lenora said.

"And then?" Lenora asked gently.

"Then . . . I smell the earth. And I can't breathe, and I know I'm going to die."

She began to whimper again and before

232

Griffin could move, Jackson gave Lenora the sign to bring Barbara around.

And Lenora did so gently.

Barbara opened her eyes and stared at them all. "I remember!" she said. "Yes, I remember. There were two of them, and yes, damn it all! One of them was a woman!"

"Did you — see her?" Barnes asked hopefully.

Barbara Marshall shook her head. "No, I'm sorry."

"But you're certain?" Griffin asked quietly.

Barbara Marshall looked up at him and nodded. "They were kind of whispering. I heard things chirping . . . like crickets, whatever. They knew where they were going, but they were watching out for other people. I think it was really late. I kept smelling the earth, but that makes so much sense — I mean, they were taking me to a cemetery. I was over a guy's shoulder. Big enough, strong enough. I know the other was a woman because of the sound of the whisper. I'd swear in court that it was a female who was whispering that way. I mean, sometimes, you can't tell. I hear songs that might be sung by a man or a woman, but . . . that whisper. I know that it was a woman."

Griffin looked up at Jackson.

He knew they were silently agreeing it was time for more of what they knew to be out there in the public, time for a press conference. They were so often in sync. He didn't always partner with Jackson; Jackson was often in the home office, juggling a couple dozen agents and cases across the country.

But it was damned good synergy when they could work together.

"Press conference," he said to Barnes.

"Now? Tonight? It's getting late."

"They'll air it all again in the morning. We might as well get started on this tonight," Jackson said. "If you don't mind, we'll have Griffin run with it from our perspective and you take over with the police."

"All right, then," Barnes said.

"Um, um, wait! We'll still have a cop watching over us, right?" Annie asked, jumping up from her chair.

Barnes nodded. "You bet. I'll get an officer to see you home now."

"And you won't . . . you won't use my name, right?" Barbara asked.

She and Annie were assured Barbara's name would not be mentioned.

Barbara Marshall and Annie were both effusive, hugging them before they left. They didn't seem at all intimidated by their FBI titles, nor did they notice Barnes seemed more shell-shocked by a hug than by a dozen decaying corpses.

Thirty minutes later, despite the late hour, they were downstairs on the steps of the station, surrounded by dozens of members of the press, including reporters with cameras and notebooks. People were raising their hands and asking questions before Griffin walked to the makeshift podium to speak. He didn't clear his throat or wave a hand in the air; he waited until the din died down and then he spoke.

"Ladies and gentlemen, we're all aware that two women have tragically died, the victims of a criminal dubbed the *Undertaker*. All law enforcements agents in the area and all agencies of law enforcement are on this case. Tonight, however, we do have information for the public. We have had several victims survive the kidnapping and murder attempts on them, and from these survivors we know two things and believe it's incredibly important for everyone out there to be aware of what we've learned. There is not just *one* Undertaker. Two people are perpetrating these vicious crimes. Secondly, we believe that one is a man — and that his accomplice is a woman."

Immediately, there was another uproar.
A woman! No one had expected such a turn

of events.

"What is the possible motive for the murders? There's still no sexual assault?" one reporter shouted.

"No, sir."

"But the victims are all women!"

"Yes, thus far, and that we know about," Griffin said. "However, everyone needs to stay vigilant. The attacks have been blitz attacks — the victims have been knocked unconscious with a severe blow to the back of the head. This is something that could happen to anyone, man or woman."

"How do you know that a woman is involved? Do you have a description? Was she seen?"

"Heard," Griffin said.

"Must be a manly woman!" someone shouted, and there was a titter of uncomfortable laughter that followed.

"Our concern tonight has been in warning the public. Please, be careful that your doors are locked at all times. Don't park in alleys; try to travel in groups of at least two. Detective David Barnes will be speaking to you about police presence and tip lines, and more on personal safety. Thank you."

Griffin turned the microphone over to Barnes and stepped aside.

He slipped away from the area with Jackson Crow.

When they turned back, Barnes was still being besieged with questions; he was fielding them well.

"Let's get some sleep — it could grow more intense," Jackson said.

"Sure."

Their hotel wasn't far from Vickie's apartment. He found himself pausing before the hotel's entry, staring out at the night.

He was tempted to head to her place.

It was late. She'd probably be in bed.

Right where he'd like to find her, he thought ruefully.

Yep, true. But . . .

There was so much at stake.

He turned and followed Jackson into the hotel. He thought Crow would go straight to the elevators; he did not.

The man wasn't much of a drinker, but he turned into the bar. He ordered two shots of Scotch and thrust one toward Griffin.

"Here's my question. And my thoughts," Jackson said. "We know — or we're pretty damned sure — that this couple knows the area really well, or at least one of them does. We're looking for a man and a woman. But how the hell did they find the bodies in the wall? They'd been in there for a hundred years. No one would have been guilty of a crime in finding them — the killer or killers would be long dead."

Griffin didn't have a chance to answer him. He looked up to see David Barnes striding toward them.

"Thought I might find you here," he said.

Jackson nodded to the bartender who returned with a shot for Barnes. Barnes swallowed it in a gulp. "That was sure hell," he said, referring to the press conference. "You guys have it down pat — speak first, and then give it to the cops!"

Jackson laughed softly. "The cops know the local score best."

"Griffin's from here. He knows the score."

"I've been gone awhile. But we were just talking about the old bodies in the wall. And I was thinking one of these killers might have grown up right around there, as in, maybe, right on Washington Street."

"I know someone who grew up right there," Barnes said.

"Oh?"

"Yeah, me," Barnes said quietly.

CHAPTER EIGHT

Closing a book, Vickie contemplated the bodies in the wall at the Pine house once again. Oliver Pine had seemed like a really nice man. Then again, if someone in his family or someone associated with his family had been killing people in or around the house in the late 1800s, it really wouldn't have any bearing on him. Except of course, it was embarrassing to have creepy ancestors. Still, probably every living person could trace themselves back to someone who had done something evil.

She'd been so tired earlier; she was surprised to realize that she'd gotten going again and read for hours. It seemed there were threads that could go together but she didn't quite have a grasp on them yet. Leaning back and idly fingering one of her books, she wondered what it was.

She thought about Bertram Aldridge. Police had thought he'd be found in the

239

Boston area because he had family there. But his mother had lived in the south side — Boston Neck — according to all the reports she found. Near the Pine house.

She felt re-energized suddenly, keying in the words Aldridge and Pine, South Boston, Boston Neck and different years, starting with 1870.

Bertram Aldridge could trace his family history back to the start of the nineteenth century. There had been Aldridges living there since the early 1800s. The family had a place near the Pine house that had stood until 1955, when it burned down.

She wasn't sure exactly what she was looking for — the fact Aldridge might have had a killer ancestor shouldn't have made him a killer — she knew of all kinds of instances in history when a killer's family had been completely normal and indeed, done many good works.

Maybe she shouldn't discount family legend — what a killer might know or suspect because he'd heard it in a number of stories passed down through the family, generation after generation?

Pondering the question, she noted a site that led to known families in the Boston Neck and South Boston at the end of the 1800s. Absently, she keyed it in, and then she paused on the first page, surprised.

The name *Ballantine* was there as well.

Curious, she highlighted *Ballantine.*

Very strange and ironic — a *George* and Mary Ballantine had lived just down the street from the Pine house from 1870 to 1900, when the house had legally been purchased by their grandson, Andrew Ballantine.

Andrew had owned the house there until 1932, when he died. His son, Mason, had sold the house to a banking conglomeration. The house had been demolished; a ten-story building had risen, offering office space in the floors above the first and retail opportunities on the ground level.

"I'm going to have to tell Dylan," she muttered aloud to herself. "He's so proud of being a New Yorker. Of course, there might have been another George Ballantine, but . . ."

She started digging around in one of the ancestry sites she liked.

According to the site, a Mason Ballantine, *born in Boston, Mass,* had taken up residence in New York City in 1933. His son, another George, had been born in 1940, and his son, yet another George, had been born about twenty-five years later, and *moved to Boston* after his son, Dylan was deceased, then his second son, Noah, had been born.

She sat back, surprised.

Of course, George Ballantine and his father had been born and raised in New York. Maybe George Ballantine had never even realized his family stretched back to Massachusetts. If you grew up in a place and your parents grew up in that place, it was the home you know.

Still, how ironic.

Bertram Aldridge and George Ballantine were both descendants of families that had lived on Washington Street, the south side of Boston, or the old Boston Neck.

Near the Pine house, where people had been murdered and hidden in the walls in the late 1800s.

Did it mean anything?

Could it possibly mean anything at all — after all this time?

Motives for murder included jealousy, hatred, revenge, greed . . .

But . . . what vengeance could someone still feel so many, many years later?

She rose, tired and restless.

Her apartment seemed really quiet — Dylan hadn't come around that afternoon, evening or night. She assumed he'd been watching over his family.

She really did need to fix what was broken with the Ballantines — she wanted to stay friends with Noah — and, really, his parents, too. She couldn't fault them too much for trying to lash out in any direction; they'd felt the brunt of trauma one time too many.

She was naturally curious, too. She wanted to know if George Ballantine knew he'd had family that had hailed from Mass!

For the time, though, she really needed to go to bed.

It was really late — and no one was going to call her.

Griffin was not going to call her.

Music would help her sleep, but her mind was racing too quickly. Once in bed, she played with the channel changer — avoiding the news. She found the old animated version of *Pete's Dragon* with Red Buttons, Mickey Rooney, Shelley Winters, Helen Reddy, and noted quickly that it was still charming. Her mind still spun between images of the dead — and far too vivid images of Griffin Pryce. But between that — and staring at the screen — she finally fell asleep.

She was pretty sure she was sleeping deeply when dreams came again — a very real dream this time.

She was there, in her bed, barely awake, and there was someone standing next to the bed. The apparition wasn't a frightening one; it was almost like an angel hovered at her bedside. A female angel in flowing white with a lovely head covered in golden blond tresses. Gentle fingers touched her, but the angel was worried. "Please, please, I need you, I need someone . . . I'm in the water. I'm in the water, and no one cares, no one knows . . . please, I need you."

The angel disappeared and she slept again. When she woke in the morning, she remembered the dream — and determined that an angel seeking her help was much better than a horde of decayed corpses coming at her.

Getting out of bed, she was stunned to realize that the bedding by her side was wet. Puzzled, she looked around for a water bottle, but she didn't remember bringing one in with her. Then she wondered if something had gone wrong with the upstairs plumbing, but there were no signs on the ceiling that anything had dripped through from the floor above.

"I don't need a cat, I need a dog. A big one. One who loves me absolutely but has big gnarly teeth and will chew up anyone who darkens my door," she murmured aloud. Then she added, "And a dog I can talk to — so I don't just speak aloud to

244

myself!"

In the kitchen, she made coffee. There was a knock on her door as it brewed. She smoothed down her hair, her heart quickening — it might be Griffin. She wished she slept in something more exotic than an oversize *Star Wars* T.

She started for the door, then realized that the sound was softer than a usual knock. She smiled, mocking herself.

It wasn't Griffin.

It was Dylan. But it would be good to see him, too.

"Come on in," she called softly. The cops watched her place — they didn't sleep in the hallways or anything, but she had to be careful — she didn't want anyone else thinking she was giving them an invitation. Of course, the door was locked. Only Dylan could enter through a locked door.

He came through, appearing before her solidly at the end of the counter. He had a worried look about him.

"You okay?" he asked her anxiously.

"Sure, I'm fine," she told him. "Why?"

"I meant to come yesterday, in the afternoon. Or at least by last evening. I wound up hanging around with my parents — they're so upset. Naturally, they heard about Fiona West — and all the old corpses that were found. My dad paces and talks to people on the phone and seems upset. My mom has done a lot of crying. Noah, of course, is concerned about them both. He is such a cool kid. But I'm sorry — I should have worried about you, too. You're really okay?"

"I am fine."

"After that many corpses?"

"Okay, so to be honest? The first night I had a horrible nightmare about them coming to life and coming after me. Last night, I had a dream about an angel."

"An angel?" Dylan asked, smiling.

"Yes, she was lost, or people didn't care, or they didn't know where she was . . . or something like that. I think I might have been a little surprised an angel would ask for my help. And I apparently fell asleep with water somehow, though I can't find a bottle of water anywhere, or a glass. But hey, an angel! Kind of beautiful — rather than zombie-terrible!"

Dylan didn't reply. He was wearing an even more seriously worried expression.

"Oh, my God. You saw her!" he said.

"What? I had a dream."

He shook his head. "No, no, you saw Darlene. I didn't think anyone would see her — I mean, not yet. I barely met her. I was going to tell you about her. I just thought I should ease into it."

"Ease into . . . ?"

"Telling you about the situation. About Darlene."

"Dylan, I don't know what you're talking about. Who is Darlene?"

"She's . . . not very good at manifesting. I barely saw her myself. I mean, it can take time. You realize you're still something, but you're not physical. I guess some people have the strength of will or soul or whatever to appear immediately, you know, right away. Maybe not. Some become really good at appearing and speaking — to those who can see and hear. I know with me, it took a while. I was there . . . but no one could see me. Until Noah. But then I could play with Noah. I could make him laugh, and that was so wonderful. But appearing . . . and speaking! It can be very difficult."

"Dylan, I still have no idea of what you're talking about. Who is Darlene?"

"Well, she's a dead girl, of course." He shook his head, as if exasperated that she wasn't understanding what he was saying. "Sorry, sorry, let me try again. Darlene is dead. And she managed to come to me. To appear to me . . . in our world, whatever or wherever that is. I mean, we're here, more or less, right? Anyway! She was the first victim in this spree — I think. They don't know about her yet. I was trying to reach her . . . she just disappeared. Even to me. They hit her on the head and put her in a box and threw her into the water. They didn't realize that the box would sink so quickly — that's what I think, anyway. But she came to you! You're going to have to tell them, Vickie. They have to know. They have to find her, get her out of the water . . . she's miserable, but she can't leave, Vickie."

"Wait? Another victim, but there was no clue about her! That's the whole deal — these guys like to send their clever little clues to the newspeople and get the newspeople to get them to the police. It's part of the whole thing."

"I know this, Vickie. I know she's dead — and I know they killed her. She came to me, and she managed to tell me."

And she knew it was true.

She hadn't been dreaming the night before. And it hadn't been an angel who had appeared at her bedside.

It had been a ghost, somehow trailing with her the waters of her demise.

Barnes called a task force meeting in the morning to reinforce everything that had been said at the press conference and to answer the questions being asked by the many detectives, officers and agents working the case.

"You really think that this is a man and a woman — a couple! — killing people?" one of the officers asked.

Barnes looked at Griffin, and Griffin shrugged and stepped forward. "There are many famous cases. In the early 1980s, you had Suzan and James Carson — they went the crazy cult way and began to kill people they thought were witches. They were caught after three kills, but they had a list. President Jimmy Carter was on that list. Fred and Rosemary West of Britain killed at least twelve women, including two of their own children. Recently, Karla Homolka and Paul Bernardo. The footage the couple took of themselves wasn't clear at first, but when it was, Karla Homolka proved to be the driving impetus in some of the sexual attacks and killing. No question about it. Yes, couples kill. One is probably the alpha — and not necessarily the male. Or maybe they both believe they're the driving force. What they're doing, however, isn't random — they stalk their victims. They plan the kidnapping — and the method with which they'll attempt to kill."

Another officer raised his hand. "But . . . weren't they rapists as well? I mean, a lot of the *couple* killers. The murders they committed, they were sexual killings, right? There's been no sign of sexual attacks on the women."

"True. But there were also spree killers Starkweather and Fugate back in the 1950s. If I remember right, Starkweather got into a fight with Fugate's father and killed him and then her mother and a baby sibling. When she came home, she watched television while Fugate cleaned up and they headed on out to kill whoever else was in their way."

"But these are so . . . planned!" someone else said. "They're sending notes, playing with law enforcement. They . . . they're kind of smart, at the very least."

"Or controlled," someone else said thoughtfully.

"And they may well start to unravel and make mistakes," Jackson said, "and that's what we're watching for. How smart are they? We don't know. They're careful not to leave forensic evidence, but what they know they may have learned online or from television. We don't believe that they are pros — law enforcement of any kind themselves. They're preying on this area. It's their comfort zone."

"And they still somehow relate to Aldridge," a young female officer said. "Fans?"

"Possibly. We just don't know yet. Again, anything you come up with, make sure you get to Detective Barnes or one of us," Griffin said.

"Two — man and a woman!" another exclaimed again. "Two, sure. A couple team? Scary as hell. That means they could walk by someone like a pair of lovers — turn around and bludgeon just about anyone."

"Yes, two to playact, plan — and help dispose of bodies. Ladies and gentlemen, we have a survivor who was certain she heard a woman's voice when she was being carried away to be boxed and buried," Barnes said. "So, everyone — extreme vigilance is necessary!"

Speculation continued. At length, Barnes raised his hand. "This is what we know. This is what to watch out for. The papers today bear our suspicions and warnings to the populace. The press conference will be carried on stations throughout the day and for the next few days — when, hopefully, we'll have caught these killers and brought them to justice. We're done here, folks. Get out on the streets — and report anything you find that may give us even the slightest clue.

Forensic crews are still working hard — our techs are scouring the internet. We will catch a break. Thank you."

The meeting broke. Griffin pulled out his phone; he'd waited, but now, he found he had to make sure Vickie was all right. Before he could call her, however, one of the officers who had been running the tip lines and working with the media came up to the front of the room where he was still standing with David Barnes and Jackson Crow.

"Sir — sirs! We've got something, I think. I'm afraid," she said.

"What is it?" Griffin asked.

"Yes, Officer Gordon, please?" Barnes said.

"Silas Warren — with the paper — discovered what he believes is a correspondence from the killers."

"A new one?" Barnes asked.

"No — one that was missed. He was going back through a pile of what they believed to be junk mail — snail mail, you know — and discovered it. Whoever first received it apparently discarded it, thinking it was some kind of a silly hoax. After the press conference last night, Silas wanted to do a recap and bring everyone up-to-date. He wanted to do a cohesive 'thus far' story."

"And he believes it is real?" Jackson asked.

"Oh, yes, he says he's certain."

"How?" Barnes snapped.

"About an hour after he brought it to his boss's attention, another letter came in that seems to fit it. They're sure the second was from the killers."

"What do the notes say?" Griffin asked.

"The one they just received started with that famous quote from George Santayana." She read from her notepad, " '*Those who cannot remember the past are condemned to repeat it.* You are fools. You missed the first — sad that there are those who never learn.' "

"All right, so what was the first clue — the one they thought to be a hoax?" Barnes asked.

The officer checked her notes. " 'So I shall begin where building began. Where all were young once, born and bred. What was once young is oldest now, to find her, see, the boldest be.' " She looked up. "I can see why whoever opened the letter first just threw it out — I mean, the first one. It wouldn't have meant anything because there hadn't been any missing women then . . . or other notes with clues on finding them."

"When was the first received?" Jackson asked.

"The reporter — Silas Warren — says the

post office date puts it at about two weeks ago."

"The first . . . two weeks ago," Barnes said wearily. "There's no hope of saving this victim. And still . . . we have to find her."

"The killers know that," Griffin said. "They want to watch us scramble, knowing that we're going to find a corpse. May I hear the so-called clues again?"

"I'll email the notes so you have them."

"Thank you," Griffin said. She flushed and hurried back to her desk.

Griffin, Barnes and Jackson pulled out their phones.

"Oldest . . . hell. There are dozens of things that are oldest!" Barnes muttered. "This is Boston, Cradle of Liberty, old Puritan stronghold. Oldest church, oldest graveyard, oldest . . . What?"

Officer Gordon came hurrying back over to them. "They just found another in today's mail," she said. "Coming to your phones, too."

Griffin glanced down at his phone as it beeped with the latest arrival.

The killers had written, "Are we having fun yet? Sorry, my friends, but this time, you will find the dead. Haha. Fresh dead. Ah, what's with the world today? No one listens anymore. Undertaker does try to give

you a chance. Alas! Get off your asses —
and the TV screens — and find the dead."

As he stared at it, Griffin's phone rang.

Vickie.

"Yeah, you all right?" he asked her.

"I'm fine, but . . ."

She was anxious. She wanted to speak, he
could tell, and yet she hesitated. He glanced
around. Officer Gordon was waiting to be
dismissed. Barnes and Jackson were studying the words that had been written.

He stepped back, away from the noise of
the other conversations. "What is it?" he
asked her.

"You're going to find another woman.
Only . . . Griffin, this one is already dead."

CHAPTER NINE

Vickie showered and dressed quickly. She was waiting impatiently when Griffin arrived, and he got there fast enough.

Dylan was there, pacing. "I know her name," he told Griffin. "I know her name, her first name, at least, and it's Darlene. She managed to tell that much."

"She died in the water, Griffin," Vickie added. "They boxed her up somehow, and threw her in the water. I would imagine they knocked her out first, too, and then threw her in the water. She would have drowned, I think."

"Wait, wait, hold up, just a minute," he said. He wasn't in the least doubtful; he was as usual, sturdy, strong, calm — and ready to listen to what they had to say.

"I thought I was dreaming last night — about angels instead of corpses," Vickie explained.

"But I saw her, too, briefly. She's not a

very good ghost. I don't mean she's a bad ghost," Dylan explained. "She's just not experienced. She can't really make herself be seen or heard well yet, even to me. But she must have seen something of what else has happened; she must have known about Vickie somehow and tried to reach her."

"So she came here, Griffin," Vickie said softly. "When she could manage to reach out, she did. She needs to be found. I think she might have been a teenager — not very old. Late teens or early twenties. Beautiful blonde girl, wearing white. White pants and a white shirt with flowing sleeves. Large brown eyes. And . . ." She paused, watching his expression. "You're not surprised. You don't think I'm crazy and you're not in the least skeptical."

He halfway smiled at her. "Dylan is standing right here," he said softly.

"Right," Dylan said.

"But . . . you're not surprised about another victim."

"No, I'm not. The newspaper found one of the clues they had apparently just tossed as some kind of silly letter," he said. "And the killers wrote in again, making sure we knew we had missed one — and would definitely find her dead."

"Oh!" Vickie said. She sank down on the

sofa, absently picking up a throw pillow and holding it to her as she stared at him. "Um — what were the clues?"

"All right," Griffin told her, perching at the end of the sofa and reading from his phone. "The first clue — the one that was missed — is this, 'So I shall begin where building began. Where all were young once, born and bred. What was once young is oldest now, to find her, see, the boldest be.' "

"Oldest," Vickie repeated thoughtfully.

"And what came next?"

"Two letters, both arrived this morning. The first, '*Those who cannot remember the past are condemned to repeat it.* You are fools. You missed the first — sad that there are those who never learn.' "

"Why now?" Vickie asked. "I mean, this poor woman was the first. Then, two women died, but you were able to save Angelina Gianni, then Barbara Marshall, Chrissy Ballantine — and now Fiona West. The killers could have taunted you with that clue before."

"I wonder if they thought Fiona West wouldn't have been found," Griffin said. "The second letter received today — soon after the first one — read like this, 'Are we having fun yet? Sorry, my friends, but this time, you will find the dead. Ha ha. Fresh dead. Ah, what's with the world today? No one listens anymore. Undertaker does try to give you a chance. Alas! Get off your asses — and the TV screens — and find the dead!' "

"What does the last reference?" Vickie asked.

"A press conference we gave last night. You didn't see it?"

"I was actually trying not to watch the news," Vickie said. "What did you say?"

"We warned people that the so-called *Undertaker* was actually two people, a couple, a man and a woman," Griffin told her.

Vickie stared at him, startled. "A woman?"

"Hey, not to be insulting, but yes, women do kill."

"Well, of course they do, but . . . I just didn't think a woman would kill this way, I guess," she said. She shook her head. "A couple, killing like this. It makes finding the truth so much harder. I mean, say you get an idea about someone, and that someone could have a perfectly good alibi because the other was the one who was busy kidnapping and killing or attempting murder at the time. And people don't tend to be suspicious of couples."

"Do you think your ghost knows anything — saw anything?" Griffin asked.

259

"She'll come back," Dylan said. "I know she'll come back. Hey, Griff, you need some coffee? There's coffee on. I'd get it for you, but . . ." He lifted his hands. "I'm not that good. You need coffee. Because the two of you have to find Darlene. She's miserable. She's lost, afraid and miserable."

"Of course, we're going to find her," Vickie murmured.

"Of course," Griffin agreed, heading to the kitchen. "We're going to drink coffee, and figure out the clues." He looked at Vickie and smiled. She nodded slowly in return.

"Yes, what was young is old. And we know that it has to do with water — though the clue has nothing to do with water, Griffin. First built and oldest now . . . well, the Fairbanks house is the oldest wood frame house and the oldest house in Massachusetts — that's in Dedham. Would they have travelled that far?"

"Yes — Angelina Gianni was found in Lexington. Same distance just about, different direction," Griffin said.

"There's a pond not far from the house — you can reach it through a parking lot for a mall and through the park. It's kind of a little treasure there, very pretty. But Griffin, what if they meant Boston, and not all of Massachusetts?" Vickie asked.

"They might mean Boston — and they might mean somewhere else. What do your instincts tell you?"

Vickie was thoughtful. "Well, you already found one victim in Lexington. And the two women who died were found outside of Boston as well, right?"

Griffin nodded, his expression tight. "Beverly Tatum was found in a Dumpster in Revere. Jennifer Hudgins was found in an abandoned school locker in Brookline, so, one might say bedroom communities. But at the least, not old Boston."

Dylan spoke up. "Come on, Vickie. Trust your instincts. What do you think?"

"The oldest house. Young once, oldest now. It's the oldest of its kind in the country, I believe. And I know that there's a pond that isn't far from the house."

"How did they . . . put her in the water, do you know?" Griffin asked.

Vickie shook her head and looked at Dylan. Dylan responded by shaking his head. "I told you," Dylan said. "She's not very experienced. And, poor thing, she's so lost and afraid and miserable. You have to find her. But of course . . ."

"Of course . . . what?" Griffin asked.

"It's not as if an hour here or there will

matter any in her case. I mean, we're not fighting a clock in the same way," Dylan said, answering for Vickie. He hesitated. "There's no question. She is already dead."

"Excuse me," Griffin told them, rising.

Dylan looked at Vickie as Griffin walked toward the door, pacing as he pulled out his phone and made a call.

"What's he doing?" Dylan whispered to Vickie.

"I don't know," she whispered back.

They heard him speaking briefly with someone on the phone. A lot of his answers were "Fine" or "Good" or "Okay" and then "That will be great."

A minute later, he hung up.

"How do you feel about an excursion to Dedham?" Griffin asked. "That was Jackson. Barnes has got cops watching our previous surviving victims. The FBI and the local police have people researching the bodies found in the Pine house. I'm hoping our press conference is enough to keep the killers at bay for a night at least, and . . . finding this young woman isn't like seeking those who might still be alive, and yet . . . well, it's incredibly important."

"Dedham?" Vickie said. "To look for her? Yes, of course, to look for her. But —"

"We'll have dive teams meet us there," he

told her. "Jackson is on the way here. Traffic is bad — it'll take about forty-five minutes, with luck, to get there. That will still give us several hours today."

"Well, yes, of course." She glanced over at Dylan. She had forgotten about telling him that his great-grandfather had lived in Boston — and his family before that. He was down on the intolerance of the Puritans. He wasn't going to be pleased to learn the truth.

But she did have to tell Griffin what she had learned. A long car drive would give her the chance to tell both Griffin and Jackson Crow.

"Of course. And I have more to tell you. As we drive, I guess?"

"About this young woman, Darlene?"

"No, I've told you everything I know about her. I was doing a lot of research last night."

"Let's head on out. Jackson can scoop us up on the street. We'll talk on the way."

"You didn't tell me anything yet," Dylan said.

"I'm guessing you're coming with us?" Vickie asked him.

To her surprise, he hesitated. Then he shook his head. "I'm going to my family's house. My dad has been absent lately — I

263

guess he's really been thrown by everything. So, he's distant with my mom. He's gone a lot — a lot. I think my mom thinks he might be having an affair. Actually, I need to follow my dad one day. But for now . . . I'm going to hang with Noah. Try to do what I can to make things good. We'll talk later, right, Vickie? Or is it something important?"

"No, no, we can talk later," she assured him.

"Good. Griffin . . . find her, please," he said, looking at the agent. "I don't know why it matters so much. I mean dead is — dead. But it does matter. We do have souls and her soul isn't at peace . . . please, make them keep looking until they do find her."

"I promise," Griffin told him.

Dylan let himself out — moving through the wall. When he arrived, he was polite and knocked. When he left — he just left.

Vickie grabbed her bag and threw it over her shoulders; she was already dressed appropriately for a crawl through a forest path to the pond, in jeans and long-sleeved V-neck T-shirt.

"Ready when you are," she told Griffin.

He stepped out ahead of her and waited for her to come out and lock the door, and then they crossed the hall and went out the main door. He left her on the sidewalk, walking down the street to speak with the patrolman assigned to watch her. The man nodded, waved to her and pulled back out into the traffic. He was barely gone before Jackson arrived in a black SUV.

Jackson Crow stepped out of the driver's seat. "I'll let you take it. You're more familiar with the roads around here."

"Sounds good," Griffin said. Jackson was already around the car; he opened the front passenger-side door for Vickie and shook his head when she said she didn't mind being in back.

"You two are the Bostonians," he said. "I have some notes to look over."

A minute later, they were headed out.

"So, Vickie, what else did you discover?" Griffin asked.

"I don't know if I discovered anything. But I did find out that Bertram Aldridge's family lived in the Boston Neck area for years and years. They were right down the street from the Pine house at the time those murders were committed."

"Family legend, talk around Halloween — maybe even breaking in and finding a peephole in the wall. So, Bertram Aldridge could have known about the false wall and told his fans about it," Griffin said.

"They were definitely there, yes," Jackson said.

Vickie turned around to look at him and he smiled. "My wife is in charge of our unit's offices back in Northern Virginia," he told her. "And she — and some of our tech people — just wrote me with the same information." He grimaced. "Angela is convinced, too, that Bertram Aldridge is somehow pulling the strings for what's going on here, even if he is locked up. Maybe he's enjoying the whole thing vicariously. Maybe there's no *maybe* to it. I've studied his past. Aldridge is a sick bastard. Angela also found evidence that Aldridge's family had been in that area a very long time."

"There's another current player who had family there, too," Vickie murmured.

"Detective Barnes?" Griffin asked. "We were talking this morning. He grew up in the area. He said when they were kids, there was an old house in the neighborhood owned by a cranky old woman and the rumor went around her son had died in the military — and she kept his body in a coffin in the parlor. He said they were terrible as kids — they used to egg the old woman's house. Well, in a way, she did keep her son. Not as a body in a coffin, but as ashes in an urn. There are all kinds of stories all the time about bones coming out of the ground when they're working on the sewers or electric lines, that kind of thing. Hey, you and I both grew up nearby — you know how stories spread."

"And some of them true, probably," Vickie said. "Gravestones are moved over time. Roads are paved over ground where the dead were buried. That's life with bigger and bigger populations. I don't think there were that many murderers who walled up their victims. Well, I guess Poe was fond of walling people up in his stories, and certainly a sick mind could take hold of that. But anyway, I was referring to George Ballantine. His antecedent — another George! — left the Boston area to head to New York in the nineteenth century. I'm kind of loath to tell Dylan what I found out. He's so glad to have been a New Yorker — without the Puritan influence in his blood."

"Depression can run in families, that's true. But so far, nothing in my experience — or in that of the profilers I know — indicates being a whacked-out murderer runs in any family lines," Griffin said.

"But," Jackson said, "some people can be susceptible to suggestion."

"And there's nothing to suggest that a family can't create a few brutal murderers a few generations apart," Griffin said.

"Here's what I'm thinking," Vickie said. "Bertram Aldridge did hear stories about the bodies walled up in the Pine house. Maybe he even peeked into a hole in the thin veneer of paneling we ripped out. At any rate, he knew about the bodies. He did communicate with our current murderers — at least one of them. It's not as if all the victims had to be left in a wall with corpses or in the ground — they just had to be left where they might or might not have been found in time. Maybe he even knew about the bodies because one of his ancestors committed the murders. And while the urge to kill may not have been inherited, having the mental disease that could cause a man to be so heinous, the stories might have been something he decided to cling to as he grew up."

"Some kids want to grow up to be cops or soldiers or whatever honorable types like their moms or dads — and Aldridge wanted to grow up to be a killer, like his great-great-granddad, or whatever?" Griffin asked.

"Maybe," Vickie said. "And maybe he knew George Ballantine's family had once been there, too, and that was why he went to the Ballantine house when he'd escaped — and why he wanted Chrissy Ballantine targeted. Or . . ."

"You know there is the possibility someone wasn't so noble in the Ballantine family," Jackson said.

"And some kind of twisted revenge might have been the motive where the Ballantine family was involved," Griffin said.

"We see Aldridge tomorrow. We can bring up all these suggestions — see what kind of a reaction we get."

"There was more — I found a researcher who had dug up a cop's notes from back then. I'll see that you all get everything I found," Vickie said. "He talks about the victims. A little late, but the article might help when it comes to seeing the victims from the wall get . . . well, they will get burials, won't they?"

"The city will be in charge of the bodies, but yes, they'll get burials," Jackson said with assurance. "I'm sure a good philanthropist out there will also see to it that they receive rites and a plaque and memorial as well."

Griffin glanced at her and smiled. "If no one else, I'm sure Adam Harrison will see to it."

She smiled and nodded. "I hope I get to meet this man," she said.

"I'm sure you will. I'm going to put

through a call to Angela, have you speak with her. Maybe you can tell her more about what you found and she can add that into what they're finding," Jackson told her.

"Um, sure."

He put through the call. Vickie was phone-introduced to Angela, Jackson's wife, Special Agent Hain in charge of cases. Angela was both gracious and down-to-earth, and Vickie discovered that the woman seemed to love research and history as much as she did.

By the time she finished with the call, they were coming into Dedham.

"How are the divers meeting us?" Vickie asked.

Griffin laughed. "They're actually getting to the pond the same way we are. Trekking it!"

Vickie found she was actually glad Griffin was a little lost when it came to exactly where he should park near the woods, and where the trail that led to the pond was — in many areas, the trees and the brush were just too thick to get through. She felt . . . useful, being able to direct him. And appreciated.

There were two other SUVs parked where they headed. The divers had apparently beat them to the site, Griffin said. Law enforcement logos showed that they belonged to the state police.

It was odd as they started down the trail; all kinds of day-to-day and very ordinary businesses surrounded the area — restaurants and chain stores. Of course, Dedham was still an old New England town, filled with lovely colonial and Victorian homes. And once they were into the trees, it was easy to imagine the raw wilderness that had been discovered by the first settlers. Massachusetts might face some brutal winters with heavy snow and ice, but the summers could be beautiful and rich and lush with foliage.

The pond, however, was loved by many for its still somewhat pristine beauty. They were readily able to traverse the one trail, and when they reached the water, the divers were already suited up.

There were four of them, and they were courteous and serious and also ready to crack a few jokes.

It was summer, but it was Massachusetts, and the pond was cold.

"Toughen up, McClaren!" the female member of the group teased the young man mentioning that the water was "Wicked cold."

"Hey, just because you've got ice in your

veins, Strickland!" he taunted in return.

A man named Beck, the head of their unit, just shook his head and talked to Jackson, Griffin and Vickie, asking them just what were they looking for.

"Our victim — first name we believe to be Darlene — was most probably boxed up in some way. She was the first, as far as our intelligence goes," Griffin told him, "and she might have been tossed in something like an old waterproofed cardboard box or something like that. Maybe even a box in plastic."

"Should have floated to the surface by now," a man named Harding said. "You sure she's in there?"

"Not absolutely," Jackson admitted.

Officer Strickland laughed. "Leave it to the Feds to send us on a fishing expedition," she said, but she was smiling and she added, "I hope to hell that we can find the victim. I really want to be able to help in any way possible with this Undertaker business."

"Thanks. I hope so, too," Griffin said.

Beck gave instructions to his people. They planned out their search grid. The divers went into the water.

Griffin, Jackson and Vickie waited on the shoreline.

The sun went behind a cloud.

Vultures flew overhead.

Things do die in the woods, Vickie told herself.

The divers had gone down in pairs. Strickland and McClaren came up first, dripping and shaking their heads.

"It's okay. We're going in again," Strickland said. "This is no small pond."

The second set of divers came up; they all regrouped and went in again.

Vickie stared out at the water. In various areas algae was thick. Lilies grew; branches stuck up out of the higher ridges in the middle of the pond.

She looked up at the sky again. It seemed as if there were more buzzards than there should have been. As if they knew . . .

As if they were waiting to feast on the dead.

The divers came up again, went down again and came up again.

Beck spoke with Jackson and Griffin. "I don't think this is going to do it. They may have to drag the pond, or bring in a bigger group. I mean, if we knew something — sorry, someone — was down there, they'd drain it even, but for that kind of work and crew and expense . . . I think someone is going to need more certainty that there's something here."

Vickie was feeling beaten — and cold. The summer sun was going down, and a chill seemed to be setting into her. She stared out at the water, listening.

And then she was certain she felt someone touch her shoulder.

She turned.

It was her dream "angel." Dylan's Darlene. She'd been wearing white jeans and a white, flowing-sleeve blouse when she'd died. Her hair was a golden blond and her dark brown eyes were filled with sorrow. "Please . . . I'm there . . ." she said.

She faded. But as she did, she pointed out into the middle of pond.

Vickie had noted a branch there earlier that seemed to stick out from the mucky earth at the bottom.

She left the divers and Jackson and Griffin talking and headed to the water's edge.

And then she walked in.

"Vickie! What the hell are you doing?" she heard Griffin shout.

She quickly reached the point where it was deep enough to dive into the water. It was icy. She hoped that her heart wouldn't stop beating out of sheer shock. But she reminded herself that she'd grown up here, in this climate. She could handle cold water.

She headed for the branch sticking out of

the water like a skeletal arm with a few lonely green leaves attached.

It was dark and murky beneath the water.

She crashed into something. It wasn't cardboard or plastic. It was wood that was halfway stuck into the earth, hidden by the branch.

She emerged.

Griffin was already in the water, his face stony and incredulous and angry, swimming hard for her.

"I've found her! I believe I've found her," she shouted.

She ignored him when he reached her. She plunged down again, feeling the slime that had formed over the wooden box. She tried to dislodge it, and, of course, couldn't. Not on her own.

By then everyone was in the water. And then the box was unstuck with a loss-of-suction sound that seemed to boom through the surrounding forest. The divers had the box.

They dragged it back to shore.

They didn't have to open the lid; it popped open as it was dragged up.

And she was there.

Sodden, a horrible ashen color, hands bruised and bloody, clothing torn, once glorious hair a sodden mass of clumped tangles.

Standing on shore, shivering so hard her teeth literally chattered, Vickie felt a horrible sense of loss and sadness.

Yes, they'd found Darlene.

She should be glad.

And she was.

Glad, and . . .

Very, very, afraid.

CHAPTER TEN

"You don't do things like that. You just don't do things like that!"

Vickie was seated in the back of a state vehicle, a blanket around her shoulders, cup of hot coffee in her hands.

Griffin was wearing a blanket around his shoulders, still drenched, but apparently oblivious to the cold. He was angry — with her.

"I do what I choose to do!" she snapped back.

He wagged a finger at her. "And that will get you killed. What the hell is the matter with you?"

"I found her!"

Another officer was coming to speak with him and he turned away and walked hard to meet him. No one else had heard the exchange, she was certain, but when Jackson Crow walked toward her with another blanket to add to the one she was wearing, she was expecting much of the same.

Instead, he looked at her apologetically.

"Ignore him," he suggested. "You just scared the hell out of him."

"You seem to be all right with what I did," she said softly.

He sat on the edge of the vehicle's seat with her. "We've all had our crazy moments of certainty when we've done something rash," he said. "He'll calm down. He'll even apologize. If I didn't believe he would, I'd have to be a gentleman and call him out," he added, giving her a rueful smile. "Griffin is just . . . invested."

He made her laugh. "Invested?"

"My dear Miss Preston! You have amazing sight and abilities — surely, you can't be that blind when it comes to Special Agent Pryce?"

She looked at him blankly. And then she flushed.

"He saved my life, of course."

"Get past that," Jackson said.

"Well, I am past it. We're both past it. And I . . ."

"For a man who speaks with the dead, he's pretty blind, too. Or the two of you are afraid. Maybe you believe you have to fight against some kind of survivors' bonding. You don't. We're all different. That is one of the reasons we come together. But people are specially drawn to one another, too. If you take a college graduating class of healthy men and women, all young, all beautiful, they'll bond — but each as an individual is also drawn to certain others as individuals. Now, we're all older than college graduating classes, but like them, we do share this strange bond. There's still the individual thing of a man being drawn to a woman and vice-versa. That's life, and a beautiful part of life. I say, in the midst of all this, go for it. But then, I'm a very happy man. I have a wife who understands me and often sees and understands the dead better than I do myself. She's beautiful and I adore her — and we're both hopelessly devoted to our work as well. Excuse me, I'm being summoned. We've got an ambulance for . . . our young lady," he added sadly. "Who was she, I wonder?"

"Darlene — I haven't managed to see her long enough to find out more," Vickie said.

"They're working on it. I'm sure we'll have some answers by the time we get back into Boston."

Jackson rose and headed for the ambulance pulling up.

Darlene — still in the sodden box — was loaded into the back of the vehicle. Forensic teams would see what they could discover before her final resting place was further compromised. She would be brought to the morgue in Boston and receive her autopsy there, as had the other women they had not saved. The police were already combing through missing-persons cases across the country, seeking her identity. By tomorrow, they'd also have dental records and DNA.

Finally, she was taken away. Paperwork was filled out, though there would be more.

Jackson and Griffin returned for Vickie, Griffin not speaking, Jackson apologizing and assuring her he'd get heat going so that they could all dry out.

Apparently, he was going to drive back. Griffin didn't even want to be in the front of the car with her.

Griffin's phone rang and he answered it. He listened to someone, and then, to her surprise, he handed the phone to her.

"For you," he said.

She realized with a sinking heart her phone had been in her pocket, drenched now. It was clearly not working.

And she had forgotten to call her mother.

"Mom!" she greeted Lucy.

"You promised to call and let us know you were okay," Lucy said. "We tried to reach you — tried and tried. I called Roxanne,

the Ballantine house, Grown Ups . . . everyone I could think of!"

"I'm sorry, truly sorry!"

"You're with Griffin Pryce and his people
again. Oh, darling, this is all so dangerous.
Where are you, what are you doing?"

"I'm fine, I wasn't involved with anything
dangerous." Seriously, the pond had been
cold — not dangerous. "Riddles and history, Mom. It's what I'm good at."

"You must come by tomorrow," Lucy said.
"Oh, God, I can't say that, can I? I mean,
you're an adult, you're a good adult . . .
But I'm your mother! And I'm worried
sick."

"I'll be by tomorrow, I promise. It's no
problem. I promise!"

"Let me speak with Griffin again."

"What?"

"Please, darling, let me speak with Griffin
again."

Vickie handed the phone back. "My
mother is still on the line," she said. "Um,
she wants to speak with you."

He took the phone. "Yes, Mrs. Preston?"

He listened for a long moment. Then he
said, "Yes, ma'am. Certainly. As you wish."

Vickie looked forward for a moment in
silence. Her mother had probably just read
him the riot act about him using her in the

investigation.

He'd probably just agreed she shouldn't be involved.

"Don't forget, we have an appointment to see Bertram Aldridge at the prison tomorrow," Jackson said.

"I think," Vickie replied, "Special Agent Pryce might have just agreed that I not be part of any more appointments."

"No, that's not what I agreed to," Griffin said.

She turned slightly in the seat to look at him.

"Then what?" she asked.

"I told her that certainly, Jackson and I would see that you arrived at their place for dinner tomorrow night, and we would be happy to join you."

The day had been long. When they reached Vickie's apartment, Griffin took her to the door; he seemed extremely hard, cold and distant. He went through the usual — having her stay by the door, walking through the apartment and then giving her an all clear. He barely said good-night.

Then he was gone.

Vickie showered and changed and decided to try the rice remedy on her phone.

Dylan didn't show up. She supposed he

was still home, and, perhaps, seeing the information on the news that a young woman named Darlene Dutton, most probably the first victim of the Undertakers — the media was using the plural now — had been found that day. Everything Vickie saw in the news was true — only specifics about her clothing, the box and the method of her death were left out. But then, to the best of her knowledge, there wouldn't be an autopsy until the next morning.

There had been no missing-persons report filed on Darlene; she had aged out of the child-care system in New Jersey and made her way to Boston, according to authorities. Her last foster parent, according to the news, said she'd been waiting to leave the state — where she'd been tossed about from home to home since she'd been orphaned at the age of seven — forever. She'd hoped to find work in Boston as a childcare worker or waitress. The city had fascinated her since she'd been a child.

Vickie thought about the poor girl; she was so glad that they had found her. Although they hadn't saved her life, it still mattered.

The news report finished in the same vein as it had since the killings had begun: residents were again begged to take extreme care in all that they did.

There was a knock at Vickie's door and her pulse quickened. The knock was too hard for the arrival at her door to be Dylan.

Griffin.

Despite the fact that a policeman watched outside, she checked through the peephole on her door.

Not Griffin.

Roxanne.

She let her friend in.

"Same cop I met before!" Roxanne said, smiling. "Thankfully, or I might have been up against the wall, being frisked. Hmm. Depending on the cop . . . hey, that might not be so bad. Don't look at me like that! I'm joking. Although, maybe I'm not. Finding a good cop might not be such a bad thing."

"I'm not looking at you in any way. I think you're just not always careful," Vickie told her.

"That's because you are, and you trust your instincts."

"Hmm," said Vickie, thinking about how trusting her instincts had just had her plunging into an icy pond to retrieve a dead body. "Anyway," she added lightly, "I think I actually can introduce you to a plethora of cops!"

They settled onto the sofa, and Vickie begged Roxanne to distract her with conversation that had nothing to do with the Undertakers.

Roxanne obliged. "So what really happened with Jared? From what I could tell, I think at heart he's a decent person. He's just trying too hard, you know? His art really is everything to him."

"He's good and I wish him well, and I just hope he stops feeling he has to be smashed or stoned to create real works of art," Vickie said. "He's a good guy — we're just done, and he needs to move on and take care of himself. He's clever and charming — and he needs to find his own way, or whatever. I truly wish him well."

"You don't think that he'd follow you up here, do you?" Roxanne asked.

"No. He likes New York art galleries. Why?"

"He's called your mom a few times."

"Oh? She never said anything."

"She doesn't want you to know."

"It doesn't matter," Vickie said. "He can call her all he likes, and I hope she's good to him. I've been honest with him. We were never going anywhere. We were really okay — just not forever, if that makes sense."

"Hey, speaking of your past, I saw your

285

other main man the other day. Hank Fremont."

"Yeah? How's he doing?"

"He looked good. Well, he always looked good. He told me he's working as an assistant manager for a food produce company. I ran into him at Pasta Fagioli, Mario Caro's family's place."

"I was just there with my Grown Ups group."

"Mario's a good guy. Anyway, Hank was there showing him a catalogue about their new organic line. We all talked for a while. It was nice. Hank, naturally, asked about you. The cops have been tight-lipped, but all that stuff about way-back-when has been dredged up in the news over and over, so, of course, he knows you're in Boston."

"I'm glad it sounds as if he's doing well."

"Oh, yeah. He told me he met the right girl; she keeps him on the straight and narrow."

"That's great!"

"We talked about having dinner — a 'for old-times-sake' dinner."

"Somewhere along the line, maybe."

"Okay, well, I'm off. It's late."

"You came over just to tell me it's late?" Vickie asked.

"I was worried — you weren't answering

your phone."

"Oh, I got it wet. I'm trying to dry it out now."

"Ahha! So you were there."

"Where?"

"At the pond. You did help them find that body!" Roxanne said triumphantly. "You always had something going for you — weird instinct! But . . . oh! So you were with Special Agent Pryce again. Cool. I can see which way that's going. Hey, the man has a future. He isn't into alcohol or drugs to get his 'mojo' going. He's tall, dark and hand-some. Studly, even. Where is he?"

"Okay, I was at the pond. Now I'm home. And he's wherever he goes, probably still working, or maybe sleeping."

"Okay, okay, I'm leaving. And you're an idiot."

"Good night. I love you, Roxanne — you're a great friend."

Roxanne gave her a huge hug. "Call me when the rice has worked, call me tomor-row — on something. Can't help but be worried. Okay? Oh, you probably have to call your mom every day, too. Sorry — just add me in, all right?"

"I will, I will. Good night."

When Roxanne was gone, Vickie locked the door and started to head back to her computer. She should have been working, looking at all her materials on Cotton and Increase Mather. Since she really thought Cotton Mather had to have been an A-one self-righteous ass as a Puritan minister, she wondered briefly why she'd been determined to write about his part in the events surrounding the witchcraft trials and those others who had been persecuted.

"To show he was an A-one ass?" she murmured aloud. She sat, and then just stared. She didn't care about her work research at the moment. She wondered if she'd see the ghost of Darlene Dutton again — she hoped the young woman would find peace.

And then again, of course, she had to wonder how it all connected, the past with Bertram Aldridge, the Pine house and the killer couple who had sent Darlene to her watery grave.

And why the hell, how the hell, was she involved?

She didn't have long to contemplate; she heard a commotion out on the street.

There was a cop out there, watching over her.

She'd thrown on sweats after taking her very long hot shower — decent enough, she decided. Stepping out into the hallway she hurried to the front door.

Her ever-watchful cop was there — questioning a man.

The man looked up. Vickie recognized Hank Fremont, looking older, a little broader and very confused.

"Vickie! Will you tell this man, please, that I'm an old friend!" he asked.

Hank appeared woebegone and lost — the way he'd always looked the few times their team had lost a football game.

She smiled. "It is okay, Officer! He is a friend," she said.

"I'm out here if you need me," the officer called.

"Thank you!"

"Wow!" Hank said, adjusting his jacket. "You're under protection, Vickie!" He started to hug her, an old friend hug, but then stopped, looking back at the cop. Vickie laughed and hugged him.

"Come on in. Roxanne just told me you were back in Boston — working with produce?"

"Yeah, a bit shy of the NFL, huh?"

"Sounds like a good job."

"It is," Hank agreed. He followed her in. "You want to make me some tea?"

"Tea?" she asked. "I mean, sure — I don't think I have much else in here right now."

He grinned. "Believe it or not, you were the best thing that ever happened to me, Vickie."

She let him in; while she made tea, he talked about the years he'd wasted, the way he'd discovered he'd wasted his years and meeting his new girl, June Jensen.

"I'd actually applied to online college before I met June, and I was so glad. She's encouraging, she's helpful, wonderful . . . I'd love you to meet her."

"That would be great," Vickie told him. "Is she from here?"

"Originally. She has family out in western Massachusetts, too. But anyway, she's working here now. She's a secretary for an ad agency. And I'm with a company called Great Organics. Whoever figured I'd be a happy man talking broccoli with old Mario?"

Vickie laughed and brought cups of tea out to the parlor. "I'm just glad."

She'd barely set the tea down before there was a really hard knock at the door.

The cop didn't let people get close if he hadn't checked them out — he knew who lived in the building and who didn't, and he was always on them to make sure they locked the door to the house itself, but people always forgot.

She had just forgotten. And the lock wasn't automatic, so . . .

She looked through the peephole.

This time, it was Griffin.

She opened the door. He swept in, looking around as if he was on high alert, ready to forge into battle.

Hank stood. "Hey!" he said. "Griffin Pryce. Special Agent Griffin Pryce. You were the cop here when . . . well, way back when. Good to see you, sir."

He offered Griffin a hand. Griffin seemed to hesitate just a second. Then he shook Hank's hand.

"Glad you're here again. Vick probably needs someone like you watching over her now," Hank said.

"It's a tough time in Boston at the moment, yes," Griffin said.

"Tough for the poor Ballantine family!" Hank said. He looked from Vickie to Griffin and grinned awkwardly. "Well, so, I guess I'm going to head on home. I hadn't seen Vickie yet — just got back into the city again myself recently. Anyway, good to see you both."

"Take care," Griffin said.

"Don't forget, we've all got to have dinner, Vickie!" Hank said.

"I won't forget," she told him.

Hank left. Griffin was still there.

"Vickie, look, I'm not trying to mess with your life, but this isn't the time to be letting people into your apartment. I know you and Hank were a big item, but if you know him now, if you're back into correspondence, or back into a relationship, you've just got to be really careful."

"Ah," she murmured. "I shouldn't see old friends, huh?"

"Vickie . . ." He paused for a long moment. "Old friends might be new enemies."

"What?"

"Hank — he was around when Aldridge escaped. He wasn't a bad kid, just an idiot kid, drinking, pot, all that, in high school. He was out in the western part of the state — now, he's here."

"You think Hank could be a killer?" she said incredulously.

"I know he was basically a carnie out with an amusement park for years. I know he's started seeing a woman who grew up on the south side."

"You know all that?"

"Vickie, naturally. We're the FBI. We look into everything. We look into everyone. Hell, we're even looking into George Ballantine!"

"Wait, wait — back up! Hank Fremont was a kid when Aldridge attacked the Ballantine house. George Ballantine was at a company dinner. That's all crazy. And George Ballantine would hardly bury his own wife in his own basement!" she said.

He was silent.

"You mean . . . you really think that could happen?"

"We really believe someone who knows you is involved, yes," he said quietly. "Look, seriously, I'm not trying to interfere with your life, your hopes, anything you want, anyone you want, but — and I'm truly sorry! — this involves you. You have to be careful."

"You're yelling."

"I'm not yelling. I'm a government agent. I don't yell."

"Yeah? Well, you're yelling."

Vickie stared at him, hands on her hips. And she suddenly felt like laughing — he really was something, he had always been a rock of fitness, ethics — and sexuality. Images tumbled before her; him in his BPD uniform, holding her and Noah as she shook, him stopping by her parents' home to see that she was okay, him in the court room, him . . . years later, standing in her parents' house again.

His face as he plunged into the water after her . . .

And she remembered Jackson Crow's advice to her as well.

She suddenly walked across the room, rejection be damned, and protocol be damned.

She slipped her arms around his neck, pressed against him and kissed his lips.

For a moment, he was stiff as a concrete wall.

Then his arms swept around her. She might have kissed him first, but he was kissing her then, and their mouths were wide, tongues plunging, and it was all ridiculously hot and wet and steaming. She was glad his arms were around her, holding her close to him, because her knees were like rubber and she was trembling and weak and still . . . ready to burst into something that was fire and electric and filled with strength and energy.

Their mouths broke apart; he seemed to be trying to get himself under control.

"Vickie, we shouldn't, I shouldn't . . ."

"Do you ever shut up?" she asked him. "For the love of God, please quit thinking!" she told him.

He stared down at her, eyes so dark and ever enigmatic. He kissed her again, this time fumbling with her flannel pullover sweatshirt, breaking the kiss long enough for the shirt to come over her head. They kissed and broke and kissed and broke, divesting clothing, backing toward the hallway and her bedroom all the while.

He paused long enough to see that his gun and holster were carefully set on the bedside table, and then they were into the comedy of trying never to lose contact while ridding themselves of all the clothing that now seemed so obnoxious between them.

She realized she'd waited forever to run her fingers over his flesh. To feel the twitching and contortion of his muscles as she touched him. To drown in the sensation of feeling his hands on her. So good, too good. She fell back, luxuriating in him resting half atop her, half to her side. Feeling his mouth again on hers, traveling to her throat, her breasts, her midriff.

His heat and energy soared into her. She halfway rose, capturing his face again, finding his lips, slipping down the length of his chest.

They rolled again, each touching the other, playing, teasing, desperate . . .

And then he stopped.

"No thinking!" she pleaded.

"Just asking. Are we . . . okay?"

"Yes! Still on birth control. No talking, please!"

"Talking can be good."

"As long as there's no thinking."

"No thinking . . . except . . . oh, yes, there, and there and there . . ."

She laughed softly, and felt his mouth on her flesh again.

"And there, and there and there . . ." she agreed.

She marveled that reality could be more sensual than ever her imagination had dared venture; she allowed herself to feel and revel in every touch of his fingers and his lips. She dared to touch and tease and hold and torment, kiss and caress . . .

And indulge in every kiss and caress, allowing him to slip down the length of her body, tease the length of her limbs . . . abdomen again, limbs again . . . around, between . . .

And she arched against him, rolled again, alive and kinetic, returning every touch and brush and stroke until he lifted her atop him, brought her slowly down, and their eyes met as their bodies joined. She knew no one else would have ever been right, he was what she had wanted, and she'd waited, and somehow, life had brought them together.

Then she stopped thinking.

She moved and writhed and whimpered,

moaned and cried out.

Then there was breathing, desperate breathing, and her heart racing as it had never raced before, a drumbeat of wonder.

It was sex, of course, just sex.

Good sex.

Great sex.

Incredible sex . . .

And after the gasping for breath and the heart pounding, it began all over again, and she was unaware of time or place. Just the scent of his flesh, the heat of him, the wonder of him.

Eventually, she realized she was exhausted.

Sated, and yet . . .

She'd never really be sated, she thought, she'd always want him. She'd known it when she had been just on the verge of eighteen.

She knew it now.

They lay together, curled side by side, and for once, he was silent, holding her.

Then he spoke softly at last.

"Maybe I should yell more often."

"Don't you dare!"

"Seemed to work well."

"What? It was me, all me. Obviously, I had to shut you up."

"Hmm. Frightening concept. I mean, you don't always end your arguments this way, do you?"

"I wasn't arguing. You were."

"I was scared," he said softly, holding her even closer.

She drew away, halfway sitting up to look at him, a frown on her brow. "Griffin, really? You can't possibly think Hank is a killer."

"I didn't know him like you knew him — he was a kid, yes, back when we met briefly. And that's the thing with the way we work — back at the main office, of course, they're drawing up dossiers on all kinds of people. Don't worry, please, it's not like Big Brother is watching — I don't even know exactly who Big Brother is, or what he watches. But yes, we have researched a lot of people. Sometimes, you just have to eliminate people. And you do have to look at anyone who was involved with Aldridge closely. So, yes, we've known Hank Fremont was back in the city after an extended time out in the Springfield area. We are watching the Ballantine family in many ways. We've investigated Grown Ups. We know your publishers, and, of course, your parents are as squeaky clean as a pair of babes." He sighed softly. "Your mom won't like this."

Vickie laughed. "You're going to tell her?" she asked.

He shrugged. "I'm thinking after the next

time or the next or the next . . . we're probably going to have to say something."

She smiled and laughed and curled back down beside him. "So, there will be a next time?"

"Please don't say there won't be."

"You know, you really had me over eight years ago."

"You were seventeen."

"I think you can actually marry at that age in some states!"

"But this is you, and me."

"And now is right?" she whispered.

"Now is right."

She knew he lay awake, staring at the ceiling, and that he was thinking.

"What?"

"I'm aggravated. No clear-cut suspects. Decaying bodies out of time, someone from the past — and a couple from the present, no forensic clues, just the dead — and the waiting. For another note to the media — and another missing woman," he said. He rolled toward her. "Well, tomorrow, we see Aldridge."

"Aldridge. Yes, who knows . . . maybe he will give us something," Vickie said. Then she suddenly bounded out of bed, looking around for a robe. She found one and grabbed it.

"Um . . . what's up?" Griffin asked, startled.

"I think I have my kids tomorrow."

"Your kids?"

"Grown Ups. My young adults. I think we're supposed to do our Duck Tour tomorrow."

"What time?"

"After school — three thirty."

"You're fine. We see Aldridge at 9:00 a.m."

"Oh. Oh, well, good! Excellent. I can do both."

"Right."

"Right."

"So, why are you still standing there?" he asked.

"Um . . ."

He patted the bed. "Come on in — we're going to have to get up early. I've obviously got to get back to my hotel room . . . it's going to be a long day. Of course, it's quite cool to make it a long night beforehand . . ."

"Oh? Oh."

"Yes, well, I guess we've both been waiting a long time."

"Too long," she said softly.

And she cast off the robe, and joined him again.

And it was a delightfully long night.

CHAPTER ELEVEN

Bertram Aldridge was seated at a metal table in a small room; he was handcuffed to the table.

There was no doubt he was considered to be dangerous, even in shackles, even behind bars.

Griffin wouldn't have thought anything about coming to see the man with Jackson, or even on his own.

There was no way not to note every detail of the situation when he and Jackson were accompanied by Vickie Preston.

They arrived punctually at 9:00 a.m.

The summer sun was rising high, but not even the brightness could dispel the air of gloom that hung over the barbed-wire fences and fortifications of the prison.

Vickie had dressed conservatively for their appointment — white tailored blouse buttoned to the throat, navy slacks and suit jacket.

But, Griffin thought, she could have bundled up in burlap and she would still be a striking woman, with her deep green eyes, near-black hair, with a lithe and shapely form. She was tall and sleek, and something in the way she walked seemed to make her glide. She was, in short, beautiful, and it bothered him on an elemental level to bring her anywhere near the sea of murderers, rapists and thieves they were about to enter.

He wondered if it had been the right decision, bringing her here. Seeing her again was probably something Aldridge would truly enjoy. And, yet, if they were going to get the man to say anything, she just might be the little edge that could make it happen.

And, actually, they didn't have to interact with anyone other than the warden and a number of the guards; the room where Aldridge had been brought was behind the security checkpoint, but before they reached the area of the general population. Griffin just had a heightened sensitivity to where they were — and he was very aware of the depravities that had been practiced by some of the inmates who were near.

Of course, Aldridge himself was disturbing enough.

The man's hair was now iron gray; more

wrinkles furrowed his brow and lean cheeks. In his youth he had been a handsome man, and while some of his appearance had faded with time and circumstance, he had maintained something of his looks, even in prison. He smiled when they entered, raising a hand halfway to greet them, then shrugging and letting his smile deepen to show that hey, he was cuffed to the table. It was easy to see how he had disarmed his victims.

Three seats waited for them. They were accompanied in by one of the prison guards, and there were two more just the other side of the barred door.

"Behave, Aldridge," the guard muttered darkly.

"Behave?" Aldridge asked. "But of course! Visitors are so rare. Not even my dear, sainted mother anymore — that blessed lady has gone on to her eternal rest! Today, I have these esteemed gentlemen and a lady. What a lady. No, sir, I shall feast my eyes — and not cause the least amount of trouble! And, of course, what a pleasure to see Officer Pryce again. Except it's not 'officer' anymore, is it? Special Agent! Oh, my. And your friend! Another 'special' agent. I am honored."

"Sure you are," Griffin said. The man was

most likely mentally licking his chops; the way he studied Vickie, his slick smile in place, made Griffin long to slug him hard in the jaw and throw a bag over his head.

"Truly. I've been in here a long time. I'll be in here until the day I die. It is a thrill to see you."

"Anything out of the ordinary has to be a thrill for you," Jackson said. "Because, yes, this is your life. You will not be pardoned. You will not escape, ever again, though I'm certain you live with the belief that you will."

"So, then, not that I would look a gift horse in the mouth, but . . . why are you here?" Aldridge asked pleasantly.

"Because you know something," Griffin said flatly.

"I know the earth is round. Winter is cold. I know that McGregor — standing guard there — is an ass, and the food here is far less than gourmet," Aldridge said, still smiling pleasantly.

"You know who I am," Vickie said, staring at him hard. "And you know something about what is going on, about the women who have been kidnapped. The women who have been saved — and the women who have died."

"Ah," Aldridge murmured. "Okay, so I know that's why you're here. And seeing you . . . I guess that's supposed to unnerve me! Make me say something. Victoria Preston! The girl who knew I was there . . . ah, yes. The beautiful creature who got away. Well, you have really come along nicely, Miss Preston. You were so ripe and gorgeous before, but now . . . let's see, your features are refined. There is an air of maturity about you that is *je ne sait quoi* . . . ? You are beyond beauty, you are compelling, seductive and just magnificent. I could go on and on —"

"But you will stop right now," Griffin informed him. He leaned toward Aldridge. "You're involved. Complicit in murder, whether you're in here or not. We will bring you up on federal charges, and you will face the death penalty."

He thought his words struck a nerve, somewhere in the man. He saw a pulse at Aldridge's throat tick — and tick again too quickly.

Death penalty. Aldridge didn't mind dealing out death — despite prison, he didn't want to die himself.

"I don't know what on earth you think I could have done. Even asshole guard over there knows I haven't so much as taken a damn step out of this place since my sentencing began. Whoops, sorry, Miss Preston. Such language before a goddess. I am sorry."

"You're lying, Aldridge," Jackson said flatly.

"Look, bizarre as it seems to you do-gooders, I do have fans out there. Oh, you wouldn't believe the women who want to marry me! Some of them are holy rollers, of course. They think if a man like me just had a really good woman, someone who loved me completely and totally, I'd be fixed. There's a real fan club out there, don't you kid yourselves. And others! Well, sorry, gentlemen and lady, there are fans out there who admire my prowess! They long to be like me — an artist with a knife, a connoisseur of the kill! Equally adept with firearms — a crack aim! Oh, and should it come up, I am nicely versed in poisons as well. A true artist of the death trade. Ah, well, if I could actually determine who was a femme fatale of my own ilk, I might consider the idea of tying the old knot. So hard to tell. So hard to figure out what truly goes on in the minds of those around us — or those writing to us, whatever the case may be."

Griffin was about to press his point when Vickie suddenly spoke again. "Mr. Aldridge, you must really miss your mother. I take it she was a good person — one who loved you and had no clue as to how you grew up to be a monster."

Again, his pulse ticked.

"She was an alcoholic whore — but she was all I had."

"I guess you grew up without love — all kinds of hardship, that kind of thing," Vickie said.

"Ah, there you go! Another redeemer. I wasn't born bad — I was made that way — and I can be fixed!" Aldridge said gleefully.

"Oh, no, Mr. Aldridge," Vickie said. "You're completely broken. I don't believe you can be fixed at all. But you did correspond with people — you do correspond with people. You're allowed two fifteen-minute phone calls a week. And you call phone numbers that can't be traced. You are involved in this and you're using me. Because you missed. You missed me because of Griffin Pryce, and you think you're going to settle a score with both of us now."

"What a clever little miss," Aldridge said.

"You need to give us something, Aldridge," Jackson Crow said. "As my partner here mentioned, you can face the death penalty. You will face federal charges."

"You're blowing smoke!" Aldridge said, but that pulse was ticking in his neck again. "You can't connect me to anything."

"Which means there is something to connect you to," Griffin said quietly.

Aldridge's fists slammed on the table, chains banging. "I didn't say that!" he snapped. "You won't connect me because I'm not involved. It's not my fault some demented soul has determined to get revenge for me. Sounds like whoever it is is pretty damned good, too." He controlled himself again and smiled pleasantly. "Yes, we do get the news in here. You fellows have nothing, nothing. You're running around holding your dicks. You don't have a damned thing."

"You grew up on the south side," Vickie said.

Aldridge quickly lowered his head, hiding his expression.

"Lots of people grew up on the south side."

"With your alcoholic mother," Griffin said pleasantly. "Hearing all kinds of rumors. You know, I just learned today there was an article in the 1880s that mentioned one of your great-great-grandparents. Jonah Aldridge. He was known to have seen a young prostitute who disappeared. She was never found. Friends tried to get the police involved, but they couldn't find anything or prove anything."

"So, great-great-grandpa was a connoisseur of death, too," Aldridge said. "Too late for you brilliant *dicks* to get him, huh? Is that why you're plaguing me?"

"No, frankly," Jackson said, "that's why we're so certain you are involved in this. You grew up on the south side. You heard family lore — you either knew or suspected those bodies were in the wall there."

Griffin leaned in, going for more. "You knew they were there. You knew where the knots were in the wood. You loved to go stare at the dead and imagine you were the one who had put them there."

The pulse was ticking at Aldridge's throat again.

Bingo.

"Since I've been in here, it's most unlikely I managed to slip out — and back in again — after adding to the body count," Aldridge said.

"It's not the same," Jackson said with a shrug, "but I'm sure you're enjoying every kill from in here. You're quite the tutor. You've taught your acolytes to find their own signature, their own means of killing. You would probably prefer it if there were knives and a lot of blood involved. But, hey . . . prison is surely boring as hell, right? Every bit of news you hear is something that

309

thrills you."

"If the news does or doesn't thrill me, means nothing," Aldridge said.

"Imagine, though. Imagine when we catch the killers, when they talk. I don't think they're actually up to par with you, Aldridge. Your dementia is controlled, almost sophisticated! And these people, well . . . they're good at being stealthy. But still," Griffin said, looking at Jackson, "I think we all know once we've caught one of them . . . that one is going to do the old cliché thing and sing like a canary."

"Yep, you will be implicated," Jackson agreed.

"And then . . . federal charges!" Griffin said.

"You think you're so clever! Well, did you know George Ballantine can trace his New York ass back to the south side, too," Aldridge spit out.

"Actually, we do know that. Your families lived on the same street," Vickie said flatly. "Did they have more money, even back then? More prestige in the neighborhood?"

"They were assholes then like they are now," Aldridge said. He shook his head. "You want to talk about murderers? Family legend? Well, my family believed Jonah Aldridge was ostracized because that old-time George Ballantine was a killer — and made it look like Jonah was the one who made people disappear. Well, my sainted-alcoholic-bitch of a mother used to talk about it all the time! The Ballantine family! They went up and up . . . and my family . . . down the tubes. You need to look at that man if you want to go after someone. Seriously. He's all fine and respected! Like hell! Check into what that man is doing, why don't you?"

"We're federal investigators, Mr. Aldridge," Jackson said. "We look into everything."

"All our looking points at you."

Aldridge suddenly stared at Vickie. His gaze was intense. "Maybe Vickie needs to be more careful than anyone else out there," he said very softly.

Griffin barely controlled himself.

He didn't speak.

Jackson did.

"Are you threatening Miss Preston, Aldridge?"

"Me? Hell, no. I'm as innocent as a babe. But bad stuff does seem to be going on. And she is such a stunning young woman!" His smile deepened. "I remember seeing you in court, Miss Preston. And I was almost thinking I was glad I'd been stopped. So beautiful. And a bullet! All over so very quickly. Such a heartbreaker! Shattering the lives of those she left behind. Of those she touched and touches on a day-to-day basis. Take nothing from that, my friends. You're not going to get anything from me. I'm not involved. You're looking for some history student who just happens to enjoy my work."

"We're looking for a couple, we know. A man and a woman."

"So I've heard. Your news conferences, warning the public. Thing is, the public just never really listens, you know. People get careless. And killers can wait until people are careless. You think you're after a man and a woman. Maybe you're wrong."

"Oh, I don't think so," Griffin said. "We have witnesses — you know that."

"Eyewitnesses are notoriously wrong," Aldridge said. "We all know that. I am so sorry, really. I've been delighted to see you, and we can talk forever, but I can't give you anything."

Before Griffin or Jackson could speak, Vickie did.

"Actually," Vickie said, "I believe you're wrong. You've just given us a great deal." She rose. And, Griffin thought, she did seem to know something — either that, or her bluff was absolutely excellent. "I believe I'll have the guard let me out now. These gentlemen can finish with you without me."

"What? Don't leave! You're the reason I've agreed to speak with these men," Aldridge said. "You came because you had to. You wanted to see me. Here I am."

"There you are. I expected something far more menacing, a monster, perhaps, in truth. You're just a man. A truly sick man — asshole, if you will. You're a little man in chains and behind bars. Excuse me, I am leaving."

She walked to the door; the guard quickly followed her.

Griffin rose as well. "We'll be back, Aldridge," he said.

"I won't see you," Aldridge said, hate now seeming to rise from him; he almost spat out the words and the pulse at his throat was going full speed.

"Yes, you will. Vickie won't be back, no. But we will be. And I suggest you think long and hard. Next time, you'll tell us everything you know, or I will personally see to it there is no way in hell the death penalty gets taken off the table for you."

"I'll be helping on that one," Jackson promised.

"You can't, you can't!" Aldridge roared as

313

they headed out the door as well. "You can't! You can't . . . I've got rights. I've got rights! You're dead, you're all dead, you . . ."

They didn't hear his final words. The door slammed on Aldridge.

The three of them didn't speak as they went through the formalities of leaving the prison.

Griffin reached for Vickie's arm to escort her; he worried she might have been shaken by the visit; that they might have put her through too much.

She was steady as concrete.

When they reached the car she turned to face both him and Jackson.

"He did give us something."

"Yes, he is involved," Griffin said.

"Through those phone calls," Jackson agreed.

"More than that," Vickie said. "I mean, he didn't give us any flat answers, but he did give us a lot. His mother was all he had. But it had to have been a love-hate relationship. And whoever is doing this now, well, I believe Aldridge has used the same type of situation to create a killer. As in someone who grew up in South Boston, poor and feeling disenfranchised, someone who maybe had a father who left the home and a mother who drank. It's a follower, yes. We need to find out who might have been in prison with him before and might have had the same lifestyle growing up. Or maybe not even a prison buddy. Maybe someone out there with whom he might have had a special relationship because they shared experiences. Someone who has been writing to him. Have you been able to get the letters he's been sent in prison? Are his letters checked before they go out?"

"Yes, always," Jackson told her. He looked back at the prison and leaned against the car.

"We can't see what he's sent out, but we can see what he's been sent, right? Copies of them?" Vickie asked.

"Yes. And, of course, our officers have read and analyzed them all. Nothing was ever said about killing, about methods of killing or about specific people. He was right — many of the letters he received are from women who think that he needs to find God and the love of a good woman, or they're letters of admiration about his looks and his skills. Those are pretty chilling," Griffin told her.

She looked as cool and confident as any law enforcement agent out there.

"Have they been seen by a Bostonian? Especially, have they been seen by a researching Bostonian? One who really knows the city?"

"Vickie, I'm not sure we were right bringing you. I'm beginning to think maybe we should get you out of town," Griffin said. "I'm not at all sure we should keep dragging you more deeply into this."

"You admitted I'm a target. I believe even more so after today — he was making allusions to people from my past. Suggesting I know the killers, that maybe I see them on a day-to-day basis. I'm a target." She smiled suddenly at Griffin — God, but he loved her face, her smile, her eyes, and the determination in them now.

"She's right," Jackson said. "We brought her in the minute we went to her parents' home to ask her help with Chrissy Ballantine. And it's a good thing — she might have already been a victim if we hadn't gotten her police protection."

"Not to mention," Vickie added, grinning at Jackson, "I have started sleeping with a federal agent — that should make me nice and safe."

Jackson grinned in turn. "Can't hurt," he told her.

Somewhat perplexed, Griffin looked at the two of them. They'd had some kind of exchange, obviously, to which he hadn't been privy.

Whatever.

It had worked.

"There are still a number of hours before you have to meet up with the group from Grown Ups, right?" Jackson asked Vickie.

"I should be there by about 3:00 p.m., ready to *Duck Tour* with them," she said.

"I thought we should pay a visit to Dr. Loeb. The bodies from the Pine house were brought to the morgue. They've brought in some anthropologists from the university, and I'd be interested in finding out what we can," Jackson said. He looked at Vickie. "So, we've dragged you to a prison. Why not add in a morgue."

"Sure," Vickie said.

"Hey!" Griffin protested.

"It's important," Vickie said. "Like it or not, you should think of me as glue now — you're stuck with me. We have to have answers. Especially after that lovely chat with Aldridge. My life is in danger. We have to stop these killers."

Dr. Loeb met them out in the vestibule; Detective Barnes, he told them, had just left.

"Sad thing, sad thing. I just finished the autopsy on Darlene Dutton. Horrible, horrible! The girl had massive trauma to her skull, but it didn't kill her. She drowned. She scratched her fingers to the bone trying to get out . . . well, unless someone had been there to see what was done, to get her out immediately . . . well, there was no hope. Even if the note that was tossed by the newspaper had been taken seriously . . . it was too late." He sighed. "Miss Dutton, so it seemed, had no family. She took busses and hitchhiked her way up here."

"We know someone who will tend to her," Jackson assured him.

"I'm glad to hear that. Anyway, I've had full reports sent to you," Loeb told them. "Is there anything else I can do for you?"

"We wanted to know if you'd discovered anything else about the bodies found in the wall where Fiona West was found," Griffin said.

"You think there's a connection? I sincerely doubt whoever murdered those poor people is still alive. No justice to be found there," Loeb said.

"We've had two scientists in from Harvard, as a matter of fact. Again, I've had the reports sent to you. We now believe they were all killed in a span of five years or so and . . ." He paused, glancing at Vickie.

"Go on, please," she said.

"Well, here's what's sad and quite terrifying, really. Each was knocked out and stuffed into the wall . . . next to the last to die. Those poor souls saw what would happen to them before it did. They were left to die next to those already rotting. Truly terrible. They were smothered, we believe thus far, with different kinds of insulation — old newspapers, cotton and linen cloth — whatever was around. Anyway, it was enough to cut out an air supply; it would kill them — and silence them, should they not die quickly enough. I'm sorry that I can't say death came easily for any of them."

"If you learn anything else, Doctor," Jackson began.

"I will call you immediately. We're still waiting on some lab tests — on our newly dead, and, of course, the long-lost corpses."

They thanked him and left. Jackson intended to head to the hospital and check in on Fiona West.

"Are you going with him?" Vickie asked Griffin.

"Oh, no. I'll be with you. Just like glue," he assured her.

Vickie had always been a fan of Duck Tours. They were fun, and she expected it would be especially fun with her group of teens.

They met at the Prudential Center where they boarded their vehicle, courtesy of a benefactor from Grown Ups.

It was even fun to see Griffin's expression as he looked at their vehicle — and the kids all playing with their "quackers" or noise-makers. He looked at her a little bewildered and shook his head.

She laughed.

The tour was great — though loud. She'd expected her group of young adults would keep their "quacks" going throughout, and they didn't disappoint. They saw the city by land, listened to a charming guide who answered questions with ease as they drove through the streets, and then their amphibious vehicle took to the water on the St. Charles River.

"You are awesome, Miss Preston," Cheryl assured her, leaning back while they were on the river and smiling. "This is too cool. Never thought I'd get to do things like this!"

"Ditto," Hardy said. He looked at Cheryl longingly.

"Never thought I'd be encouraged to make so much noise — when learning history, of course, Miss Preston," Art said.

Cindy was quiet and Vickie worried about her. But as they were coming in, she turned to Vickie. "This is what I want to do! I want to be a tour guide. I want to use all this stuff and learn more and more — and be a tour guide!"

"Sounds great," Vickie told her.

Vickie wasn't sitting with Griffin; he had taken to the back with a group of students and a young couple; she was in the row ahead with Cheryl, Hardy, Art and Cindy.

"You know, Miss P," Hardy said, lowering his voice. "I think this situation is a little cold on your part."

"What's that, Hardy?"

"Making the Fed sit back there. He's your guardian, huh?"

"I think he's more than that," Cheryl teased.

Vickie hoped that she wasn't flushing, or giving herself away in any measure.

"We're both out with the group of you. Doesn't matter where we sit," Vickie said.

"She's good," Hardy told Art at his side, nudging him.

Art grinned at her.

"Oh, in many ways, I'll bet!" Cindy said, laughing. She quickly sobered and apologized. "Sorry, didn't mean anything. I'm grateful for you, Miss Preston. Really grateful."

"We'd never get opportunities like this if it weren't for you," Art said.

"And Grown Ups," Vickie reminded them.

Tad flicked his fingers in the air. "Money is easy to give — well, I imagine. If you have a bunch of it, I'll bet it's easy to part with some. Time. That's what people never have for kids, so it seems. Anyway, if we're obnoxious, just smack us down. Because we do appreciate your time."

Tad used his "quacker" and made a lot of noise — others joined in.

Eventually, the tour was over, and they returned to the Prudential Center.

The next trip with her group was the aquarium, the following week.

"I'm so excited," Cheryl told her. "My friend is with your friend, Roxanne Greeley — they just went to the aquarium. I do love fish! And they have beluga whales. And penguins and . . . well, I love aquariums."

"I love them, too," Art said. He looked at Cheryl adoringly.

Cheryl, it had seemed, however, was usually closer to Hardy.

Vickie always felt a bit odd when her group broke off and left. They were all just about to reach their eighteenth birthdays; they were fully formed. Young adults. They were just a few months younger than she had been when she'd moved down to NYC. She still worried about them. She always hoped they got home safely.

"Young doe-eyed love, eh?" Griffin asked, standing closer to her as they waved to the last of the kids.

"Which one?"

"Art. Seems to have it bad for Cheryl. And that little Cheryl. She is a minx. But an interesting one. Wise — and cunning! — beyond her years. Taunting Art in turn, though she seems to gravitate to Hardy."

"Ah, the all-seeing mind of the mature male!" she teased.

"We need to head to the Ballantine house," he told her, turning serious.

Vickie felt her nerves tense. "Has something happened?" she asked quickly.

He shook his head. "Not that I know about — but Jackson received a call from Chrissy Ballantine. She asked if we'd come by. She specifically mentioned you, but she talked with Jackson first and suggested Detective Barnes might like to come, too."

"You think she might have remembered something else?" Vickie asked.

"Maybe. I don't know. I keep hoping. We've looked in so many directions. I do believe Aldridge is involved, but since torture isn't ethical, we have to try to finesse him. Threaten — and hope to trip him up. Naturally, we looked into Reginald Mason

— the guy who broke out with Aldridge years ago. The two had something. They escaped that day through a shaft they'd built in the walls in the laundry room — each covering the other constantly. So, they definitely had a bond. But Reginald Mason was actually released six months ago — humanitarian reasons. He was dying of cancer, and he wasn't faking that. He did, indeed, die. Thing is, Aldridge always liked knives. Reginald Mason was in prison for two strangulation murders — asphyxiation, though not quite the same. I'm tempted to dig up the man and find out if he's really the one who died."

"I'm sure they checked on that," Vickie said.

"Ah, well. Key word there — *they.* He had a parole officer, but the guy checked on him twice in the two months he lived outside of prison. He visited a man in bed."

"But — surely, the doctors in the prison system would have known if the man really had cancer or not."

"Yes. But as we all know, sometimes cancer is brutal and swift. Sometimes, there are cases of regression. At any rate, I'm going to say Aldridge did know about the bodies in the wall. But how he's conveyed so many things to his fan club, I don't know."

"Cell phone. He's allowed a couple of calls a week."

"I still think there's someone out there, some way, somehow, doing . . . something," he finished lamely. "Detective Barnes said it was a tough place growing up. He remembers hearing about old murders and about Quaker ghosts and that there were three shootings on his block when he was a kid. Anyway, we'll see what else he might have." He was quiet for a minute. "Him — and Ballantine."

They drove, though it was a matter of blocks. They were the first to arrive; Vickie almost went to the kitchen door, she'd been so accustomed to doing so years earlier. But Griffin headed up the front walk to the porch and the mammoth old colonial doors.

He lifted his hand to hit the buzzer, but the door opened for them.

Chrissy Ballantine was in slacks and a sweater, looking a bit thin and bit pinched — and very worried. But she smiled as she greeted them. Vickie felt a bit awkward; Chrissy reached for her though and pulled her into a hug.

"Whatever you might have heard, I'm an idiot," Chrissy said. "Vickie, I'm so grateful to you. You saved Noah — you saved me. I don't know . . . I might have babbled. I might have been looking for someone to blame. I'm so sorry. Forgive me?"

"Of course."

"Come in, come in."

Noah came running down the stairs as Vickie and Griffin entered. He threw himself into Vickie's arms. "You came! I'm so glad. Thank you for coming over!"

The ghost of Dylan followed Noah down. He grinned at Vickie and Griffin happily.

"It's super to see you, Noah," Vickie said.

"Likewise, young man," Griffin told him.

"Well, come in, come in. I've made some iced tea and have some snacks. Where are my manners? There should be more. It's almost dinner time," Chrissy said, looking confused again. The woman was really off — as if something was really wrong.

"Chrissy, we're supposed to be at my parents' place for dinner, so please, don't worry. We don't need anything at all," Vickie said.

"Oh! Yes, well, I'm sorry. To be honest, I needed to apologize," she said. "And, I was wondering . . . well, I know certain things were supposed to be kept quiet. But people do leak . . . they say things. And then it becomes tell a friend, tell a friend . . .

anyway, a lot of people know one of the victims remembered bits and pieces of what had happened when she was hypnotized."

"Mom, maybe we should move into the parlor and let them have some tea," Noah said, sounding very mature.

"Yes, please!" Chrissy said.

A minute later they were seated in the parlor. Dylan had followed; he stood by the mantel, leaning against the wall. He was somber, not doing anything to try to throw any of them into acknowledging his presence. He looked worried.

They all had glasses of iced tea. Vickie wasn't really hungry, but Chrissy was so anxious that she accepted a little quiche. Then, finally, Chrissy took a seat herself.

"I just keep hearing more and more. I'm so worried. Not so much for me — there's a man watching the house, of course. I mean, we're lucky, we can afford our own help . . ." She broke off and smiled at Noah. "I wish George was here — you talked to your dad, Noah, right? He said that he wouldn't be home for a while?"

"Yes, ma'am," Noah said. "I don't think he knew you were going to ask the agents and Vickie over. I didn't know." He paused and smiled at them. "I'm really glad you're here, though. I'm happy to see you."

"You, too," Griffin assured him.

Vickie realized then that Chrissy Ballantine had purposely not told her husband about inviting them over; she also thought Chrissy might have been planning on Noah being somewhere else, too.

She'd wanted to talk to them alone.

"Poor Noah!" Chrissy murmured. "He was supposed to have baseball practice this afternoon. His coach called in sick! My darling, you must be so bored with your poor old mum being such a scaredy-cat!" Chrissy said.

"Never bored by you, Mom," Noah assured her. He smiled. "I love you."

"And I love you!" Chrissy whispered.

There was no way Chrissy could possibly get Noah to just leave.

And, therefore, she wouldn't say what she had intended to say.

"So," Griffin said, apparently as aware of the situation as Vickie, "you were curious about us using hypnotism. You think you might know something that you don't know you know, Chrissy?"

"I just think . . . well, I mean, I guess the other woman didn't know she knew anything, right? It was Barbara Marshall? One day, we should have a survivor's group, maybe. I'm so sorry. And the latest victim . . . I don't know . . . how do you judge pain and fear and trauma? But for Fiona West . . . did she know she was walled-up with old corpses?" Chrissy shivered.

"Fiona hasn't been able to give us anything, I'm afraid. And she's still in the hospital," Griffin told Chrissy.

"Okay, so, would you like me to come to the station — and see the hypnotist?" Chrissy asked.

"We could have her come here for you," Jackson offered.

Chrissy flushed. "Oh, no. I can come to the station."

"Well, I'll let you figure all that out," Vickie said, rising. "Noah, I was hoping I could have a word with you, upstairs."

As she'd hoped, Noah glanced at her and nodded, assuming she wanted to talk to him about Dylan, and would not try to do so in front of his mother.

"If that's all right with you, Chrissy?" Vickie asked.

"Sure."

"Come on, cool, I'll show you my latest superhero action figures!" he told Vickie.

He headed out of the parlor and up the stairs. Vickie followed, desperately curious about what was going on downstairs, but glad to give Chrissy the opportunity to talk.

Apparently, Noah wanted to talk to her, too.

Dylan hadn't followed them; he was remaining downstairs.

At the door to his room, Noah looked back. He urged Vickie in, checked to see they weren't followed and shut the door.

"Vickie, I'm so scared."

"What is it, Noah, what's wrong?" she asked him.

"My mom, my dad . . . I don't know what it is. He never comes home anymore, Vickie. And my mom cries all the time. She hates it when Dad is out — and she seems scared when he's home. Vickie, they're not even sleeping in the same bedroom. They had one big blowout fight. Neither of them wants me to know, but . . . I may be a kid, Vickie, I'm not stupid."

"Oh," Vickie said. She lifted her hands, trying to make him feel better. "Parents fight sometimes. Mine fight, and they're like the two sweetest and most easygoing people ever. We might all think differently about a situation. And, Noah, this whole thing has the entire city on edge. Your mom . . . she was buried alive, Noah. She had to have been so scared. But I think her having us here . . . it will be good. She can come to the station and see the hypnotist, and when she's done, I'll ask Griffin and he'll see to it she gets some help, some counseling. I'll do anything I can for you, you know that."

Noah nodded, seeming a little relieved.

"Dylan is here. He's been with you," Vickie noted. "What does he say?"

"He's mad — he's mad at our dad."

"Oh?"

"For being gone," he says. "For not being around when we need him most. I think he wanted to follow dad." He giggled suddenly. "Actually, he tried to hit Dad the other day. It was funny. You could see Dad felt something, but . . ."

His voice trailed.

"We'll do everything we can," she promised him. "And," she added, a finger to her lips, "let Dylan know I'd like to speak with him. When you can, huh?"

"Sure."

"Noah?"

Chrissy was calling. Noah opened the door and yelled out.

"Yeah, Mom?"

"Vickie needs to go. We don't want to get her mom and dad worried, too — or ruin their dinner!"

"On my way down," Vickie said.

She hugged Noah fiercely. "You're a great kid," she told him.

He smiled. "You were always the best, Bick-bick. I love you, too, you know."

"Love you, kid!" she said, adjusting the baseball cap on his head. "And you call me anytime — about anything, all right?"

"Yep, I will," Noah promised.

Vickie hurried down the stairs. Chrissy, Griffin and Jackson were standing in the foyer.

Dylan was protectively close to his mother.

"We'll see you at the station, then, Mrs. Ballantine," Griffin said. "And thank you so much. Noah, cool to see you."

"You guys, too," Noah said.

Then they were out the door.

"So — so what happened downstairs?" Vickie demanded, the minute they were in the car.

"We're about two seconds from your mom's place," Griffin said.

"So, we'll talk there?" Vickie asked.

"Oh, no. No, no. We're going to have dinner. I'm not having the wrath of the Preston duo down on me," Griffin said.

"So, tell her. Just tell her," Jackson said. "And we'll talk after."

"Tell me!" Vickie pleaded.

Griffin sighed. "Chrissy Ballantine is suspicious of George."

"What?" Vickie said incredulously. "Of

him . . . cheating on her. Of . . ."

"She suspects him of murder — of having an affair, and, with his girlfriend, committing the murders," Griffin said.

"No! How, why? I mean . . ."

"Told you — two seconds to your mom's place," Griffin said, as Jackson parked the car. "We will talk later. For now, Vickie — so that your parents don't violently throw us onto the street — smile!"

CHAPTER TWELVE

Griffin tried to keep the conversation off the deadly situation at hand.

And for a few minutes, it worked. Lucy and Philip Preston greeted them at the door and offered drinks and their second round of snack food, cheese and meats and crackers and other little finger foods. They accepted pops, but declined alcohol — Griffin didn't want to be off in any way, even a hair. Jackson seemed to share his state of mind.

Lucy asked about Vickie's Grown Ups group and she told them cheerfully about the excursion that day.

"Not on your own, right?" Lucy asked sharply.

"I enjoyed every minute of it," Griffin assured her.

Lucy nodded. "And you, sir, Special Agent Crow?"

"Jackson will do just fine — I am, after

all, a dinner guest in your home, Mrs. Preston."

"Lucy should do then, too, just fine," Lucy Preston said.

"Well, I understand you actually live in the DC area now," Philip said.

"Northern Virginia," Griffin said.

"Nice area. But anyway, we wanted to treat you with a taste of home so Lucy has made her ever-famous New England clam chowder and we are having baked scrod *and* lobster tails!" Philip said, proud of the cuisine, as if he was announcing a win at an awards ceremony.

"Excellent," Griffin said, "thank you so much."

"Can I help, Mom?" Vickie asked.

"I think we're all set, table is done . . . just got to get our food out of the oven. Now, agents, I have to admit, I'm not sure this would be the most healthful meal! The scrod is lovely of course, but we do bake it with a butter and graham cracker crust."

"I'm sure it's going to be delicious," Griffin said.

"So much in life is absolutely delicious!" Vickie said, giving him a slightly mischievous look.

He kept his cool. He knew he cared about Vickie; really cared. And he knew she loved her parents — he was not getting himself into their bad graces.

"Scrod, always," he said pleasantly.

As it happened, he helped take the large tray of individual scrod dishes out of the oven; Jackson and Philip carried out sides and Vickie poured the drinks. And while there was talk of food and plates as they set up, they'd barely been seated and taken their first bites — applauding the meal, which was delicious — before Philip brought them all point-blank back to the kidnappings and the murders.

"We have followed every inch of the news," he said. "So, a couple. Amazing. Boston is full of couples. Sadly, we've also had our share of very bad people. The Boston Strangler. There was Alfred Gaynor, though that was out in Springfield. In recent history? Bombers. But even then, how do you see such a killer? With a couple . . . I see how people might not notice a nice young couple following them, but . . . how in God's name to you find out who they are? Do you start stopping every duo on the street?" He swung around to stare at Vickie, caught with a dish of slivered-almond green beans in her hand. "And you! What is it — how are you figuring out where these bodies are, and, Vickie, if you can do that, why can't you figure out who is doing all this and have these men arrest the crooks?"

"I, uh . . . Dad!" she protested. The dish landed hard on the table. "You're asking me? You and Mom are scholars — always with history. How do you think I come up with all this?"

She faced her father down pretty darned good.

He lifted his hands — and looked at his wife.

"We're just scared, that's all," Lucy said softly.

"Mom, we've established that," Vickie said. "And everyone is going to be scared until these people are caught. So, we're working as hard as we can in that direction."

Lucy looked from Jackson to Griffin. "I know we're coming across badly. We all know that your quick reactions years ago probably saved Vickie's life," she said. "And I guess . . ."

Her voice trailed. She looked at Vickie's father.

Philip wagged a finger at Griffin. "You just don't leave her. You just don't leave her — not even for a minute. Do you understand?"

Of course, it was really very serious.

And he nodded solemnly.

"Sir, I will not leave her."

Philip leaned back and looked at his wife. "So, we're fine. I told you, they're slee— told you they're together. I think they wanted to be before. I suppose this fellow does have some ethics."

"Dad!" Vickie protested.

"Vickie, dear, really, we're not living in the Dark Ages!" Lucy said.

"Well, let's get it all on the table. My point here is that, if you're *together* anyway, don't make it any kind of a part-time deal. You watch her. You don't let anything happen to her," Philip said.

"That goes for you, too, Jackson Crow," Lucy said.

"Special Agent Crow is married," Philip said.

"He'd better still lay down his life for my daughter!" Lucy said.

"Yes, ma'am," Jackson said.

Vickie groaned, flushing to a brilliant shade of crimson.

"He's got a wife," Philip said.

"This is what we do," Jackson told him quietly. "Angela would expect me to do no less."

There was silence for a minute. Griffin wasn't at all sure what to say.

Philip solved that for him. "Your intentions better be honorable!"

"Absolutely, sir," Griffin said.

"Well, we really should eat," Lucy said. "Mr. Crow — how's your scrod?"

"Delicious," Jackson said. "The best I've ever had."

Vickie looked over at Griffin and shrugged.

Dinner went on; the conversation veered from Massachusetts to Virginia, DC and the West; scrod and clam chowder and grits and tacos.

"Apple pie for dessert," Lucy announced. "Cradle of Liberty and all — American as apple pie!"

And so they enjoyed dessert and coffee, and then Jackson rose, thanking the Prestons for their hospitality and the delicious food — and once again avowing that one of them would personally be with Vickie at all times.

"And for the love of God! Take her to a shooting range. I was actually a crack shot with our skeet group years and years ago," Lucy said. "I'll bet she can be pretty good."

Both of Vickie's parents hugged her tightly.

Then, to Griffin's surprise, they hugged him. And then Jackson.

They headed back out on the street, to the car.

"So what now?"

"It's late. Bed. And we start again tomorrow."

"Bed," Griffin couldn't help but repeating, adding solemnly, "with a rather strange blessing from your parents."

"No, no, no," Vickie said.

"I just made a promise!" Griffin protested.

"Yes. No. I mean, what about George Ballantine? What else did Chrissy say to you? She really suspects *her husband*?"

"Let's get somewhere. I don't want to talk about this on the street," Jackson said.

"My apartment," Vickie said.

Twenty minutes later, Vickie was seated on her sofa, legs curled beneath her. Jackson was in the chair across from her.

Griffin was standing by the front window, looking out between the drapes.

"So?" Vickie persisted.

"It was strange," Jackson said. "Chrissy was so nervous and speaking so quickly — she was afraid Noah would come back down. She said George was behaving very weird — ever since they'd come home from the hospital. He'd leave early for work, and he'd call and say he was going to be very late. She called his office last night, and he wasn't there."

"So, he may be stepping out. Midlife

crisis, something like that," Vickie said.

Griffin spoke, still looking out the window. "She wants very badly to be hypnotized. She's thinking maybe she did hear or see something right before she was struck on the head. If she's hypnotized, she thinks she might know. As it is, she and George are sleeping apart." He turned to look at Vickie. "She's sleeping with her door locked. And she's afraid he'll eventually realize she's not just suspecting him of an affair — she's suspecting him of being a murderer, of trying to murder her."

"But . . . when Aldridge broke into the house years ago, they were both at a dinner. There were witnesses."

"Aldridge was evidently in the house before they ever left," Griffin said.

"Oh, no, no. I can see a man and a wife having problems — and we all know husbands have killed their wives and vice versa, but Noah was in the house! They both adore Noah. He was a miracle for them," Vickie protested.

"We're not telling you what is or isn't, Vickie. Just what Chrissy said," Griffin reminded her.

"And," Jackson said quietly, "we've already informed Detective Barnes and our local contacts — Ballantine will be watched now."

"Watched — and followed," Griffin added.

"Can't be, it just can't be," Vickie said. "Noah . . . This would be devastating for him. I mean if George proves to be guilty in any way . . ."

"It's a long shot," Griffin said. "At the moment, we can't let anything go."

"He had nothing to do with Aldridge being in his house, I'm certain. Even if Aldridge had gotten in before he and Chrissy left that day. I can't believe it. I won't believe it. He loves Noah," she insisted.

"And you're probably right," Jackson said.

Griffin came and hunkered down before her. "Vickie. We've still got nothing. We've got the dead, and we've got those we've managed to save. We think there's a connection between the murders that happened years and years ago, but what, we don't know. We believe a man and a woman are pulling this off together. We pull on every thread, no matter how fragile."

Jackson stood. "I'm heading out. I'll see you in the morning. Chrissy is coming to the station first thing. I figure you want to be there?" he asked Vickie.

"You bet," she said.

"No kids tomorrow?" Griffin asked.

"Next up will be the aquarium, two days," she said.

Jackson left and Griffin walked around, checking her windows, securing the door. Vickie watched him. "Is there still a man on the outside? I wonder what he thinks."

Griffin laughed softly. "Well, here's the good news — what he thinks doesn't matter. I have your parents' blessings. Go figure on that one!"

"I will admit they took me quite by surprise. But then again, they're 'not living in the Dark Ages, you know.' "

She smiled and turned, heading into the bedroom, stripping in a leisurely manner. She heard him follow, heard the gun and holster go down on the bedside table, and then he swept her up, and they fell, laughing, onto the bed.

It was still a wonder.

She was still in awe. Touching him was amazing.

Feeling his touch in return was the greatest eroticism she could imagine . . .

No, she'd never imagined something so wonderful, something that combined such combustion and fire and vitality with . . .

Such emotion.

It was new, of course. All new. And yet she was certain she'd never tire of him. Maybe when they were older. Or if they were exhausted after nights with a sleepless baby or running around after toddlers or . . .

She was way, way, ahead of herself. Of everything. And yet . . .

He lay beside her, arm draped over her naked torso. And she realized his eyes were open and he was watching her. He tenderly smoothed back a lock of her hair, fingers brushing over her cheek as he did so.

"It's amazing," he said.

She lowered her head quickly, suddenly a little afraid. She had now touched all this, known all this. Before it had been a back-burner dream, a memory of longing.

And now it was real.

"Well," she said softly, afraid to be too serious. "We . . . this . . . us together . . . is, after all, blessed in a very strange way. Fate, maybe? Oh! Or, did you just mean me? I'd like to think I'm good. Well, no, I'm a liar. It's just instinct. It's just . . ."

He swept atop her, lifting her face, meeting her eyes.

"People are lucky in life sometimes. They meet each other — it's right. And sometimes they meet each other but the time isn't right. When they're incredibly lucky, somehow, times goes by, and they meet again, and then they're very, very lucky in life."

She realized she was trembling when she reached up and touched his face.

"I'm incredibly lucky," she whispered. "And when I'm with you . . ."

"Everything else goes away," he finished softly.

"But it's always out there, isn't it? How do you do this . . . day after day? Always?"

"I'm good at it. And we save lives. And . . . now . . . there's you."

She didn't want to take that any further. Not at that moment. She didn't want to know anything about his past relationships or love life; there had certainly been one.

But at the moment, she couldn't even remember her own.

Because the past just didn't matter.

He lowered his head and kissed her slowly and tenderly, and the warmth and scent of him swept around her. The kiss was soft and gentle and seemed to speak volumes . . .

And then, of course, it changed. And it was passionate and as demanding as the one she returned, and then their hands and lips were all over one another's bodies and they made love again.

When she slept that night, she didn't know if she dreamed . . . or if an angel in white did drift silently into the room where the two of them lay tangled under their covers.

"Oh, I'm so sorry," the ghost seemed to murmur.

"Darlene," Vickie murmured, saying the name aloud.

"I will find you!" the ghost whispered. And then she faded.

At Vickie's side, Griffin stirred, but did not wake.

When morning came, Vickie was left to wonder once again if she'd been dreaming, or if the ghost of Darlene Dutton had stopped by, determined it was a bad time, and disappeared.

She hoped the ghost would come again.

Darlene had been the killers' first — they might not have been as organized. They might have made mistakes.

There was something . . . just maybe, Darlene might remember.

Chrissy Ballantine arrived at the station accompanied by a burly security man who had been hired by her husband.

The company was legit; Hard Core Security had high ratings by every possible measure.

Griffin knew for sure, because he verified all the information they'd received from headquarters, just as he'd made a point of researching Donald Baugh, one of the two men assigned the duty of watching over Chrissy and the Ballantine house.

Baugh had no problem sitting in the antechamber, drinking coffee and reading, while Chrissy joined him and Jackson, Detective Barnes and Vickie in the conference room. Baugh didn't even seem curious as to exactly why Chrissy was there; apparently, he hadn't been given instructions to question Chrissy's actions. His only job was to follow her and keep her safe.

According to Chrissy, she and Baugh — or Carl Lumley, the second man from Hard Core Security hired by her husband — went together to bring Noah to school in the morning.

They went together to pick him up in the afternoon.

They talked about it in the conference room while waiting for Lenora Connor.

"I feel good about the protection detail. The men are quiet. They call at night several times just to check on us, even though they've watched all the while. They watch over Noah and me, of course. My husband, George, is convinced no one would come after him. He's a man. And, of course," Chrissy said, "he's right. These people have only gone after women. And girls who have barely become women. My heart so aches for Darlene Dutton. She was so young —

and praying she might find something in life."

Chrissy still seemed nervous.

"I have been so privileged, in so many ways, I can't imagine life for that poor child. Not that I wouldn't have given anything we ever had if it could have . . . could have given me back Dylan!" she said in a whisper.

Griffin glanced at Vickie. She walked over to Chrissy and gave her a hug. "I know how much he loved you," she said.

Chrissy nodded and then frowned. "But you never knew him. We lived in New York before — before the accident."

"I've seen his pictures — the way he looks at you in family photos. And I know how Noah adores you, Chrissy," Vickie said.

"And we all die in the end!" Chrissy said. "So, you think I'll get to see him again?"

"Definitely," Vickie told her with conviction.

Chrissy smiled and Lenore Connor walked into the room with nice timing. She was calm and very pleasant, speaking easily with Chrissy and setting her at ease. She explained she didn't care if Chrissy sat or lay down, just as long as she was comfortable.

There was something just amazing about the woman's tone of voice, Griffin noted, admiring her ability. The rhythm and cadence of her tone were more soothing than many a sedative, he was certain.

He realized everyone else in the room breathed, opened their eyes, and looked at one another now and then — all to keep from falling beneath the woman's spell themselves.

"First, Chrissy, we're going to go back a few years. It's winter. You and your husband are going to a business dinner. Do you remember anything special about that night?"

"It was cold," Chrissy said.

"And the dinner?"

"With Mr. and Mrs. Schwartz. Barney Schwartz is a banker."

"And the house, what about the house that night, Chrissy?"

"Noah was playing . . . even little, he had imaginary friends. He was so delightful. He laughed so very often. I hated to leave him. I hated to leave at all. But . . . we had Vickie. She was good with Noah. Noah loved her. It was all fine. It was all fine until . . ."

She broke off; her eyes were closed, but her brow was puckered with a serious frown, and she was evidently distressed.

Lenore gently set her hands on Chrissy's. "It's all right. It's in the past. You're safe.

349

Noah is safe."

"They called us. We went straight to the police department. Noah was there and I held Noah and I was grateful, of course, that Vickie was okay, but . . . Noah. Noah was what mattered."

"Your husband was with you all the time?" Lenore asked her.

"At dinner, yes . . . not before. He . . . came home just about an hour before it was time for us to get ready and go to dinner."

"Was he different in any way? Concerned, anxious?"

"No, just . . . in a rush."

"Okay, Chrissy. It's okay. Noah was fine. Vickie was fine. But then, just a bit ago — you weren't so lucky. You were buried alive in your own cellar. You're fine now — you're safe. But do you remember being buried?"

"I couldn't move — I could barely breathe. I felt the world pressing down on me. I saw blackness, so much blackness . . . and earth. I could smell the earth. Musky. The scent was so strong."

"What happened before that, Chrissy?"

"I was in the kitchen. I don't know. There was something. A little noise. I don't think it even registered in my mind. George . . ."

Lenore glanced over at Griffin. He gave her a small nod.

"What about George?" she asked gently.

"He often comes quietly into the kitchen. He likes to come up behind me, slip his arms around my waist. I thought it was George. I was sure it was George. I was evening smiling . . . and then . . ."

Chrissy stopped speaking, her voice breaking away in a whimper.

"And then?" Lenore said.

"The pain! The pain."

"Your head — you were struck in the head. You probably fell. Do you remember any scents, and sounds, people speaking, voices?"

"A woman," Chrissy said. "I think . . ."

"Yes?"

"I think she's the one who hit me. And someone whispered it had been too hard. And she said no, and really, what difference did it make? And he said I wouldn't know the darkness, wouldn't fear the coming . . . and then, then I smelled the earth, I felt such a sensation of the earth. And darkness, terrible ebony, such darkness and a miasma . . . death."

Chrissy began to twitch. Lenore made a sharp sound, snapping her fingers. "Everything is okay, Chrissy. You're okay. You're with us, here now, safe and well."

Chrissy's eyes flew open. She looked

around at all of them — they were all still watching her, perplexed — and wondering.

"It was George, wasn't it?" she asked, tears spilling from her eyes.

"Not necessarily," Griffin told her gently.

David Barnes shuffled his feet behind Griffin and he glanced up; Barnes was ready to bring George Ballantine in for questioning — maybe not a bad thing.

Griffin looked at Jackson to see if they were in agreement. They were. Jackson and Barnes left; he and Vickie stayed with Chrissy and Lenore.

"Even with hypnotism, Mrs. Ballantine," Lenore explained, "we can entwine what we expect with what really happened. You thought your husband was behind you, but that's because you always had the sensation it was George when someone was behind you like that in your kitchen."

Chrissy looked at Vickie and Griffin, her expression a little desperate.

"So, I didn't help. I didn't change anything," she said dully.

"You helped tremendously," Vickie said with assurance.

"How?" Chrissy asked.

Griffin stepped in. "You've helped solidify a point, Mrs. Ballantine."

"Chrissy," Chrissy said automatically.

"Chrissy, we know two people were in your house. We had been told that one of the two killers is a woman, but now, that's a certainty — two witnesses have identified a female voice. You've helped tremendously," Griffin assured her.

"But I haven't helped myself!" Chrissy said thoughtfully. "I'm either the biggest fool in the world, or I've destroyed my marriage with horrible suspicions and distrust." She started to cry softly.

Lenore patted her hand. "We all have doubts," Lenore said. "You're being way too hard on yourself. Mrs. Ballantine, you've been through incredibly trying situations — you were nearly killed. You're really an incredibly strong woman."

"You are, Chrissy," Vickie assured her.

"But what do I do?" Chrissy whispered. "Go home — sleep in the house with a man I believe to be cheating on me at best, killing people at worst?"

"Chrissy, let's think on that for a bit. It's early. Detective Barnes is making arrangements now to have a question-and-answer session with your husband," Griffin told her. "For now, you're safe to go home. We'll have an officer on with the guard from Hard Core Security — and we have vetted him, Chrissy, he's a good guy, truly bound to protect you. We'll be watching George, and we'll talk to you before the two of you are back together. Unless, of course, you feel really uncomfortable going home. And if that's the case, we'll make other arrangements for you."

Lenore stood and smiled at Chrissy. "Trust in these people. They're good cops and good agents. And don't worry about yourself. Not that a good therapist wouldn't help. I can leave you my card and you feel free to call me for help, okay?"

"Thank you," Chrissy said, accepting the card.

Griffin thanked Lenore; they all bid the hypnotherapist good-bye.

"Should we make some temporary living arrangements for you, Chrissy?" he asked.

Chrissy shook her head. "I'll be fine going home. I don't want to Noah to think his mother suspects his father of . . . of trying to kill her. I have to be crazy. I have to be all wrong. I mean, he couldn't have known Bertram Aldridge — I know he wouldn't have let him into our house to hurt Noah! I'm so sure of it," she finished softly, almost as if her assurance was really a prayer.

"I can go with Chrissy and hang around with her," Vickie offered.

He stared at her, arching a brow. "I rather

made a promise I'd be with you," Griffin reminded her quietly.

"Yes, but that doesn't mean every second of every day. I'm sure it does mean you wouldn't dream of leaving me unprotected, but I won't be. I'll be with Chrissy and Noah. And outside will be one of Boston's finest, and Donald Baugh. And you won't be long," Vickie told him.

Griffin heard the steel in her voice. She was determined. And she was right.

He nodded. "Chrissy, you'll be okay with Vickie?"

"I would love to have Vickie with me!" Chrissy said.

"Then that's it. We're off," Vickie said cheerfully. "And you get to go be an agent, hopefully find out what is going on and let Chrissy have some peace! Remember," she added quietly, "George Ballantine does know you from before. He'll be more comfortable with you there."

She was right again.

"I'll get Baugh and he'll see you both to the Ballantine house," Griffin said.

"I feel so bad," Chrissy said.

They were sitting together in the back seat of Donald Baugh's plain black sedan.

They were being followed by an officer in

an unmarked blue Volkswagen Touareg.

Chrissy was still restless and shell-shocked.

Vickie didn't try to suggest Chrissy shouldn't feel badly. She had nearly been killed; she didn't trust the man she loved, the man who should have been making it better for her, day by day.

"Chrissy, there really may be a completely plausible explanation for George's behavior. He may feel guilty himself, Chrissy. Men can be strange."

"There's an understatement," Chrissy said.

Vickie smiled. "I mean as in, going way back in human evolution. Men were the hunters, women the homemakers. Men were the protectors. Maybe he's going through something himself because he blames himself for what happened to you. Maybe he was careless with the lock and the alarm."

"He's horrible. I do always have to remind him. Of course, he's been better — way better! — since the attack on you and Noah all those years ago. He's just preoccupied so much of the time. Business and investments. But . . . he is still a good-looking man. And he's got confidence, an aura of power. Women like that. He could be having an affair. With someone younger. Someone young and beautiful," Chrissy said. "If I'm lucky," she added with a whisper, "it's just someone young and beautiful, and not someone young and homicidal."

"Chrissy, George is very good-looking. But you're an extremely lovely and charming woman. I swear to you, that's true — I'm not just trying to make you feel better. But right now, you don't know anything."

They stopped at a traffic light, near the Paul Revere house and Chrissy's own home. Vickie looked out the window, watching the mill of people thread through the area.

"No, I don't know anything," Chrissy said. "Which might make me the horrible one. I'm just so lost right now — so afraid."

Vickie started to respond to her, but her words suddenly stopped.

For a moment, she hadn't realized just what she was seeing. A handsome couple stood just down the street from the ticket booth and entrance to the Paul Revere house. They were a very pretty couple, he tall and blond, she tiny and golden. At first, they were just smiling — looking up into one another's eyes.

Then, they kissed.

And then, Vickie got a good look at the man's face, and then the woman's.

She gasped aloud.

The woman was Roxanne, her best friend . . . who never picked the right man.

The man was . . .

Hank Fremont. Hank, suddenly back in Boston from the western section of the state. Hank, who had claimed to be in love with a new woman, the right woman for him, who made him follow the straight and narrow. But he had said her name was June Jensen . . .

And it was no old-friend-sisterly kiss he had just shared with Roxanne.

"Vickie, Vickie, are you all right?" Chrissy asked anxiously.

Vickie turned to her. She shook off her surprise.

"Um, yes, sure, of course. I'm sorry. I drifted there."

"Poor thing, you must be exhausted, helping the police and all," Chrissy said. "And with having to work — although, you might make enough off royalties for your old books to live okay. But I guess you love your work? I'm rambling. You're exhausted and you must be starving, and I'm rambling."

"I'm fine," Vickie assured her.

It was fine; it was great if Roxanne and Hank had found some kind of happiness together.

But . . .
Why were they both lying to her?

George Ballantine hadn't wanted to come in at first; he'd suggested that it was a bad time.

Barnes had told him that it had to do with his wife and the safety of his family; put in that position — unless he wanted to look like a heedless ass guilty of something — he had little choice.

He was led to the conference room. Barnes and Jackson sat on one side of the table, George Ballantine was at the end and Griffin sat next to him across from the others.

"You know, I am a busy man," he told them apologetically. "And in my life . . . there's just been so much upheaval. I feel like a hamster on one of those wheels, just running and running."

"Boston isn't much different than New York City huh? Mile-a-minute pace?" Griffin asked him.

"Not all that different, no," George agreed.

"I guess you knew that when you moved up here — your family did stretch back to the south side of the city," Jackson said.

"Huh?" Ballantine said, frowning.

"Oh, come on. Surely, you know your family lived here back in the 1800s," Griffin said.

"Tough times, back then. Hey, that's when those grisly murders happened — when those people were shut up in the Pine house, where we found Fiona West," Barnes said.

Ballantine lifted his hands, as if truly baffled. "Yeah, I had family back here, my dad's side. I grew up in the city — the city meaning New York City. My mother's people came to the east from Colorado. What does my background have to do with any of this?" he asked.

"We're just curious. Because Bertram Aldridge came from South Boston. You didn't happen to know him at any time — before he broke into your house? He did break into your house — you didn't just let him in?" Griffin asked.

Griffin watched the man. He's reaction didn't seem feigned. His eyes popped with surprise.

Then he frowned.

Then he grew angry.

"What?"

"We have to ask these things, George," Griffin said.

"Routine, of course," Barnes said, using

his best by-the-book detective voice.

"Routine?" George Ballantine seemed to growl the word, but his voice was low, as if he hadn't really had the breath to shout. He shook his head. "You're accusing me of letting a serial killer into the house where my baby was playing? Are you daft?"

"Okay, George, we know you've been through a lot. We think you're a good man," Griffin said. "So, what the hell is going on with you? Your wife almost died. And suddenly, you're out at all hours. You don't come home. What's up?" Griffin asked.

"What? You've been following me?" Ballantine asked.

"Not as well as we should have been," Barnes muttered.

"George, talk to us," Jackson said.

The man shook his head, bewildered. "I'm not a killer!" he protested. "You can't really believe I would . . ."

"Your wife was found in your own house, George," Barnes reminded him.

"You were there. You were the one who called it in," Jackson reminded him.

"I never knew Bertram Aldridge. I never let him into my house. If anything . . ."

George's voice trailed.

"If anything, what?" Griffin asked quietly. George Ballantine's head suddenly dropped into his hands.

The man sobbed.

"It was my fault. It was all my fault!" he said.

Chapter Thirteen

When they reached the Ballantine house, Vickie's mind was still plagued by the deception being played on her by her friends.

It made no sense.

Why didn't they just tell her the truth? She and Hank had been over nearly a decade ago! As far as Roxanne went, her friend was known for picking the wrong guys, but from what she had seen and heard from both of them, Hank Fremont was on his way to improving his position in life. And she had never been enemies with either of them; she and Hank hadn't had any kind of a tumultuous split. High school had ended; they had gone their own ways. And she had stayed friends with Roxanne all through her years in NYC, even if it had been mostly through emails and social media and the occasional visit.

She wished Dylan was here, but she

hadn't expected him to be at the house. If he hadn't been with his mother, he was probably doing his ghostly best to stand guard over his brother.

"Vickie? Tuna sandwiches okay for lunch?" Chrissy asked.

"Lovely," Vickie assured her. "Will you excuse me for a minute? I'm going to call my mom."

She did so, thinking it would be a very good thing for her parents to be reassured earlier, rather than later. She told her mother that she was at the Ballantine house, that Chrissy wasn't doing so well and that a policeman and an armed private security guard were right outside.

"I guess we can't stop Griffin from doing his job," her mother said. "As long as he trusts the cop and the guy outside, right? I watch TV. I know cops can be dirty."

"Don't worry, Mom. Griffin and Jackson and their people are thorough. They check out everyone," she assured her mother.

Was that really true? She didn't know. It sounded good at the moment.

"I'm so sorry for Chrissy. She's having trouble bouncing back from the attack?" Vickie's mother asked her.

"Yes, but I think she'll go into therapy now. That will help," Vickie said. She hesitated. She was an excellent researcher — it was one of the things she did, along with trying to make sure she strung together what she learned with entertaining words.

She was really good at researching the past.

That should mean she could research the present just fine, too.

"Mom, I don't remember if I mentioned this when we were at dinner. Did you know Hank Fremont was back in Boston?"

"Oh, Lord above us!" her mom said. "Vickie, you're not thinking about . . . Hank?"

Vickie laughed. "No. I'm sleeping with an FBI agent — with your blessing, remember?"

"Ouch, oh, daughter dearest! Must you be so blunt?"

"Hey, you were the blunt one. You weren't born yesterday, remember?"

"Okay," her mother said softly, "so I'd much rather you have a healthy sex life that I know about rather than lie awake each night worrying. Of course, I'd like it best if you just came home, you know."

Vickie laughed. "Not too cool. I think that would make you and dad uncomfortable!"

"Ohhhh . . . so! What about Hank, then?"

"Did you know he was back in town?"

"No. We were kind of friendly with his parents, but they moved to South Carolina years ago," her mother said. "I heard he was doing okay, though. That he was working — at a real job with prospects. I never particularly thought he was right for you, but I think he's a decent enough human being these days."

"Yeah. I'd like to think so," Vickie murmured.

"Why? Has he been bothering you? If so, I'll call that G-man new guy of yours myself and see Hank leaves you alone!"

"Mom, he hasn't bothered me in the least. Through the years, though, you've stayed kind of friendly with my friend Roxanne, right?"

"Of course, darling, she was always one of your best friends. If you recall, Roxanne was over here on Christmas Day. Oh, and we saw her at church on Easter and went to brunch with her after the services. You know she's a sweet thing! I worry about her, too."

"Yep. Okay. So, I'm with Chrissy, and two good guys with guns. Talk to you tomorrow, all right?"

Her mother agreed. Vickie hurried back into the kitchen, hoping to catch Chrissy in time to stop the tuna sandwiches.

"Chrissy!" Vickie said.

Chrissy started, dropping a can of tuna.

"Let me get that!" Vickie said, hurrying over to fetch the fallen tuna. "Would you mind, I'd like to see a friend who owns a great Italian restaurant, Pasta Fagioli. Do you think we can get Donald and the cop to go to lunch with us?"

"Go to lunch?" Chrissy said.

"Yes, just go out to lunch. I'd like to see my friend Mario for a minute."

"I . . ."

"Going out will be good for you, and Noah isn't due home for hours, right?"

"No, we leave here to pick him up right at three. He hates it, of course. Prefers to hop the bus and walk with his friends. He's such a good kid. So wise beyond his years! He knows we might still be in danger, and so he just bites down hard, forces a smile and does what is needed."

"Noah is extraordinary," Vickie assured her. "I'm going to step out front. Donald will be right there and I'll tell him we want to go out."

She didn't know if Mario would be able to tell her anything about Roxanne and Hank, but he did seem to be her best hope.

Although . . .

She didn't know why it bothered her so much.

They were lying to her.

They were apparently a couple.

And they both knew the city of Boston like the back of their hands.

No. She was becoming as paranoid as Chrissy.

And still . . . Like Chrissy, she had to know the truth about the situation.

Because, hopefully, the truth was far better than where her imagination and suspicions were taking her.

George Ballantine was a big man, tall and fit, and customarily friendly but dignified.

At the moment, he was anything but.

The big man sobbed.

"It was me," he wailed. "It was me."

"You and a mistress did commit murder?" Barnes asked, completely thrown by the confession.

"What? No, no. Murder — me? No, no, I just caused it all."

"George," Griffin said, keeping his tone at a low, even keel. "You didn't kill anyone, but you think you caused it all."

"Before the breakout — before Bertram Aldridge and Reginald Mason broke out of prison — I was part of a service club. You know, we're the guys who wear the funny hats. There was a meeting because one of our members was an attorney who had been asked to do a write-up on the state of our prison system, the pros and cons of the death penalty, and so on. I wound up doing the main work on the letter to the parole board. In my summations, I quoted cases in which the death penalty might be a proper punishment — because our prisons seem incapable of keeping people in. Well, in the end, there were all these papers and write-ups flying through the state legislature. One of the prison wardens wrote a scathing return on how the system was completely capable of keeping men incarcerated." Ballantine exhaled on a long breath. "You see?"

"You think that Aldridge and Mason broke out — just to spite the man who wrote the rebuttal?" Jackson asked, frowning. He leaned forward. "Aldridge is a sick man. A serial killer. Ballantine, you didn't turn him into a killer. Most men in prison dream of escape. The clever ones study every way possible and look for any chink or weak link in the system," Griffin told him.

"If you're blaming yourself for Aldridge, Mr. Ballantine," Jackson said quietly, "you've taken your assumed power of persuasion as far too great a burden, sir."

"Not even I hold you responsible for that," Barnes muttered.

"It's more than that," Ballantine said.

"Did you put your wife into the pit in your basement, Mr. Ballantine?" Griffin asked him.

"No! Oh, God, no!" Ballantine said.

"Do you know who put your wife in the pit in your basement?" Jackson asked.

"Of course," Ballantine said, distracted.

"Of course? Then who the hell was it?" Barnes demanded.

"The Undertaker! Hell, we all know that. The Undertaker — or the Undertakers!"

Griffin saw the weariness that shook Barnes and the frustration on his partner's face.

Yes, of course, they all knew that.

"Mr. Ballantine," Griffin said, "I'm finding it hard to believe your guilt is just over Aldridge's escape. Your wife was nearly killed. She needs you, and, apparently, you disappear for hours. You don't come home when you should."

Ballantine nodded. "Yeah, well, I sit in Boston Common," he said.

"Why the hell are you doing that?" Barnes demanded.

Ballantine suddenly looked at Griffin. "I'm not having an affair. I didn't kill anyone. But what happened to Chrissy was my fault. She could have died because of me. I'm sure as hell not having an affair now, but I was! It was a younger woman. There was all the talk about the dead women on the news. I was shaken up — couldn't help but remember Aldridge, and from the beginning, his name was in the news, comparisons to the last such case to shake Boston and all. I don't know what hit me. Midlife crisis? There's an excuse that truly sucks. I love Chrissy. I've always loved her. And I adored Dylan, like I adore Noah now. I was out — I was out when Chrissy was attacked in our own home. And I'm the one who probably forgot to set the alarm, like I forgot to set it years ago when Aldridge was in the house. I don't know what or why, and I don't know how to ask for forgiveness. Maybe I can't. She's gone. She's out of my life. I cut it off, but it didn't matter — I think she was through with me, too. Got tired of her older man. Thing is, I was a wicked good liar when it was all going on, and now I can't stand what I did, and maybe I was off with this woman — having forgotten to set the alarm — and caused Chrissy to be attacked. How low could a man be?"

"You know we'll have to check this all out," Griffin told him. "What was the woman's name?"

"What?" Ballantine said.

"The young woman you were seeing. What is her name?" Jackson said.

"Oh. June. June Jensen."

"Where does she work? What does she do?"

"She's an artist. I met her sketching in the park," he said.

"And where does she live?" Barnes asked.

"I — I don't know. We met at a hotel off of Beacon Hill," Ballantine said.

"Do you believe this shit? I don't think I believe this shit," Barnes said.

Ballantine just shook his head. "I don't care what you believe. I can only imagine what Chrissy believes. And Noah . . . I don't know what happened. Honest to God, I just don't know what happened. I never even thought of straying before."

Barnes shoved a notepad toward Ballantine. "Hotel name, dates and times you met — and a description of June Jensen. Her phone number, please."

Ballantine wrote it all down. Jackson stepped aside, took out his phone, and dialed the number that Ballantine wrote down.

Griffin looked at him as Jackson waited. He hung up without speaking.

"No connection — pay-as-you-go phone.

We can put the techs on it, but . . ."

"It's been tossed. It's going to be in a Dumpster somewhere," Griffin said.

"What? She's real, I'm telling you — June Jensen is real," Ballantine said.

"She is — and somehow, Mr. Ballantine, she was using you. We really do have to find her," Griffin said.

He didn't add that if they did . . .

They might be on their way to solving the puzzle.

June Jensen could be just a woman who had chosen to indulge in an affair, using a throwaway phone and what idle time she had. Maybe she was in a bad marriage, maybe she'd gotten out of a bad affair.

And maybe she was one of the Undertakers, and she had used Ballantine. She had gotten to know him; she knew when he was out, when he worked . . .

And maybe she even knew he always forgot to set the alarm.

And just when his wife might be alone.

Pasta Fagioli was busy, but Mario greeted Vickie at the door. He had never actually met Chrissy Ballantine, but he was great with her, not betraying in the least that, of course, he'd heard of her — she'd been all over the news several times.

Mario found a table for Chrissy and Vickie.

And he found a strategic spot for Donald Baugh and their cop, as well. Chrissy wasn't worried in the restaurant; the Undertakers snuck up on people. They took them by surprise.

Like old friends kissing in the street.

The problem was, of course, she didn't get a minute to speak with Mario alone. Maybe by the time they left, the lunch crowd would thin out.

"This is one of the best Italian restaurants in Boston, I swear," Vickie told Chrissy. "I think Mario's dad was born here, but all four of his grandparents were born in Italy, different regions, and so the restaurant offers specialties from Rome, Naples, Tuscany, and so on."

"How nice."

"All the pastas are homemade," Vickie told her.

"Do you think my husband has come here without me?" Chrissy asked.

"I have no idea," Vickie said flatly.

There was a couple at a window table; the man was older, the woman much younger — by at least twenty years. Chrissy was staring at them.

"I'll bet he's someone's husband. And

she's just after his money," Chrissy said.

"They could be father and daughter, Chrissy," Vickie protested.

The man gave the young woman a box. She opened it and looked up at him with shimmering eyes of delight.

"See," Chrissy said.

"A present for a daughter, Chrissy. It happens. I go out with my dad. He's bought me great presents over the years.

"Sure."

The young woman leaned forward; she kissed the man.

"That kiss is on the lips," Chrissy said. "Oh, and will you look at that? Lots of tongue going there with that kiss, too. Father and daughter?" she asked Vickie.

"I certainly hope not," Vickie said.

Taking Chrissy out to lunch was not proving useful.

But then the door out to the street opened; Hank Fremont walked in. He was alone.

"Isn't that the guy you were dating in high school, Vickie?" Chrissy asked. "He really was so good-looking back then. He's matured okay, but he's young for all that puffiness in his face . . . kind of drawn-looking and all. Sorry. Guess I'm in a bitter mood."

"It's okay."

"Your other friend Mario seems to be asking him to wait . . . there are no tables now. Why don't you ask him over here?" Chrissy suggested.

"That's okay —"

"Really. Ask him over. You don't want to see him just standing there, do you? Ohhhh! Especially because, look now. Mario is pointing us out to him."

And Mario was. Mario waved to her, and then Hank, looking hopeful, waved to her, too.

She waved back.

Chrissy smiled and waved, making a motion to indicate that he should come over to him.

Hank did, thanking Mario before weaving his way through tables filled with diners to reach them.

"Ladies, good afternoon."

"Hank, you remember —"

"Mrs. Ballantine, of course. It's a pleasure to see you."

He didn't ask her how she'd been doing. Maybe he didn't want the answer.

"And you, too, Hank. Have a seat," Chrissy said.

"Thank you. It's really kind of you to share your table," he said, drawing out the chair between them at the four-top to join them. "Mario has been doing great things with this place. I believe it has raves in all the tour books — great for business, hard on locals and friends!"

"I haven't been in here before," Chrissy said. "But Vickie says it's wonderful."

"How's everything with you, Hank?" Vickie asked. She realized that Hank, too, was staring at the couple by the window, the older man, the younger woman. "Tell Chrissy about what brought you back to Boston."

Hank drew his attention from them to look at Vickie. He smiled. "I'm working for a relatively new and small company called Great Organics. I believe in the product. I've been out to some of the local farms. Yes, we in Massachusetts can have wicked bad winters, but we have really lush earth, too — pristine forests, though that doesn't really help me a lot — but some great growing conditions. I'm happy."

"That sounds wonderful," Chrissy said. "No pesticides, right?"

"No chemicals — great scarecrows. Kind of fitting with New England, too, right?"

They were chatting with one another — and glancing at the couple by the window now and then.

For a moment, Vickie thought something tensed in Hank's face; as if he experienced a moment of true anger — but quickly got it under control.

"They're something, huh?" Chrissy whispered, seeing where Hank's attention had been.

Hank gave a little shiver, shaking his head and turning away completely.

"Ugh, right?" Chrissy said, possibly thinking George Ballantine was out somewhere, looking much like the older man here — not so great with eye candy on his arm, but rather sad as people around him wondered just how much money he had in his bank account.

"Yeah, sorry, who am I to judge?" Hank said.

Chrissy gave him a brilliant smile. "Sometimes we can't help it, right?"

"I think your 'ugh' kind of summed it all up," Hank said. "Maybe it's not the age difference. I think it's just obvious . . . I mean, that's prostitution, really. Sex for money or gifts or power or whatever. I'm sure I've known people with large age differences who are really in love. I just don't think that's the case."

"So, what do you think he does for a living?" Chrissy asked. "And where do you think he's from? I don't think he's local. White area where his wedding band should be. He's probably a salesman."

"I beg you, don't judge all salesmen harshly," Hank said.

The two of them seemed to be enjoying themselves, playing their create-a-scenario game. Vickie interrupted to ask them to order the eggplant parmesan for her, and then she slipped from her seat, heading toward the host stand.

She didn't see Mario at first; he was in the hallway to the kitchen, leaning against the wall. He saw her and flashed a smile. "You doing okay, Vickie?"

"Fine, how about you?"

"I need a breather. No, a smoke. I should have quit. I've mostly quit. Is there such a thing? Anyway, come with me, if you can. I want to step out for a cigarette."

"Sure," she said.

She stopped by the table Donald Baugh and the cop were sharing to point just outside. The cop said he was trying to quit, too, but maybe he'd have a cigarette.

"Don't make guarding me cause you to pick up a bad habit again!" Vickie begged.

"Wish I could blame it on you," the young cop said, grinning. "I can use the air. Donald will order for me and watch over your table." He grew serious. "You do know the man who just joined you?"

"Old high school friend," she said.

Did she know him? Not really, it had been years.

She knew he was a liar.

Mario was waiting for her by the door. She slipped out to join him.

"Thanks for the company," he told her.

"You must be wiped out all the time. The restaurant is crazy busy."

"Yeah, I done good, huh?" he said lightly. "I always wanted to be in the business, too. I love going back in the kitchen when we need a cook. I remember thinking once the only thing I wanted to do was get away — be somewhere new and cool, be *someone* else, maybe. You know, I majored in this, right? I hadn't even known you could major in being a glorified host, really."

"School of hospitality, down at FIU, right?" Vickie told him. "And, yeah, you done good. It seems now most of us are, at the least, still standing, which is good. I had a roommate from an inner-city school who had lost ten of her classmates to gun violence, drugs and alcohol, or vehicular accidents before her first day of college. I know Roxanne's ex, Trent, is doing time, but hey, look, Hank never did time, and now he's back — thrilled with his job."

"Yeah, and the stuff he's selling — it's just

prime!" Mario said.

"You did check out his business, right?"

"Locally owned," Mario told her. "And the company doesn't discriminate against Rhode Island, Connecticut, New Hampshire or any other state. But they really work to provide the freshest, cleanest produce from the state of Massachusetts."

"That's nice. I'm glad he's happy. What about this June Jensen he's dating?"

"I think I saw her once," Mario said. "Actually, I think he was trying to get her to come in here for lunch. She ran off on him."

"Ah, so she is real!"

"Did you think she wasn't?" Mario asked, and then laughed softly. "Forgot what a thing you two had been. Yeah, I guess he'll always have a thing for you. But no, I think he really is seeing a pretty young woman."

She'd gotten nowhere, Vickie thought.

"I'd always thought, now that Hank is so on the up-and-up of life, I kind of thought it would be cute if he and Roxanne got together. They'd make a gorgeous couple," she said.

"I guess they would. A blonde goddess for a blond god." Mario grinned. "Maybe it will happen. Who knows — you're right. It might be great for both of them. If, of course, Hank is the right guy, now. Roxanne is such a great person. I guess we have to sit there like a pair of yentas and hope that they see it, figure it out — and that it is right!"

Mario walked away to crush his cigarette out by the Dumpster behind the restaurant. Vickie waited for him. He grinned, took her arm and told her, "Thanks, Vickie. Thanks for the support. We've been written about for helping out with Grown Ups. We wouldn't have been involved, if it weren't for you. Not that our food isn't great — it is. But hey, that's life. Publicity and name recognition — name of the game. So thanks."

"Absolutely, my pleasure."

"Might want to wave to your cop — let him know we're going in."

Vickie waved.

When she returned to the table, their food had been served.

Hank and Chrissy were talking away as if they were very old friends.

Maybe they were closer than Chrissy knew. Maybe Hank had slipped into the Ballantine house with his accomplice — the mysterious June Jensen, or Roxanne? He had strength. He could easily have knocked her out and dragged her around, buried her.

And maybe . . .

God, no. Not Roxanne. Roxanne had been her friend as long as she could remember.

Then June Jensen.

Thing was, what was up? Was Hank cheating on June with Roxanne . . .

Or cheating on Roxanne with June, or was it all part of a plan that was yet to be fathomed?

And maybe it was all totally innocent.

Vickie knew that Chrissy and Hank both seemed to be happy through the meal. She was pretty sure she smiled and replied and spoke at the proper moments.

Finally, they were handed a check. Hank insisted on getting it.

They rose to leave.

Donald Baugh and the BPD cop rose to leave.

They all said goodbye to Mario. As they stood on the street — the cop nearby as Baugh went for his car — Hank looked back toward the restaurant.

"That wasn't . . . that wasn't June in there, was it? With the older gentleman?" Vickie asked him.

"June?" Hank asked her, startled.

"June Jensen, the woman you were dating. I'm sorry — I could be way off, but I thought someone mentioned to me the fact you two had broken it off," Vickie said.

"Dear, I'm so sorry!" Chrissy murmured.

Hank studied Vickie speculatively. "We did break up. Well, I don't know if you can call it a breakup. She just . . . she just disappeared out of my life. Funny thing, she was never on Facebook or any other social media. I had her phone number. I guess she was just done with me. The number she gave me is disconnected."

Was he watching her to see if she was suspicious? Or because he was really curious as to how she knew what was going on in his life?

He smiled at her. "But it's okay," he told her. "It's really okay. Somehow, I know I'm going to be okay."

Baugh was there with the car. Hank moved in to give her a hug goodbye. She pretended she didn't see; she hopped into the car.

Chrissy Ballantine stepped into his arms for a big hug.

They both waved from the car and started the drive back to the Ballantine house.

"Too bad that young man didn't seem to have it together before, when you were young," Chrissy said. "Seems like he's coming along. But . . ."

"But?" Vickie asked.

Chrissy grinned. "I always liked that cop-turned-agent," she said softly. "Griffin

Pryce. You could see it in his eyes — he really cared what happened to people. He cared about you, and he cared about Noah. And I admit, well, I guess you know — I wanted to blame this on you somehow. I needed to blame someone. I'd had a perfect world — it was completely destroyed when Dylan died. Then, somehow, God gave us Noah. And I had a perfect world again. Then you and Noah were nearly killed, and it was as if we went through this period of waiting, almost as if we were underground. It wasn't terrible — I wasn't aware of it all the time. We had Noah. Nursery school and kindergarten and grade school. Christmas shows and Easter dramas — he made the best carrot ever, once! But you know how cicadas go to sleep for years and years and they're suddenly up and flooding the region again? It's as if we were asleep. As if we hid from the danger for years — but it was always there, underground, waiting. Anyway, thank God for you — and Special Agent Pryce and that lovely therapist, Lenore. I am strong, and I am going to make it. But the evil has been there all this time — and if the evil is George, then damn him to hell, and if it's not, then God forgive me. Odd, though, I have this strange sense that it really is coming full circle — and that, for whatever it might cost, we are reaching the end."

Vickie looked at her. She'd never heard such a long speech from Chrissy Ballantine; she'd never imagined what was going on in the woman's mind.

But then, it was always so hard. Knowing what someone else was really thinking.

She squeezed Chrissy's hand. "You're very special, Chrissy. Noah is lucky to have such a great mom. So was Dylan."

Chrissy nodded. "Sometimes . . ."

"Yes?"

"I just wish I could see him one more time. Dylan, that is. Just one more time so that I could tell him what a great kid he was — what a wonderful, caring, giving adult he would have proven to be. Is there a Heaven, Vickie, do you think?"

"I'm sure of it," Vickie said. She lowered her head, wondering why it was she could see Dylan so clearly — that Noah could see him, had even seen him when he'd been an infant — and Chrissy, who longed to do so with all her heart, could not.

When they reached the house, Vickie saw that Griffin and Jackson Crow were seated on the porch; they quickly rose as Baugh drove the car into the porte cochere, waving and walking around to meet them at the kitchen door.

Chrissy Ballantine was quickly out of the car, rushing up to the agents before opening the door.

"Did you talk to him? Oh, God, is George a killer? What's going on? You did find him, didn't you?" she asked.

"Shall we go inside?" Griffin asked her, glancing over at Vickie as she got out of the car, and nodding to Baugh.

"Inside? Yes, sure, but . . . is he a killer?"

"Chrissy, we don't believe George is a killer," Griffin said.

"No?" Chrissy asked, fumbling with the lock.

"No," Jackson said as Griffin took the keys from her to open the lock.

Chrissy fumbled to put in the alarm code. "Come in, come in — I lock up and put the code in right away. He's not a killer. He's just a . . . a louse? I love George. If he were a killer, though, I'd help see him fried or locked away forever, I promise. But . . . okay, yes, let's sit. The parlor. Far more comfortable there, less awkward. Can I get you something? We just ate. Vickie's old flame was there . . . he was very nice, had a lovely time with him. But have you all eaten? What can I get you? I'm doing all the talking. I want you to be talking."

"We'll go sit. Come on," Griffin smiled at her, such a gentle smile. She loved the way he could be so hard when necessary — but so kind to those in distress.

He looked at her curiously, arching a brow.

He wasn't the jealous type, she didn't think. He was more curious.

Hank Fremont — showed up at your lunch? he seemed to be wondering.

She shrugged, and they all headed into the parlor.

Chrissy looked at her watch. "Two o'clock," she said. "We have a bit of time before picking up Noah. I've tried really hard to keep my thoughts and feelings from him, but . . ."

"He's a smart kid. So, here's our suggestion," Griffin said. "Talk to your husband. He went through a few bad times of his own. We're going to be investigating George's friends and business associates, but one instinct you've had has been right all along — George would never hurt Noah. He would never willingly do anything that would hurt Noah."

Chrissy swallowed nervously and looked down at her hands. "But he was cheating. You can't say that, because you're agents."

"We can't say things your husband needs to say to you because it wouldn't be right,"

Griffin said quietly.

"George needs to speak with you. He will. In fact, I believe he'll be here soon," Jackson told her. "I think you're both good people. I hope you figure things out."

He had barely spoken before they heard the kitchen door open and close. They heard the little pings the alarm gave off when it was being reset.

"Chrissy? It's okay," George called. "It's me!"

"In here, George," Chrissy told him.

George Ballantine walked on into the room. The man looked as if he'd been crying.

He glanced at Jackson and Griffin and then Vickie, and he nodded an acknowledgment to them.

"Thank you," he said softly.

Then he walked over to where his wife was seated and he went straight down on his knees, burying his head in her lap.

"Forgive me. If you can't forgive me, I beg you find a way to go on and be happy. Oh, Chrissy, I am so, so sorry."

Chrissy set her hands on her husband's head. She looked across the room at the three of them, baffled, grateful.

"I forgive you, George," she said softly.

"Chrissy, you don't even know what I did!"

"You didn't kill anyone, George. I forgive you."

"But . . . I . . ."

"I always wondered what I'd feel, if and when something like this happened," Chrissy said. "I know now. I still love you. We've both hurt. We've both managed different ways. You can tell me everything, but you don't have to. Truth can hurt."

"Chrissy, yes, there was a young woman. When I was with her, I could forget . . . I could pretend. But not really. So help me God, I could never forget that I love you."

Griffin rose and Jackson and Vickie followed suit.

If there had ever been an exit line, it seemed George Ballantine had just uttered it.

"We'll see ourselves out," Jackson said.

Chrissy nodded. "One moment — just one moment," she said.

Griffin, Jackson and Vickie headed to the kitchen.

"Give them that minute," Jackson suggested.

They waited in the kitchen. Shortly, Chrissy came in, smiling. "Ah! The Justice League!" she teased. Then she hugged

Vickie and then Griffin and Jackson. "Thank you," she said. "Thank you."

"None of this is over. Please take extreme care," Griffin said.

"Yes," Chrissy whispered.

They went out.

Chrissy locked the door. They heard her set the alarm.

They headed to the car. Vickie went to the back seat immediately. She could look through the bucket seats that way, listen to and speak with both of the men.

"So?" she demanded, as Griffin geared up the car. "George is innocent. You've proven him innocent? But you're watching him. So what is going on?"

"George had an affair," Jackson said.

"Not a good thing, but not something I believe the FBI would usually find to be earth-shattering?" Vickie asked.

"We think he might have an affair with the wrong woman," Griffin said.

"Oh. You mean . . . ?"

"We think she might have been one of the Undertakers," Jackson said.

"Ah. But . . . how? Why? Oh, okay, so this woman is one of the Undertakers. And you think she got close to George and learned about his house and how to get in? I guess that's possible, but what about the women who were kidnapped before? Do you think she had affairs with other husbands, too? Barbara Marshall isn't married. Her guy is in the military."

"I think the Undertakers are ice-cold killers," Griffin said. "I think they used whatever machination would work for them in any situation. But this woman he was seeing doesn't seem to exist. We ran the name, but eliminated everyone we found. She didn't have email, or an address other than a hotel — the hotel where she met up with George. Oh, and where she got him to make the arrangements and use his credit card. Her phone was pay-as-you-go with no way to trace it. She was seeing him . . . and then she disappeared. He'd told her it was over, so he hadn't thought anything about it. He said she understood. And then she disappeared. A godsend for George. But we can't find her — or a trace of her — either," Griffin said.

"Police and home office are still trying every angle," Jackson told her.

"What was her name? Or what name did she use?" Vickie asked.

"June. June Jensen," Griffin said.

Mario's wonderful eggplant parmesan seemed to erupt in Vickie's stomach.

"June Jensen?" she repeated.

"Yes." They'd reached her complex. Griffin pulled the car to a halt, turned off the ignition, and it seemed his head nearly spun as he turned to look at her.

"You know her? You know this woman?" he asked incredulously.

"No. But I know someone who does."

CHAPTER FOURTEEN

They made it to Vickie's apartment, inside, doors locked.

And then they talked.

Vickie paced as she told Griffin and Jackson about her afternoon with Chrissy.

"You know Roxanne Greeley," she said, looking at Griffin.

"Of course. Your best friend. You've known her since you were kids," he replied.

"So, I'm driving with Chrissy and I look out the window and there — right in front of the Paul Revere house — is a couple, and they turn out to be Roxanne and Hank Fremont," Vickie said.

"Vickie's old high school flame," Griffin said to Jackson, who just nodded.

"But they knew each other all through high school. Why was it unusual that they were on the street together?" Griffin asked.

"They weren't just together. They were *together,*" Vickie explained.

Griffin and Jackson glanced at one another. "Maybe . . . maybe something is going on between them," Jackson said. "Is there a reason there shouldn't be?"

"Yes. No. Oh, God, don't look at me that way!" Vickie exclaimed. "Trust me, it has nothing to do with me being jealous. I knew years ago Hank Fremont was welcome to the best life he could have — as long as it was without me. But the thing is, I don't know why they lied to me. The last time I was with Roxanne, we were commiserating over her lack of talent in picking good guys."

"Maybe Roxanne is worried you would be upset," Griffin suggested.

"No, no, you're missing the whole thing here. Sure, that's possible, even though Roxanne seems delighted you're in my life, Griffin, which, one would think, would make her ready to spill the truth immediately. It isn't Roxanne who actually lied to me or — I should say — gave me a totally different story. It was Hank. He came to see me — you know that, Griffin. You saw Hank."

"Yes, so . . ." Griffin said.

"He told me his life was going great. He'd met the right woman. She brought out all the best in him. He was happy — moving forward," Vickie said.

"Roxanne is your best friend," Jackson reminded her.

"No, no — Hank told me the name of the woman who had brought out the best in him. He told me that her name was *June Jensen.*"

"We need to speak with Hank," Griffin said. "Now. Do you have a phone number for him? An address?"

"No. But we can call Roxanne," Vickie said. "I'm assuming she knows where to find him."

"You're certain they're actually seeing one another?" Jackson asked her.

"Their tongues were down in each other's toes — yes, there's something more than a friendship going on. Oh! I took Chrissy to Mario's restaurant. Hank walked in while we were there. I didn't ask him point-blank then — I went to talk to Mario because he's worked with Hank through his business. He's working for something called Great Organics. Mario buys produce from the company through Hank."

Griffin glanced at Jackson. "It's a real company."

"If a restaurant has gotten produce, yes," Jackson agreed.

"Anyway, I asked Mario about Hank, and — as far as Mario knew — Hank was still with that woman, June Jensen."

"Let's find Roxanne, and then we'll find Hank," Griffin said. "Call her, please."

"And what do I tell her?"

"That you need to speak with her. Find out where she is," Griffin said.

He felt his phone buzzing in his pocket; he saw Jackson was reaching into his pocket for his phone as well.

It was a message from Detective Barnes.

" 'New clue to papers — we've got another victim,' " Jackson read aloud.

He started dialing Barnes.

Griffin read the text that followed.

1721, Puritans slipping, but hanging around.
The dead are quickly filling the ground.
The talkers are a mix. Oh!
Doctor, doctor, give me a fix. Let not the church prevail.
Bumps here and there, pustules everywhere.
Like a bell you'll hear me wail.

"Vickie?" he said, handing her his phone so that she could read the message.

She glanced at him, and then glanced at the text, her features tense.

"In 1721, there was a horrific smallpox

epidemic here, right?" he asked her.

She nodded. "Yes, and it was the first use of vaccinations — different from today, of course. They made a cut on the person to be vaccinated. Then they smeared it with — or kind of inserted — the pus from someone infected . . . sometimes right from the bodies of the dead. I was actually just reading something about this because of the Puritans in Boston. Ben Franklin was actually a kid back then, working for his brother's paper. He was right around fifteen, I think. He made up a name when he was writing. There were some people who thought that inoculating people was like murdering them. Others, desperate, thought they had to try anything. It was pretty amazing — led to a lot of what we do today."

"Okay," Jackson said, returning his phone to his pocket and looking at the two of them. "I'm going to head to the station and meet up with Barnes."

"Obviously, we have to get on this immediately," Griffin said. "But we need to find June Jensen, too."

"Barnes is sending a sketch artist out to the Ballantine house, then we'll have something to go on. Still, it would help to locate Hank Fremont and find out what he can tell us," Jackson said.

"All right — Vickie has her books and computer and everything here," Griffin said. "She can call Roxanne, and see if she can get her over here. Then, while we're waiting, we can work on the latest clue, while you connect with Barnes and see what you can find out about the most recent victim. We need to confirm we even have one, because if the clue is in . . ."

"Then a woman has been taken," Jackson said. "Let's do it."

He headed for the door and was gone.

Griffin looked at Vickie. She pulled out her phone and called Roxanne.

"Hey," Vickie said.

He watched as she listened, spoke and listened again.

"No, I kind of need your help with something. No. No, I'm at home. You're close? That's great." Vickie looked over at Griffin; he could hear Roxanne speaking, and then she stopped. "Okay, seems we're on the same track today, huh. Anyway, thanks so much — see you when you get here."

She hung up and looked at Griffin. "She's with a group of kids. They just finished up for the day. She had them sketching on the Common. She'll be here as soon as possible." She shrugged. "Roxanne said she wanted to talk to me, too."

"Tell you about her and Hank?"

"Maybe."

"Okay, so, back to the clue," Griffin said. "It refers to the great smallpox epidemic of 1721. Puritans — and people dying."

"Okay, by then the initial charter had been pulled. The Puritans were still a major force, but a new church was being built by a more liberal group. Ben Franklin was born into a Puritan household, but as he came to adulthood, he was definitely one of our first liberals — he was a deist. He believed in a greater power, but also in reason and science and the arts and all that. Of course, he was still a young man, and 1721 was a year when everything was changing, people were beginning to rebel against the authority of the crown . . . and, of course, there was the smallpox outbreak."

"It was common knowledge then that those who had suffered from the disease and survived were immune to it in the future, right?"

Vickie nodded. "I was never a fan of Cotton Mather — I mean, really! His stance on witches! But it's true that, after all that happened, his life pretty much sucked. Bit by bit, he lost influence, lost his position at Harvard . . . lost most of his children. But he was a supporter of the inoculation. He did study medicine at Harvard, but the idea of inoculation came from one of his slaves, Onesimus, an African. There was a huge controversy between the physician, William Douglass and Cotton Mather. Anyway, Douglass had been educated in Edinburgh and argued that they didn't know what they were doing and would kill more people than they would save. But there was a local doctor, Zabdiel Boylston, who was in favor of inoculating. Remember the times — a lot of people believed smallpox was God's way of punishing people for sinning — and taking any information from someone from Africa was like dealing with heathens and the devil."

"Okay, what about this Zabdiel Boylston?" Griffin persisted. He looked at his phone and read aloud:

" '1721, Puritans slipping, but hanging around.
The dead are quickly filling the ground.
The talkers are a mix. Oh!
Doctor, doctor, give me a fix. Let not the church prevail.
Bumps here and there, pustules everywhere,
Like a bell you'll hear me wail.' "

"Okay, so Cotton Mather wasn't doing so well . . . once the witchcraft trials became an embarrassment, his hold on his congregation began to falter. And Zabdiel Boylston had to hide in his own home — both men were attacked. But . . . 'Like a bell you'll hear me wail,' " Vickie said.

"A church?"

"Not a current church," she said thoughtfully. "Cotton Mather was the minister of the Second Church at the time, and the Second Church changed buildings and areas many times over the year. But back then . . ."

She paused, hurried to a table, and flipped open one of her books. She turned back to stare at him. "Yes! It was in North Square. Originally Clark's Square — changed in the 1700s. Part of the Freedom Trail now. In old pictures, you can see how it was just down the street from the Paul Revere house."

Griffin didn't have a chance to reply. There was a knock at the door. Griffin glanced through the peephole; it was Roxanne.

He let her in.

"Hey!" she said, looking at him oddly. Griffin realized Roxanne hadn't expected to find him there; maybe she'd come to tell

Vickie about her new relationship, and had thought she'd have some private time with her friend.

"Hey, Roxanne, please, come in. We're hoping you can help us," Griffin said.

"Oh?" Roxanne looked warily from Griffin to Vickie.

Vickie didn't waste time. "Roxanne, we need you to tell us where to find Hank."

"What? Ah, me? I — uh . . ."

"Roxanne," Vickie said. "I think it's great you two are together. But we need to find Hank. It's really important."

"He's . . . he's supposed to be at my place tonight around seven. I'm not sure where he is right now — he's working," Roxanne said. "But . . . how . . . I feel like an idiot. I wanted to tell you, but it was all so strange and so fast! I was feeling badly for him . . . the new girl, the love of his life, was suddenly gone. He said she disappeared into thin air! He was really hurt, thinking she'd been playing him all along, using his money, asking about his past, telling him that she'd make everything right, and make him right, and then . . . then she just disappeared. Her phone number was no good. And she stood him up, and then stood him up again. So, the two of us were just there, in the Common, watching kids play and people walk and I held his hand, and he looked at me, and . . . it's just awkward, because at one time he was so crazy in love with you."

"We were kids then!" Vickie said. "Oh, Roxanne, don't be silly, please! I'm happy if you're both happy."

"We really need to see him. Is there any way he can see you sooner?" Griffin asked.

"I can call him," Roxanne said. "But what do you want me to say? I can tell him it's important you talk to him. I'm sure he'll come quickly, then."

"Just ask him if he can meet you now. It's critical," Griffin said.

Roxanne put through the call. She looked at Griffin warily as she spoke, but she didn't say anything about Griffin, the police, the FBI or anything else.

She had just finished her call when Griffin's phone rang; he excused himself to answer it.

Jackson was on the other end.

"We've got our missing woman. Gail Holbrook, twenty-nine, mother of two. She failed to show up to pick the kids up from school this afternoon. The school called her husband; he got his kids and headed home and found the back door ajar — and a bunch of groceries on the floor in the kitchen," Jackson said. "Any progress on the clue?"

"Vickie seems to think North Square — near the Paul Revere house, and again, near the Ballantine house. The Second Church — Cotton Mather's church — used to be there. It was there during the time of the smallpox epidemic," Griffin told him. He lowered his voice, walking away. "We have Roxanne here. She's gotten Hank Fremont to head to her house, now. Hank is a question mark in this thing himself. He's back in town right when all this goes on. He knew Vickie — Vickie had been with him — she rejected him. He has to know this city right and left."

"I'll get down to North Square with Barnes and get a host of cops down there with me. Go ahead and meet up with Hank Fremont. See what you can find out. When you can, bring Vickie and get on down to meet me."

They rang off. Vickie was looking at him.

Roxanne was staring at him nervously, too.

"You don't think Hank . . . oh, no, no, no!" Roxanne said. "No — I, uh, I've um, I've been with the man! He can't be part of any of this."

Griffin smiled grimly at her. "Roxanne, we're really trying to find out more about June Jensen. We're hoping he can help us."

"Oh. Oh, well, she does sound like an evil witch — bitch witch. Wicked mean, getting Hank to fall for her and all and then just disappearing."

Roxanne was speaking too quickly. Either she was nervous about Hank herself, or she was nervous about their business with him.

But she sighed. "Okay, well, he's coming to my place. Now."

"Okay, let's go."

They were talking about a matter of blocks from place to place; Griffin suggested they walk — it would be as quick as anything else. Both women agreed.

As it happened, they neared Roxanne's apartment from one end of the block as Hank was approaching from the other.

Griffin wasn't sure — did Hank see them and give a little pause?

The man's schoolboy smile was quickly in place as he hurried forward to meet them.

"Roxanne, you didn't tell me that Vick and Special Agent Pryce were with you."

"I didn't? I'm sorry, Hank. Really," Roxanne said. "They needed to talk to you."

"Oh?" he said, not flinching, just appearing puzzled as he looked from Griffin to Vickie.

Roxanne turned and fled up the steps to her building. "Did you want to come in?"

"Sure," Griffin said. He lifted his hand, indicting politely that Hank should go first.

The man did.

A few moments later they were all seated in Roxanne's small parlor. Her building, like many turned into apartment complexes and condos, had been built in the late 1800s. It was small, and the parlor was planned around the fireplace and the old carved mantle.

"Ah . . . sit down?" Roxanne asked. She sat herself; she almost seemed to plop into one of the old chairs that was part of her sofa grouping.

They all joined her. Hank was on the chair next to Roxanne's. He seemed to be sitting on the edge of the chair. He was smiling, still. A ploy to cover his nervousness?

"So, what do we need to talk about?" he asked. He glanced over at Roxanne. "Okay, okay, so we should have spilled the beans really quickly. Roxanne and I are seeing each other. But you two are seeing each other, right? I mean, the moment you walked into Vickie's life, I was a goner. That's all in the past. All silly. Oh . . . This isn't about Roxanne and me seeing each other, is it?"

"No, it's not," Griffin said.

"Then . . . hey, my business is solid. I

work for good people, and I work hard and I do a good job," Hank said.

"No one is questioning your business," Vickie said quickly.

"We need to know about June Jensen," Griffin said.

Hank's face seemed to darken and pinch. "She's not a good person," he said.

"But what can you tell us about her? Where does she live? What does she do?" Griffin asked. "How can we find her?"

"You said she had family in the western area of the state — out where you'd been working," Vickie said. "And she works for an ad agency."

"I didn't meet her out in Springfield," Hank said. "I met her here. In Boston. I'd applied for and gotten the job with Great Organics and moved back here. About two months ago. I met June when I literally crashed right into her one day."

"Where was that?" Griffin asked.

"Actually, it was right outside of Mario's place," Hank told him. "I knocked papers out of her hands and I picked them up. And we were both laughing and I asked her if she'd like to have drinks. Then I apologized and kind of stumbled over myself, thinking she might be married or have a boyfriend. But she said 'Sure.' She said she'd been out of the city for a while and just taken a job with an ad agency. She was glad to have a friend for drinks. We had drinks, two nights later, we had dinner. And then . . . it went from there."

"So where was she living?" Griffin asked.

Hank knotted his fingers together. "I don't know. Crazy, huh? But she had some kind of a magic to her. She said she had room-mates — it was best to meet at my place all the time. She was . . . yeah, I guess magic is the right word. She was encouraging. She listened to me. When we talked, I'd go all the way back to my childhood, and she'd just listen and never judge. She was so cool."

"What about Facebook or email?" Vickie asked.

He shook his head. "We never emailed. We called or texted one another. And she told me she loathed social sites. She wouldn't go on one."

"And you've tried calling her on the number you had, right?" Griffin asked.

Hank nodded. "Disconnected. She just disappeared. She smiled one morning and left and said she'd meet me later in the Common. I sat there for hours. She didn't come back. I tried it again and again . . . and then realized she was just done with me. I was sitting there one night when

Roxanne came and listened to me . . . and she touched me and . . . well, Roxie is real. Solid and real and we know all about each other, the good and the bad — we've known each other forever!"

"Hank, we'd like to send a sketch artist here," Griffin said. "Are you willing to help?"

"Of course!" Hank said.

Griffin rose and Vickie quickly followed his action. Roxanne and Hank rose as well.

"You think this woman has done something?" Hank asked. Then he let out a whistle. "Oh, my God! You think she might be the woman who is part of that killing team, the Undertakers?

"She's not that big — I mean, she may be cold when it comes to dating, hell, I didn't find out all that much about her, though she found out just about everything regarding me. We talked about what was happening, of course, I mean . . . everyone talked about it. A woman had already died when we met, maybe two of them . . . I don't really remember now. But Aldridge's name came up, and I talked to her about what had happened to you, Vickie, at the Ballantine house and . . . oh, God! But no, she couldn't be. I mean, she was pretty, vivacious, fit, yes — but she was no hulk! I can't see her putting a body anywhere, honestly."

"Maybe her partner is big," Vickie said quietly.

"Oh, no, no, no! Don't look at me like that. Vickie, for the love of God, I might have been a selfish creep in high school, but you can't believe I'd kidnap or kill anyone!" He turned and looked at Roxanne and his look of loss and hurt appeared to be very real. "You can't believe that of me. Oh, Lord. I would never hurt anyone. I'm a big jerk trying to fix my life, not a murderer."

"Hank, as I said, we need to find June Jensen. You weren't the only man that she was seeing. She wasn't with you every night, right?" Griffin asked.

"No. Like . . . every other night. Sometimes two in a row . . . and sometimes she couldn't see me for a few days," Hank said.

"I need the phone number you used for her," Griffin said.

"I told you — the number is disconnected," Hank told him.

"I need the number anyway," Griffin said.

"Well, it's off my phone now. I mean, I was angry with her, and after I realized what I was feeling for Roxanne . . ."

"Do you remember the number?" Vickie asked.

He was thoughtful, then slowly said the

phone number. Griffin quickly took it down. He compared it to the number that George Ballantine had given them for June Jensen.

It was the same.

He looked at Hank, who was still staring at him like a kid in the principal's office.

"She also used this number with another man, Hank. One way or the other, you're well rid of her," he said softly.

Hank slipped an arm around Roxanne. "Don't I know it!" he said softly.

Griffin wasn't certain if Roxanne appeared to be assured or not. Her eyes were wide as Hank hugged her and she stared at Griffin.

"For now, I'd actually like Roxanne to come with us," Vickie said. "We're doing some Boston research. I could use her help."

"Ah, sure. Do you need me?" Hank asked.

"Just Roxanne," Vickie said.

"Oh. Okay," Hank said. He moved away from Roxanne. "Call me?" he asked her.

"Of course — as soon as we're through," Roxanne said.

"Hank, may I have your address?" Griffin asked. "We need to send out a sketch artist. This could be very important."

Hank glanced at Roxanne. "Of course. I want to do anything in my power to help the law in any way I can." He rattled off his address; like most people in this area, it wasn't far. Not even a half a mile.

"I'll be there," Hank assured them.

"Thank you," Griffin said.

Hank left first. When he did, Roxanne spun on Vickie. "How could you? Oh, my God, how could you? Things were suddenly going good for me. I believed that . . . we were old friends. We seemed to be perfect together. He's working — he has a good job."

"Roxanne, I didn't tell you that you had to go with us," Vickie said. "There is no evidence Hank did anything. He was simply with a woman who has been behaving very strangely — and doesn't seem to really exist. I — I just wanted to give you an out if you wanted one."

"I don't know what I want — I don't know what I think or feel," Roxanne said. "I want to cuddle up in the dark and pray you find who is doing this and prove that Hank isn't involved. And, then, of course, Hank will trust me because I didn't trust him now!"

"Go, please. You don't really need me. And I'm serious. I want to go into my room and curl into a ball for a while. Please. Just leave me alone for now," Roxanne said.

"Roxanne, I'll get a man outside your door. Just in case."

"Just in case Hank comes back? But I'm in love with him!" Roxanne said.

"Just so you'll be safe, whether Hank comes back or not," Griffin said firmly.

Roxanne appeared stricken still.

But they had to leave.

They had to get to North Square.

More and more, Griffin was convinced the murderers were playing with Vickie; she was the one who was going to have to figure out the answers.

Roxanne nodded miserably. "I don't know what to do. I want to call him back. I can't believe Hank could hurt people," she said.

"We can't stop you, Roxanne. Whatever you choose to do, there will be an officer outside your building, all right?" Griffin asked.

Roxanne nodded. Then she let out a wailing sound again. Vickie hugged her; Roxanne held still for a minute and then hugged Vickie back.

Griffin caught Vickie's hand, finally getting her out the door.

"There is a woman who is dying — we have to go," he told her, once they were outside the door.

"I know. Hey, there is no policeman out here," Vickie said.

"But there will be," he assured her, calling

414

Barnes to ask him to send someone.

"Come on," he said to Vickie.

"The cop isn't here yet," Vickie said firmly.

"She can't really be that in love with the guy yet!" Griffin protested.

Vickie very slowly and pointedly raised a brow to him.

"All right, all right, we wait for the cop."

They did — luckily, it wasn't long.

They hurried to the North Square area.

When they reached it, at least a dozen police cars were already lining the street. Griffin showed his credentials to get through. On the corner, he met up with Jackson and Barnes.

"What did you get from Hank Fremont?" Jackson asked.

"Our June Jensen is the same woman who was seeing George Ballantine. Disappeared in the same way — same disconnected phone number." He turned to Barnes. "Can you send an artist to this address? We'll get sketches from both men, see how they compare — and get the picture out in the press," Griffin said.

"Right away," Barnes said, taking down the address. He lifted a hand, calling over one of his officers, but before the man could reach them, he turned to Vickie.

"North Square. Down the street from the

Paul Revere house. Near the Ballantine house. You've got the Pierce-Hichborn house right next to the Paul Revere house. You've got the Mariner's House, still operating as a hotel, but that's later, right?"

"Yes, 1800s," Vickie murmured.

Griffin watched as Vickie slowly looked around. She looked from house to house down the street.

"We've got people going through the historic houses — management couldn't be more helpful — everyone wants this stopped. But you're free to go in anywhere you like, anywhere you think you may know something that someone else doesn't, or might feel something, or . . . anything," Barnes finished lamely.

He turned to give the information regarding Hank and the sketch artist to one of his officers.

Vickie still stood in the street.

"Anything?" Griffin asked her softly.

"I know the church stood there," she said, pointing.

"They've contacted the building manager. He's on his way," Jackson told her.

"I keep thinking they find something different every time," she said. "A Dumpster, a grave, a wall . . . Chrissy Ballantine's own basement floor. This will be different. Not a forgotten grave on church land, not a wall . . ."

She pointed suddenly, just half a block away, on the street.

There were two barricades by the side of the street; they had been drawn there when road workmen had finished for the day.

"What about . . . under the pavement somehow? People were just working there, right?"

"A cable line was dug up in the area recently," Barnes said.

Vickie started walking that way.

For a moment, Griffin watched her go.

He felt something in the air, like a wisp of cloud. It slowly materialized.

He saw it was the young woman in white. Darlene Dutton.

Vickie seemed to start; to turn and see her. And, though he was now some distance, he was certain the ghostly apparition spoke, and Vickie heard her.

He hurried to catch up with Vickie.

As he did so, the very ethereal image of Darlene Dutton began to evaporate, and to disappear entirely.

"Vickie, hey!" he murmured, catching her arm.

She turned to look at him. "She tries so hard . . . she can't seem to form words, and she can't seem to stay, but she tries so hard to help. She may not always be seen or heard, but she is watching and listening as much as possible, as often as she can. She said smallpox, Griffin. 'Remember, it was smallpox!' "

"Does that mean we should be looking at Zabdiel Boylston?" Griffin asked.

"I don't know, Griffin, I don't know. Boylston is buried in the Walnut Street Cemetery, in Brookline. I don't think she's going to be that far, but I don't know — they left victims out of the city before."

"They talk about the waning of the hardcore Puritans. The year 1721 is considered to be the year the Age of Enlightenment began to arrive in the Americas. Hardcore Puritan — Cotton Mather?" Griffin asked.

Vickie nodded. "Definitely . . . the son and grandson of hardcore Puritans. Beyond a doubt. And it all began to wane, and he really lost his position in life. But Darlene referred to smallpox and . . . oh, Griffin!"

"What?"

"There!"

Griffin turned in the direction Vickie was pointing.

A line of old broken road stones was piled up and surrounded by barricades — and a circle of rounded "no parking" stones.

In the waving light, they appeared to be a pile of . . .

Pustules!

"Do you think . . . ?" Vickie asked softly.

"Yes, I think," he said.

Barnes came striding over to them, anxious. "Beneath those cement elephant turds?" he asked. "Hell, yeah, they look like giant pus caps in the shadows there."

He hurried on ahead of them, shouting for officers to help him.

Griffin caught Vickie's hand and they hurried after Barnes.

Jackson and a dozen police left their positions and hurried over as well.

Bit by bit, they dug through the pile.

Old paving stones were hurled aside as well.

Beneath it all was an old ice box, a chain wrapped heavily around it.

Small! Griffin thought. *Good Lord, too small to hold a human being.*

The box was locked, and by the grunts of the men trying to move it, apparently heavy.

Someone hurried over with a large bolt cutter and broke the chain around the box, then they nearly tore off the door.

Stuffed inside in a grotesque twist of humanity, there was indeed a woman.

CHAPTER FIFTEEN

Griffin and Jackson had gone on to the hospital; as impossible as it had seemed, fire rescue had moved in, gotten the folded and twisted body of Gail Holbrook out of the small box — and discovered that she was alive. Her pulse had been faint; her air so nearly gone. Had they been as much as another five or ten minutes in finding her, one of the young EMTs had told them, she wouldn't have made it.

"As it is, she's got a dislocated shoulder, cracked ribs . . . not sure what else," he told them. "Maybe it's a darn good thing she was knocked out cold — and, as far as I can tell, she didn't regain consciousness. If she's lucky, she'll never remember how she was in that box."

Forensic crews were going over the scene.

With all the commotion, Vickie was afraid she'd be in the way. She knew the cop assigned to her — same guy she'd had the day she'd met the kids at Mario's after they had gone to the Paul Revere house. He was young and sharp and she thought he seemed good at his job.

Griffin, of course, had wanted her to stay with him, telling her that she was making him one hell of a liar.

Truth was, as much as she wanted to be with him, she needed time alone. She wanted to go back over what she'd read about the murders in the south side in the late 1800s. And, she hoped maybe, if she was alone, the ghost of Darlene Dutton might appear again.

The cop accompanied her into her apartment; as Griffin always did, he went through the apartment room by room, and reminded her to lock the door once he was out. She thanked him and did so.

When he was gone, she headed for her desk — but then veered into her room, finding nightclothes and heading on into the shower. The street had been dusty and dirty, and the fall of steaming water was delicious.

She half expected the ghost of Darlene Dutton to appear in the mist of the bathroom after her shower.

Darlene did not.

Refreshed, she headed out, made tea and went straight to her desk.

Vickie logged on to the internet and looked up the pages that had been written about the notes in the diary of the nineteenth-century cop, Joseph MacDonald. Only two people had actually been mentioned by name — Mary, the prostitute. Flannigan, the day laborer. Then, of course, he'd talked about the doctor who had just disappeared.

She was actually reading over the notes when she noticed she had messages on one of her social websites. Some were from friends, a few were from her Grown Ups kids.

The notes from the kids were nice — they were mostly thank-yous.

But there was another note, and that one excited her. It was from Alex Maple.

"Hey. Alex Maple here," it read. "Would love to meet with you." He'd left a phone number.

She drummed her fingers on the table. It was late now; she figured she'd call him first thing in the morning. She wrote a note back to that effect. There was no reply. Morning would be good. She wasn't even sure what she could glean from him. The murders had happened so long ago. The dead were in the hands of scientists; they would receive decent burials. Eventually. They couldn't be avenged; it was far too late.

They knew George Ballantine's ancestors had lived near the Pine house. They knew Bertram Aldridge had come from the area. The police had positively cleared Pine himself of wrong-doing. What else could they learn?

She wasn't sure.

But as she stared at the screen, she felt a presence, and she turned. Darlene Dutton was there. She appeared more solid than she had on the street.

"Hello," Vickie said very softly.

Darlene nodded, a sad smile on her lips.

"You saved her," she said softly.

"Darlene, were you there? You were right — we wouldn't have found her without you, you know," Vickie told her.

"I'm so glad to have helped!"

"But how did you know where she was? Did you see them put her there?"

"I only saw the man leaving."

"What did the man look like?" Vickie asked, hopeful.

But Darlene shook her head. "He was wearing blue, I know that. Blue jeans and a Harvard sweatshirt. The same sweatshirt every tourist in town seems to wear. I didn't see his face. I didn't even see the color of his hair, and I didn't know what he was doing at first. I had come to the corner . . . I guess I was there because I had loved the Paul Revere house so much. And when I saw you . . . I figured you knew the woman was somewhere near and I'd seen the guy there, and those cement things looked so much like pustules . . . But I couldn't seem to stay. I couldn't seem to speak. I'm so glad you found her. So glad."

There was a knock at Vickie's door. Darlene immediately began to fade.

But it wasn't a hard knock; it wasn't a real knock.

"Darlene, please, please stay. It's Dylan. Dylan, come on in!" Vickie said.

And Dylan appeared. For a moment, the image of Darlene faded.

Then it solidified.

"Vickie, they thought my dad did it! Okay, so I know he strayed. But . . . you know? Thank you! They made up tonight. I mean, I didn't hang around for the whole thing, but you should have seen my dad. I never saw him so humble in my life! So good to my mom, really. And she's the best person in the world. She forgave him." He suddenly seemed to realize that Darlene was in the room. "Hi, Darlene," he said softly. "Did you know anything, did you see anything?"

Darlene managed another sad smile. She

repeated what she'd told Vickie, and Dylan listened gravely.

"Ah. But Vickie, my dad told a cop what the strange woman — June Jensen — looked like. It sounds as if she may be involved."

"Maybe. I know the police have another person who knew her. Between the two images, it's likely they'll get something useful!" Vickie said.

"I'm going back to my house," Dylan said. "I just wanted to check on you. I'm not ignoring you, Vickie, I swear. It's just that my family . . ."

"You do need to watch over your family, Dylan. Noah — Noah needs you now," Vickie said. She smiled. Her ghost was apologizing to her for not "haunting" her. Nice.

Dylan stretched out a hand to Darlene. "Want to come with me? We'll just check up on my house and then maybe, if you can, walk around the area. See if we can find anything that might help as well."

Darlene looked at Dylan's hand for a minute. "I'm not . . . I'm not good, like you are, at staying . . . at staying around," she said.

"You'll learn. You're really great!" he told her.

Darlene took his hand.

Dylan looked at Vickie again.

"I'm okay. Go."

The two of them seemed to dematerialize as one. She smiled, watching them go. She rose, and as she did so her phone rang.

It was Griffin, telling her he was just outside.

She ran to the door and let him in, looking at him anxiously.

"Gail Holbrook is hanging on," he told her. "They're pretty sure she'll survive. She'll be in a few casts, but she's not in a coma — just heavily sedated. It will be a while before we can talk to her."

"But she is hanging in."

"Yes."

Vickie threw her arms around him. He pulled her to him and held her tight.

They were still so new . . .

She couldn't just be held. She kissed him. And touched him.

"You smell deliciously like a summer's day," he told her. "And I'm a mess."

"And I don't care," she said.

"I can shower."

"Tonight, that will take too long," she said.

And it would. She slid out of her robe and tee with his help, turned her hands to his clothing, pausing to walk backward to the bed, kissing him in between steps, feeling

426

his hands on her, so seductive in their need.

As always, he paused to carefully place his gun and holster down.

Then he crushed her to him, still half-dressed, and made love while he was still crawling out of his clothing. And only when it seemed they were both assured that they were still touching, breathing, together, did they pause long enough to talk again.

"Dylan came by. He said his dad has been great — he's very happy. He said the cop came and the sketch was done. I should turn the TV on — they were going to put the sketch out tonight."

Griffin sighed impatiently.

"What? What happened?"

"Well, we got two sketches, you know. One from George Ballantine — and one from Hank Fremont."

"Yes?"

"Well, we expected they'd come out very similar. They didn't. The artists are going back to both men tomorrow. They're going to try and see if they can make them combine. There are techs down at the station, too, trying to see if the compositions are close."

"There can't be two different women using the same name — and using men in the same way, disappearing in the same way!"

Vickie said.

"I agree. I'm sure we'll still have something by tomorrow."

"By the way, I got a message back from Alex Maple."

"Who?"

"Alex Maple. The Harvard grad who did a great paper on the old South Boston cop, MacDonald. He's the one who wrote about the people who had disappeared — those who are probably the victims found at the Pine house."

"Ah."

She knew that he was wondering if anything from that far in the past could help. He lay on his back, staring at the ceiling, and pulled her closer to him.

"Can't hurt to find out what he can tell us," he said.

"To be honest, he sounds like someone I'd really like to meet anyway — he did some pretty cool research to come up with all the information he did. A lot of people rehash what's already known in history — he went out in the field and found new information."

Griffin was quiet for a minute. Then he said, "We've really got to be exceptionally careful now — if we don't get one composite sketch out by the morning, we'll use both of them. I really believe this woman — this June Jensen — got close to both George Ballantine and Hank Fremont to get closer to the old situation. I think, for some reason in his twisted head, Bertram Aldridge had it out for George Ballantine. That's why he nearly killed you and Noah in the house. And June Jensen's affair with George now would have given her all the information needed to get in the house and attack Chrissy Ballantine." He paused a minute. "Getting close to Hank Fremont meant that she could get closer to you — get information on you. I can't shake the feeling that we're coming close to an end — and that scares me. You've got to be careful with everything that you do."

"Hey," she said, rolling up on an elbow to look down at him. "Not to worry. I don't try to shake my good cops — I try to buy them cappuccino! I am careful — not afraid or alarmed at having help close at hand. I am careful — you know it. Absolutely careful."

"I know. But be really hypervigilant, okay? If you meet with Alex Maple, you even want to let the cop on duty join you for coffee or lunch or whatever. Have someone with you at all times."

"Absolutely," she promised.

He smiled, reached for her, and pulled her down to him for a kiss. She wondered if — had the time come when they'd been together forever — they might have given in to exhaustion and slept then. Not in a bad way; just in a comfortable sleep-is-necessary survivor way.

But it was all still so new. And so they made love again. And finally slept, and when the sun rose and Vickie stretched her arm across the bed, Griffin was gone.

There was a note on his pillow.

She smiled. It didn't say "I love you" and it wasn't accompanied by a rose. The note said, "Hypervigilant!"

And it was accompanied by a time for when they'd meet at a gun range that night, and a P.S.: "Don't worry. The cop will know the way!"

"Actually, that is an 'I love you' from Griffin," she murmured aloud, and she rose, anxious to get the day going and hopefully meet up with Alex Maple. And, of course, later that afternoon, she'd have her excursion to the New England Aquarium with her Grown Ups group.

George Ballantine's June Jensen had a headful of short dark curls, wide lips and blue eyes.

Hank Fremont's June Jensen had a sleek bob of rich auburn hair. Her mouth was large and generous, and her eyes were dark brown. Fremont's girl was sketched as wearing a well-tailored shirt and business jacket; Ballantine's June had on a frilly, low-cut blouse.

"Eyes and hair are easily changed," Jackson commented. "Here's the thing — when you put them together on a computer screen, you do have something of the same face shape."

"I want to see both Ballantine and Hank Fremont again," Griffin told Jackson. "I want to see what their reactions will be — and if they see the images as the same woman."

"I have a feeling she's a chameleon," Jackson said. "Walking down the street, she can doff a wig and a jacket, and even pop out contact lenses. She's probably not a redhead or a brunette."

Griffin let out a sound of aggravation. "So we get the pictures out on the news — and say she may not look like the pictures at all." He frowned, studying the screen image in which one of the computer techs had tried to combine the pics. There was something about the face shape that seemed familiar to him.

"What is it?" Jackson asked.

"I don't know — I can't quite get it. But I think I have seen this woman."

"Maybe after you've seen Ballantine and Hank Fremont again, it will come to you."

"Maybe. Are you coming with me?"

"Yes, and after, I'd like to go back to the prison again. Aldridge knows something. I know he does. We have to get him to tell us what's going on," Jackson said.

Griffin agreed.

They started with the Ballantine house. George was home. He told them he was going to take the week off and stay close to Chrissy.

Chrissy seemed to be happy. While George led the way to the parlor, Griffin was alone with her in the kitchen for a minute.

"Do you think I'm an idiot?" she asked him quickly in a whisper.

"An idiot? Why?" he asked.

"Forgiving George. They say women should be strong and leave a cheater."

"Chrissy, 'they' haven't lived your life. Only you know what's right for you."

She smiled and gave him a kiss on the cheek. In truth, he didn't really understand the underlying psychology of any of it.

Maybe Chrissy was just so glad to believe her husband wasn't a murderer that discovering an indiscretion meant nothing.

Or maybe she was just a very good woman, understanding both she and George had been through rough times, and marriage was something both parties had to work on. Maybe she was able to forgive — and move forward.

In the parlor, Jackson already had the sketches out, showing them to George Ballantine.

"I thought it was a wig," George said. He looked at Griffin as he came into the room. "A good wig." He glanced at his wife, shamed embarrassment on his face. "It was a good wig. It never came off. And, I didn't say anything. She might have been coming back from cancer treatments, for all I knew."

They thanked George and moved on to find Hank. He wasn't at his residence, however, and when they checked in with Roxanne Greeley, she told them when she had called him back the night before, he had already been in bed and said if she wanted, he'd see her that evening.

She sent a text to Hank for them and tried calling; there was no response. But just as they were leaving Roxanne's, he called back. He was on a service call out in Framingham, but would be happy to see them if they wanted to come to him, or later that afternoon.

They agreed to meet that afternoon; Hank would come to the station.

Jackson spent part of the drive to the prison on the phone, calling Adam Harrison to see they'd have easy access once they got to the prison. The officials there were not fond of making arrangements for a prisoner like Bertram Aldridge to be interviewed.

But arrangements were made. And Bertram Aldridge appeared to be delighted by the visit — though he frowned when he realized that Victoria Preston wasn't with them.

"We told you she wasn't coming," Griffin told the man.

"She's something, though, huh? I mean, you buffoons and the police never would have found all those women without her, would you? Now, I admit, two died — no, three died — before you were involved. That one in the water . . . Darlene Dutton. Too fast. Fools. If they're playing a game, they started out botching it pretty badly. I mean, if your victim drowns right away and no one even believes you have a victim, what kind of masterful planning is that?"

"You know who is doing this," Jackson said flatly.

"I'm in here. I haven't had any correspondence — at all — since you clowns came to see me. No, I just get the news. I don't care what they say or what they try — everyone gets the news," Aldridge told them.

"But one of the major events was at the Pine house, South Boston," Griffin said. "Is that why you hated George Ballantine? He had family from the same place, but his family moved on and he turned into a rich and prosperous man?"

Aldridge leaned forward. "His family were cutthroats."

"What makes you say that?" Jackson asked.

Aldridge leaned back. He started to cross his arms over his chest, but his shackles stopped him. He shrugged and leaned forward.

"I had a great-grandma who used to talk about the old days when I'd stay with her. She remembered the murders from when she was a kid. Said she saw the doctor who disappeared there. He had been a wealthy man, and she was pretty sure he'd been done in because he was rich. He'd brought a whole ton of money — in gold — with him to start up a practice. She believed a fellow named George Ballantine killed him — for the money. 'Course, after, he had to hide the money. But here's the crux of the thing. Turned out my ancestor was suspected of the crimes and shunned. My ancestor — who didn't commit murder and sure as hell didn't wind up with the gold."

"And that's why you murdered women with a knife — women who had nothing to do with your past or Ballantine's past?" Griffin asked.

Aldridge smiled — the look on his face was the closest thing to a glance into pure evil that Griffin had ever seen.

"I murdered women with a knife because it got me off. Because I loved the spill of blood. I loved their screams. I loved looking into their eyes and seeing they knew they were going to die, but somehow hoping until the last second they were not. I murdered women with a knife, Special Agent Pryce, because it was pure, primal pleasure." He leaned back suddenly. "But I was younger then. The act itself was so important. We learn patience with age."

"Federal charges can be filed, Aldridge," Griffin reminded him. "I can see you on a gurney now, a needle in your arm."

"Yeah, yeah, yeah. The federal government can go after the death penalty. But, it ain't easy — we both know that. You'll never connect me," Aldridge said.

But Griffin was certain he had unnerved the man.

"You get the news," Jackson said.

"And I think you'll be surprised quite soon to discover that we are on to one of your people," Griffin continued.

Now he was certain something in the man's face changed.

"No, you're not," Aldridge said, and then added quickly — too quickly, "Not that I have any people."

"Well, we'll see you again, Aldridge," Griffin said, rising.

"Gotcha!" Jackson said, rising.

Aldridge's chains rattled against the table. "Assholes!" he screamed after them.

"Yeah, pretty much so," Jackson muttered as they left. "Though, I wonder what will happen when we post images of our mystery woman. Aldridge gets the news — he'll see we're on to something."

"We can hope. This June Jensen might just be a run of the mill gold digger or user. But I don't think so. And I think we did get something from him today," Griffin said.

"What's that?"

"These killers have moved around. They get what they want, when they want it. They've got some kind of decent financing."

"Which might suggest George Ballantine."

"Or someone who found the stash that belonged to the doctor killed in the late 1800s," Griffin said. "Aldridge knew it was there — maybe Aldridge had used some of it. I think we need to head back to the Pine house. Let's assume, too, the money was in gold or silver. Anyone using it now would have to go very carefully."

"Or take a loss on the black market."

"But even then, we're looking at some nice income — usable income — at today's rates. The killers have money. They have easy access to a car. They know Boston, because they had to know just the right time to dump the refrigerator with Gail Holbrook in it," Griffin said. "And, here's the thing. I believe they're known in the neighborhood — and no one is surprised to see them when they're on the Freedom Trail, or around the Paul Revere house — or the Ballantine house."

"Let's head on out to find Hank Fremont."

"Yeah, but let's get ahold of Barnes right away. I don't think we should wait. Hank Fremont may be able to help us and we can put up another image after. But for now, let's move. Let's get the images — with the police overlay as well — up on the news."

"I agree," Jackson said. "Something has to break. They must have made a mistake somewhere, and involving the public now with our mystery woman might help us recognize that mistake."

"Let's pray that 'June Jensen' herself *is* the mistake," Griffin said.

Vickie met with Alex Maple at a café just outside Faneuil Hall.

She always loved coming there, and since it was both vibrant and historic — originally built in 1742 by Peter Faneuil as a gift to the city — she figured it was a place Alex Maple might like — and where her cop — a man named Justin Hornsby that day — could comfortably sit and enjoy coffee and the beautiful summer's day as well.

She'd worried about recognizing Alex; she shouldn't have. No one wore the scholarly nerd look better. He was tall and bone thin and slouched slightly as he walked. His hair was brown and shaggy and fell over one eye.

She wondered if she might resemble a nerdy scholar, too — they looked at one another and said each other's name carefully as Alex approached Vickie's table.

She laughed and rose to greet him.

"I was — and wasn't — surprised when I got your message," he said, pulling out the chair opposite her. "Naturally, I've seen the news and know that the bodies were found at the Pine house. And, of course, I sent what info I had to the anthropologists working on the bodies from the wall. Otherwise, I've got to tell you, not too many people get into scholarly papers written about events that may or may not have happened back in the 1800s. But I know your name, of course. We're about the same age. I was in high school in Brookline when Bertram Aldridge escaped and went after the Ballantine house — with you in it. I looked you up, after you wrote me, of course," he told her. "I admire the work you're doing with Grown Ups. And, of course, I looked up your book. Nice style! I haven't figured out how to convey what excites me in my research without boring people to tears."

"What are you doing now?"

"I've got a guest spot at Harvard. I'm hoping for a full-time position."

"You went there for college — my dad was a professor there."

He nodded and smiled. "Great teacher. I had him years ago. After looking you up and checking on your books, I figured you had to be his daughter."

A waitress came. They ordered coffee.

"I'm trying to find out anything else you

can tell me about the situation on the south side. The police really did nothing?" Vickie asked.

"I don't think it was so much a matter of them doing nothing. I think that they had no idea of what to do. Remember, that was way back, as far as forensic science went. And, sadly, a lot of people in the area then were immigrants, many were just traveling through. When they disappeared, there was no bloodshed seen anywhere. They were just gone."

"You'd have thought the bodies would have smelled. That someone would have known."

"Farms were still far apart. From what I understand, the Pine family seldom lived on the farm. The odor of manure from the animals must have been strong and maybe some kind of natural substance was used to keep the odor down," Alex told her. "Anyway, I found something of interest the other night. I was going through papers written by guys who came long before me. I guess some people have been curious through the years. Anyway, a guy named Hugh Belford — Harvard class of '39 — also wrote on the subject. He honed in on the doctor who had planned on opening a practice in Boston on the south side. Doctor Marquette, Alain

441

Marquette. Witnesses said that Marquette treated a Jonah Aldridge when he first arrived in the area, so Jonah Aldridge definitely knew Marquette. When the man's brother, Robert, arrived in town, he accused Aldridge of killing his brother to steal his money. There was quite an uproar over it all. Apparently, though, he was never arrested and nothing was ever proven. Aldridge was an outcast from that day forward. I don't know if that helps you any or not."

"Do you know where the Aldridge home was?"

"Right on Washington. But it was torn down decades ago. I think there's a building there now that houses offices and shops. Whatever — apparently, Aldridge sure as hell never appeared to be rich. His family would have definitely been considered blue-collar, lower working class. I'm curious. I guess those horrible people somehow knew about the bodies in the wall at the Pine house, but . . . even so, how do you think that affects these kidnappings and the deaths?"

"The killers are most probably hiding in the throng of Boston's day-to-day movement," Vickie said. "But to go from place to place, to manage to get wooden boxes, refrigerators and all, and to get around — they have to have some money."

"So, you don't think George Ballantine is involved?" he asked.

"I don't. But I'm not sure what the police think — or the agents, or if they all think alike. And, God knows, I don't consider myself an expert. But I do know George and his children — I mean, his son — and I know that his family loves him."

"Yeah. BTK killer — bind, torture and kill. He was a regular Joe," Alex reminded her.

"Yes."

"Oh, of course, here's something else to think about. We know the Aldridge back then also had a number of children."

"Yes, but the Aldridge in prison now doesn't have a family — neither a wife nor children," Vickie said.

"Doesn't have a wife — that doesn't mean a man didn't have kids."

"True, and something to think about. Though how we might find an illegitimate child, I don't know. However, I can suggest that to the people who investigate for a living. They can track down women he was known to have had relationships with. Non-killing relationships."

"Who knows? Maybe he did kill the baby

mama, just not the baby," Alex said.

"Good point."

"Anyway, if you think of anything I can help you with at any time, I'm here." He smiled. "Actually, I tend to be available. I have a habit of talking too much history. Or hanging around at art galleries. Love art."

"I have a friend who majored in art at Boston College," Vickie said. "I should introduce you some time." Of course, now Roxanne was involved with Hank. Still, people could be friends. "She's great — works with the kids for Grown Ups, too."

"Nice," he said.

They chatted a few more minutes. Vickie wasn't sure what she'd gotten from him, if anything.

Except, of course, a stronger belief that Bertram Aldridge was pulling the strings.

He must have known about the bodies in the wall at the Pine house.

And, he must have known, too, there was a hoard of gold which had belonged to one of the victims in the wall. It hadn't been found — that anyone knew about. Of course, this was assuming that one of the bodies in the wall had been the doctor, Marquette, and he'd still had a stash when he'd died, and his killer had hidden at least some of it — afraid to use conspicuous treasure from a dead man.

The nice thing was, she figured, when they did part ways, she'd found a new friend. She liked Alex. They promised to keep in touch.

When she rose to leave, she saw that her cop, Justin Hornsby, was casually folding his newspaper and rising, too.

She headed toward her apartment, glad to know Justin Hornsby was behind her.

She passed an electronics store and paused. The news was showing from TV screens in a variety of sizes. Two images were shown — sketches of June Jensen.

They were then overlaid, shown as one. Though the woman had appeared very different at first, the overlay showed the facial structure — nose, chin, eyes — were shaped very much the same.

Something about the image caused her to frown.

Did she actually know the woman?

Maybe she had seen her on Boston Common, or walking the street — or maybe even in a restaurant. She might have passed her in a ladies' room, or been behind her in a grocery store line.

She shivered.

Yes, at some point, she had been close to that woman. She recognized something.

Something familiar. But it was disturbing. She should know — she should . . . something.

She just didn't.

She hurried on; she did have the kids this afternoon, and she was anxious to see Griffin again. Maybe together they could figure out what it was in the picture that seemed so very familiar.

Griffin called Vickie, determined he'd be in touch with her throughout the day.

She answered cheerfully; she'd met with Alex Maple and her very fine officer — Justin Hornsby — had kept a close watch. He was, naturally, behind her now.

"Do you think you might have learned anything from Alex Maple?" he asked her.

"I think so. One of the victims in the wall — I theorize, at any rate — was a doctor named Marquette. He'd come to Boston with a lot of money. Sam Aldridge way back then was suspected of doing away with him, but there was no body. The money vanished. So — theory — Bertram Aldridge knew about the bodies in the wall and he gave the information through some code via his phone calls and letters that led his killing duo to the money. They've used it on this spree of theirs — to get around, probably to

446

buy the clothing and wigs and whatever else this June Jensen has been using. Hey — the image with an overlay — did George or Hank recognize her as the same woman?"

"We haven't seen Hank yet. He's late. We did see Aldridge, and, after we spoke with him, we have pretty much a similar working theory," Griffin told her.

"And then there is this," Vickie said. "Alex wondered if there might not be an illegitimate child of Bertram Aldridge out there somewhere."

"I never heard of him having children, but if he had a kid when he was young and no one admitted to it . . . anything's possible. I'll get people looking into it, though that's a task that could take a lot of investigators a very long time."

"I know."

"But your new friend did have a good idea. We'll get on it. And you — what are you doing now?"

"I'm going to head out to the aquarium. Think my cop will mind if I walk?"

"I think you're talking four blocks, maybe five," Griffin said.

She laughed softly.

"I doubt he'll mind," Griffin told her. "Keep in touch. I don't like it that we haven't heard from Hank."

"Want me to call Roxanne?" Vickie asked.

"We called her. No response."

"I thought a cop was watching her place. Because of Hank."

"Yep. He says no one has come or gone. He told me he knocked, but just lightly. She hasn't done anything wrong — he's just there to protect her and he thought she might be sleeping."

"She might have been up all night, worried about not trusting him — or that he could be a killer."

"There was a shift change, but one officer stayed until the other was at his post. Unless she went through a window, she's in there, just not answering anyone. I'm going to give her a few more minutes, and then we can start getting worried."

"I'll try her. Maybe she'll answer me."

"All right. Well, we're at the station waiting — we've got feelers out, trying to search the black market for old gold. And I've got blueprints here of the building where the Aldridge family once had a house. Looking for stash sites. Luckily, I have a task force of computer geniuses here, too."

"They might have moved the money."

"I don't know — they might not want to be caught with it. This woman is moving around the city on an assumed name. She doesn't exist. We're checking nationwide records, too, trying to find out if she might be using the identity of someone who died, or if she's just playing it as she goes. I'm going to get back to work. Keep in touch. Please, stay in crowds. Be safe."

"Don't worry, I know Officer Hornsby will protect me, even if a beluga whale jumps out of the water."

"Seriously."

"Seriously — I'll be in public, well-populated places. I'll be in a throng of adolescents soon, in a busy tourist spot. I'm going to watch for Officer Hornsby at every turn. And I'll keep in touch," Vickie promised.

He hesitated on the line, thinking he should say something. Something more. Something about his feelings for her.

"Hey, don't forget we're going to the gun range later."

"I'm ready!" she assured him. "I'll call Roxanne and get back to you," she said. "Griffin, I am worried."

"If you don't get an answer, the cop will go right in."

He hung up and stared at the mountain of papers and architectural plans before him.

Hank had promised to show up. He wasn't

answering his phone, he wasn't at his residence and he hadn't gone to Roxanne's apartment. They'd called his work; he hadn't reported in since leaving Framingham.

His fingers itched as he held his cell phone. He was ready to break down the door to Roxanne's if she didn't respond to someone soon.

His phone rang. Vickie.

"Did she answer you?"

"Yep, she says she's fine, and she hasn't heard from Hank."

"Okay, thanks."

"Sure. See you soon?"

"I'll come to the aquarium if I can," he promised.

He hung up still feeling that something wasn't right.

He stood and walked into the conference room where Jackson and Detective Barnes were also going through records, papers and tip-line info.

"We need an APB out on Hank Fremont. I don't like this," he said.

"I was thinking the same thing," Jackson said.

Barnes nodded. "Consider it done," he said, rising.

"And," Griffin added, "Vickie reached

Roxanne — but I don't like it. We need to get into her apartment."

Again, Barnes nodded. "Consider it done," he said.

Barnes left the room. "Jackson, you can deal with Hank when he comes in, right? I'm going to head to the aquarium. I don't like Vickie being alone."

Jackson didn't try to tell him Vickie wasn't alone, or that the BPD officers were among the best in the country and she had one guarding her. Sometimes, the person needed for a particular task was you, yourself.

"I can handle Hank just fine — assuming we find him," Jackson said. "Go, watch over Vickie."

"Thanks," Griffin said.

And he left the station, heading for aquarium.

He was only halfway there in a mass of Boston traffic when his phone rang. It was Jackson.

"They broke Roxanne's door because she wasn't responding. She wasn't there."

"How could she not be there?"

"She actually went out a window."

"Okay. I'm getting to Vickie, as fast as I can."

Vickie's phone rang right after she hung up

451

from Griffin.

It was Roxanne.

"Hey, you okay?" Vickie asked her.

"Yes. Are you headed for the aquarium? You have your kids there today?" she asked. "I'm on my way to join you."

"Why aren't you at your apartment? You should be with your protective detail!"

"I wasn't sure they were really protecting me. I — I'm scared. I need a friend. I'd feel better with you."

"Roxanne, I'm really angry with you! That was crazy — you had people watching you!"

"I need you — I need a friend!"

"All right, all right, but you be careful, and you get with me now, okay?"

"Yes. Right away."

"Where are you now?"

"Faneuil Hall area. I'll head back to our favorite coffee shop."

"Great — I will be there as quickly as possible and I'll find you," Vickie said and hung up.

Her phone rang again almost immediately. She thought it was Roxanne, calling back, maybe with a change of heart. If not Roxanne, Griffin.

If not Griffin, her mother.

But it was none of them. The voice on the other end of the line was young and hushed;

scared, Vickie thought.

"Miss Preston, it's Cheryl. Your Grown Ups student, Cheryl Taylor."

"Hey. What's wrong? Are you not going to make the aquarium today?"

"I don't know. I really need to talk to you. Please, can we meet somewhere?"

"Where are you now? I was on my way to the aquarium, but I'm pretty early. I'm by Faneuil Hall."

"I'm in the cemetery."

"Cemetery?"

"Yes, people here, but it's quiet, I can be alone . . . there's a cop following you, right? Or that handsome Fed. I mean, you're okay, right?"

"Yes, I'm fine. Who are you afraid of?"

"I don't know . . . I'm hanging around here, at the Granary."

"It will take me a few minutes. But yes, I have a cop. And yes, I'll come to you. Stay put."

She turned and waved to Justin Hornsby — letting him know that she was changing directions. As she walked, she called Roxanne and told her where she was going and why.

"Poor kid is probably in trouble. Maybe the wrong guy," Roxanne said. "I'll head for the Granary instead of the cemetery."

"I don't know who to worry about more."

"I'll be okay. I promise. You get close to me. Please. Then I'll hover and you can nod when you see me, let me know if you need time with her alone, or if maybe I can help."

"All right. Stay safe!"

The aquarium was actually a much shorter walk.

She thought about Cheryl Taylor and thought it maybe had something to do with either Hardy Richardson or Art Groton. Both boys liked her — that was obvious. But she was a very pretty girl with her tiny, sexy body and vivacity. Hardy liked to flirt and say wild things; Art was quieter, gazing in wonder at her all the time. Had they gotten into a fight over her? Or had one of them threatened her?

She knew, of course, that sometimes those from abusive homes or situations could lean toward being abusers in return. Unless, of course, the cycle was broken.

She hurried around the Old State House and on to Court Street and then around the corner to head for the Granary Burial Ground. Turning back, she smiled and waved to Justin Hornsby.

He waved back. She didn't know why he didn't just walk with her.

When she reached the cemetery, she

didn't see Cheryl at first. She walked around the old slate graves and marveled at the age of the cemetery, the air of nostalgia, sadness and history about it. She was ready to call Cheryl back and ask where she was when the girl stepped nervously from around a tree. "Hey!" she said to her softly.

"Hey. There's a bench over there. Want to sit?"

Cheryl nodded nervously. "Where's your cop?"

"Right back there," Vickie said. She pointed around the graves, smiled and waved at Justin Hornsby. He smiled and waved back.

Cheryl let out a long sigh. "He's going to kill me," she said.

A sudden loud scream erupted. Both Vickie and Cheryl leaped up and looked toward the street. There had been a tremendous crash — a car had veered around another car and slammed into two others. People were screaming.

"What the hel— heck?" Vickie murmured, automatically remembering Cheryl might use any language herself, but an adult should be careful.

"A baby carriage! There was a baby carriage in the road."

"Come on — let's get closer. I don't see

Officer Hornsby now. He's probably moved out to see if someone needs help," Vickie said.

"No, no, come back . . . we have to stay back! He'll see us. He's going to kill me!"

"Who?"

At that same moment, Vickie saw Roxanne a few rows away in the cemetery. Her friend lifted a brow to her, looked toward the street, and shook her head.

Then, Roxanne seemed to pale, going dead still, staring.

Vickie whipped around again.

Hank Fremont was also at the cemetery, heading toward her. He paused, seeing Roxanne was a distance across the ancient stones and sarcophagi.

"Come on!" Cheryl said, grabbing her hand and heading through the stones. "Come on, please."

For a moment, Vickie was pulled along at Cheryl's impetus. Then she stopped. Roxanne was there. And Hank had been going after her.

Cheryl tugged back on Vickie's hand. "Vickie! We need to go to the crowd, and I have a friend back there and . . ." She turned.

Hank and Roxanne were together. Walking toward her and Cheryl.

"Come on!" Cheryl said. "Now, run!"

"Wait!" Vickie protested.

Maybe Hank was a killer.

She hadn't seen him in years. She'd known him as a kid in high school — she did not know the man he had become.

She did know Roxanne. Her best friend.

Something wasn't right.

Suddenly they were behind a maintenance vehicle. "Down!" Cheryl urged.

Though wary, Vickie ducked low, then looked around the big dusty vehicle. She gasped; Roxanne was screaming, falling to the ground.

But Hank wasn't hurting her. Hank was prone on the ground as well.

"Oh . . ." Cheryl murmured. "Look! He got them — he got them!"

And as she looked, Vickie saw a man running toward them.

It was Hardy Richardson. Vickie gasped, starting to rise. It was all getting too crazy.

Hardy was there? Hardy had just saved them from . . . Hank?

But Cheryl's next words startled her; they didn't fit.

"Hardy! You can't kill me — I don't care what *he* told you! You can't kill me. Look, I got her for you! See, I got her for you."

"It might as well be Grand Central Station here!" Hardy spat out furiously. "And you went to her for help. You made it look like it was all me."

"What the hell?" Vickie demanded. She did not adjust her language that time. She stared at Cheryl.

Then she knew. Take away the schoolgirl hair and switch up a few things and . . .

Cheryl was the woman in the sketch artist's renderings. And looking at her now . . .

It was always so hard to tell a young woman's age. Cheryl was so petite, but . . .

Maybe she wasn't just seventeen!

"No, no," the girl said.

But even as Vickie looked at her, she saw Hardy moving out of the corner of her eye.

He was gripping a piece of an old marble tombstone.

And it was coming down on her head.

Griffin discovered Vickie was not at the aquarium. Most of her high school kids were there, waiting.

The minute she didn't answer her phone, his instincts went on alarm. He didn't have to try to reach Officer Justin Hornsby. Hornsby dialed him.

"The cemetery. There was a crash in the street. People screamed — I thought someone was near death. I turned and she was gone. She was just meeting a kid, Special Agent Pryce. She was just with one of her kids . . ."

Griffin was pretty sure he swore. "You've lost her. Where?"

"At the Granary."

Griffin didn't wait for more. He left the aquarium. He ran. His car was there, but the Boston traffic was jammed.

Running was faster.

He made it in a matter of minutes. Cop cars were there already, but it was a scene of mass confusion; they were dealing with the accident on the street.

He raced into the cemetery, shouting Vickie's name. And as he made his way through the stones, he nearly tripped.

Over the prone body of Hank Fremont.

And at his side, hand in hand with him, was Roxanne Greeley.

He hunkered down, feeling for pulses. Both were alive. He saw blood dripping down their foreheads; residue of broken tombstones mingled with the blood.

He rose, shouting for help. Officer Hornsby pushed his way out of the street crowd and jumped over a barrier to come running toward him.

"Get help for them — get an ambulance," he said.

Hornsby was on it immediately — he yelled into the street, demanding EMTs on the double.

Griffin rose and looked around the cemetery. He hurried around slate and marble stones, death heads and sarcophagi.

His phone rang. Jackson.

"It's the kid, Griffin. One of Vickie's so-called girls. She's using the identity of a dead teen from Worcester County. They just found her body in a weir last night. The real Cheryl Taylor. Watch out for the girl. It's got to be her and Hank."

"Vickie's missing, Jackson, I'm here, where she disappeared. Granary. It's not Hank, Jackson. Hank is on the ground with his head bashed in. Along with Roxanne Greeley. It's only been a matter of minutes. I'm combing the cemetery. She has to be here somewhere."

"I'm on my way."

There was a maintenance vehicle parked up against a section of tombstones.

Griffin hurried to it.

There was a woman on the ground. His heart froze. Her head was so matted with blood that he had to stoop down . . .

He turned her over.

Not Vickie.

It was Cheryl Taylor.

Or the woman who had claimed to be Cheryl Taylor, teenager. And June Jensen adult.

Her eyes, glazed, stared up at him.

She was dead.

Vickie awoke with a searing pain in her temple. For a moment, all she could feel was the pain. And then she realized the darkness, and, when she tried to move, realized she couldn't. She was in a tight space.

She was in a box.

A coffin-like box.

But she could hear something.

Like dirt being shoveled over her.

"You're an ass, Hardy!" she shouted. "This time, they're going to get you. They'll find you and Cheryl or June or whatever the hell her name is. And, guess what? They're going to see to it you get a needle in your arm."

The noise stopped. She felt a shift, as if someone had lowered himself right over her.

"Guess what?" Hardy asked.

"What?"

"They are going to get Susan. Oh, that's her real name. Susan. Susan Malloy." He laughed. "And she's twenty-three. All grown

461

up. And she was good — for a while. But women! Who can trust them? They can be the worst! That brat was going to tell you it was all me. That I forced her into sleeping with men for information and I raped her and subjugated her and she was afraid for her life and all that rot . . . biggest pile of bull anywhere! Want to know where we met? Wait, don't answer, save your air. We met through my dad. You know my dad. Bertram Aldridge. She was one of those women in awe of a prisoner like him. She was his fan, yeah. Sicko herself. Who do you think came up with the idea of burying people or shutting them into things, huh? She liked the torture of it. She liked to bet me just how long someone could stay alive. Oh, and she was the jerk who threw the first girl into the water. What a fiasco. I mean, torture? She wasn't tortured long. She had to have died pretty quick. But hell, the newspaper even ignored us then. We had to be more careful next time. And then, there you go! Two dead women and someone finally starts paying attention to the clues. Thing is, I didn't even care about Chrissy Ballantine. That one was really for my dad. Did you know that a Ballantine killed people years ago — and look at George Ballantine now! A pillar of society. A rich man. People were murdered for all that gold. Well, about half of it, anyway. We got the rest. When Dad broke out years ago, he knew he probably couldn't get to George himself. But he could do worse — he could kill his other kid. Use the kid, maybe, to find out if that gold was still around — hadn't figured out where it was yet — but he could make George give it to him . . . and then kill the kid. That's the worst torture in the world, so I've been told. My dad told me. Said it was torture that my mother had lied about having me — she tried to tell him that there was something wrong with him, so she kept his baby from him! Go figure on that. But . . . ah, well, I may not be able to get that FBI agent, but killing you will be torture for him, right?"

"How did you do it all?" she asked.

"Dad was a great teacher. Hit 'em, and hit 'em hard, first. Then they don't scream. And, while it lasted, Susan was good. Cheryl. Susan-Cheryl-June," he said laughing. "But you see, I hit her more than hard. I gave some damned good whacks to those friends of yours, too. They never saw me coming. They'll have no idea what happened. Well, of course, they didn't know me to begin with. Hey, it will be pretty cool if they keep thinking your old pal Hank is the culprit! God! Was it fun watching them. And now, wow. They won't have you. You were the one who kept solving the puzzles. You know, they all came from stuff you taught us — stuff we learned on your excursions. Figured if anyone was going to get the clues, it would be you. But alas . . . oh, alas! Now they have to find Vickie — without Vickie's help!"

Earth; she could smell the earth all around her.

"One might have thought you had divine help." Hardy laughed softly. "If I believed in divine help."

"Better watch out!" Vickie said. "There is divine help. Darlene Dutton. She's the first girl you killed. She's still walking the earth. She helped me find Gail Holbrook last night. I do have divine help."

"Oh, Miss Preston. I'm trying to be respectful, but really — blow it out your ass! Whoops — don't! Save all the air you have, wherever it might be."

"And the FBI agents, Hardy. They found Angelina Gianni because the ghost of her mother came to help."

Air . . . she would run out of air. She was in a box, and he was burying her. They'd been in a cemetery, but . . .

There had been commotion everywhere by the cemetery. He couldn't be calmly burying her there. How had he gotten her out of the graveyard?

And had he killed the woman named Susan whom she had known as Cheryl?

What about Roxanne, and Hank?

What about breathing . . . ?

She did need to quit talking. But what the hell could she do? Could she scratch and claw her way out of the dirt — wherever this dirt might be?

She felt the ground shifting again.

He was rising. She heard the weird sound of him throwing dirt on the coffin again.

Then he spoke once more.

"Don't worry, baby. We'll see how good your FBI guy is. The papers will have received the clue about you. And, I won't be worried, though I really doubt he'll get it. I'll be gone — got all the fake papers I need. I'll be on an island somewhere, soaking up the sun and some good tequila. And I'll find me a new Susan/Cheryl/June. I'll write! Oh, wait. No. I'll send flowers now and then."

Laughing, he rose. Vickie could barely move.

She had to! she told herself.

Had to move, had to fight, now. He couldn't have sealed the box well. He wouldn't have had the time.

Use her strength and her air carefully, very carefully. Think about the situation, how to twist, get her limbs in position . . .

How to live.

Griffin, along with Jackson, Barnes and a horde of officers, went over the cemetery, foot by foot.

A witness remembered a man supporting a woman out of the cemetery to a car.

Another remembered it as well. The woman had been crying or hurt, but the man had seemed to have it all in control.

The car was a Buick, one man said.

No, a Chrysler.

No, a Ford.

It was blue; it was black. No, it was a deep green.

With every minute that passed, Griffin fought to keep from growing frantic.

Then they received the call from the newspaper. The clue was in.

Remember last night!
The Puritans, raw, the physician in chains.
The teacher is taught, poor lady, distraught.
What will you find?
Just the remains.

"What the hell?" Barnes said, disgusted.

Griffin stood there, tense, torn and thinking. "The physician," he said. "We thought that the long riddle referred to Zabdiel Boylston last night. But . . . pustules . . . the road, the place. Puritan — he used Cotton Mather last night. Tonight, Zabdiel Boylston. He drove away. Drove somewhere. With all this going on."

"She's not here — not in the ground here," Jackson said.

Griffin felt something. A light touch on his arm.

He turned; it was the ghost of Darlene Dutton. She began to fade almost immediately.

But Dylan was there.

"She saw them leave. She knows who it is — it's Hardy. Hardy, one of the other so-called kids in the group," Dylan told him. "She heard him muttering to Vickie, as if she could hear him. Talking to her, even though she was out cold. He was heading for Brookline."

"Brookline," Griffin said aloud. "She's going to be somewhere near the grave of Zabdiel Boylston."

"Stop that! I'm running out of time!" Hardy told her. She could hear his voice again, even though there was more dirt between them now.

But she had gotten her arms and hands wedged up in front of her chest.

And her wooden coffin hadn't been sealed.

She was able to push at the wood.

But he was still there; still shoving dirt on her.

"Save your air, you idiot. Hey, I gave him a good clue. And if you happen to push through, it's going to be all over for you. I have a knife, too. I'm not my father's child for nothing, Miss Preston. He told me how to cut and hurt — and how to cut and kill."

She paused for a minute.

"Yep, give them time. I gave them a good clue. I play a game fair, Miss Preston. But if you're not good, I won't have to abide by the rules. Should have hit you harder. I did want to give you a chance to wake up, though."

She held still, listening, waiting.

And she realized that it was becoming harder and harder to breathe.

Dirt was falling on her from cracks in the wood. If he kept going she was going to be smothered by the weight atop her and the earth filling the coffin.

And her head was still pounding, a horrible, sharp pain that managed to throb as

well . . .
Wait? Pray?
Asphyxiate in the earth . . .
Or die in a sea of blood.

Griffin was ahead of the others, out of the car as if he was the fictional Flash. He'd used the time riding in the car to study the cemetery map.

He knew right where to find the grave of Zabdiel Boylston.

Of course, the killers had used a natural degradation of the earth to bury Barbara Marshall.

In an old cemetery, that could be anywhere. And now the light had waned.

He leaped over old slate stones and monuments, running hard. And then he saw a light; just a pinprick.

It was Hardy. He was still there, standing over the grave. He was using a flashlight.

Griffin's heart was thundering.

He ran and dodged the old stones and the trees with their branches as gnarled as old bones.

And then, he almost stopped.

There was a sudden explosion of earth and a splintering of wood. Like some kind of an avenging angel, Vickie was bursting out of the earth, out of the ground that

469

would have been her grave.

And Hardy was screaming — furious. Kicking at her. And raising his hand. Griffin saw in the pinprick glow of the flashlight the man was holding a knife. And Vickie wouldn't have the power to fight in any way, to stop him.

Griffin nearly flew over the last graves.

He tackled Hardy a split second before the knife could fall on Vickie as she slipped backward, trying to crawl out of the grave.

He rolled with Hardy, slammed a fist against the hand holding the knife.

The young man let it go.

He stared into Griffin's face, laughing.

He felt the ghosts of Dylan and Darlene Dutton coming up behind him.

He resisted the temptation to kill.

But he slammed his fist against the laughing jaw of Hardy Richardson.

Jackson ran to the scene, followed by Barnes and more police officers. EMTs rushed forward with them as well.

He left Hardy Richardson lying on the ground; they would take over.

He rushed to Vickie's side.

She was covered in dirt. There was blood on her forehead. But when he lifted her into his arms, she smiled at him.

"What took you?" she asked.

"I'm just not as good without you," he told her.

And she smiled.

EPILOGUE

Boston, Massachusetts
One week later

"Hold steady, remember there is a little kickback," Griffin said.

Vickie gave him an almost imperceptible nod. Her concentration was completely on the task at hand. She held his Glock with both hands.

Aimed as instructed.

Fired.

Damn good.

"Hey, you could be a crack shot," he told her.

She smiled and told him. "I'm going to be. Hey, I'm heading to Virginia with an FBI agent. I'm going to be the best!"

"Okay, well, that's good for today. We're due at your parents' for dinner."

Vickie laughed delightedly. "You can be stoic — incredibly strong. Dare I rhyme and say heroic? And yet, my mother makes you

472

tremble!"

He smiled, took the Glock and slid it into the holster at the small of his back, then drew her into his arms, protective glasses and ear muffs and everything.

"You love your parents. I want them to like me. Trust me, my mom can be scary as well. You'll get to be on the other end soon enough."

They left the range and headed to her parents' condo. They were only in the city a few more days and Vickie, Griffin knew, was trying to see them as often as possible.

To his surprise, Lucy and Philip greeted them at the door without looking at Vickie with searching, concerned eyes. They naturally asked how they were doing, but they'd stopped treating Vickie as if she was incredibly fragile.

"Dinner is ready," her mom said. "Vickie, get the glasses, please. Griffin, there's a big pitcher of tea in the fridge . . . oh! I guess your tea is better than our tea."

"It's pretty much the same, Mrs. Preston," he said.

"Virginia! You know, Phil, we are retired, and we may have to move," Lucy said.

"Oh, my God! Dad out of Boston," Vickie said.

"Virginia is a great state — and Massachusetts and Virginia were both incredibly important in the founding of the country. Bostonians went to Virginians for help, you know. I should be just fine if we moved. And you'll be on the border of DC. Not a bad place at all."

"Oh, dear Lord," Vickie told Griffin, "they are going to move."

"If it makes them happy, hey . . ."

Lucy sat down and Griffin saw that she was trembling slightly. "Virginia is fine. But Vickie — they have a division of Grown Ups there? Are you sure you want to go that route again?"

"Yes, Mom. Susan/Cheryl/June wasn't a kid at all. And the son of someone like Bertram Aldridge . . . not sure he ever had a chance. There are kids who will have a chance. If people give them a chance. I love working with them, Mom. I love my kids here — and I'm taking a group of them to the aquarium before we leave, just as I had planned."

"She's really stubborn," Philip warned Griffin.

"That awful boy! Was he really seventeen?"

"No one really knows. He was born under a different name — they're still trying to sift through all the records," Griffin said. He paused. "The one thing they have fathomed is that his mother was Priscilla Hampton. She was one of Bertram Aldridge's first victims. Aldridge taught Hardy that women were meant to serve — and that, when they failed to do so, they needed to be put down."

"And Susan/Cheryl/June was a petty crook from the time she was in grade school," Vickie added. "She was the one with the right connections to get falsified papers so she could get into the school system here — as a teen — and get into the Grown Ups program."

"Well, she's gone," Lucy murmured.

"Yes," Griffin agreed.

"But Hank and Roxanne are both out of the hospital — and doing great!" Vickie said.

As the meal went on, Griffin was glad to see Lucy and Phil Preston really seemed to be okay with their daughter leaving town.

He also believed they'd soon be relocating themselves.

They left at about nine and returned to Vickie's apartment. She spun in his arms and said, "You're wonderful! You're so good to them!"

"I have an ulterior motive," he told her. "I'm running after their daughter."

"I think you've caught her," Vickie whispered. And she kissed him. Like usual —

maybe even more desperately, passionately and urgently since that night in Brookline — they doffed their clothing bit by bit, a little frantically as well, as they made their way to the bedroom.

They lay together as the night went on, and Griffin talked more about the Krewe of Hunters and the great people Vickie would meet. They were involved with a theater in the area, too — long story, but she would love it! — and in truth, Northern Virginia was a great place to live.

He wasn't sure when he fell asleep. But he woke when he heard Vickie stirring.

He heard a whisper from the parlor; he fought the temptation to reach for his gun. He recognized the sound of the whisper.

It was Dylan, softly calling for Vickie.

She rose and grabbed a robe. He swung his legs over the bed, sliding into a pair of jeans, and he followed her out to the parlor.

Dylan was there with Darlene Dutton.

"Hey," Vickie said. She frowned. "Is this . . . did you come to say goodbye?"

"Leave you?" Dylan teased. "No. In fact . . ."

"In fact?" Vickie asked.

"We're here because you can't leave. Not right away, anyway."

"What? Why? What's happened?" Griffin asked.

Dylan looked at Darlene. It was evident that he didn't want to say what he had to say.

"Your new friend . . ." Darlene began.

"What new friend?"

"The college guy. Alex Maple."

Griffin felt Vickie tense and he slipped his arm around her.

"What about him?" he asked.

"He was attacked outside his house tonight. He was left for dead."

"But he's not!" Darlene said quickly.

"He's going to need you, though. Because he was left with a letter on his body. A letter of warning. Vickie, you're going to have to see this letter."

Vickie looked at Griffin.

"Of course," he said softly.

"Come now!" Dylan urged.

"Is it even seven in the morning?" Vickie asked.

"Does that even matter?"

Griffin's phone began to ring.

It was Detective Barnes.

He listened as the detective urged him to stay awhile at least, there was something going down, something very bad for Boston.

"We'll be right there," he promised.

Vickie reached for his hand.

"We'll be with you!" Dylan promised.

They headed back into the bedroom to get dressed.

"There is one thing to all this," Griffin told her.

"What's that?"

"It seems you'll now be haunted forever by two ghosts, and not just one."

"Hey," she said softly. "Let's just be happy for them, huh?"

She was dressed, that quickly. She started out of the room again.

"Vickie," he said, and she turned back, looking at him expectantly.

"I love you," he told her.

She grinned. "About time!"

"Really? What about you?"

"I've said it a dozen times."

"You have not! Not even once."

And so she said it, and said it again and again.

And then he stopped her.

"We do have to get to work," he reminded her.

She grinned, and they headed on out.

ABOUT THE AUTHOR

New York Times and *USA Today* bestselling author **Heather Graham** has written more than a hundred novels. She's a winner of the RWA's Lifetime Achievement Award, and the Thriller Writers' Silver Bullet. She is an active member of International Thriller Writers and Mystery Writers of America. For more information, check out her websites: TheOriginalHeatherGraham .com, eHeatherGraham.com, and Heather Graham.tv. You can also find Heather on Facebook.

The employees of Thorndike Press hope you have enjoyed this Large Print book. All our Thorndike, Wheeler, and Kennebec Large Print titles are designed for easy reading, and all our books are made to last. Other Thorndike Press Large Print books are available at your library, through selected bookstores, or directly from us.

For information about titles, please call:
(800) 223-1244

or visit our website at:
gale.com/thorndike

To share your comments, please write:
Publisher
Thorndike Press
10 Water St., Suite 310
Waterville, ME 04901